Foolish Aspirations

An April May Snow

Southern Paranormal Fiction Thriller

By

M. Scott Swanson

April May Snow Titles

Foolish Aspirations

Foolish Beliefs

Foolish Cravings

Foolish Desires

Foolish Expectations

Foolish Fantasies

Foolish Games

Seven Title Prequel Series

Throw the Bouquet

Throw the Cap

Throw the Dice

Throw the Elbow

Throw the Fastball

Throw the Gauntlet

Throw the Hissy

Never miss an April May Snow release.

Join the reader's club!

www.mscottswanson.com

Letdowns will get you,

And the critics will test you

But the strong will survive,

Another scar may bless you.

Sia – "The Greatest"

Chapter 1

I stand next to the old orange pickup truck and look out over the dock for what I feel will be the last time. It seems like only yesterday, John Michael and I sat on the weathered boards looking out over the now calm water of the channel. We would count the ski and bass boats of the vacationers while he chomped on his unlit cigar, and I pondered the meaning of my life.

He is gone now. The small dock had offered a safe haven for me as I healed my wounded pride and constructed a plan for my future. Despite my nostalgia for the old boathouse, I know it's time to venture out and start my journey anew.

The garage door closes, and my eyes are drawn to Shane. I can't look at him without smiling.

"I almost forgot." He raises a small cooler shoulder high. "I packed you a lunch so you wouldn't have to stop unless you wanted to stretch your legs."

I'm not sure if it's the recent loss of John Michael, Shane's paternal grandfather, or his kind gesture, but my throat tightens as my eyes mist with tears. "Thank you," I croak.

"Nothing special. Just some chicken salad and pasta."

"It's special to me." I look away from him as I take the cooler. I'm struggling not to get emotional.

"You'll call me when you make it to your parents' home?"

"Yes. Your truck?"

"No hurry. I'll drive your car to Guntersville this weekend and swap out with you."

I force myself to look him in the eye. When I do, I know more than anything I want to stay. I've grown accustomed to his easy smile and perpetually needing a trim, thick chestnut hair. His golden hazel eyes seem to always seek out the secrets of my heart.

"Are you sure you'll be all right? I mean, it's not like I've got something waiting on me. I can stay a few more days if you'd like."

He favors me with a crooked grin that has no humor in it. "Nah, I'll be fine. Besides, you do have something waiting on you."

"No, I don't." I wrinkle my face.

"You've got a big successful life waiting on you."

"Now you're being silly."

He steps closer, now inches from me. "I'm not being silly at all. April May Snow is going to take the world by storm. They'll never know what hit them."

I grunt an unladylike laugh that nearly turns into a sob. "You're full of it, Shane White."

"Don't doubt me. I'm psychic and can see into the future," he jokes.

"For your sake, I hope not."

We continue with an awkward stare. My feet feel as if they are sunk in the concrete, and I know I'll never get in the truck of my own volition.

Shane gestures toward the pickup. "Time to fly, April."

The other night, it was a major fail, but maybe we had it all wrong. It's stupid, but I must know, and if I don't risk it now, when will I? I close the distance between us and kiss Shane.

When I was ten, my brothers explained how a car battery works. Curious, I promptly found a nine-volt battery and put it to my lips. Kissing Shane gives my brain the jolt my lips felt that day. But this sensation is a flood of emotion that spikes my core temperature and loosens my knees.

No twin circular welts on my lips today.

I realize he never embraced me as he pulls back, and our lips part. "If you leave now, you'll miss the rush hour traffic in Chattanooga."

I don't take it personally. Mama always told me I can be a bit much for some people. But I also know I grow on people. Shane is going to be in love with me. He just doesn't know it yet.

Hopping up into the truck, I say, "You're going to be able to hang out this weekend, right?"

"Saturday."

"I'm going to hold you to it."

"All right then." He laughs. "Be safe, and don't forget, call me to let me know you arrived home."

When I arrive, the only vehicle in the lake house's driveway is Dusty's huge black sixty-seven Impala. That's a good thing. I'll have time to get my nerves together before I pitch the new circumstances of my life to Mama.

I know I should have listened to Shane's advice and called her first.

I ring the doorbell three times and begin to call Dusty's phone before he opens the door. His quizzical expression morphs into joy.

"April!" I brace for impact as Dusty picks me off the porch in a bear hug. "What a surprise."

"I wasn't sure you were going to answer the door."

"If you hadn't lost your house key again, you could have let yourself in."

"How did you know—" I shake my head. "Never mind."

He cocks his head to the side and squints. "Why aren't you in Atlanta?" His eyes dart to the strange pickup truck with a full bed and trailer in tow. "Uh-oh, Wee, Cheatham, and Howe was a wipeout?"

Dusty's brain works like that. The warp speed his mind can process facts into a complete and accurate tapestry of events, makes lightning bolts seem slow. If a perfect IQ score is two hundred, Dusty's score would be two hundred and ten.

"For the thousandth time, it's Master, Lloyd, and Johnson, and I'm on furlough."

He steps to the side and lets me in. "For how long."

"I don't know. The FBI sort of has their office locked up right now."

Dusty bursts into laughter as he holds a fist to his mouth. "Snap. Are you serious?"

I give him my best death stare. "I don't find it humorous."

"Sorry. I sort of find it funny after what Uncle Howard told you about those folks."

"I'm sorry. I thought my parents lived in Guntersville, Alabama, not 'I told you so.'"

"Oh, don't get your dander up. You have to give me the opportunity to get used to the news. It's a bit of a shocker."

"I know. Right?"

He starts laughing again. "No. There were thousands of warning signs leading up to that cliff, and you did the Thelma and Louise right over the edge anyway."

"Stop it! Don't laugh at me."

He sobers and leans against the kitchen counter. "I am sorry. I know you had a lot of hope pinned on that position. I wish they had been what you hoped they were."

I let out a long breath. "Thanks. Hindsight always being perfect. I wish I had listened to all the warning signs. I was caught up with their high-profile client list, but after seeing how they operated, the only thing I think I'll miss is the guaranteed salary."

"Money's easy, April. Integrity and a passion for what you do is much more valuable."

Spoken like a true independently wealthy thirty-two-year-old.

I've met a lot of brilliant people. Most of them are unable

to monetize their superior intelligence. Like our father, Dusty earned a doctorate in physics from Auburn University, which puts him into the near-genius category. Unlike most super-smart folks I know, Dusty had parlayed his interests into a business that made him a multi-millionaire before he was thirty.

You'd never believe it by looking at him. His tightly curled red hair is tied back and reaches the middle of his shoulders. He has gauges the size of quarters in his ears and full ink sleeves on both arms, giving him the appearance of a heavy metal roadie. I'm sure he'd love to be a roadie as a side gig if his busy schedule permitted it. His "work" clothes consist of holey cargo shorts, frayed canvas flip-flops, and concert T-shirts from obscure bands. Presently he has allowed his full beard to get out of control.

I reach up and tug at the whiskers. "You need me to get Daddy's hedge clippers?"

He grins and pulls at the tip of his beard. "I'm going for the ZZ Top look."

"I'd say you're there. Another week you'll be a double for Rip Van Winkle."

"Ha-ha, you're too funny." He sighs. "What gives with the loaded truck?"

"Like you said, the position didn't work out."

"You're moving home? Just like that?"

My face tightens. "Not just like that, Dusty. It's sort of a trau-matic event."

He raises his hands. "I'm not making light of it. It bites. But you wanted to be in Atlanta. Why not just find a different job?"

It's a good question. One that would take too long to explain if I even could. "It's just temporary."

Dusty frowns at my deflection of his question. "You haven't discussed moving back home to Mom or Dad. Have you?"

"Geez, Dusty. What's with the hostile cross-examination?"

"I don't have a dog in this hunt, April. I'm trying to give you a bit of brotherly advice. Things would go a lot smoother if you could at least come up with a decent story about "A" what happened with the job and "B" why you are moving home rather than staying in Atlanta."

He is right. I hate it when Dusty is right.

Chapter 2

Mama arrives home an hour later, and I still haven't put together an argument that I believe will carry my case. And I fancy myself a defense attorney.

I know I'm in deep trouble. Mama acts as if she is genuinely pleased to see me and begins preparing chicken enchiladas for dinner immediately after giving me a hug. Mama all but hung up the apron and potholders on the weekdays ten years earlier when she started her real estate company. Today is Monday. She also didn't mention the strange truck and trailer in her driveway piled high with my possessions.

I get the impression she thinks if she doesn't bring it up, the truck will magically disappear.

She slides the two enchilada trays, one chicken and one faux chicken, Mama is vegan, into the oven. She turns her attention to making fresh guacamole and salsa.

Mama is like that. She can make the most challenging task seem simple.

The deft slicing with her paring knife is so quick it's mesmerizing. I can't imagine how many nicks I would have on my fingers if I attempted to emulate her.

I stare at her face in hopes she will look up and break the silence. I need to talk to her about my plans, whatever they may be. She is not ready. She is working through her aggravation.

Despite the present rigid set of her full lips, Mama is one of the most beautiful women I've ever met. She is a tall woman at five-nine, with a generous portion of her height being long legs. Her cheekbones are high set, and her eyes a rich brown that reminds me of hot cocoa on a cold winter's day. Her most stunning feature by far is her luxurious head of hair. The few silver strands in her otherwise chestnut brown mane only highlight and enhance her beauty. Mama, with her hair combed out, is an impressive sight.

"Baby, can you set the table for five?"

Every muscle in my body relaxes. The exile is over. "Yes, ma'am."

"Thank you."

Grateful for the break from the silent treatment and pleased to be given a task, I decide now is my opening to broach the subject of the orange pickup truck in the driveway. "Mama, what would you say if I decided to move back home for a while?"

"I'd say someone kidnapped my daughter and replaced her with an impostor. Why?"

I feel my ears heat up with embarrassment and carry the silverware to the kitchen nook. "I'm just not sure if I'm ready to live by myself in a big city. Maybe I should come home for a year and then try it out."

"That's nonsense, April. You lived in Tuscaloosa for seven years by yourself."

My family is so logical. It's aggravating when you need to float a little white lie to save face. "Right, but you have to admit Tuscaloosa is not on the same scale as Atlanta."

"Poppycock. How is a year at home going to help you transition? Besides, what would you do for work?"

The water stops in the sink, and I hear the paring knife click on the cutting board. I look up from setting the silverware, and the disbelief on Mama's face pierces my heart. "You lost your job," she declares.

"I didn't exactly lose it," I try to explain. "The firm got shut down the day I was supposed to start."

She closes her eyes and whispers, "Oh, my foolish girl. You're going to be the death of me."

"Don't be mad, Mama."

"I'm not mad. I'm concerned about you. What are you planning on doing now?"

"I don't know." As soon as I said it, I knew it was the wrong thing to say. One thing about Snows is we're all planners. We make plans, and we work toward our goals. Heck, I'm uncomfortable right now because I don't have a clearly delineated action plan.

"I'd suggest you figure it out, April. Your Uncle Howard warned you about those folks. Didn't he?"

Here we go. I did end up in "I told you so" Alabama, "Yes, ma'am."

Mama swings her finger like an orchestra conductor. "He warned you, and you argued with him. You told him he was just one of the naysayers. Goodness! How will you pay back all that student loan debt we told you not to take out?"

"I'll think of something, Mama." My voice sounds pathetic and whiny.

"You better, and quick." She shakes her head. "You know Dusty went to college for nine years and doesn't owe a single dime to anyone."

"Now that's not fair, Mama. Dusty writes those stupid spook books, and that's what paid for his school."

"No, he showed ingenuity and has always worked to provide what he wants for himself. On the other hand, you expect everything to come to you because you are April."

I flinch as if her words were fists. "Well, thank you for the understanding shoulder, Mama."

She sets her jaw, and her eyes narrow. "Don't you pull that with me, missy. I've been there for you when you needed a hug and a shoulder to cry on about some boy not liking you or some teacher giving you a bad grade. But I also know when someone needs a swift kick on her derriere. I refuse to be the enabler of this bad habit you have developed over the years."

"Bad habit?"

"Yes! April, you spend more time and money preparing to do something than anyone I know. The time for preparing to work is over. You're an adult. It is time to put your nose to the grindstone and get busy doing your life's work. Whatever it is."

"I'm trying. It's not my fault the firm closed."

"No. Well, I guess not." She begins to wind down. "But you did decide to turn a deaf ear to your uncle's warning."

"Yes, ma'am."

She sighs heavily, and she appears ten years older. "Child, you're killing me."

I'm still sore from her uncharacteristic outburst but seek to lighten her mood. "Admit it. It'll be fun having me back at the house. We can catch up."

"Baby, if I thought this is where you wanted to be, I'd be positively thrilled you are home."

I give a quick shrug. "It's where I want to be for now."

She nods. "All right. But I'm not sure where we are going to put you."

That makes me laugh. "I'll be able to squeeze everything into my old room. I promise it won't disrupt anything you have going on."

Mama checks the timer on the enchiladas, then crooks a finger at me as she leaves the kitchen. I follow her up the stairs to my room. "April, I took you at your word." She opens my bedroom door. "We've made some changes."

Chapter 3

My room no longer exists. It's been turned into a functional real estate broker's office with a massive L-shaped executive mahogany desk dominating the left side of the room. Multiple oak built-in bookshelves form the back and right walls. An old-school drafting table and stool stand next to the leather love seat opposite the desk. There are enough electronic equipment and flat-screen monitors mounted on the walls to make the CIA envious.

"Oh," I whisper. It comes to mind that I haven't been home since the day of Susan's wedding, and that was four months ago.

"Yeah. I don't think we're moving all that."

"Downstairs?"

"Dusty and all of his equipment. Don't even ask about the guest bedroom. Chase knocked out the separating wall between it and his room two months ago."

"I wasn't expecting this."

Mama opens her eyes wider. "Wait. I just thought about something."

She turns and leaves her office, formerly known as April's room, and quick steps down the stairs. I follow her through the kitchen and out the sliding back door toward the boat dock.

I understand as we reach the brick stairs. "Oh, Mama. I can't stay in the old party room."

"Why not?" she asks.

"It's spooky out here, and that old party room has some of the largest kamikaze camel crickets known to mankind."

"Nonsense. Crickets never hurt anyone." She opens the door and flips the light switch. The old fluorescent lights hiss and blink as they struggle to life. The harsh blue glow illuminates long discarded fishing poles, blow-up rafts, and life jackets. "This looks big enough for your furniture."

"It smells like mildew." I crinkle my nose.

"It's nothing some bleach and Pine-Sol won't cure." She turns to me, and her smile is self-congratulatory. "This will be a nice bachelorette pad if I say so myself."

I sigh. It's no use arguing with Mama once she feels she has a suitable solution to something.

"We'll get the boys to help clear out the clutter after dinner. You and I will bleach the floors and walls, and once it dries tomorrow night, get the boys to move your furniture inside. We'll pull your truck and trailer into the boat garage tonight in case we have some weather." I watch the woman I most want to emulate take charge of the situation. I fear I will never be her equal, and I am positive I will never make her proud of me. My doubts cause large fissures to run through the assertive, confident personality I developed over the last seven years. April, the leader, scholar, and woman with a hundred contingency plans, is receding.

My arms cross my chest, and I clutch at my sides. I want to fight the transformation, but it is as if the April I want to be is being eclipsed, and I have no control over the change.

I am, once again, Mama's foolish girl.

My lungs are burning, and every muscle in my body is spent eight hours later when I step into the shower. I lean against the tile wall as the scalding water blasts years of dust and unidentified grime from the party room off my body.

I partially dry my hair and take note of the time. One in the morning? If this is the first day home, it should motivate me to get my life back on track—sooner rather than later.

Crashing onto the living room sofa, I regret not having dried my hair all the way. It will be a curly mass of confusion in the morning.

My sore body relaxes, and as I drift off to sleep, I have visions of camel cricket carcasses in the corner of rooms and thick cobwebs hanging from the rafters. My new bachelorette pad. Home sweet home.

The following morning, I catch a ride into town with Daddy. He suggested I spend the morning visiting with my Uncle Howard, Daddy's younger brother. Howard owns a law firm in Guntersville.

Daddy routinely works from home in the lab he built on the backside of the lake house. But he has a team meeting at Redstone Arsenal and said he could drop me off on the way.

That's a win. I can detach the trailer from the truck, but I'm not ready to unpack the truck bed until the party room above the boathouse airs out a bit.

I'm beginning to sweat as my nerves act up. I love Howard, but since he warned me about Master, Lloyd, and Johnson, I may be in line for another helping of crow. Plus, he made me promise that if it didn't work out with MLJ, I would work for him for half a year.

Working for him until I receive another offer sounds like a brilliant idea. The six-month commitment not so much. I'm sure it won't take but a few weeks to get my next opportunity lined up.

"What are you working on for the arsenal?" I ask Daddy.

He shoots a quick glance at me and grins. "I could tell you…"

"But then you'd have to kill me," I finish his favorite line that

I walked right into. Daddy is the physics equivalent of a renaissance man. He started with the arsenal as a twenty-something genius in the eighties working on safer fuel cells for the space shuttle after the Discovery disaster. In the last few years, he has been working on something that he can't even tell Mama about.

When he isn't working for Redstone Arsenal, he teaches a science class at the Junior College or tinkers with his perpetual motion machine. The project is his lifetime passion.

Daddy pulls into one of the angled slots in front of my uncle's law office. Howard Snow's office sits one block down from the Guntersville courthouse. It has an impressive ten-foot-tall solid mahogany front door. That's the first and last remarkable thing you can say about his law office.

"I told Howard you were coming. He doesn't have court this morning. I'll be back before noon to pick you up."

That seems like a long time to visit with Howard while he is at work, but we'll have to deal with it since I am down to bumming rides because I can't unload the pickup truck yet. "Okay. Thank you for the ride."

"No worries. Have fun."

I open the large door and step inside. The foyer smells like stale coffee and decaying papers. It is a few steps down to the hardwood floor covering the office. A desk on the right and one on the left sit vacant. A door across the foyer in front of me is open. "Hello?"

"April?" There is a rustling commotion inside the room/ Howard pops through the doorway. "It is you. Ralph said you might be stopping by this morning."

Howard is a man of average height like my daddy. Still, his penchant for business lunches and his love for cobbler has given him a soft rounded look, unlike the sturdy appearance of his brother.

"Yes, sir. He just dropped me off."

"He is not coming in?"

"No, sir. He had a team meeting at the office."

Howard comes and takes my hands into his. The Snow side of the family are huggers and hand-holders. The Hirsh side of the family, not so much. "Vivian told me what happened to you. I'm so sorry, love."

Mama has been busy. Great.

"Please come to my office and tell me all about it."

I explain the events of what was supposed to be my first day at Master, Lloyd, and Johnson. How when I arrived, the FBI was walking the three partners out of the fancy law offices in cuffs. The firm's computer equipment and file cabinets were loaded onto a moving truck caravan. I was informed I was out of a job, just like sixty other people who worked for the firm.

Howard was listening so intently that I found myself explaining how Shane White came to my rescue. Then how his grandfather planted the seed in my mind that I may need to take a step back by moving home temporarily, to move forward.

Howard shakes his head. "That's quite a heartbreaking tale. I'd heard those were some shady characters, but if I'd known to what degree, I might have argued a bit more forcibly."

"It wouldn't have helped." It was easy to be truthful with Howard. He is never judgmental, and his lawyer-client privilege seems to extend to his relationship with his niece.

He favors me with a wan smile. "True. But all the same, I would feel better if I had argued the case effectively." He cocks his head to the right. "So, what now?"

"My plans?"

"Of course, dear. You do have a plan, do you not?"

My shoulders droop. "I don't. I know I need one, but I just can't. You know? The last one worked out so swimmingly well; why bother?"

"I see." Howard sits with his hands clasped together on his desk. I am unsure if he is thinking or waiting for me to formulate a plan.

"I suppose I was hoping you might have some ideas. Since we are in the same line of work."

"I see."

I bite the inside of my lip. I'm not sure what wise advice I hope Howard will share, but the silence as he stares at me is unnerving. Still, he did ask for me to inform him if things didn't work out with MLJ.

"April, the population base is thin in Guntersville and getting thinner every year. Business isn't great. Remember I asked you to come work with me for six months if things didn't work out with your Atlanta firm. I can't think of anything I'd rather do than bring my niece on board and show her the ropes of this old and illustrious profession."

I have no idea what direction this conversation is going in. "I understand."

"Well, I don't believe you do. While I don't have enough work to bring another attorney on full-time, I have a considerable need for a paralegal. I also have a rare case I can't cover due to time constraints."

I think he is offering me a job as an assistant. Awkward. "I'm an attorney, Uncle Howard, not a paralegal."

The left side of Howard's face creases into a wry smile. "No, you're unemployed. Graduating from law school does not make you an attorney. Passing the bar exam and practicing law makes you an attorney."

"I don't sit for the bar until next month." The state only offers it twice a year.

Howard chuckles. "I believe you just made my case, counselor."

His point has some merit. I've already burned two months waiting for the Master, Lloyd, and Johnson position. Now I'm a few weeks out from taking the bar exam and only a few months from some significant student loan payments.

"I appreciate the offer, but I don't want to mislead you. As soon as I pass the bar, I'll be heading back to Atlanta or a different major market."

"You'll find I am always grateful for the help, whether for only the summer or if it turns into a permanent partnership one day."

Permanent partnership? The significant difference between our visions of my career path startles me. He knows I have always had my eye on big city law.

Still, working for him this summer while I study for the bar —I scan the office—and putting the filing to some semblance of order at this office could be mutually beneficial. "What are you proposing?"

"Just basic contract drafting, some consultations, nothing too difficult, mind you." He looks down. "Some filing, bookkeeping, and possibly collections."

I laugh. "I agree on the filing."

He looks up and grins. "I'm afraid it has gotten away from me. But it won't only be office work. I have a contract to fill in for the public defender's office. The court is always running short on defense attorneys. Ever since the budget cuts in two thousand and eight, they've jobbed many of those cases out. I get the lion's share of them. They're mostly plea deals. The name of the game is more about saving time and money than actual justice as of late."

"It sounds interesting enough. What are you offering in the way of pay?"

He sighs. "I can offer fifteen dollars an hour, but not a penny more."

It's hard to swallow. I spent seven years in school and ran up substantial student debt to secure a job I could do with two years' worth of vocational school.

As Grandpa Snow used to say, "You can eat a bird in the hand." I stand and extend my hand to my uncle. "You have a deal, sir."

"That's wonderful. I look forward to working with you, Counselor Snow."

"You know I was planning to hold out for free lunches, but I didn't want to risk overplaying my hand." I joke.

Howard smiles. "If the work is good, I'll throw that in as well."

"So, how about a company car?"

"Now, you've overplayed your hand."

I shrug. "You can't blame a girl for asking."

"No, you can't. Can you be here tomorrow at eight?"

"As long as I get my truck unpacked this evening."

Chapter 4

Howard has to take a call during our conversation about the upcoming Alabama football season and eminent championship repeat. I wave goodbye to him as I lip "thank you."

I have the urge to walk around the square, an activity I enjoyed when I was younger, while I wait for my ride home. The heat and humidity have begun their climb upward, but it's only enough to remind me that it is summer.

The visit with Howard did not go exactly as I expected. I walked into Howard's office, prepared to whine about how unfair the world was, and eek a couple of decent leads out of him. Instead, I leave with a temporary job that seems more like a paid internship with someone I respect and admire while preparing for the bar next month.

Not a bad turn of events. It has me pumped enough to map out April's life plan two-point-o.

I walk through the park in front of the Marshall County courthouse. I stare at the names on the war memorials. It makes my hair stand on end as I consider that Wesley Greenwood, an aviator candidate I met this summer, would be earning his wings about now.

The thought makes me uneasy. Wesley is an accomplished and resourceful man. So much so that I briefly flirted with the idea of a long-term relationship with him.

Still, the idea of him being in harm's way is unsettling, and I hurry from the otherwise pleasant park.

Fant's, the longtime general store on Gunter Avenue, is just up the street. I get a strong urge for nostalgia. Grandpa and Grandma Snow always took us there when we would come into town during our summer-long visits to their farm.

I'm clueless why the old store has always held so much magic for me. There are certainly stores with a better selection, even as close as Boaz, as Mama would always point out when I would ask her if we could go there.

I suppose it is just another touchstone in my life. Something that reminds me of who I am and from where I come.

Today I need that solace of something familiar that holds a sacred memory of my innocence.

As I step onto the alleyway leading from Gunter Avenue to Blount Avenue, a scream makes me jerk to the right. I roll my left ankle as I turn.

Stooped over, clutching at my ankle, I assess the situation further down the alley. A girl, possibly eight, clasps her hands to her stomach as she sits on the asphalt. Two teenage boys stand around her.

Something clicks in me. I limp at an awkward trot down the alleyway, unconcerned that I must look like some crazed blonde female version of Quasimodo.

All the better to scare the little punks away from their victim.

"Hey! What did you two do to her." I yell.

The little girl howls in pain again.

The shorter of the two boys steps back. His eyes are startled wide open.

The other boy gives me a bug-off look as he kneels by the girl and extends his hands toward her. "Let me see, Emily."

"Leave her alone."

"She is my sister, lady." He shoots me a sideways glare, then returns his attention to his sister. "Let me see how bad it is, Emily."

"It hurts—" she sobs.

I take in the helmets, knee and elbow pads, and skateboards as if they miraculously appeared. Bless it. I certainly read this situation all wrong.

Convinced that I have shelved my crazy, the other brother returns to his sister. "C'mon, Em. You got to let us see how bad it is."

My ankle is really sore. I lean over and rub it as I look toward the alley entrance. It seems so far to walk on a sprained ankle.

"It's bad, Tommy. Really bad."

Her voice draws me back to the children. Her expression is serious, and her lips tremble.

"We'll get it fixed. But you got to let me see it."

"You have to promise, Tommy."

"Promise what?"

She draws in a deep breath. "You have to promise me that you won't let them amputate it."

I stifle a laugh. Oh, this little girl is *good.* I wonder if this is the dynamic folks saw when my brothers and I were young.

"I promise I would never let someone hurt you."

"We'd punch them in the nose and then kick'em in the balls if they tried to cut it off, Em." The brother who almost ran from me is a tough talker.

"Okay. But you promised."

Emily holds up her right hand toward Tommy and her other brother. My gorge rises, and I nearly lose it. I must turn away. Her right pinky waggles at a gruesome angle toward the back of her hand.

"Oh, Emily. I think it is broken."

"That's gross," the other brother says.

"Shut your mouth, Scott. You're not helping."

Emily's voice becomes shriller. "But they can fix it, Tommy. You said they can fix it."

A shiver runs up my spine. My fingertips tingle. I know I shouldn't because it will only worsen my situation, but I can't let her be in pain and scared that someone will amputate her pinky.

"Guys, sorry for the intrusion, but I can help."

Tommy frowns at me. He is a tough character. "Are you a nurse or something?"

I move closer. "No, but my brothers and I used to do stunts off ramps with our bicycles."

Scott grins as if I am making that up. Fair. I did just roll my ankle while walking.

"We used to jam our fingers all the time, and we learned tricks on how to fix them so we wouldn't have to go home early." I lower myself to the pavement next to Emily. "Hi, I'm April."

She squints her eyes warily as she focuses on my face. "I'm Emily."

"Pleased to meet you. I wish it were under better circumstances." She is not warming up to me. These kids are a tough crowd. "Can I take a closer look at your finger?"

She presses her lips into a thin line. She sighs and sticks her right hand over my lap. I take it in my hands and make to study it at length.

"This isn't bad at all, Emily. It's a simple dislocated knuckle. I can fix this if you want."

"That's not like any dislocated finger I've ever seen. That's broke," Scott says.

I ignore him and look pointedly into Emily's eyes. "It is your choice, Emily. Do you want me to try?"

"Will it hurt?"

"I can't promise that it won't, but doesn't it hurt right now."

She nods her head.

I wink at her. "Okay. I need you to keep it still the best you can and if you feel a tingle, just know that is supposed to happen. It is your pinched nerves coming back to life."

"That ain't no pinched nerve."

"Quiet, Scott," Tommy scolds.

I fold my hands over Emily's and gather the energy floating in the air. There always seems to be an overabundance of it in Guntersville. I condense it into my core as I focus on healing

Emily's finger.

Electrical pricks dance along the palms of my hands. Emily's eyes open wider, and I offer her a reassuring smile.

Unnatural heat builds between our hands as the healing process takes hold. I relax, knowing that my wackadoodle paranormal skills may prove helpful for something today.

"What do you want to be when you grow up?" I ask Emily as I wait for the heat to subside, indicating the healing is complete.

"I want to be either a princess or a spy." She leans in toward me.

"Those sound like two great choices." I tilt my head. "Why can't you be both?"

"Can I?"

"Girls can't be spies," Scott says.

"Dude, Belle Boyd—Mata Hari—" Tommy says.

"Who?"

"Dude, you've got to read more."

I whisper in Emily's ear. "Don't you ever let someone tell you that you can't do something." I lean back and arch my brows. "Promise?"

Emily favors me with a determined expression. Frankly, if I'm being honest, it is a tad on the scary side. "I promise."

The heat has dissipated from our hands. I make a flourish of releasing her from my grasp. "Voila!"

Emily holds her hand in front of her face and grins.

"Try it out," I say.

She bends her pinky several times, and she flashes her tiny teeth as she looks at Tommy. "It's fixed, Tommy. She fixed it!"

He raises his eyebrows. "I see that."

"She didn't do nothing," Scott says.

Emily holds her hand up toward Scott and makes an ugly face. "It's fixed." She punctuates it by sticking out her tongue.

"How did you?" Tommy asks.

I struggle to my feet, twenty-seven is feeling pretty old today, and the healing "gift" always transfers a portion of the pain temporarily to me. "I think we should go get a Coke and some candy. My treat. What do you think?"

Sugar is always an excellent deflection against difficult conversations.

Daddy picks me up back at the alley where the three Wake siblings are showing off their skateboard skills to me.

"Who are your friends?" He asks as I get into his truck.

"The Wakes, do you know them?"

"Chris's and Lia's kids?"

I grimace. I'm out of practice with the small-town ways. "Sorry, I didn't think to ask their parents' names."

He grunts. "It would have to be. What did Howard have to say."

"Mostly that he wished I had listened to him. But then he offered me work until I finish the bar." I beam toward Daddy. "I don't know why. It's just an administrative job. But for some odd reason, I'm looking forward to it. I think it might be a fun distraction.

He appears to consider the information carefully before answering. "At least you can show some experience on your resume for future job interviews."

"I know. Right? I'm super excited."

"That's good, April. I'm glad you're happy."

Daddy's tone doesn't match his words. "But what?"

He shrugs. "Nothing, baby."

Chapter 5

I see my car parked at the lake house as we pull into the drive. My stomach does a flip. If my old Prius is here, that means Shane has arrived.

"How did your car get here, April?" Daddy asks.

"My friend, who loaned me the truck and trailer, drove it up from Atlanta so we could exchange."

"That is some sort of special friend indeed."

With all my heart, I hope Daddy is right. I'd love for Shane to be my special friend. "I can't wait to introduce you."

I hop out of the car and quickstep across the drive to the deck. I look through the sliding glass door, not there, and then to the lower dock. I see two big men squatting beside a tackle box on the weathered gray boards. Their backs, shirtless, are to me.

My brother Chase is the golden-brown back on the right with "Barbarian" tattooed on his right shoulder blade. The lower-case letter "I" appears crammed in the tattoo because the ink used to read "Barbara." She was Chase's first, and as far as I'm aware, only serious girlfriend.

The other masculine back speeds up my heart, and I feel lightheaded. It's only been a day, and it feels like I haven't seen Shane in a month.

I jump the last three steps off the deck and jog down the

concrete path toward the water. I slow as I reach the dock and walk silently toward them. The men, deep in their conversation, don't appear to notice the slight vibration my steps cause.

"Hey!" I holler loudly.

Shane and Chase tilt their heads toward me, squinting against the sun's brightness. Okay, they did hear me coming.

"Hey, April," Shane says with an easy smile.

My breath catches in my chest as he rises to face me. Impossibly, I'd already forgotten how chiseled his upper body is, and I struggle to tear my eyes from his exposed nipples. "I was expecting you to call before you brought my car."

"I had a break in my schedule. I thought I'd take advantage of it and surprise you."

I move in and hug him. Breathing in his scent, he smells like honey and orange flowers with a hint of musk to me, and I close my eyes and enjoy his smell like a cupcake. He gives me a squeeze and releases me.

"Your brother Chase is showing me these spinners he has been using for smallmouth with some success."

"I told him I couldn't swear they'd work with those Georgia bass, but it works just fine on Guntersville Lake," Chase interjects.

"I'm always up for trying something different to improve my chances," Shane says. "You can't get in a rut."

"You know, I've got extras of these. You need to take a few." Chase hands him the spinner and then taps him on the shoulder with the back of his hand. "Oh man, I forgot to show you the Striker King." Chase squats down, hovering over the vast camouflage-patterned tackle box, and Shane follows suit.

I'm shocked as I watch the two men rifling through the tackle box and discussing different lures. I know Shane likes to fish, and he is only distracted by the opportunity to talk with another angler. He wouldn't make me feel like a distant second to a stupid fish lure on purpose.

I'm not going to lie; it does sting my ego a little. Well, a lot.

I almost do the intelligent thing and creep back to the shelter of the lake house, where I can hide out until my ego recovers. Instead, I decide Shane's had a momentary lapse, and once he really sees me, he'll want to hang out with me.

"Shane, do you want to ride to get some ice cream?" That must be a better offer than squatting on an old dock in blistering heat sorting through fishy-smelling lures.

Shane turns his head and squints again. "Huh?"

"Ice cream. You like ice cream, remember?" Now I just sound stupid.

His brow furrows. "Yes."

"Well?" I gesture in the direction of the driveway. "Do you want to go to the ice cream parlor?"

Shane considers the proposition carefully before he replies, "Nah. I'm good. You go ahead if you want, though."

It's as if someone pulled my beating heart out of my chest and dropped a sixteen-pound bowling ball on it. I'm crushed.

The boys have already turned back to their stupid bobbers and floats. I fight back the urge to grab a pack of barbed hooks and see how many I can attach to them before they break out of their lure trance. Dejected, I close my mouth before catching a fly in it and retreat toward the lake house.

My walk up the concrete path to the patio is more embarrassing than any walk of shame I took during college. Nothing shameful ever happened with Shane, and nothing ever will from the looks of it.

I slide the glass door a little too hard as I enter the kitchen. Standing at the kitchen sink, cleaning some strawberries, Dusty quickly scans from the entrance to my face.

"You're at seventy percent of the force required to shatter the glass out of the doorframe."

"I just can't right now, Dusty," I reply as I turn to examine the glass and wonder if he is telling the truth or making his observation up on the fly.

Dusty holds up a strawberry. "Want one?"

"No," I snarl.

He pops it in his mouth. "I was kidding anyway."

I sit down on one of the stools on the opposite side of the counter and watch him continue to clean strawberries. Watching Dusty's thoughtful attention to cleaning each berry and listening to the running water has a calming effect on my nasty mood. I hold my hand out, and Dusty drops a golfball-sized strawberry into my palm.

I bite it in half. The juice, tart and sweet, makes me pucker my mouth slightly as the full-bodied taste covers my palate. There is no mistaking the berries that come from our strawberry patch. Some of my earliest memories of home come from eating strawberries and blackberries right off the vine.

"Chase, Shane, and I got your stuff moved into the party room. Let Chase and me know what you want to be moved around later if you don't like how we laid out your furniture."

"You didn't have to do that."

"It was our pleasure."

"Well, thank you."

"You're welcome. Dad said Howard offered you a part-time job?"

"Yeah."

"That's good. A little spending money can take the pressure off. Keep you from making a hasty decision on your next job selection."

"What does that mean?" I bow up.

The corners of Dusty's lips flare up into a grin. He looks down at the berry in his hand. "Just saying the next time you step out there, I'm sure you'd prefer it to be with a quality organization."

"That's true." I hold out my hand, and he drops a few more berries into my palm.

"Preferably one that'll be open long enough for you to draw your first paycheck."

"Dusty, so not funny."

He doesn't bother to hide his grin now. "I was wondering. I know you don't care for it, and this is just a thought, but I'm in the research stage of my next book—I thought maybe you could do some odd jobs around here for me too."

"Geez, Dusty. I'm just in between jobs temporarily. I'm not desperate enough to be your maid yet."

Dusty leans against the counter and barks out a laugh that makes me sit up straight. His head drops back as he continues with his out-of-control howl, his red beard swaying as he shakes his head. He holds his breath as if trying to gain control, and his body begins to shake with irregular tremors as tears stream down his cheeks.

Despite my best effort to remain outraged at his comment, I begin to giggle. It's been this way for as long as I can recall. Dusty is given to fits of uncontrolled laughter. His laughs are incredibly contagious.

He regains his composure and swipes the perspiration off his forehead with the back of his hand. "No, I don't need my kid sister picking my dirty shorts off the floor for me. I'm a big boy, and I can do that myself. I need someone with real talent when I go on site. Most of the time, it'll be weekend work. I'm sure we can work it out with Howard and your commitment to his law firm. That is if you're interested."

"I thought Miles helped you with your research trips."

Miles Trufant, one of Dusty's band friends from high school, was at one time an up-and-coming nonfiction writer in his own right. Miles earned his doctorate in psychology from Vanderbilt. His thesis was on the dangers of superstitions to the development of the human mind. They paused their friendship because of their differing views when it became too challenging to have a civil discussion. The pause turned into professional dislike, culminating in Miles working for two years to discredit and disprove all thirteen stories Dusty reported in his first book.

Miles was unable to disprove any of the stories.

In typical Dusty fashion, unexpectedly, he called his frenemy and asked him to join him on the subsequent site visit. Dusty promised to share all documentation regardless if the site proved truly haunted or a fake.

Neither will talk about what transpired the night of that investigation. Still, I know both men ended up in the emergency room, according to Chase, who took them a fresh change of clothes. Miles and Dusty have been an inseparable team since.

"He does. And Miles is an excellent researcher as well as writer, but he is not psychic."

"What?" I can't believe this is coming up again.

"April, my work would be so much easier with a psychic."

"Dusty, no. You know I can't risk that."

"Risk what? That your powers will get stronger? April, you've said it yourself. They're getting stronger on their own no matter what you're doing."

"Only because I keep getting put into weird situations that bring them to the forefront, Dusty."

"Listen, all I'm saying is if they're going to be coming to life anyway, you might as well use the talent for some extra cash until you get your next lawyer gig lined up. Besides the lawyer gig with Howard."

"Cute."

He cracks a smile. "Come on. You know we have fun when we investigate. It'll be like the old team getting back together."

"The old team that almost got you killed. No way, Dusty. That hoodoo stuff scares me."

"Of course, it does. It scares everyone. Why do you think my books pull in a million dollars a year? People love to be scared."

"Not this chick." I point at my chest.

"Sorry. I just thought you might want to make some extra money. Given your current employment status, I didn't think you could exactly turn down easy cash."

"You bite!" I slide off the stool and stomp out of the kitchen.

"Okay. No need to get upset. I just thought thirty dollars an hour might be of interest to you. You know, on a three-day weekend, that's over two thousand dollars before taxes."

I freeze in my tracks and walk back into the kitchen. "How's that?"

"A three-day weekend is seventy-two hours. I'd have to pay

you every hour you're traveling with me. I mean, that is what would be fair, right?"

"Right. That would be fair," I reply as the idea begins to seem a little more palatable to me.

"So, does that mean you're in?"

"Are you throwing in meals?"

Dusty's face twitches. "Of course, meals are included. What do you think I am, a mule driver?"

The paranormal has always given me a severe case of the heebie-jeebies, but I can earn in three days with Dusty what would take three weeks to make with Howard. Not to mention, I know the two of them will work through any scheduling conflicts. I extend my hand to Dusty. "Deal."

"Excellent! The next trip is in eight days. I'll get you the particulars a little later in the week."

I should be happy. Earlier this morning, I was concerned about making a living. Free room and board are great, but it's hard to pay my student loans or put gas in my car without an income. Now, I have a nice income stream lined up that will allow me time to prepare for the bar exam and find my dream job.

Then why am I feeling anxious? Easy, the more I use my paranormal "gifts," the more often they pop into gear and the stronger they grow. I really want them to just go away.

But you can't deny your heritage, especially when you're the lucky girl to win the double recessive freaky gene lottery. Daddy's mama, Granny Snow, is rumored to have cast out demons in her younger years. If you met her you would agree with me that it must be poppycock.

Granny in her youth, standing straight, might have been a smidge over five foot tall. Now I'm forced to bend my knees when we hug and she feels pleasantly soft like a marshmallow —not exactly Archangel Michael if you catch my drift. Still, I swear there are times she has an odd glow around her head. It has nothing to do with her cotton ball white helmet hairdo.

My Nana Hirsch, Mama's mother, is a witch. I don't mean

she is some crotchety old woman who scares the bejesus out of the neighborhood kids. Although she does that with regularity too. I mean, Nana is an actual hex-bag hiding, voodoo-doll-pin-sticking, potion-making witch.

My Grandpa Hirsch met her a couple of years before he was deployed to Vietnam. He fell head over heels in love with her immediately. Everyone in the family agrees Nana must've slipped him an extra-strong love potion. He was an extraordinarily handsome man with a beautiful disposition, from what I'm told.

On the other hand, Nana Hirsch is a beautiful woman who is outright odd and scary. I've never met a woman stranger than my Nana. Still, once you get past her oddity, she can be fun to visit.

I never bought into the whole "Witch" act when I was a little girl. I played along with what my older brothers told me about her. It was less out of respect for her and more as an insurance policy in the event I was wrong, and Nana really was a witch. I was perpetually terrified of being turned into a camel cricket.

My entire belief system turned upside down the day I became a woman. While I suppose other young women only deal with the anxiety and fright from the sight of their first menstruation, I had the added surprise of coping with the voices and visions.

The voices came flooding into my mind. Loud and eager, each scratching at the interior of my brain. Each spirit was anxious for its story to be heard. The noise was deafening.

As horrifying as the voices were, the visions were much more disturbing. I could not touch a single object or go into a room without seeing some past event or a blur of what would soon happen. The scenes would flash in brilliant colors behind my eyes so quickly that I sometimes could only make out snippets of the event. It was like watching a movie fast-forwarded while you sat three inches from a big-screen television.

The scenes left me disoriented and dizzy. I'd slump to the left if I were seated as I lost equilibrium. If I were walking, I'd fall onto my side unless I was able to clutch hold of a desk or table on my way to the floor.

After two weeks, with great reservation, Mama took me to Nana Hirsch's on the behest of my daddy. On the way out to her trailer in the woods, I remember believing that my mama might be ready to abandon me at Nana's.

The fear of isolation at Nana's focused the visions for the first time. The images behind my eyes slowed, and I heard only the voices of Mama and Nana.

Nana had me finish off a nasty dark liquid as she described ways to tune out the voices and the visions. She explained when the "gift" arrived, the valve was wide open. It was like a fire hydrant, but I held the key to decide how much flowed through the valve and what I wanted to see and or hear. I also, she explained, could seal the pipe.

The vision calmed me as we approached Nana's trailer. The calm was quickly replaced with a foreboding knowledge of the power of my "gifts." I was horrified as everything Nana and Mama said followed the script from the earlier vision I had traveling to Nana's trailer. Even when I attempted to raise a question or objection I thought would alter our visit, I only helped pull the foreshadowed events quicker into reality.

I wasn't scared after the training class with Nana. I was terrified. No one should have the ability to see the past and future with such clarity, much less at the age of twelve. From that day forward, I rarely opened the valve of my "gifts" intentionally.

Mama and Daddy never spoke of the incident again. Dusty figured out on his own what was happening to me. Until I left for college, he would come to me and beg me to "read" an item for him. Sometimes it would be a rock, a plank from an old barn, and on one occasion, and one of the most extended visions I ever experienced, the family bible of a family from Montgomery, Alabama.

I've always been concerned when I read an object, I might not be able to reclose the valve on the voices and visions. Or worse, get caught up in some unseen vortex that pulls me into an alternate plane. I have no reason to think this. Neither of my grandmothers has ever hinted at some dangerous wormhole in the veil. It is just a gut feeling I can't explain.

Now that I'm older, another concern has clawed its way into my mind. Lately, I've wondered what it would mean if I changed my approach and used my "gifts" to my advantage. What if I used them to read people's thoughts and emotions rather than try to decipher them like an average person. The idea started as a tickle in my mind. Now, as situations like what happened with my job at Master, Lloyd, and Johnson, and Shane's unexpected disinterest earlier on the dock, it's an outrageous itch that wants to be scratched. I worry if I ever crossed the line and began to use my "gifts" actively, they would take hold of me in an all-consuming addiction.

Chapter 6

I'm in the family room watching a *Flip this Dump of a House* marathon when Shane makes an appearance. Sadly, his shirt is on now. "Hey, April. I just want to let you know I'm heading back home."

"Are you not going to stay for dinner?"

He favors me with a sexy smile, and my skin tingles. "Nah, I've got to get back tonight. I'm on duty for the rest of the week."

"How's Dr. Hamlin?" I worked for Dr. Hamlin while I was in Atlanta.

"Good. She just promoted me because of the certification you helped me get when I went to Cincinnati."

"Congratulations. What's your title now."

"Dr. Hamlin's right-hand man." He grins.

I know I won't get clarification out of him. Usually, I don't like men who keep secrets. For Shane, I would make an exception.

Speaking of exceptions, I need to cut him some slack. I'm aware of his fondness for fishing, and he just got carried away discussing his hobby with another fishing enthusiast.

He did make a point to see me before he left. Shane is a wise man. After having time alone to consider our relationship, I'm sure he realizes we would make a dynamo couple.

I make my way over to him and hug him, leaving my arms draped around his waist. I look him in the eye, then lean in and kiss him on the lips. I break the kiss and say, "I appreciate you loaning me the truck and bringing my car to me. That's beyond the call of duty."

"Hey, I wanted to. I'll be back in a couple of weeks."

My heart soars, and the flames of lust are stoked to a fevered pitch instantly. "Really! That's great, Shane. We can go tubing, eat at Rex's and build a fire in the pit at night."

Shane's lips curl back, exposing his bright white teeth. "Yeah. Maybe we can work some of that in-between."

"In between?"

"The fishing tournament. Chase and I are entering the upcoming fishing tournament."

"Oh. Oh, my bad." I attempt to hide my embarrassment poorly.

"April. Hey, look at me." He slides a warm finger under my chin and gently turns my face toward him. "You're a beautiful woman. You're so smart, and you'll make some lucky man a great partner someday."

"But?" I croak.

That blasted, devastatingly sexy smile graces his face again. "Baby, too much is sometimes too much. I'm a simple man."

My face crumbles into a sob, and I'm relieved Shane pulls me into a hug. I feel raw and exposed as he holds me tight. He pats me on the back and breaks from me without looking me in the eye. "See you in a couple of weeks, April. Stay out of trouble."

I watch Shane's slow gait to the front door. He opens it, turns, and gives me one last wave before closing the door behind him.

The click of the door closing crushes me for the second time in less than an hour. My self-confidence is shredded.

I don't want you to think I'm in love with Shane. I have too many things I want to accomplish to be tied down with the burden of being in love with a man and having to worry about his needs and wants. However, I'm seriously in lust with

Shane. I wasn't expecting much. A steamy kiss to unhinge my knees, have him cop a feel so I could brush his hand away and tell him to cut it out. Is that too much for a girl to expect? Obviously, it is.

The score, plus two on the job front and minus one in the sexual column. Overall, I'd put today in the winning category. So why am I feeling like a total loser?

Daddy calls us to dinner and lays out bowls of his five-cheese baked ziti. I take a mental note, I must kick my non-existent exercise program into overdrive now that I'm back home. It's easy to consume two to three times the necessary daily caloric intake when my family is cooking if you're not careful.

"Your father says you got a job with Howard, April?" Mama asks.

"Yes, ma'am. More of a paralegal. But it'll help for now."

"It will do you good to get back on that horse quickly," Daddy comments.

"I hired her too," Dusty announces. "She is my team's new psychic."

I notice Mama and Daddy exchange one of their concerned looks. "It sounds like she has a full dance card now," Mama says.

"I like your new dude," Chase interjects.

"Shane is not my dude. We're just friends."

"He is cool. Not like those pretty boys you usually date."

My ire begins to rise. "We are not dating."

Chase nods acknowledgment. "So are y'all like exclusive or what?"

I close my eyes and try to contain my aggravation. "I guess it would be what, Chase."

"I don't know what you're waiting for. He is a great guy." Chase shoves an enormous amount of pasta in his mouth.

Mama and Daddy cast their eyes downward and shake their

heads slowly.

Dusty adds. "Make sure to let Chase know if you kick Shane to the curb."

"What? I'm just saying the dude is cool, is all."

"Shane is not my boyfriend!" I say too loud.

"Guys, it's not appropriate to talk about your sister's love life," Daddy says.

Oh my gosh. This is what drives me nuts about being home. Everyone is in your business, even when you don't have any business going on.

"I was just saying it'd be cool to have him around," Chase grumbles.

"Chase Snow, enough," Mama says.

Chase gives a shrug of the shoulder before he becomes distracted, wrangling noodles onto his fork. He has always been a direct speaker, too light on the social graces.

Part of his issue is he has an insatiable natural curiosity. I can't fault him for that. I suffer the same affliction.

Still, Chase lobbying for Shane as if Chase needs another friend is beyond the pale. Chase has accrued an eclectic collection of friends from all levels of society. Everybody in Guntersville knows Chase, and moreover, everyone loves Chase.

"We'll get up to your room as soon as we clean the kitchen. Okay, April?" Mama says.

"Yes, ma'am."

"I wish we had been able to get it painted first. I suppose we can get that done easily enough later."

Something about the permanence of paint hooks under my skin. I know I'd be trapped forever in Guntersville if the walls were ever painted. It's not logical, but that's what I feel. "We don't need to paint the walls, Mama. I won't be staying long anyway."

"Oh, don't be silly. I've been meaning to clean the party room for years now. This is a great excuse to get busy with it."

I lay on my bed in the old party room converted into my bachelorette pad. My hair's still wet from my shower, and my eyes are wide open and fully adjusted to the dark. I admire the silver quarter moon through the sunroof of the party room and feel the soft upward and downward bob of the large boat-house on the lake.

I close my eyes and attempt to open the paranormal spigot ever so slightly. I smile as the vision of three children jumping off the boathouse roof appears. It's not a vision, just a mem-ory of a summer day long gone. Chase, long, lean, and blond, dives in, leaving no ripple on the lake's surface. Dusty, full-bodied with bright red curly hair, pulls his thick thighs against his chest as he strikes the water butt first, sending a plume of water to lick at my legs as I stand on top of the party room roof.

I'm a pencil-thin little girl and stand on the roof's edge. My brothers cheer me on as they wade below. They plead for me to jump. Finally, I pinch my nose with one hand and leap off the tin roof.

My thin body slides quickly under the dark water as I plunge straight to the bottom of the lake. My feet sink deep into the thick mud below.

I swim upward, following the last bubbles from my lungs when something grabs my left ankle and holds me in place. I flail with my arms trying to purchase the surface as my lungs begin to ache and burn. A second hand clasps my wrist, and momentarily I am in between a tug of war. The hand pulling on my wrist wins and draws me to the surface.

The concern is etched on Dusty's meaty face. "I wasn't sure you were coming back up, Tinker Bell." His voice echoes in my head as if I heard it rather than remember my brother's young voice.

I lay in bed, wondering why that vision. It must be because I rolled my ankle today. That's all.

Slowly I run my hand over the left ankle that, to this day, has nerve damage from the strange hand that grabbed me in the water. An injury I've never mentioned to family or friends.

Chapter 7

I enter the front door of Snow and Associates for my first day of work. A small plaque bearing my name is on the anteroom desk to the right. I run my finger across the top of the shiny nameplate. "Counselor April Snow." I like the sound of it.

Howard's sweet gesture warms my heart as I realize, he has already done more to welcome me than Master, Lloyd, and Johnson did the entire time they recruited me.

My nose takes over, and I see a little white bag and a small coffee. I don't have to open it to know it's a breakfast biscuit from Ms. Bell.

I walk to the office door and knock on the casing. Howard angles his face up from his laptop screen. He pushes his glasses back and smiles. "Good morning. I didn't hear you come in."

"Thank you for breakfast."

"Hmm. You're going to need it, I'm afraid. Ms. Castle is on her way in to change her will again. The pleasure is all yours, counselor."

I notice a concealed grin on Howard's lips. "Again?"

"Yes, again. It sounds as if one of Ms. Castle's many nieces has done something to irk her sensibilities once more."

"Okay." I want to go back to my desk without asking the next question, but I can't help myself. "How many times has she changed her will?"

"Lord. I honestly wouldn't know. It seems like she has revised it at least two or three times in the last year."

"Goodness. Is her family fighting over her money that fiercely?"

Howard chuckles. "Heavens no. Other than her social security check, a rundown farm and a ten-thousand-dollar burial policy that woman doesn't have a cent to her name."

"Then why on earth would you allow her to spend money on changing her will?"

"Because the woman is seventy-nine years old and I was brought up in an era of respecting my elders' wishes. Besides, if it gives the woman some twisted petty pleasure cutting a relative out of her will, who am I to judge. I have a few odd vices myself."

"It's unseemly to take payment for unnecessary legal work."

"My, my, a barrister with a conscience. They say that is rarer than a talking pegasus." Howard turns his attention back to his laptop.

"Do you mind if I show her how she can alter the will online to save her the money?"

"Please, be my guest. If you can change her ways, so I don't have to hear her horror stories a couple times each month, go right ahead. You be sure and tell me how that works out for you."

I exhale loudly to indicate my displeasure and return to my desk to enjoy my breakfast. I'm secretly appalled by Howard's cavalier attitude about taking money needlessly from a widow living on a fixed income. I've always considered Howard to be one of the "good guys" when I was growing up. I always fancied him as a hero in the courtroom who fought to get wrongly arrested people their freedom again. Never would I have imagined the sparse client population of Guntersville had led him to feed off the withering bank accounts of elderly women.

I unwrap the parchment paper from the biscuit. My mouth waters as I recognize the golden butter biscuit overflowing with meat the color of brown sugar. I hold in my hand a Marshall County famous tenderloin biscuit from Ms. Bell's Meat and Three.

Let me explain. Ms. Bell's butter biscuits melt on your tongue like peppermint candy. You don't really chew her butter biscuits. You just take a bite and savor them as they dissolve in your mouth.

Honestly, it must be magic. I don't cook, but everyone in Guntersville who does cook has tried some variation of biscuit recipes to replicate the taste and experience of eating a Ms. Bell's. It's been concluded that it's impossible to make a biscuit that'll dissolve in your mouth and taste so good without using magic.

As good as her biscuits are, the tenderloin her son Jasper makes for the biscuits is unworldly. Jasper is a master griller and barbecue specialist with no equal. They call him the butt whisperer. I know, it's a funny-sounding moniker. There is an art to cooking pork butts, and Jasper is the Michelangelo.

As famous as he is for his pork butt, his tenderloin is revered as a special gift for someone important in your life. I'm feeling special right now.

I once heard Jasper cooks his tenderloin for five days at an extremely low temperature, and that's how his meat is so tender. My brother Chase is a competent griller, too. He claims that's total bull. Chase says the only thing you'd get from five days on the grill is some delicious beef jerky.

Jasper is the defensive coach for the Guntersville football team and their basketball coach in the spring. Consequently, he only works at the Meat and Three during the summer months. That always makes a tenderloin biscuit a limited time offer. The line that forms outside of Ms. Bell's on summer mornings can be twenty deep.

Steam tendrils roll off the top of the biscuit as I lift it to my mouth. In anticipation of the culinary delight, I close my eyes. The front door opens.

I'm sure I look like a victim of a severe case of lockjaw to the diminutive woman standing in front of my desk. Her skin possesses a translucent quality. Her hair, while cotton ball white and wispy thin, is made up with impeccable care. Her teal pants suit, while a bit dated, looks sharp and crisp on her small frame.

"Ahem, ahem." The elderly woman clears her throat while not making eye contact.

Slowly, regrettably, I lay my treasure back in its parchment paper and wrap it lovingly around it as if it will somehow hold the warmth to the biscuit. "Yes, may I help you?"

"Yes, dear. I am here to see Howard. I mean attorney Snow."

"Can I tell him who's calling?"

"Certainly. Dottie Castle."

"Oh, Ms. Castle. We've been expecting you. My name is April Snow, and Counselor Snow has asked me to help you with your will today."

"Are you an attorney?"

"Yes, ma'am."

"You don't look old enough to be an attorney. You did not get your degree from some online program, now did you?"

"No, ma'am. I graduated from the University of Alabama."

"Well, I suppose we won't hold that against you, dear. Not everybody can get into the University of Georgia."

"Yes, ma'am." I gesture toward the seats in front of me. "So, what changes do you need to make to your will, Ms. Castle?"

She steps to the left and cranes her neck toward Howard's partially closed door. "Is Howard back there?"

"Yes. He is preparing for a big defense case this afternoon." the white lie uncommonly smooth for me.

With a sigh, Ms. Castle takes a seat. "Now I expect the normal client-lawyer privileges. This all needs to be held in tight confidentiality."

"I understand."

"Those girls can be right down hateful about such matters."

"Yes, ma'am. I understand completely." I open the folder Howard handed me earlier and I turn on my laptop. "Now, I heard you want to remove someone from your will."

"Yes. My grandniece Jill Bates."

That's the thing about Guntersville, it's a novelty that I've never met Dottie Castle, but the first relative she mentions, BAM, I know Jill Bates.

Jill Bates runs one of the two locally owned hardware stores in Guntersville with her husband, Walter. They have two daughters, Mindy who is a few years older than me, and I believe I heard she married some guy in North Carolina and Tiffany, who is two years younger than me. We were on the cheerleading squad together in high school. The last I knew Tiffany was running the local beauty college.

"I see. Now before we go any further, Ms. Castle, I want to explain that we'll treat today as a free consultation. For smaller estates, sometimes it makes more economic sense for you to simply adjust your will online, print it out, and have a notary sign it." I turn my laptop around so Ms. Castle can see the form online. Her look is blank and confused. "I'll walk you through it. It's easy. You'll see."

"I don't understand. Howard always takes care of these things for me."

"Yes, ma'am. But it cost two hundred dollars each time Counselor Snow makes a change for you, and if you're on a fixed income, that can become pretty expensive."

"But Howard has been our lawyer ever since Gil and I bought the business."

The name Gil brings back memories. Gil on the Hill at one time had been a dominant force in the new and used car market in Guntersville.

When I was a child, Guntersville was known as the used car capital of the southeast. Each year there were over twenty-five thousand cars sold in Guntersville. An impressive number of vehicles considering the city has a population of fewer than eight thousand people.

In the late nineties, after twenty years of the Castles being one of the most influential couples in Guntersville, Gil on the Hill was raided by FBI agents who collected information on the business for the previous two years. The company had a two-fold purpose.

First, Gil on the Hill was a processor of used cars of disreputable origin. Not unheard of in these parts before digital odometers.

A vehicle would be stolen in Texas, brought to Alabama, the odometer changed, new paint, seats, floor mats, and a fake VIN plate added. The revitalized vehicle would then be sold as a "Program" vehicle. The second aspect of the business had to do with Gil's expensive dependency on cocaine. He financed his habit by laundering the money of one of the many drug rings that flourished in Guntersville at the time, often referred to as the Dixie Mafia.

Gil Castle would have been much better off to have just paid cash for his drugs. He would've gotten off with a year or two in minimum security and then a few years of probation if he were just a user. Having been part of the financial operation of the drug ring, he was caught up in the RICO act, and all assets of the Castle family and businesses were seized.

The scandal was massive enough even as a seven-year-old, I was able to commit some of the tawdry details to memory. The couple's fall from grace was swift and permanent.

As it was, Gil never served a day of jail time. He disappeared into thin air without a trace. The legends of where Gil Castle is now are many and light on facts. If I had to guess, Gil is part of a concrete slab resting on the muddy floor of the Guntersville Lake.

"You know what, Ms. Castle? I'm just going to fix you up right quick and let you get on with the rest of your day."

I reach out and pat Ms. Castle's hand, meaning to reassure her. The image is fast and grainy in texture. Too quick for me to make out details other than the face of a man under duress. The metallic taste of fear overwhelms my taste buds, and I can feel intense anger. Still, there is no auditory with the flash. I list to the left as my equilibrium goes screwy.

"Miss Snow, are you all right?"

I shake my head to clear the cobwebs and straighten my posture. "Yes, ma'am. I just felt faint for a moment. Now let's take care of this paperwork."

Chapter 8

Howard leaves for lunch with a client at noon. He promises to bring me back a chicken salad.

I do some light filing for him and then come to the end of the task list for the day. I flick on my laptop and do a job search in Huntsville, Alabama. Nothing is even remotely of interest. Besides, there is one aspect of living in Guntersville that will require positions in other cities to up their compensation packages for me to apply. Being pragmatic, free room, and board is a serious perk.

I'm deep into an ad about a human resource director position in Nashville that I'm not qualified for when the front door opens. I assume it's Howard returning from lunch. Instead, a well-dressed man with salt and pepper hair strolls into the office like he owns the building. We lock eyes. His brown eyes are so bright and alert they seem to cut to the secrets of my soul.

He straightens to his full height as apparent confusion flashes across his face. "Oh, excuse me, I didn't realize Howard had hired an assistant."

"I'm actually his niece, April."

"Niece? Right. I'd forgotten he had a niece." He extends his hand. "I'm district attorney Lane Jameson."

I shake his hand briefly and am forced to conceal my smile.

He is incredibly easy to read. Lane's energy level is only eclipsed by his sexual force, yet his body language is utterly calm, collected, and professional. "Pleasure to meet you, Mr. Jameson."

He looks over my shoulder. "Is Howard in his office?"

"No, he is at lunch."

"I see." He takes his phone out and taps in a number.

"I doubt you'll get him. Howard is having lunch with a client and probably will set his phone to airplane mode."

Lane raises his chin and grins. "That stops voice mail from working now?"

"No, but some folks don't check voice mails right away. If you leave the message with me, I'll make sure Howard calls you." Sue me, I'm nosy. My reasoning sounds lame even to me, but from the look of Lane's facial expression, he is debating if he wants to leave a message with me.

I like his eyes. Something about him makes me lean forward while we talk.

"Yes, I suppose that would be all right. Please inform your uncle I'll need him to take on the Charlotte King defense. I couldn't arrange council representation for her given my team's present caseload." He holds out an inter-department envelope.

"That's it?" I ask, a bit disappointed as I accept the envelope.

His lips curl into a smile. He has a smile way too sexy for a man of his age. "I'm afraid the rest would fall under client confidentiality rules. But please ask him to get with Ms. King as early as his schedule will allow. Hopefully, he can negotiate a plea bargain for her. I believe it would be best for all parties."

Still disappointed, I take out a sticky notepad, jot down the message, and stick it to the envelope. "All right, I'll give it to Howard, and I'll make sure he gives you a call."

"Thank you." Lane begins to leave before turning. "And congratulations on the job. I can't tell you how happy I am to see Howard finally hire some help."

I open my mouth to tell him I'm just temporary and set him straight. But before I say a word, he closes the door.

My original intent as I walk into Howard's office is to put the folder on his desk. But my curiosity gets the best of me.

I check the time and figure I have at least fifteen minutes. I sit down in Howard's cool cushy leather chair and kick back with my feet on his desk. I flip through the folder of Charlotte King.

The first thing I notice is even though we are the same age I've never met her. That's two people today, a record. But she does live near Boaz, so it's doubtful she went to our high school.

I take note that the report says she has four children that were referred to DCS when she was taken into custody. Mama would be thrilled if I were that productive having babies rather than earning a law degree the last seven years.

Unfortunately for Charlotte King, that's where the positives come to a screeching halt. It would seem her husband, a Mr. Alan King, liked to party hard. Charlotte, understandable with four kids, took exception to Alan's good timing ways. In the last five years, there have been three domestic disturbances reported to the police. One even had Alan spending the night in the local pokey—for his own protection. Charlotte had pulled a shotgun on Alan, and the police were too chicken to take it from her. Alan told the officers it would be easier if he just went with them so Charlotte could feed the kids breakfast in the morning since it was a school night.

Some folk's logic is beyond my comprehension.

Like most runs of bad luck, it gets worse for Charlotte. Alan recently showed up dead under his home with a nail hole in his forehead. He presently occupies a refrigerated six-foot drawer at the local medical examiner's office.

It's fortuitous for the killer that Alan was a master carpenter. That ensured the pneumatic nail gun, the murder weapon of choice, was handy for his killer. At least that's the murder weapon the police have ascertained put the twenty-penny nail hole in his skull. I'd say it's a solid clue on the surface.

I find myself staring at the angry black and red hole in the center of Alan King's forehead. I can't help but wonder what possesses someone to remove the nail they drove into a man's skull. I mean, he is dead, right? That's what you wanted, right? Why would you remove the nail? That's weird to me.

I study Charlotte's mugshots. She looks like a woman at the end of her rope, not homicidal in the least, just ready for a heavy-duty nervous breakdown. I know, you can't always tell people's nature by the look of their eyes. But I've found often it's a pretty accurate indicator.

All this leaves me wondering what he did to push a mother of four to kill the father of her children. Sure, the domestic disturbances were indicating a less than harmonious relationship with her husband. But most women don't kill their man just because they honkytonk. They might leave them, but murder them? That doesn't seem right.

The motive the police give is the fifty-thousand-dollar accidental death life insurance policy Alan carried. The police's theory is Charlotte planned to collect the money and be rid of her troublesome husband all in one swift move.

Convenient, yes. But again, that doesn't make sense to me. First, how stupid would Charlotte have to be to think the insurance company is going to consider a single nail hole to the forehead an accidental death? Second, if she is a woman capable of shooting a nail into her lover's skull. Why did she have to go through three reported domestic disturbances, and no telling how many unreported disputes, before she finally lost her temper and killed the man? And lastly, their home looks to be leaning toward expensive for our area. How long will fifty thousand dollars last a widow and four children? None of this makes a bit of sense.

I hear the front door click and drop my feet to the floor.

"April?"

"Just putting a note on your desk, Howard," I say as I push the file back into the envelope.

Howard comes around the corner, a bag, and a drink in his hand. "Who from?"

"The district attorney, Mr. Jameson?"

"Did Lane have something for us?"

I hold the Charlotte King envelope out to Howard. In turn, he holds out the paper bag, and we exchange. "Plea bargain request."

"Chicken salad." His eyes drop to the folder. "Charlotte King."

"Who's that?" I ask in hopes of covering my snooping tracks.

"Just a young mother of four caught in a bad circumstance. The police believe she finally had her fill of her bi-polar husband and drove a nail into his forehead."

"Bless it, what does a guy gotta do to get a woman that mad?"

Howard flashes a smirk and sits in his chair. "Just wait, you'll be surprised how mean marriages can be when they start going off the rail." He thumbs open the folder. "Even so, I have a tough time believing her capable of this. Not saying I haven't been surprised before. But, despite all their arguing, everyone who knows them reports they were crazy about each other. Just sometimes, the crazy got too loud for the rest of the neighborhood."

"Lane asked that you get with her as soon as possible. He made it sound like you may have already spoken with her?"

"No. I knew the detectives were interviewing her, but I wasn't sure Lane planned to press charges or assign the case to me."

I struggle with being overly spontaneous. There are times I really wish I could put a leash on it. It's part my brain and part my mouth—put the two together, and they become a lethal combination. My mind runs full throttle, determining how a diminutive woman who's been submissive for years one day grows a set of kahunas and doesn't just kill her man. She drives a nail into his forehead. The mouth part is asking the question I thought was contained in my head.

"Can I work Charlotte's case?"

Chapter 9

"Work Charlotte's case? What do you mean, April?"

I experience a full-body blush as I realize I'd voiced my desire. "I can't try the case, but I can do the legwork for you. I can interview Charlotte for you, lay out a case brief for her defense, and you represent her at trial. That's a fantastic way for me to get some real case experience and maximize my contribution to you."

I'm also dying to find out for myself if Charlotte really offed Alan. But I think it best to keep that to myself.

"That won't be necessary, April. What I know of the case, I believe the best for all parties is to hammer out a plea bargain on this one. You must understand as it stands, she would be tried for first-degree murder with a plausible motive. You don't want to rely on a jury when it's someone's life at stake."

I recoil. "Why on earth not? Especially if they're innocent. You just said you doubted she did it."

Uncle Howard frowns. "Whether she did or didn't do it is almost irrelevant. If she takes a plea bargain, she is looking at twenty years or less. She could be out in ten with good behavior and still see her children graduate high school."

I'm dumbfounded. "But if Charlotte didn't do it, she shouldn't have to miss raising her children."

"Let me ask you this, what if she didn't do it, but you fail to prove it to the jury? You do realize she could be looking at the death penalty? I'm sure it's highly unlikely the state of Alabama would put a woman, let alone a mother of four, to death, but she would spend the rest of her life on death row." Howard leans forward. His eyes lose their softness as he stares at me. "Does that seem like a gamble you want to take with someone's life?"

"But that's not justice." My voice sounds tinny.

"No. I suppose it's not. But it is the safe play." He waves dismissively. "Thankfully, it's not our decision. We just advise, and Charlotte will have to make her own decision. She will decide if the gamble is worth it. But I guarantee I'll be trying to convince her to take a plea bargain until the end."

Something is burning inside me. My stomach rolls as heat races up the side of my face. This isn't fair. If Charlotte is innocent, she'll miss raising her children for a crime she didn't commit. What if the police did a sloppy job and just looked for the quickest way to close the case? Injustice is one of the emotions I've never dealt with well. "I want this case."

Howard snorts a derisive laugh. "No. There is no case. I appreciate your ambition and your desire to defend her, but your desire is misplaced."

I widen my stance. "I want to talk to Mrs. King first. What's best for her is freedom if she is innocent."

"In a perfect world, I would agree with you. But this is far from a perfect world. You will come to find in the court system that only fools seek perfection. Those of us who have survived this noble profession have learned how to compromise and negotiate the most favorable deal we can for our clients."

"That's not good enough!" I don't care to just survive. I want to win and, in the end, help someone during their greatest need.

Howard stifles a laugh. "Perhaps you're correct, April. Nevertheless, I believe you have something pressing to attend to."

"What's that?"

Howard points to the bag in my hand. "Your croissant will be soggy from the chicken salad if you don't hurry and eat it. That would be a shame."

"I think I'm losing my appetite," I grumble.

Howard crosses his arms. "Fine, you want to speak with her; I won't stop you. If she tells you she wants to go to trial, I won't stop either of you. But I promise you April, if you end up getting Charlotte put away for life, it'll haunt you to the end of your days."

His words feel like a two-ton yoke strapped across my shoulders. I want to say I changed my mind, and he can handle the case. That he is correct, the plea bargain is in Charlotte's best interest. The thing is, I just can't. "Thank you."

"I hope you're thanking me when this is all done."

The jail visitation hours are past, and I can't schedule a meeting with Charlotte until the following morning. That's disappointing. To prepare for our interview, I borrow the folder Lane brought us and study it beginning to end.

Driving home, my stomach cramps. Nerves. I'm having severe second thoughts about what I've done. I realize now, this is for keeps. This isn't a litigation project in a kangaroo court to earn a grade in law school. This woman's life will be impacted by my actions. My confidence begins to fade. I wonder if I'm up to the task. More frightening if I'm not up to the case, it'll be Charlotte who's hurt and not me.

It becomes more apparent to me Howard spoke with complete wisdom. Wisdom derived from years of holding people's futures in his hand. How ominous is it to know my preparation and performance determines the trajectory of another human being's life? I begin to wonder if I've chosen the wrong field.

But I know Charlotte is innocent. She must be. And if Charlotte is innocent, I'm the only person who can and will help her. Regardless of my fear, I need to do what I can to help.

The lake house's driveway resembles a public parking lot.

There are no less than ten vehicles in the drive. Noticeably absent is my daddy's black Silverado.

I pull onto the grass next to a nineteen-sixty-seven Chevelle. I gather my belongings and head to the sliding glass door.

My brother Chase is leaned up against the kitchen counter, talking on his phone. He waves at me, covers his phone and whispers, "Guess who I'm talking to."

I pull a Coke from the fridge. "No clue."

"You don't even want to guess?"

I pop the top of the Coke. "Nope."

Chase returns to his call. "Nah, man. Forget it, she is grouchy today."

"I'm not grouchy," I protest.

Chase looks in my direction and mouths, "Yes, you are."

"I am not. For your information, I've had a great first day at Snow and Associates."

Chase turns his back to me. Cupping his phone to his ear, he slips into the den as if it's a call requiring privacy.

"Who are you talking to anyway?" Not that I care. It's none of my business who Chase dates. But his sketchy behavior has piqued my curiosity.

Chase waves me off over the top of his head, and my temper snaps at his dismissive gesture. "Hey, don't you shoo me. Who are you talking to?"

"Shane. We're setting up the schedule for the weekend after next." Chase covers his phone. "You want to talk to him?"

"Why would I want to talk to him?" I pick up my backpack and purse, passing him on the way to the den. "Geez. What, are you two dating now?"

Do I want to talk to Shane? Yes, I would love to talk to Shane. If he had called me rather than Chase. I don't want a second-hand phone call from anyone.

I plop onto the sofa and rifle through the King folder. Nothing changes my mind as I review the details again. I'd be more at ease if I understood why I'm so sure Charlotte is innocent.

Being realistic, there is plenty of circumstantial evidence to lead a jury to convict Charlotte of killing the father of her four children. The prosecutor's proof being of the weakest type is no comfort since I have zero information of my own to dispel the validity of his assertions. If I hope to prove Charlotte innocent, I'll need to do some major investigating and find Alan's real killer.

I frown at the picture of Alan's body curled just inside their crawlspace access. Alan's body found under his house after being missing for three days is a bad break for us. While it proves nothing, him being murdered at home tends to convince police, and often jurors, it was a domestic homicide. It's no wonder the cops believed Charlotte was the murderer and never bothered to investigate any other potential suspects.

"Hey, Tinker Bell. What time did you get here?" Dusty says as he tops the stair coming from the basement.

"Just a few minutes ago. Guess what?"

Dusty flares his eyes open wide in mock excitement. "What?"

"Guess who has her first case?"

"Really? Well, hot dog. That's cool, baby sis. Shoplifter, church fund embezzler..."

"Murder, first-degree."

Dusty grits his teeth and pulls back his lips. "Well, I guess there is always the jump off into the deep end to learn how to swim method."

"What's that supposed to mean?"

"Nothing." Dusty shakes his head and continues toward the kitchen. "Serious, though, congratulations on the new opportunity. I know you have to be thrilled."

"Yes. I'm looking forward to the challenge."

"Hey, listen. Since you're here, the guys and I are planning our trip to Paducah. I'd like you to sit in if you can."

"Oh, Dusty, I think I've got enough to do right now with this case."

Dusty's eyes narrow. "I have pizzas coming from Torino's."

Usually, offering Torino's pizza to anyone in Guntersville

would do the trick. Nobody turns down Torino's pizza. But as attractive as the offer is, I'm intent on figuring out how to get Charlotte off the hook. "Thank you for the offer, but I already have a full plate with this case."

Dusty's raises his eyebrows. "You'd be on the clock. Thirty dollars an hour. I pay cash money tonight."

And here's the thing. I don't know if Dusty knows I'm hurting for spending cash or if I look hungry, but he is hitting all the right buttons tonight. As much as I need to prepare for my interview with Charlotte the next morning, I can't resist the offer. "Where did you say y'all are going?"

"Where we are going. You've already committed to the research trips, remember? You're my psychic. And the case is in Paducah."

"Padu, who?"

"Paducah, Kentucky. We received a report of a poltergeist on the fourteenth floor of the old Osborne Hotel. I read about the hotel a few years back, but at that point, it was just odd smells and shadows. Nothing serious. Nothing that we could really film and write a story about."

"Then why are we going?"

"Things change. A few months ago, the hauntings increased. Guests began reporting apparitions dressed in early twentieth-century clothes. Items have been flying across rooms. Voices have been heard in the walls." Dusty shrugs. "You know me, it takes more than a few bumps in the night to sell books. But when one of the maids hung herself on the fourteenth-floor last week, it bumped the Osborne Hotel to the top of our list. Who knows, it may even be good enough for the lead story in the next book."

My lips part in mortification. I love my older brother. But he is one serious freak. His face lit with excitement as he mentioned the maid hanging herself. That's just messed up.

I don't want to give you the wrong impression about Dusty. I'm sure he is as upset about someone killing themselves as anyone. But in the world of paranormal, suicides transpiring near a haunting can be an indicator of high supernatural activity.

You can dismiss it as coincidental, but it occurs too often for me to ignore. Suicides can be vibrant markers where a spirit has remained on this side of the veil. Where they have remained in the realm of the ordinary living.

I say ordinary living to delineate between the average person and those of us cursed with paranormal "gifts." Ordinary in that their mind refuses to acknowledge a ghost when it manifests in their presence. When the living are forced to recognize the spectral, it can end with devastating consequences to the individual. They tend to believe themselves mad and, in the end, kill themselves because the reality drives them insane.

There is the off chance the maid was a psychic and was unaware of her "gifts" until she began work at the hotel. Psychics see ghosts all the time. You get used to it, manage it, or take up residence in an eight-by-eight padded wall cell at Bryce Mental Hospital.

But in my experience, the spectral sense the paranormal power of psychics and seek us out. It's unfathomable to think the maid was psychic and experiencing her first encounter as an adult. No, we're dealing with a spirit with epic juice.

Dusty is right, this could be big. It takes a powerful spectral being to affect the living.

I follow Dusty into the basement. I'm shocked at the expanse of equipment turning our old playroom into a control center that rivals a special forces communication station. There are seventeen large-screen monitors mounted on the walls in the main living area. The entire perimeter is lined with counter tops creating eight separate workstations complete with personal computers, pull out keyboards and executive leather chairs. A myriad of expensive-looking video and audio equipment, scanners, and odd hand-held devices litter the countertop where there are no workstations.

"What in the world is all this?"

Dusty pulls at the red whiskers under his chin. "You like?"

"It is definitely impressive. What is it all for?"

"Audio sensitizing, magnetic resonance, chemical chromatics, atmospheric gas computations, and general historical research. You're not a stranger to this. You know how much science goes into paranormal research."

Miles, a too-skinny man with a tall Afro and Coke-bottle glasses, approaches. "Well, look what the cat drug in."

"Better to be dragged in than covered up," I shoot back.

Miles grins as he pushes his glasses back up the bridge of his nose. "The boss tells me you're back in the program."

"Just temporarily. I've my law degree now; as soon as I get full employment, I'll cut out again."

"That's cool. It'll be nice to have someone with your talent even if it is temporary. Have you met the team?"

"I was just about to introduce her," Dusty says.

"I got it." Miles crooks a finger for me to follow. "You'll be glad to know your brother isn't doing this by the bootstraps anymore. It's a lot safer for the team now."

Miles stops behind a young woman typing furiously on a laptop covered in decals. He taps her on the shoulder. "Liza."

The woman glances over her shoulder. Her eyes are sharp and questioning.

"Liza, this is Dusty's sister April. The new team member we were talking about. She will be going to Paducah with us."

Liza lets out a sigh, swivels her chair, and stands. She is a few inches shorter than me and thinner. Like my brother Dusty, both arms are covered in colorful tattoos. Her artwork consists of intricately detailed crucifixes, serpents, and skulls. Her expression turns harsh, and I consider backing up a step.

"Hopefully, you're as talented as Dusty claims."

I begin to say something self-effacing, I get it, it's her turf, but it's not necessary. She sits and spins back to her laptop. Conversation over, Liza returns to her work.

Miles gives me a quick shrug as if to say, "what can you do about it?"

He slides over a few feet and rests his hand on the back of an athletically built man. The man turns and immediately flashes a welcoming smile.

"Luis, I want you to meet April. Dusty's sister."

Luis extends his hand as he stands. "It's an honor to meet you. I've heard so many good things about you from Dusty."

I like Luis immediately. But it's hard not to love somebody who is beautiful and greets you with a smile so warmly the very first time you meet.

"Definitely my pleasure, Luis. Quite an operation y'all have put together here. I'm excited about being on the team." I'm not just being nice. I do have a spark of excitement building inside me. Paranormal adventures are scary, and at their worst downright dangerous. Still, you'd have to be dead not to get a kick out of the rush of adrenaline. Plus, they make exceptional stories assuming everyone makes it home.

"Well, I know we're definitely excited about having a true psychic. It will certainly make our job simpler. Safer too."

That's the second time in just a few moments I've heard the word safer. My stomach rolls uncomfortably with nerves as I realize the team is counting on me to help them stay safe on the subsequent investigation.

My newfound taste for adventure evaporates.

In twenty-four hours, I've gone from being responsible only for myself to having several lives in my hands. First Charlotte and indirectly her children and now Dusty and his team. I'm not comfortable with the added responsibility.

"It's been ages since I went on a hunt. I hope I'm not too rusty to help."

Luis waves his hand. "Oh, you don't have to be so modest with us. We're all family here." He gestures over his shoulder. "I'm charmed to finally meet you, I don't mean to be rude, but I need to get back at it."

"Oh, yes, please. Don't let me keep you."

Miles motions for me to return to Dusty. Dusty is speed pecking at his keyboard.

"Pretty impressive operation, brother. I'm proud of you."

He looks up. "Don't let all this equipment fool you, April. No amount of computer software and hardware replaces true talent. Your recruitment is essential for this Paducah project."

I'm a frog's hair away from running from the room like my hair's on fire. The entire team is acting like Beelzebub himself checked into the fourteenth floor at the Osborne Hotel.

"Team, let's huddle up." Dusty moves across the room and takes a seat on the overstuffed sofa in the center of the room. "First, since there may be an opportunity for video and audio on this trip, we'll be taking a full complement of equipment. Travis, Jason, and Chet will be traveling with us to help with the gear. Vehicle accommodations will be tight, so think pleasant thoughts of closeness."

Liza groans, "Chet?"

"Yes," Dusty says. "With all the equipment to position and wires to run, we'll need the extra hands."

"Just make sure the big lug keeps his hands to himself. Otherwise, he won't be much use for pulling equipment around with his hands cut off," Liza threatens.

"I told you, I explained everything to him. He should be on his best behavior. If not, we won't use him on any future assignments." Dusty turns to Miles. "Okay, one more time for review and for April's benefit, history."

Miles opens a spiral notebook and begins to read. "Osborne Hotel built circa nineteen twenty-two by William J. Osborne, a local real estate developer later turned entertainer and politician. The building is listed as fourteen stories tall with the fourteenth being the penthouse."

"Who needs a penthouse in Paducah, Kentucky?" I ask.

"You have to remember the time; Paducah has several rivers that converge at its port. Earlier in the century, steamboats visited the port regularly."

I decide it's best just to listen to Miles's history course.

"The hotel had only a brief period of profitability before the collapse of the stock market in twenty-nine killed off most of the trade. Followed by an extended period where the property changed hands several times before finally in the seventies, it became a homeless shelter. It was recently purchased by James Caldwell, a young entrepreneur who's made his money in synthetic fuels. A few months back, he renovated the building, kept its historical designation, and reopened it as a five-star hotel."

I can't help myself. "And why do you need a five-star hotel in Paducah, Kentucky?"

"That's probably a question better left for Mr. Caldwell. You can ask him if we see him." Dusty inclines his chin toward Liza. "What do you have for us?"

"Like we discussed earlier, before the happenings last month culminating with the maid's suspected suicide, we have a bunch of nothing. Sounds, drafts, odd smells... nothing that couldn't be explained by the fact that it's an ancient building."

"And now."

"Best guess?" Liza puckers her lips then clicks her tongue. "I don't know, Dusty, it seems odd the building would lay dormant for decades with no issues and then suddenly have a poltergeist. If I were to put my money on it, that's what I'd assume."

Dusty nods in agreement. "Well, I think it best we approach it as a poltergeist until we know better. That should keep us on our toes, and if it happens not to be, we at least played it safe."

"My turn?" Luis asks.

Dusty gestures with his hand. "Go ahead."

"I've increased the power by twofold on the MRI recorder. With any luck, I can record enough pixels to fill in any image we capture."

"MRI? That works?" I ask.

Luis smiles in my direction. "Well, that's the hope. It depends on if the energy of the spirits is reflective or not. If it proves not to be we have an expensive toy. If it reflects, I hope to at the minimum get a good outline. With an outline, we can fill in the rest for the story's illustrations."

"Isn't that just like painting the picture?"

Luis waggles his hand in front of his face. "Sort of, maybe. One person's painting is another person's enhancement."

"If it's there, we need the shot," Dusty insists.

"We'll get the shot," Luis says.

Despite Luis's assertion, I have my doubts. Before I left for Tuscaloosa, I'd been on a number of these ghost hunting trips with my brother. Surprisingly, poltergeist and ghosts are not as camera shy as most people believe. In fact, we had the opportunity to film several spirits. While the ghosts themselves are not shy, producing a photo that looks like anything besides fog is elusive. There were countless times we knew we had a Pulitzer winning shot. Only to be later disappointed by an image of a faint outline of something, a blur or worse nothing but an overexposed photo.

I let Luis and Miles explain all the new equipment to me while we wait on the pizza. My brother has laid out a serious investment in the research aspect of his business between the hardware and the custom software.

But that's what makes Dusty different from the other ghost hunters. His level of detail and integrity is in a league of its own. All other paranormal writers are more fiction than documentaries. But not Dusty. Dusty has the real goods, or he doesn't publish it.

"Pizza's here," Luis says as he points at a screen that shows a delivery girl standing at our front door.

Dusty hops up and jogs to the stairs. "I got it."

Luis waits until Dusty clears the stairs. "I'm not sure if Dusty moves that quick because he loves his pizza or if it's because it's Renée Love delivering."

"The boy does love his pizza," Miles says before narrowing his eyes. "But now that you mention it, I don't believe I've seen him take the stairs that fast for anyone else. Maybe we should set a timer on him for the next few deliveries and compare."

I move closer to Luis's monitor to see if I can get a better look at the delivery girl. I can't see her face because of the Torino's pizza cap. It's difficult to see much other than she is petite, considering khakis and golf shirts aren't the most flattering attire.

"Have y'all gone through puberty yet."

Liza swivels her chair to face us. She warns the boys with an icy glare.

"Ooh, the Rat Queen speaks," Miles says.

"I'm being dissed by Steve Urkel. Is that supposed to concern me?"

"You both are too beautiful to be arguing," Luis says. "What's your take, Liza? Do you think the boss is sweet on Renée?"

Liza's white skin flushes. "How would I know? I don't have time to keep up with your lame, non-existent love life. But I'll say this, if he does like her, he better wear protection. There is no telling where all that piece of pepperoni has been."

Luis and Miles lean back, their eyes open wider as their mouths part. Unless Liza has a personal issue with Renée her reaction is odd.

Something else weird. When Luis asked Liza her opinion, there was a disturbance in the room's energy. It was as if a warm breeze emanated from Liza and blew past me, warming my face.

Interesting.

Dusty comes down the stairs with three large pizzas breaking the awkwardness of the room. He looks at the four of us, and his eyebrows knit. "Did I miss something?"

"No. All good here," I say. "Do you need me to get some drinks from upstairs?"

Dusty points to the far corner at a short fridge under the counter. "Help yourself."

I open the fridge and ask everyone what flavor they want as Liza gathers paper plates and a roll of paper towels from a cupboard I missed earlier. Her face has returned to its natural porcelain white.

"You have it going on here, Dusty. If you had a bathroom, you'd never have to come out of your dungeon."

He laughs as he puts two pieces of meat lover's pizza on his plate. "I looked into it. But Mom and Dad didn't like the idea of the plumber having to cut the concrete to run the pipes. They sort of got turned against anymore remodeling after the mess Chase made when he knocked out the wall between the guest-room and his."

"Aw, man. This one is all veggies," Miles complains.

"Mine." Liza grabs it away from Miles.

"That's why I got three." Dusty pushes the third toward Miles.

"Why are you two setting up house? Are you going to live here forever?"

He snorts a laugh. "Where would I go? My best friend lives upstairs, my parents live here, and we're sitting in my office. Pretty darn convenient by my estimations."

Miles is eating directly out of the pizza box in his lap, and Dusty's looks like a heart attack pill. Liza and I lock eyes, and she lifts the veggie pizza toward me.

"Thanks." I open the lid and continue with Dusty. "But what about when you remarry?"

"What? Do you know something I don't?"

Miles and Luis are staring at me with goofy grins of expectation. I sense they desperately want me to ask about Renée. Liza has turned pink again, and I have the odd sensation of sitting next to a warm oven. I better keep my mouth shut.

"No." I take a bite of my pizza. Blech. Too many veggies.

I throw away my paper plate and Dr. Pepper can. I'd prefer to stay and socialize with my new team, but I hold the fate of a widow and four children in my hands. After eating my fill of pizza, I excuse myself from the group, collect my backpack and purse, and leave for my waterfront apartment.

Despite the stress of Charlotte's life, depending on the success of the defense I prepare, I'm eager to get started. I've got a burning desire to earn the woman her freedom. Besides, if past performance is the best indicator of future success, I must win my first case and get my career started on the right foot.

I pull my clothes off and slip into a soft pair of shorts and an oversized T-shirt. I consider sitting at my desk and opt for sitting cross-legged on my bed. I lay the folder out in front of me and spread the pictures from Alan King's murder across my bed.

The second time looking at the pictures is less startling. The hole in Alan's head begins to appear more like a sharpie mark the longer I study the medical examiner's photos.

I scribble my notes onto a legal pad. I'm unsure how much time I'll have with Charlotte in the morning, and I need all my questions answered in our first meeting to be effective. I must be able to witness her body language and voice inflection as she answers me to know if my gut is right or if it's wishful thinking.

The big question, "Did you kill Alan?" is the key to everything. I can't decide if it is best to ask it first in a straightforward manner or slide it in at the end once we have developed a friendly rapport. I should ask her at the start and follow up with the question again at the end of our interview. Would that make me seem stupid to her? Who wants a forgetful attorney?

I lose steam. I didn't realize how much energy the day sapped from me. It was a tremendous amount of excitement and stress. More than I ever anticipated.

The random thought pops into my mind. I could save a lot of time if I hold Charlotte's hands and read her memory. If her consciousness isn't haunted by the crime, I'll know she didn't kill Alan. I quickly push it down.

I get an uneasy feeling just thinking about it as the tingly spider climbing up my spine sensation begins. Something inside me wants me to use my "gifts." Still, the thought of using my powers on an unsuspecting Charlotte makes me feel filthy. Dirt, you can't wash off with a scalding hot shower.

The gentle rocking motion of the dock combines with my exhaustion, and my eyelids droop lower, closing momentarily.

I'm just resting my eyes.

I force them to open again. I'll lay back against my pillows and try to get comfortable while reviewing Charlotte's interview with the police.

The sound is nearly imperceptible but does not escape me. I know the sound well. In an instant, I'm eight years old again, struggling for air. I freeze and listen for the voice of the ghost from the lake in my mind.

Instead, I hear the thump, thump against the bottom of the dock, vibrate up through the party room's slatted wood flooring. My heart threatens to beat out of my chest. My breathing becomes shallow and fast. Why doesn't it show itself?

For twenty years, the ghost has been content to make noises and occasionally whisper my name. Whisper my name so close, it's like a lover's lips at my ear.

"April, April."

Will it speak tonight? I pray, no. Instead, the burning sensation on my ankle begins. I scratch at it to no avail.

You think I'm crazy. Maybe I am. I might even grant you it's all psychosomatic. But I swear to you, my ankle burns as if something hot is wrapped around it. The same way it burned when I was eight.

Chapter 10

Exhaustion finally overtakes my fear. I don't dream and for that I'm grateful.

Waking, I check my phone. I have ten minutes to grab a shower, dress, and be at the jail which is fifteen minutes away.

I proceed to take the quickest shower of my life. As I pull on my clothes, I try to remember if I put on deodorant. I'm sure I didn't but gather my shoes and backpack and run out to my car anyway.

Shutting the door, I realize my hair is still damp and my pants outfit badly crumpled. My shoes look uber-cute, that's a positive.

If my good luck holds, Sheriff Blake will be patrolling a different road this morning. Driving my car like a possessed woman, I might arrive at the county jail only a few minutes late.

I slide into one of the angled parking slots in front of the jail and jump out. My car gives several loud knocks of the engine before it finally stops. That's not embarrassing.

I'll have to deal with that later. I run up to the glass doors. Remembering I'm still barefoot, I stop and pull on my shoes.

The receiving room is a hive of activity. Business is brisk in Marshall County this morning.

I sign in at the front desk and follow my assigned escort into the prison complex. As I trail the guard over the highly buffed floors with deep scars under the shiny wax, I realize this is my first time inside a jail. I've been brought in for questioning a few times over a misunderstanding but have always managed to explain myself and not be arrested.

That's good. A felony conviction can really cut your legal career short.

I take it all in, the dim lighting, the peculiar smells and silence that speaks volumes. Yeah, I'm good. I'm glad I never did anything to earn me a free room.

"I must inform you your conversation will be taped," the young guard tells me as we stop in front of a steel door.

"No, that's totally unacceptable."

"The detectives require it of all interviews." The guard adds a dismissive shrug of the shoulder.

"No. That's a complete breach of confidentiality. There will be no taping of this meeting." I move closer to him. "Do you understand?"

He narrows his lips. I can tell he struggles with the conflicting instructions between the detectives and me. He unlocks the door and motions for me to enter.

As I pass in front of him, I add in my most threatening voice, "I better not ever hear a tape of this meeting coming from the prosecution."

He doesn't reply. And I look down at his tag. "Officer Brady. Are we clear?"

"I heard you the first time."

I step into the cell. The door clicks then locks behind me.

Charlotte King sits at a small table in the center of the room. My client is a short woman roundly built with a kindly, sad face. Trying to make the situation lighter, I force an overly warm smile as I approach her. "Charlotte? I'm April Snow."

She starts to rise and extend her hand, but the wrist chains catch and force her to short arm her greeting. She frowns as she sits back down.

"One moment," I say.

Turning to the two one-way windows, I gesture toward the dark glass. "Seriously? Is this really necessary?" I'm part venting my frustration and part checking if the audio is active in the room. It would not surprise me if I hear a response from the viewing office even though they're not supposed to be listening in on our confidential consultation.

That leads my mind to wonder if they are videotaping the interview. I scan the room and find the video camera in the corner. I take a sheet of paper from my legal pad and a Band-Aid from my purse. Standing on my chair, I'm able to cover the video camera. I walk back to the table and sit down.

"There. I just had to do a bit of housecleaning first."

Charlotte appears amused. "I don't think they're gonna like that much."

"Yeah well, it won't be the first time I put a knot in somebody's knickers."

I take a few seconds to scan her face and observe her body language. I want to get the full measure of her. She becomes uncomfortable with the silence and I decide to ask her the only question that I really need answered.

"Charlotte, did you kill Alan?"

She looks me dead in the eye and without hesitation, replies, "No. I'm not gonna lie, we've had some intense arguments from time to time, but no I wouldn't lay a hand on Alan. As weird as it may seem to you and the rest of the world, I love him. My children and Alan are my life."

So far, so good. I believe Charlotte King. "Can you explain how he came to be under your house? Found dead after over a hundred volunteers searched the woods around your house for him for three days?"

"No." She shakes her head and clasps her hands on the table. "No, but I sure wish I knew."

"Is there anybody that has a reason to hurt or possibly even kill Alan."

She blinks hard then shakes her head for several seconds. "No. I mean, don't get me wrong, Alan's rubbed more people wrong than you can imagine. He can piss off the pope. But I can't think of a single person he knew who would hurt him—well, more than a well-deserved punch in the face. I've never known anyone to be mad enough at him to kill him. Most everyone knows he is—was—a smart mouth and never meant anything by it."

"Tell me about the nail gun, Charlotte."

Her face flushes. "That nail gun is nothing but a stupid reason the police are using. I mean think about it, unless the man was passed out drunk, there is no way in the world someone gets close enough to use a nail gun on him."

The answer made me uneasy. "You've thought about using the nail gun before?"

"I already told you he has a knack for getting under people's skin, and that includes me. But I can tell you if you're going to use the nail gun the only way to have done that would be to take the guard off it. If the police want to take the time, they can check that guard's never been tampered with. But either they're not mechanically inclined or they're too friggin' lazy to check it."

That's the answer I'm looking for and I smile. "Have the police talked to you about a plea bargain?"

"A what?"

"A plea bargain—it's where instead of us going to trial you admit to some level of guilt or claim no contest to a lesser charge rather than go to trial."

"Why would I want to do that? I didn't do anything."

"I understand. But you need to know that you could be looking at the death penalty."

Charlotte's facial skin tone grays as fear replaces her combative stance. Her jaw clenches as she stares at her hands. "If I'm not there to raise my babies, it's the same as a death penalty to me. If it's all the same to you, I'd rather take my chances than admit to something I didn't do. Doesn't seem right to lie."

"Okay then." It's anything but okay. I have no doubt that Charlotte King is innocent. Still, I have major concerns if she will be allowed to return home and raise her children.

It's awful how the King children had their dad taken from them. If I fail Charlotte, it would be a tragedy as they will be without either parent to care for them. That's a burden that crushes in on me making it difficult to breathe.

"I'm going to have to do some digging to find information that'll throw doubt on the circumstantial evidence the police used to charge you, Charlotte. I refuse to lie to you; we have an uphill battle on our hands. If you can think of anything or anyone that I need to interview, I need you to tell me immediately. The smallest facts might be the difference between you going home or spending the rest of your days in jail. Do you understand me?"

"Yes, I do." Her stare is taking on a distant appearance.

I gather my folders, push them into my backpack and begin to stand.

Charlotte reaches across the table. The chain just long enough for her to lay her hand on mine. "Thank you, April. I appreciate you doing this for me."

The vision comes with more force than usual, weakening my knees so quickly they nearly buckle. It's loud and bright, and I feel a chill in the air. It takes a second for me to determine the time and place and gather my bearings. Made more difficult being the point of view is different from usual. I'm looking at me. I'm in the middle of the football field, in my cheerleading outfit being escorted by my brother Chase who's decked out in a rare tie and sports coat. A moment later a tiara is placed on my head, and I remember it's the night I was crowned homecoming queen of Guntersville High School.

I squint my eyes as I pull my hand slowly from under Charlotte's. The vision dissipates.

"I know you probably don't remember me. But I remember you from school." She draws a ragged breath and exhales. "If anybody can make this happen, you can."

"You went to Guntersville?"

She nods her head. "I was a year behind you. Alan is from

Boaz and he bought property out there after high school as a wedding gift."

Unconsciously, I rub my hands together and think about the vision just played in my head. I feel the shame of not remembering Charlotte who remembers me so vividly. It drives my desire to help clear her name. As if it somehow will atone for my self-centered past.

"Don't take this the wrong way, but before we go to court, you might want to get a manicure."

Charlotte's matter-of-fact statement shocks me out of my self-loathing. I quickly examine my nails. They're an absolute disaster. "Yes, I was moving last week. They are looking rather snaggly."

"My cousin Tiffany Bates runs the beauty college down on Church Street. You need to stop in there and let her work on you. A good manicure always helps your confidence. And I need me a confident lawyer."

I begin to mention Tiffany's great aunt had been into our office yesterday. I think better of it. It would just bring up the question of why Dottie was there, and I didn't want to get into the fact the vengeful woman was writing Tiffany's mom out of her will.

"You know, that's an excellent idea. And I don't have a regular manicurist yet. Thank you for the recommendation."

"Well she'll talk your ears off, but she really is the best around these parts."

I sling my backpack onto one shoulder and start for the door. As I wait for the guard to key the lock, I feel Charlotte's stare attentive on my back. I turn and offer a smile I hope is confident. "We've got this Charlotte. You'll be home with your children in no time." I only hope I'm not fibbing.

Chapter 11

I'm deep in thought about Charlotte's case, trying to keep the gray clouds of doubt away as I enter Snow and Associates.

"April, is that you?"

I hear Howard's feet come off his desk and slap the floor. "Yes, Howard."

"So how was your meeting with Charlotte King?"

"I'm still convinced."

He peeps his head around the corner and his eyebrows rise. "My, did somebody have a rough night?"

"Funny." I run both my hands through my wildly curly blonde hair to subdue it. "It's my beach hair look."

"Too bad we're six hours from the beach," Howard says with a smirk. "I must go to the courthouse for two depositions this morning, and I probably won't be back until after three. Do you think you can hold down the fort?"

I look pointedly at the silent phone and then around the empty office then nod. "It'll be tough, but I think I can manage."

Howard disappears into his office, and I hear him rummaging through paperwork. "I forgot to ask you, the DA and I are having dinner tonight. Would you like to come?"

"I'm not sure I can, Howard. I've taken on more projects than I have time for here lately."

Howard walks past my desk toward the door. "Actually, it was a rhetorical question. Meet us at the Black Angus at seven."

It's hard to look a steak dinner in the mouth, but a fancy dinner reservation does move the manicure up on the priority list. "Do you think it would be a huge problem if I close the office early this afternoon? I still have some items I've not cleared up from the move."

Howard considers my request for a moment, and I fear I'm going to dinner with skanky fingernails. "No worries. Just forward the office phone to your cellphone. Don't forget, Black Angus at seven."

I busy myself by reviewing each of the three King family domestic disturbances. Then I pull the arrest records for both.

Alan drank a little too much and liked an occasional fist-fight. Around here that would just put him in the "one of the boys" category.

Charlotte has a ticket for failure to make a stop at a stop sign and the notation about the shotgun waving during one of the domestic dispute calls. Otherwise she has a spotless record. Well before the arrest for first-degree murder.

It's obvious I'm missing something. There is no mention of any physical violence in any of the domestic disputes. A whole lot of hateful name-calling, I suspect some alcohol induced, and a lot of threats with no appearance of any follow through. How does that escalate into one of them dead? How does a fifty-thousand-dollar accidental life insurance policy motivate anyone to kill the father of their four children? One thing is clear, I don't have near enough information to answer that nagging question.

By two-thirty, I'm beyond bored and make the executive decision to close the office. I forward the office line to my phone and lock the door. I hurry over to the beauty college. I refuse to be seen at the Black Angus tonight with broken and chipped nails.

Church Street is four blocks down from Howard's office. I could've walked faster than the time it took me to get in my car, pull out of my parking spot and find a parking spot pseudo close to the beauty college.

When I step into the salon, I wonder if they run some sort of promotion on Tuesdays. All six of the dryers are running with women of different ages and ethnicity under the hoods. All four of the hair cutting stations are occupied, too. Two women are at the back which is the manicure station. I make my way to the counter, worried I may not be able to get service today. A short blonde approaches, pushing her hair out of her face with the back of her hand.

"Hi, do you have an appointment?"

The woman resembles Tiffany but I'm not sure. "Oh, I'm sorry. I didn't realize I'd need one."

"If you don't mind the wait, you don't need one." She flips open a spiral notebook and examines the sign-ins. "It's a little late in the day for a coloring, maybe it would be better if we schedule you for in the morning."

"I... I wasn't here to get my hair colored." I pinch a bit of my hair and examine my natural dark blonde coloring. "I'm actually looking for a manicure today."

She blushes. "Of course, I don't know why I said that. That'll work out better. I have an opening for a manicure in fifteen minutes. I just need to finish up with Mildred first."

"That's fine."

She recovers her smile. "Great. Your name?"

"April."

She prints my name on the appointment book, then sets the pen down. I wonder if she will recognize me, but she looks distracted from all the clients in her shop.

She stares at me for a second. "Okay, if you can make yourself at home, I'll be with you in a jiffy."

"Thanks." I take a seat to wait.

I flip through a celebrity magazine that's over a year old. It's not holding my interest. My mind wanders to my meeting the night before with Dusty's team. I'm not sure if it's the flash vision I just experienced with Charlotte or not, but the idea of opening my "gifts" fully begins to worry me.

In high school, I used to help Dusty with his research. It was fun to go on the ghost hunts with him. The whole idea was a bit of a lark to me despite my encounter with voices when I was younger and still didn't know how to block my psychic senses.

Of course, I believe in spirits. Mostly because I've seen them off and on most of my life. But I didn't understand how Dusty could sell ghost books to a population that's never seen a ghost themselves. The idea seemed preposterous to me, but I had a fun time being with him even if I was enabling his delusional dream.

It's always been Dusty's dream to be an author. The fact Dusty sees ghosts too, albeit with only a small fraction of the regularity I do, makes me feel like less of a freak. So, if he wanted to hunt them, and document them in stories and books I wasn't going to complain. There was the bonus of a little sister being allowed to tag along in the adult world of her older brother.

The summer of my junior year in high school, Dusty and I made no less than eight excursions. The first two times we took Chase with us. We soon found his patience for such things was limited and he had zero paranormal abilities in him.

The last excursion we planned for the summer was a trip to the old Freeman Plantation. It's less than an hour drive from the lake house, and we expected it to take only a few hours. That's the night ghost hunting turned from amusing adventure to a grim business for me.

Dusty was informed there were apparitions in the old mansion for the better part of thirty years. Mostly it sounded like minor energy forces, manifesting themselves in poorly formed fog silhouettes. There were reports of unexplained cold drafts in the air, too. With less than exciting reports, the plantation was relegated to the last excursion of our research that season. It held the least promise of something worthy of being recorded in Dusty's book.

The reports were woefully understated.

The moment I stepped onto the Freeman Plantation I began to hear the voices. They were angry. They were hostile. "Get out, you worthless trash. You have no right to be trespassing here, demon spawn." Not exactly very welcoming, and if I'd had my druthers, I would have immediately left, as the voices requested.

As I mentioned, Dusty has some paranormal abilities. Fortunate for him, he'd argue otherwise, his "gifts" don't have the same bandwidth as mine. Sometimes he hears and sees exactly what I do. Other times he sees no more than what an average person would see or hear. For that reason, as we entered the plantation gate, I turned to him and said, "You heard that, right?"

"Heard what?"

"You're joking. Please tell me you heard that." Dusty shook his head. "Well, I just had something tell me we needed to leave right away. And not in that pleasant of terms."

"Are you sure? Nobody reported voices."

I rolled my eyes in frustration. "Why would I kid about that?"

Dusty shrugged. "I don't know."

"I want to go home."

"No. Come on, April. Don't chicken out on me."

"Sorry. I want to leave, like right now."

"But this is good stuff, I mean, if it's talking to you there might be more to this than just a few fog clouds and changes in temperature. This is huge, April. It could even be the lead for my first book."

There Dusty went with the "first book" statement. It was impossible for me to refuse him when he used the saying because I knew it held the hopes and aspiration of his life dream. How could I ever refuse to help either of my brothers accomplish what they wanted most in the world even if I might never understand the goals they desire.

I held my ground for a few more seconds, insisting I was scared and needing to leave. Always knowing I would eventually give in to his request, but confident he was aware of my trepidation.

As we made our way to the front porch of the old plantation, the voices continued, and I became filled with a sense of impending doom. They were more hostile than any voices I had ever heard prior.

When Dusty pried the swollen front door open, the voices immediately stopped. But they were replaced by sounds of heavy breathing and heartbeats. I crammed my fear back down into my gut and followed my brother into the mansion, hiding behind his girth.

"Do you smell that?" I asked.

"Yeah, the mildew is pretty heavy in here."

It wasn't mildew I was smelling. It smelled like rancid meat thrown in the garbage a week before pickup during the summer. The noxious smell was so overbearing, my stomach began to roil, and I wondered if I would be able to hold my dinner down.

The first time I felt the breath on the back of my neck, I nearly peed myself. I grabbed hold of Dusty's belt and plastered myself to his back.

"What's up?" he asked.

"Something just breathed on my neck."

Dusty spun about, and I was inches from his belly. "There is nothing behind you?"

"Something was breathing on my neck. I didn't say I saw it. I just said I felt him."

"How do you know it was a him?"

"Only a guy would be creepy enough to do that."

Dusty grinned and turned in the direction he was going earlier. "Just keep close to me, and if it happens again jerk on my belt twice."

I wasn't sure what repulsed me more. A ghost breathing on my neck, or my brother telling me to tug on his belt twice. If I'd not been so scared, I'd have protested. If I had half a brain, I would have ran out of the building and set a new land speed record.

Nothing else happened while we were on the first floor. I eventually became used to the rancid smell of rotten meat, and the ghost must have lost interest in the back of my neck because I didn't feel him again. The heartbeat and the heavy breathing sounds continued but faded back into my subconsciousness.

If we had left then, everything would've been fine, and my view of the world would not have been forever warped.

Dusty led the way up the stairs to the second floor. Halfway up the flight a board caved in and if not for Dusty's quick reflexes, he would have fallen through to the dark basement below.

"Wow, I didn't see that one coming," he said as he pushed up with his hands from the staircase. He then stepped over the broken runner board and continued up the flight.

Every inch of my skin began to tingle as if a thousand ants were crawling on me. I started to get sharp shooting pains up the back of my neck forcing my eyes shut from pain. When I closed my eyes, my mind filled with visions of young men in leather jackets and blue jeans. Because of the pain, it took a moment to put the vision into a coherent context. It was as if I was watching the movie *Grease* for the hundredth time.

"Are you tugging on my belt, or are you just going a lot slower than I am?"

I had Dusty's belt pulled a full six inches from his waist. I immediately released it. "Sorry."

"No trouble. I just wasn't sure if I needed to be looking back behind you for the mad breather."

The first room we came to, I saw nothing. We checked a shared bathroom. Again, I neither felt nor saw anything.

As we approached the last room upstairs, the skin tingling began to itch incessantly. I couldn't help myself, I started to scratch at my forearms. "Let's go, Dusty."

He shone the flashlight behind me. "Just this last room. Then we can go."

Dusty opened the last door and I followed him inside. He stopped so suddenly I ran into his back.

"Do you feel that?"

Yes, I felt the twenty degree drop in temperature. But I couldn't answer my brother presently. Terror had turned off my ability to speak. The young man hanging from the chandelier by a noose stole my ability to communicate.

"I said, did you feel that temperature drop?" Dusty turned to me tilting his head quizzically to the side. "What is it?"

I pointed in the direction of the chandelier. "Man, hanging from the chandelier."

Dusty shone his flashlight in the direction of the chandelier. Leaning forward he squinted as he tried to see what I saw. He stepped toward the center of the room.

I grabbed his belt. "No, don't."

"What? I want to see what you see."

"Let's go," I pleaded.

When the dead man's eyes opened, I released Dusty's belt and nearly fell on my butt. As I started to back up, the man's neck stretched, cracked, and elongated further. At first, I thought it was my imagination. As Dusty continued forward, the man's neck extended another foot and by the time Dusty reached the center of the room, the man's feet were inches from the floor.

"I think I'm starting to see mist or fog," my brother said with the apparition directly in front of him their noses nearly touching.

"Dusty, don't," I croaked.

The dead man's feet touched the ground. He reached out for my brother's collar, and as his hand clasped the fabric, he pulled Dusty's face toward his as he bit my brother's nose, Dusty let out a bloodcurdling scream and the apparition moved his second hand around Dusty's neck.

Dusty turned violently and the apparition lost hold of him. "Out! Now!" Dusty yelled as he ran toward me. A stream of blood flowing off his nose.

We pin balled off each other as we made our way through the doorway. Dusty beat me to the stairs somehow, and before I could yell a warning he broke through the rotted board in the middle of the staircase.

He caught himself from going all the way through the floor by extending his arms outward. He was trying to push up through the hole, but with no effect. I stepped over him and tried to help pull him up by his arms. Beneath him, where the basement should've been, molten lava exuded sulfuric gasses that stung my throat and burned my eyes as it spat globs of hot red earth up toward my brother's dangling feet.

I continued to pull at Dusty ineffectively. Our exertions only exhausting us.

"You have to go get help," Dusty panted.

"I can't just leave you here."

"Well, this isn't working."

"What about the ghost?"

Dusty looked over his shoulder. "He must have to stay in that room."

I had a cold knot in my stomach. Something told me Dusty did not have the right of it. My fear was confirmed seconds later as the body of the man stepped out of the bedroom. His neck stretched grotesquely behind him reaching back into the room. I couldn't say anything. I could only point.

Dusty looked over his shoulder. When he looked back in my direction, I saw genuine fear in his eyes for the first time.

"That's just wrong!" he hollered.

I remembered my brother's belt and thought if I could grab hold and leverage against the stair above him, I could help pull him up. As I moved to grab his belt, he did a dip maneuver on the stair and kicked one of his thick legs up onto the ledge. In seconds, he extracted himself from the hole. I don't believe I've ever seen a big man move that agile before or since.

He grabbed hold of me and half carried, half dragged me down the rest of the stairs. Within seconds we were outside, panting against his truck.

"Mother of pearl, I can't believe I didn't get a picture of that."

"You're not going back in for a picture," I told him.

I could sense Dusty processing his desire for a photo versus the risk. I did not breathe easily until I saw him frown. "Yeah, I suppose that's a bit out of my league just yet." He raised a finger and pointed at the house. "I'll be back for you."

True to his word, Dusty did return to the Freeman Plantation four years later with a full crew and all the current paranormal electronics available to mankind. The pictures he and Miles obtained were little more than shadows. It was not the highly detailed grotesque dead man with the stretching neck. That vision had to be painted by Dusty's words. The story was the lead tale for his book. Not his first book, but his second.

I often wonder what would've happened if Dusty failed to pull himself out of the stairway hole that night. I did see the apparition pull his collar. Dusty claims he never felt the ghost's hand around his neck, but even he couldn't deny the teeth marks on his nose.

I'm left to wonder if the spirit could have done him bodily harm or if it was my imagination. Either way, the fear was real. And in some ways, it's never left me.

Chapter 12

"April?"

I look up from my trance, and Tiffany is standing in front of me. "Sorry," I say as I stand.

"No. I'm sorry. That took longer than I expected, Honey. When Mildred gets started on one of her stories, since she does most of the talking with her hands, it's impossible to give that woman a manicure," she explains as she ushers me to the back of the salon.

"Just have a seat here, April."

We take seats opposite the worktable. The young woman squints her eyes as she sits on her chair. "Do I know you?"

"Are you Tiffany?" I ask.

"Guilty as charged." She points her finger at me. "April Snow. Gosh, I'm so sorry. I should've recognized you right off."

When I was a senior in high school, my cheer squad had the responsibility of teaching the middle school squad while their sponsor was on maternity leave. It was a lot like herding cats. Tiffany was one of the girls way too cool to take instructions from anyone other than an adult.

"Well, that was like a lifetime ago," I offer.

"More like somebody else's life. It sure would be nice to go back and change a few decisions along the way."

"I'm sure we all feel that way occasionally."

She stares at me. Tiffany has dark puffs below her eyes and way too many crinkles at the edge for a woman her age. Her lips curl up, and she huffs. "Man, I'm sorry I was such a twerp back then."

"Were you?" I don't know why I'm letting her off the hook. It just seems like the right thing to do.

She lifts my hands and inspects my nails. "You know I was." She wrinkles her nose. "I declare, girl, what do you do for a living? Dig graves by hand?"

I follow her line of sight to my nails. "Can you work magic? I have an important business dinner tonight."

"I can't help you with the business dinner thing, but I know nails. Do you have a color in mind?"

"Orange, maybe?"

"Absolutely not." She turns in her chair and pulls a candy apple red bottle from her caddy. "It's still hard to beat the classics, especially for fancy business circles."

I think to argue the point. Dinner with the Guntersville DA and my elderly bachelor uncle is hardly mingling in fancy circles. Still, Tiffany is the professional in the field of cosmetology. "I'll defer to your expertise."

Tiffany grins. "You won't regret it."

Tiffany is part of the extended Castle family, but she lived a far different life than her Great Aunt Dottie. If my memory is accurate, she never knew her dad, and I specifically remember her mother having a drinking problem. As a troublesome vice, her mom's alcoholism ran a distant second to her mom's proclivity to hook up with violent men in a never-ending carousel of the father of the month.

I wouldn't know this if my mama didn't volunteer at the women's shelter. I was venting one night to Mama how awful the middle school cheerleaders were, specifically Tiffany, who instigated most of the disruptions. Mama sulled up and began to tell me how I was spoiled, and I should be more sensitive to girls who didn't have as easy of a life as Daddy and she provided for me.

When I countered that I felt Tiffany was just using her home situation as an excuse, it was the equivalent to dropping a lit match onto a puddle of gasoline. Mama blew up on me, and I couldn't get a word in edgewise.

Mama grew up in a trailer out in the woods. She lost her daddy to the Vietnam conflict before he had the opportunity to hold her, and her mama is a witch.

Mama had a few things to overcome in her life. Consequently, she gets a little salty when people fail to consider we don't all begin at the same "start line."

I remember being so angry at Mama for yelling at me about Tiffany. It took all the self-discipline I had not to dish it out to Tiffany the next day.

Predictably, she once again disrupted the routine I was trying to teach the younger squad. Still, I was mature, redirected the outburst in a professional manner, and had the team go back to learning the dance in only moments. I handled it maturely, not because I learned an altruistic truth from Mama about underdogs. It was because Mama mad is a scary thing.

After the fiasco of losing my dream job on my first day, I'm less sure life events can't sap your energy level and natural desire to do good. Remembering our past, specifically, my past opinion of Tiffany using her family circumstance as a crutch, makes me uncomfortable now. Especially since moving home I have felt a significant shift in my personality and how I react to obstacles. Where I once met challenges head on with confidence that I will succeed, I find myself tentative and even—more than I care to admit—complaining rather than doing.

That's not how I normally handle things and I don't like the sudden change.

Tiffany is doing well enough for herself. She has overcame her own obstacles to become a salon owner. Tiffany certainly seems to be a successful entrepreneur while enjoying her work.

She works quickly with clippers and then an emery board. The concentration on her face as she labors to repair my damaged nails intrigues me. "I'm surprised you're not just supervising."

"These girls are almost trained. They really don't need any supervising."

The woman working next to Tiffany clicks her tongue. "Girl, you know straight up you're too much of a busybody just to supervise the girls. "

"Glenda, 'A-B' conversation."

"Just making sure you're not caught in any fibs."

I don't know Glenda. She appears to be in her mid-thirties. Her dark hair is straightened to a mild curl, and her facial expression perpetually fixed between 'Don't mess with me' and 'Girl, you crazy.'

"Are you two partners, Glenda?"

"She wishes. But like I said, she is too much of a control freak to have a partner."

Tiffany taps Glenda on her arm. "You pay attention to your customer. I'll pay attention to mine."

Glenda rolls her eyes and continues to work on the octogenarian customer's nails, who was falling asleep in her chair.

I turn my attention back to my hand and am shocked that Tiffany is already painting the nails on my left hand. I pull my right hand up and examine her artwork. It's as if I come in every week. All the damage has been magically reversed.

"Good?" Tiffany asks without lifting her eyes from the brush stroke on my nail.

"More than good."

"You can keep them that way with just twice a month visits."

"I'm convinced." It's too hard to explain to Tiffany that I'll only be here for a few weeks, two months at the most. Either way, it will be smart for me to keep them up while I'm interviewing.

"I talked to your cousin Charlotte today." That sort of popped out of my mouth.

Confusion flashes across Tiffany's face. "Why, how did you do that?"

"Her cousin's being framed!" Glenda interjects.

I ignore Glenda. "I'm helping with her defense. Charlotte is who recommended you to me."

"How is she?" Tiffany asks.

"You haven't visited her?"

"I should have." Her eyes cast down. "I just don't know what to say. It's all so sad."

"Sad that her husband is dead or sad that she is in jail?"

"Both. Plus, the kids. I mean, they're with her sister-in-law right now, and Rachel's good with kids, but she won't want to keep them forever. She has two of her own. Lord knows I wouldn't know what to do with them."

"What's really sad is not having Alan around for carpentry work anymore," Glenda remarks as she paints her client's nails purple.

"Hush up, Glenda. I can't believe you'd be thinking about how this would inconvenience you."

"All I'm saying is the man did excellent work. Smelled like a distillery, but he fixed my back porch in just a few hours, and at half the price the other folks were quoting me."

"Alan was a good guy?" I ask.

Both women stare at me with brows raised.

"No! I said the man did excellent work. Other than that, he was a total jerkwad. Plumb crazy too," Glenda says.

Tiffany nods agreement. "True story. He had a habit of rubbing everybody the wrong way just for the fun of it."

"Well, if that's the case, can you think of anybody that might've wanted to kill him? If you don't think Charlotte killed him."

"Charlotte couldn't have done it. That sort of violence is just not in her," Tiffany says.

"And Alan wasn't the kind to have enemies who would be wanting to kill him. They might want to kick his tail and teach him a lesson, but definitely not kill him," Glenda adds.

"That's where I am. I don't think Charlotte did it either. But somebody killed him, and if I can't come up with a plausible alternate suspect, it's gonna get hung on Charlotte. Besides, the prosecution has the motive of the fifty-thousand-dollar accident insurance policy."

"Horse puckey. If Charlotte did kill him, she did a horrible job of making it look like an accident. She'll never see a red cent of that payout. Hello, you can't use the insurance policy as a motive if she won't receive it." Glenda shakes her head. "That's just stupid."

"Well, Jacob was the arresting officer," Tiffany mumbles.

"No, kidding? I didn't know that," Glenda says.

"What's the matter with Jacob?" I ask. Jacob and I were good friends in high school, but I have fallen out of touch with him in the last seven years.

Tiffany sighs as she paints the nails on my other hand. "Jacob is a sweetheart, but some days he may not be the sharpest tool in the shed."

Glenda clicks her tongue. "Yeah, he always has been sort of dumb when it comes to people, but the boy is some serious eye candy."

My memory of Jacob was a broad beefy lineman with a baby face who played on the high school football team both ways on the line. I always thought of him as a brother, and the "eye candy" comment catches me off guard.

"What do you think?"

I think I could be a hand model. "You are a true magician, Tiffany."

Her face flushes. "I'm glad you're happy. I appreciate a challenge, but how about you use a shovel to dig the next hole."

"Deal."

Tiffany leads me to the counter. We set an appointment for two weeks, and I pay her.

"I appreciate you helping Charlotte, April."

"It's my job, Tiffany."

She narrows her eyes. "I know. But there is a difference between doing something because it's your job and doing it because you really want to help someone. You're asking the right questions, that's more than anyone else would be doing for her."

As I leave Tiffany's, I realize my old student has taught me something I'll need in the days ahead. I'll need more than my education and intelligence to fix Charlotte's situation. I'll need passion. Passion for helping someone, not for the money or the win, but because she is in need.

Unfortunately, the case is even more confusing to me after speaking with Tiffany and Glenda. One thing is certain, my to-do list is getting longer. I need to talk to the Officer, that sounds so weird, Jacob Hurley, about the arrest. I also need to get by Charlotte's house and snoop around and see if it helps me visualize the crime.

I might lower the partitions in my mind in hopes of receiving a few clues from the other side of the veil. I know I said I shouldn't use my powers in the "real" legal world, but a woman's life is at stake. As my brother, Chase, would say, "Go big or go home."

Chapter 13

I'm only five minutes late to Black Angus. Given I learned about the dinner this afternoon and hadn't fully sorted through my clothes, they're piled on my kitchenette table, I consider myself on time.

The Black Angus Grill is located outside of Albertville on what used to be an antebellum plantation turned ranching operation turned restaurant. Black Angus is one of the few places in Marshall County to take a date to impress. Originally it was supposed to be the keystone to a massive country club golf operation. The golf course is overgrown now, and only the restaurant remains.

I park my car and speed walk to the entrance. Typically, I'd be looking forward to a big juicy slab of beef from this culinary treat. Their steaks melt on your tongue. However, I have a cold knot of dread, irritating my stomach. For the life of me, I have no idea why my anxiety level is climbing.

The hostess ushers me to a booth in a dimly lit corner at the back of the restaurant. As I approach, my uncle and Lane stand.

"There she is. I was about to call the Marines," Howard jokes.

I steal another quick glance at my watch. "I'm only five minutes late."

"I'm just teasing. Have a seat."

Howard motions for me to sit on his side of the table. I oblige by sliding into the booth. "I hope you didn't order for me, too."

"I know better than to commit such a faux pas, even though I know exactly what you're going to order."

I ignore my uncle. "Mr. Jameson, how are you this evening?"

"Lane, please."

"All right, Lane."

"I'm doing well. Very well, thank you." He lifts his tumbler and smiles. "Would you like one?"

I realize the source of the cold knot in my stomach. I'm leaning forward toward the mesmerizing eyes of the distinguished gentleman across the table from me. His gaze, fully attentive, has a hypnotic quality to it. When Lane talks, half of what he says I don't comprehend because I'm watching his practiced expressions.

As if his level of attentiveness and directness isn't disconcerting enough, there is a fascinating unreal quality to the man. It's as if Charlton Heston stepped out of a digitally colored version of the nineteen fifty crime noir film *Dark City* and is asking me to enjoy a drink with him.

I struggle not to grin when I look at him because I can't get the silly vision out of my mind. I'm sure my amusement will pass as I become more familiar with him.

"Yes, please," I manage to say.

"What would you like?"

I panic and point at his tumbler. "I'll have what you're having."

"Scotch?" He arches his eyebrows. "My, aren't you just full of surprises."

No, I don't drink scotch. I also believe anybody who tells you it's possible to develop a taste for it is a liar. It's merely the "Lane" effect on my brain.

"I must say I was surprised but pleased to find you at Howard's office this morning."

"Really?"

"Yes. I've been after Howard for the better part of two years to hire some help. I admit I'm surprised you're working for him. Having graduated from Alabama, I expected you to fly into a big city and sign on with a high dollar law firm rather than share a shingle with your uncle."

"Now I may have misled you there, Lane. I don't recall telling you April was working full time for me. She is only taking a little breather before she does exactly as you say," Howard says.

"Really?"

Lane's intense stare almost has me spilling the beans of my whole sad brief employment at Master Lloyd and Johnson. How a witness holds up under his cross-examination is beyond me.

"Sure," Howard continues, "April was rightfully concerned if she hired in immediately with one of those multi-cubicle law firms, it would be years before she'd litigate a case. Worse, she might spend her entire career doing nothing but drawing up contracts. April hopes to log some real court experience first before continuing her professional development with a larger firm."

My appreciation for my uncle's ability to spin a golden story out of my complicated career detour cannot be higher. He not only extricated me from the embarrassment of explaining my situation in a long lengthy discussion, he made me sound like someone who had their act together. Someone who has a plan for the rest of their professional career.

Which I absolutely do not. I wish I were the girl my uncle is describing to Lane.

In an epiphany, I realize Howard is the sneakiest of smart people. When you look at him in his ill-fitting brown suit, not so good haircut, and sloppy demure, you tend to forget the man's exceptional intelligence. He can win the intellectual battle while you're still attempting to square the fact the man who looks like he hasn't the sense God gave a goose is twice as smart as you and three times as quick.

"That is incredibly mature and far thinking." Lane bobs his head. "I hate to hear you are temporary, but I certainly understand real talent does not stay in Guntersville if they have other options."

"How's your golf game, Lane?" Howard pries the spotlight off me.

"Not. I hardly have any time to play, and when I do, it's so embarrassing, I wish I hadn't."

The next hour and thirty minutes, I sip on expensive bitter scotch once the ice cubes melt sufficiently to cut the taste. I snack on deep-fried onion rings and devour a medium-rare steak that's proportioned for a three-hundred-pound man. The entire evening, I might as well be invisible. Which truthfully is a blessing.

"April."

Lane calling my name causes me to jump.

"I did want to speak with you regarding the Charlotte King case. I assume Howard informed you of the generous plea bargain I offered."

I give a quick nod, and he continues.

"It's simply a horrible situation." Lane tugs at his tie knot. "I typically would not offer a plea bargain given the strength of evidence, but the thought of four children being forced into the care of strangers, no matter how fine of people, vexes me terribly."

"Evidence? What evidence?" My voice is a higher pitch than I intend.

Lane straightens his back. "You read the folder, right April?"

"Of course, she has, Lane."

Lane shifts his view from me to Howard and back. "That evidence, April. It pains me to say it, but the woman is guilty."

I'm astonished that Lane is serious. It's as if we're conversing about two different cases.

The folder I reviewed is light on facts and heavy on circumstantial evidence and unsubstantiated speculations. Compromising, to say the least, but hardly a case with a preordained outcome if taken to trial.

"I could easily try her for first-degree murder and send her to prison for the rest of her life." He shrugs. "We have enough evidence to recommend the electric chair, but that's not acceptable punishment for a mother. You need to persuade her to take the deal. You do understand, don't you?"

I look to Howard, and he offers no help as he raises his eyebrows. "I don't know," I stammer.

"You don't know?"

"I can't explain, but I have a feeling Charlotte is innocent."

Howard lays a hand across my hands on the table. I did not realize I was wringing them in a fretful manner.

"What April is trying to say, Lane, is she wants to maintain the assumption that Ms. King is innocent until she has completed her own exhaustive research. Then she'll reach her own unbiased conclusion. If Ms. King is guilty, she'll persuade her to take the deal when and if it becomes apparent it's in Ms. King's best interest. It isn't necessary to rush such matters."

I appreciate Howard clearing up the conversation. I should remain silent. Keeping my mouth shut is not in my nature.

"No, I mean, I've spoken with Charlotte, and I've reviewed the case ad nauseam; I don't see a case worthy of your time to prosecute."

The transformation of Lane's expression from soft and understanding to thinly controlled outrage is immediate. "I assure you there is more than enough evidence in the brief to win a conviction against your client, ma'am. Luckily for Alan King, the decision to prosecute is mine, and I will see justice done."

"Yes, sir."

"I want you to understand the gravity of the situation. The grand jury reviews the merits of the case next Wednesday."

I nod my head as I bite my lower lip. I can't think of a thing to say. My mouth has put my back in a corner and then abandoned me. Typical.

Lane sighs, "I hope for Ms. King and her children's sake you are correct. I sincerely would not want four children to know their mother was executed for killing their father. Still, once a case is in the hands of the jury, it very well may be the outcome. I'm sure I do not need to remind you a jury is a fickle beast made of twelve parts. A very fickle beast indeed."

So, this is how it's played. Everything's chummy and casual if I go with the flow. But the moment I take a stance against the consensus, it becomes all hard edge and chippy.

That's fine with me. I grew up with two competitive brothers. When someone decides to play rough and lean on me, I'm wired to push back, not submit.

If I can't be on Lane's team because I follow my gut, I'm good with it. I know whose side I'm on. I'm on Team Charlotte, and I'm not scared of a fight.

Chapter 14

I pace the floor of my room. I'm fit to be tied. Even changing into my favorite PJs hasn't alleviated the growing tension and frustration I feel from my discussion with Lane. Plus, I have a bowling ball in my gut from eating a steak I had no business eating.

I'm perfectly miserable. It's all I can do to fight back the urge to scream.

I search through the King case once more. I add my notes collected from the beauty college today and hope to see the dots to connect what has eluded me to this point.

No such luck.

I need sleep but know it will not come. I pull out my laptop and scan the legal profession job boards. After a few minutes of fruitless searches, I decide my time is better spent watching silly baby goat videos.

Wait. There it is. My dream job appeared magically on my screen. A law office in Louisville, Kentucky specializing in mergers and joint ventures, has a listing for a junior account representative position.

I like the idea of being assigned to existing accounts. I've also been to Louisville once for race day. From what I remember, admittedly I'd had a few too many mint juleps, and was at least mildly inebriated, I like Louisville. The ad also claims the position has a competitive salary and full benefits. That means it must pay well. Right?

I click the link to their online application, fill in the pre-requisite header information, and attach my resume. I can't help but smile and get a warm glowing feeling all over as I press the send button.

This is the one. This is the job I was meant to have, and all the recent difficulties have led me to this climactic moment.

Even though I've only applied for a job, I feel a tremendous sense of accomplishment. I turn off my laptop and sleep through a restful, dreamless night.

Chapter 15

The last half of my first week at Snow and Associates has been like whiplash. If our week started out slow to boring, we made up for the slow start the last three days of the week. I am clueless how Howard was managing the flood of requests during the busy periods without help.

True, none of it is highbrow law. Still, I'm seeing all manner of legal issues. The exposure is honing the many different specialties of law I studied the previous seven years. At the least, it will have to do wonders for my preparations for the bar exam.

I genuinely enjoy working as a team with my uncle. Howard is patient and takes the time to explain any items I don't understand. He is a great teacher. I'd forgotten how easy it is for him to make me laugh. That's been a bonus to the work environment.

Howard is still buying my lunch too, which is the best.

What's not cool is my agreement to work with Dusty this weekend. We were so busy at the firm I'd forgotten about the trip to Paducah until Dusty reminded me Thursday night after dinner.

I have a significant case of cold feet. It's no reflection on Dusty and his team. They've all been welcoming and encouraging. It's the idea of unleashing my "gifts" that has me concerned. No, scared is more accurate.

Last night when I attempted to beg him off, he didn't fight fair. He told me it was fine by him if I bailed, but the rest of the team was looking forward to working with me, and it wasn't right that I led them to believe I was looking forward to working with them.

As I watch the team load the last duffel bags and cases of gear into the van, I'm convinced not only that I shouldn't go, but we should cancel the trip in its entirety. I have a bad feeling about this trip. A metal scraping on bone sort of feeling.

On Dusty's signal, we all get in the van. Dusty asks me to ride shotgun so he can discuss a few details with me while he drives us to Kentucky. Not to be dramatic, but when I step up into the van, it feels like I'll never make it back to the lake house.

It could be the details of the case. The more I contemplate the case notes, the more they don't make sense. The troubling aspect of the Paducah poltergeist, as we've begun to call it, generally paranormal entities are or are not. If a full apparition is in costume from an earlier period, typically, it's been in existence since that era. It's highly unusual to have an apparition suddenly appear in the present and not have existed earlier.

The few eyewitness accounts list the spirit as a fully formed vision. Not mist, smoke, or some undulating mirage in the air. They specifically said a man dressed in turn of the twentieth-century attire. The nineteen-twenties or thirties, to be specific. So, where's the poltergeist been all this time? Asleep? Why has it only been seen recently?

Another aspect, and more troubling, is the maid's suicide. Something about the details just makes me itch.

There are two manners in which the maid could have come to her demise. She could have hung herself willingly out of desperation. Assuming it was spirit related, she may have feared she was going insane. The theory is plausible as ghost sightings, especially repeated sightings, can have that effect on someone.

In the second scenario, the poltergeist took control of her body and forced her to hang herself. If it's the second, that's a powerful spirit, and we're walking into some significant trouble.

The van rolls down our street, and we turn onto highway seventy-nine. "You okay?" Dusty asks. "You're awfully quiet."

"Just tired. We had a busy week at the firm."

Dusty clicks the low playing radio off. "Yeah, that's one of the reasons why I want to get to Paducah tonight. We all need a good night's sleep for tomorrow."

I turn my head and survey the dark night only occasionally pierced by a barn light in the distance and listen to the random bug cracking against the windshield. How can I be near so many people and simultaneously feel so alone?

"But we're good. Right?" Dusty favors me a smile.

"Yeah, we're good."

"All right then. Hopefully, we'll get us some scare the living daylights out of you pictures of a ghost tomorrow to headline the next book. God willing and the creek don't rise."

I'm reasonably sure God doesn't have anything to do with what's in the old hotel in Paducah. The uneasy feeling making my skin tingle tells me we would be wise to set the bar lower than a poltergeist's photo. Possibly completing the excursion with everybody in one piece is a more reasonable goal.

Chapter 16

I expected we'd spend the night at the Osborne Hotel. Instead, Dusty pulls the van into the parking lot of a seedy motel just outside of Paducah. At first confused, I realize Dusty doesn't want us to deal with the introductions and unloading of our gear tonight. I'm grateful for his planning and for the opportunity for a good night's rest. I've not fully realized the depths of my exhaustion from the first week of my new working life.

Dusty has proven he doesn't hesitate to make sure his team has the most current and technically advanced equipment in the field of paranormal research. When it comes to creature comforts, he can be a skinflint. I shouldn't be surprised when he hands me a room key, announcing Liza, and I will be roommates for the night. I can't complain, all six of the men are bunking in a second room.

I won't lie. I'm filled with an awkward apprehension as I accept the key from my brother. Call me a princess, but my experience with sharing a room is like, umm—never. Growing up, being the only daughter in a family had a few perks.

I'm also not excited about the prospects of Liza and I being the best of roommates. Sure, we have the same plumbing and all, but I get the feeling that's where our commonality comes to a sudden end.

She lifts the key from my hand. From the tight set of her jaw and squinting eyes, I get the vibe she is not too thrilled about the sleeping arrangements either.

"I call the bed closest to the bathroom," Liza says as she pushes the door to our room open.

It wasn't a question, but I have no preference. "Okay." I have more crucial details to tend to, like what's that weird odor in the room?

She tosses our key onto the dresser and slings her backpack onto her chosen bed. "Do you plan to shower or what?"

It crosses my mind; Liza is advising me I need one. I did have a nervous sweat going on during our drive to Paducah, but I think I'm too tired. "I wasn't planning on it."

"You got to pee?"

"No. I'm good."

Liza pulls off her T-shirt and walks to the bathroom sink. The artwork on her porcelain skin is so profuse I can't take in all the illustrations before she disappears from my view into the shower and commode area.

"Good because I take a long shower." The door clicks shut behind her.

"Alrighty then," I whisper. I check my phone for the time. It's only eight. As tired as I feel, I'm sure I won't be able to sleep just yet.

I consider checking out the motel office to see if they have vending machines. Going on the hunt for a candy bar would kill some time, but I'm not hungry. It would just be nervous eating, and I don't need the extra carbs this late at night.

Sitting at the foot of my bed with my hands in my lap, I can't decide what to do with myself. I can review the King case I loaded on my laptop. No. I'm sick of reading the same notes repeatedly. It could be helpful to brush up on the Osborne Hotel history Miles gave us. Meh, that seems pointless since I'll see it for myself in the morning and get more information from being in the building than any report could provide.

The last option, turning on the ancient TV, almost wins.

Oddly, after being in a van with seven other people for a few hours, I need social interaction, not mind-numbing activity.

I haven't spoken to Shane since that awkward "me kiss—he no kiss" moment at my parents. A quick conversation, long if I'm lucky, could answer a few lingering questions I have about our relationship status. I enter his number as I fluff the paper-thin pillows on my bed closest to the door. I stare at the sliver of dingy glass the green vinyl drapes fail to cover. I wonder if a passerby can see me on my bed. I'll need to check that out before I go to sleep.

"Hello?"

Shane's smooth, robust voice hits me with a little tingle below the belly button and brings my full attention to the call. "Excuse me, but one of my friends told me this is the number to call if I need a pickup truck. Or is it just a pickup. Bless it, I'm just not sure which it is now." It's stupid, but I tried being direct with the kiss at my parent's. I feel keeping it light, and flirtatious is the best tactic now. Besides, I don't really want the sting of rejection again if he isn't interested.

Shane lets out a slow, deep chuckle that brings a smile to my face. "Girl, you're all kinds of messed up. What're you calling me for April? Are you all right?"

"Yes. I'm simply curious about what my friend in Atlanta is up to."

"Work. You?"

"I'm working too. Did I catch you at a bad time?"

"I'm with some patients."

"Oh, I'm sorry. I'll let you go."

"Nah, they won't mind much."

I burrow my back farther into the pillows. "Are you still coming to Guntersville for the fishing tournament next week?"

"Wouldn't miss it."

I clench my fist in triumph and decide to double down. "Any chance we can go to dinner?" Warmth flows from my chest to my ears when I ask.

"Sure, I believe we have a whole busload of us going to dinner Saturday night. It'd be great if you can come too. Maybe you can invite your other brother Dusty."

I close my eyes and deflate in defeat. I know, I know. It's not like Shane hasn't made it abundantly clear we're only friends. Excuse me if I find it difficult to accept.

One, because he has looked at me in "that way" before indicating he finds me attractive. Two, because I'm exceptionally in lust for Shane, and I'm rarely this into a guy.

I'm not sure if I want a long-term relationship with him, I haven't gotten that far in my fantasy where he does a one-eighty and falls madly in love with me. Okay, that's not true. I do believe the name April May Snow White is uncannily perfect. But even if "Until death do us part" doesn't happen, I still want a hot and steamy short-term relationship with him. "Oh."

"Chase told me you're working for your uncle?"

Great. So, Shane called Chase but not me. That's right. Twist the dagger in my heart, Shane. "Yeah."

"That's cool. I'm glad you were able to get a job and practice law so quickly. I know you were worried about that when you were in Atlanta."

My aggravation is kicking in, and I don't feel much like talking anymore. "Yeah, but I'm really waiting for this opportunity in Louisville to come through."

"Really? You have an offer to move to Louisville?"

Well, of course not really. But it sounds good in a pinch, and right now, it's important to me to let Shane know I'm well, and my life is coming together just as I planned. "Yes, but I need to compare it to the other verbal offers I've received once the contracts arrive. It's a crucial decision, and I can't take it lightly."

"Sure. Yeah, I get that."

"Well, I'll let you get back to work."

"Okay. Hey, April."

If I could punch myself, I would. Something about the man's voice makes my heart jump, and I loathe myself for not being able to kill the spark of hope in my gut. "Yes, Shane."

"Thanks for the call. I think it's the first time a woman who wasn't a family member has been thoughtful enough to call me just to talk. Kinda cool, you know."

I sigh and hope he doesn't hear. It's my issue, not his. I know from experience he would make a spectacular friend; I just don't know if I can do the "friend" thing with Shane. "Well, I was just thinking about you."

"Thanks. I'm looking forward to seeing you Saturday."

The consolation prize is not what I hoped for. "Yeah, me too, Shane. See you Saturday."

I set my phone on the dresser after disconnecting. Honestly, I have no idea how to process the Shane relationship. It's virgin ground for me.

Liza wasn't kidding. The shower is still going strong, and massive steam tendrils are leaking out from under the door. I have entirely too much nervous energy to stay in our room. I decide I want the candy bar.

Chapter 17

I enter our room as Liza emerges from the bathroom. The hotel room door clicks shut behind me. Liza drys her short raven black hair with a towel as her body drip-dries nude.

"I'm so sorry," I say as I back into the front door.

Nonchalantly, she glances at me via the vanity mirror. "What for?"

Heat flashes across my face as I look away from her. "I should've knocked before I came in."

Liza huffs with the roll of her eyes before frowning. She stops drying her hair and wraps a towel loosely around her slim body. "Sorry. Dusty said you were kind of a prude."

I'm no prude! Well sometimes. About some things. "If you're not embarrassed, I'm not."

Liza ignores me as she puts toothpaste on her toothbrush and brushes her teeth.

I watch her until it feels like I'm staring and then divert my eyes. I don't feel like turning on the TV, but there is nothing else in the room more interesting to look at than Liza.

The awkwardness is killing me.

When I move my hand, the candy wrapper crackles, and I'm overjoyed to remember I have something else to turn my attention to other than Liza. The cellophane wrapper is ridiculously loud since the room is silent since Liza turned off the water.

Liza catches my action in the mirror and turns to face me. "Did you get that from the lobby?"

I don't know what it is about her that makes my face flush. "Yes. I asked through the door if you wanted a candy bar too. I guess you didn't hear me."

Liza presses her lips into a thin line as she cocks her hip. "You could've bought three for the price they probably charged you for that one. These places are highway thieves." She stretches to her backpack, unzips it, and pulls out a plastic bag tossing it onto her bed. "If you need a sugar fix, I never leave home without. Help yourself."

"Thanks." I take a bite of the chocolate covered nougat bar I bought from the front desk while staring at my favorite type of candy bar on top of Liza's stash. I nearly break a tooth on the petrified candy bar. "How long have you been teamed up with my brother?"

"For a while," Liza says as she drops her towel and pulls a T-shirt over her head.

"Did you go to college together?"

"Nope."

"Meet at a supernatural seminar or something?" I laugh nervously at my own joke.

Liza pulls the sheets up to her neck as she gets into bed. She flicks off her nightstand light. "April, I don't do this." She waggles her index finger between the two of us.

"Do what?"

Liza slaps her pillow a couple of times and turns her back to me. "Girl talk."

Girl talk? I'd settle for talk.

I seethe as I watch the back of Liza's head in the dim light. I wonder if she can feel the hot stare on her still damp hair. I've never suffered dismissive people well. Especially when I don't know what I've done to offend them.

The Milky Way comes mindlessly to my mouth then I hesitate. I hate this brand. What is nougat anyhow?

Setting the candy bar on my nightstand, I walk to the bathroom to brush my teeth. On the way to the bathroom, I snag one of the Payday candy bars from Liza's stash.

Chapter 18

I can fault Dusty for being cheap with the motel rooms. But when it comes to food, Dusty is a fantastic boss. There will be no cheap biscuits for his team. We walk across the street together the next morning to have a proper sit-down breakfast at the diner across from the motel.

The eight of us take a long table in the center of the diner and place our orders. Last night's sting from the cruel candy bar event fades into my distant memory as I admire the steaming breakfast plate. The "All-American" value meal I ordered consists of scrambled cheese eggs, a double order of hash browns, four slices of bacon, and a stack of pancakes large enough to share with the entire team if I want to. I'm not offering, though.

Dusty is polite enough to wait until everyone has finished most of their meal and started their second cup of coffee before beginning to interject the business of the day.

"Liza, given we're not positive what we're up against, you must be prepared with your instruments on a moment's notice. As much as possible, I always want us to remain in designated teams. Each team is to report to the control station every fifteen minutes on their walkie-talkie. Each member will always keep their body camera on. No exceptions to that rule." Dusty looks pointedly at the Early twins. "And I shouldn't have to say this, but no solo research projects. Anyone caught going rogue on their own will earn a bus ticket home."

My gut clenches tightly. It has nothing to do with the monstrous pile of bacon I consumed, and everything to do with Dusty's level of caution. I understand his reason for vigilance. There is always the possibility a research project can go south quickly. All the same, it sharpens my focus and tweaks my anxiety. We're about to go poke a ghost.

Liza gives a curt nod of her chin without looking up from her raisin toast. I can't help but doubt her level of commitment, given her perpetually sullen attitude. The idea of Liza being all that stands between me and an unnatural death by a phantom or poltergeist is not comforting.

"April."

Dusty calling my name startles me. My fork clatters onto my plate. "Yes."

"Given your skill set, there is a high probability you'll be the first point of contact if we're successful in locating paranormal activity. Since the spirits often seek you out, I'm teaming you with Liza. I don't want her to have to respond to you being in a crisis. I want you two together. But that means the two of you will need to be flexible and able to swing to the aid of the other teams if necessary."

Just peachy. I should have guessed I'd get teamed with little Miss Sunshine. If my anxiety was unwarranted earlier, now I have a good reason to be not just nervous, but scared. I have zero confidence Liza wouldn't take her sweet time in saving me from a paranormal event. I also have no idea what her skill set is that Dusty holds in such high regard or why he feels she needs to be near me during the investigation.

I raise my hand. Dusty's face tightens as if I've lost my mind. "You don't have to raise your hand, April. If you have a question, just ask it."

"Sorry, you just seemed to be on a roll. I was wondering why you're teaming up Liza and me. Maybe it would be better to team each of us with a guy."

"No. Like I said, you're the highest probability of the first contact. If something goes wrong, I want Liza by your side. If a spirit needs to be expelled, she will be the only one who can help you."

My shoulders slump. Simply great. Liza is a supposed expeller.

Understand me; a practiced expeller is worth their weight in gold if you cross an evil spirit. It's that true expellers are as scarce as hen's teeth, and there is an overabundance of folks claiming to have that dangerous and challenging skill.

The paranormal world is full of hacks and wannabes, especially expellers. They are attention seekers who want to walk around a room, burning sage and mumbling some stupid chant without a shred of talent or understanding. The best-case scenario is they're a waste of money. Unfortunately, they are just as liable to raise the ire of a hostile spirit in a flash, putting a research team in mortal danger.

Spiritual expulsions run from moving a ghost out of a room to permanently banishing them from a location such as a house. Then there is the hardcore stuff folks lean on the church to cleanse. Some of those priests lack the necessary skills too, but at least the church has standards.

Claiming to be an expeller is also a matter of perspective, like claiming to be able to run. A person can run slow, fast, or be an Olympic track medalist. The wide variance of abilities aside, most of the expellers I've met are simply hacks.

Dusty typically can smell a fraud from a distance. Liza claims they've worked together for a while. I assume she has some skills, or Dusty would've already moved on to another expeller.

"Miles."

Miles flips open his notebook. "We have an appointment with Mr. Caldwell at nine a.m. He'll give us a tour of the hotel and then show us our control room so we can set up our equipment. I plan on having Jason and Chet set up the audio equipment on the fourteenth floor. Travis will work with Luis setting up the photography and the infrared equipment."

"Sounds good. That keeps with the everyone has a partner aspect as well."

Miles raises a finger. "One other point to bring up. And it's a bit disappointing. Reports are that since the maid hung herself, the apparition has been dormant."

"You're just now telling me this?" Dusty rarely loses his temper, but his face turns as red as his hair.

Miles shrugs. "You know how these things go. Just because the apparition isn't showing itself today doesn't mean it won't appear when we invade its territory."

"All the same, you know how expensive these trips are to put together. It would've been nice to have that bit of information beforehand."

Liza interjects as she put some more orange marmalade on her raisin toast. Her eyes don't meet theirs. "If it's there, it'll either be agitated by my presence or drawn to April." She angles a look at me. "Assuming April has the skill level you say she does, Dusty."

I've never been fond of my "gifts." They truthfully scare the bejesus out of me and all things being equal I'd rather not have my talent. But Liza's tone irks me.

If I weren't having the same concerns about her skill level in her role, it might have escalated into an argument. I suppose her doubts are as fair as mine, but she can't belittle me without cause. I tilt my head and narrow my eyes in her direction. "Don't worry about me, illustrated girl."

Liza remains too interested in her toast. I think I catch the hint of a smile before she takes another bite. Hmm. I might like her.

"Do you two have a problem? If so, we need to get it worked out now." Dusty's glare shifts from Liza to me.

"No problem here," Liza mumbles with a mouthful of toast.

"I'm good," I assure my brother.

Chapter 19

You can do all the research you want on the internet about any city in America. Despite the technology of the maps and the plethora of photos available to you, it's never the same as walking the town.

As we enter the riverfront section of Paducah, I get a multitude of tingles. Nothing particularly strong, just light tingles. The city is rich in history, which means it has a corresponding number of souls floating in the ether looking for the opportunity to express themselves. It's not exactly like walking through a cemetery. Still, large older urban areas tend to cultivate a collective strength of residual energies from the deceased. Thank goodness for Nana's coping strategies from decades earlier.

I catch Liza's gaze in the rearview mirror. She raises an eyebrow, and I know she feels it, too. Good. Maybe she is as skilled as Dusty claims.

Pulling into the parking lot across from the Osborne Hotel, the voices tumble over my mental barrier, melding into one crescendoing unintelligible articulation. The noise is deafening inside my head. I struggle to strengthen my internal defenses. With effort, I'm able to move my mind along the path of control until I only hear a whisper. Even they are layered from multiple entities and garbled.

As we pile out of the van, Liza sidles up to me. "You good?"

I nod my head briefly, despite my nausea. I've never experienced morning sickness. But if it's half as bad as the queasiness I get in a spirit rich area, I may rethink the childbirth idea and just adopt.

"Good." She rubs her forearms. "Because there are a lot of entities here, and they're not exactly excited about seeing me."

I study Liza's features. It startles me to realize she is genuinely scared. We share the same concerns. Now, both of us are at the mercy of Miles's research, and Dusty's ability to keep us all safe. I'm not feeling particularly secure in either of them to deliver the goods.

Liza and I fall in behind the six men. They all seem oblivious to the paranormal disturbances, even Dusty.

As we follow them into the hotel, the voices oddly fall silent. I look at Liza, and she frowns. "What?" I ask.

"Something nasty is in here," she whispers.

"Everything went silent for me."

She scowls. "There is something evil in here, scaring the rest away."

The men have fanned out in front of the concierge desk. They're speaking to someone, but their broad shoulders are blocking my view. I slide to the right, and as I pull up beside Travis, I see a man of average height and build. That's all that is average about the man. His suit is impeccably tailored. His facial features are chiseled and intriguing, his eyes golden-brown, and most importantly, he exudes a natural magnetism that forces a smile to curve onto my face as I watch his movements intently.

His hand extends to me before I realize it. I favor him a smile before accepting it. His palm is warm and slightly calloused.

"What a pleasure to meet you, Ms. Snow. I'm James Caldwell, the purveyor of this establishment."

I want to kick myself. If there were anything I'd change about myself, it would be how my body reacts when I meet an attractive man for the first time. I mean I'm in my late twenties, it's not like I'm some middle school girl that should get all hot and bothered because a member of the other sex says hello to me. I'd like to write it off as having a long dry spell. The truth is it wouldn't matter if it's been a year since my last relationship or if I were in a relationship now. If I meet a good-looking guy for the first time, I usually blush, stare, and must force my gaping mouth shut.

You'd think it wouldn't be that big of a problem since it's only when I find a man attractive. Unfortunately, I have an eclectic taste in men, which means I continually have this schoolgirl reaction if I'm meeting new people. Honestly, it's exhausting.

"Pleasure to meet you, Mr. Caldwell." His eyes linger on me before he gives a brief grin and turns his attention to Liza.

"And you, Ms. Gowen." He furrows his brow. "Are you all right?"

Liza has a green hue about her. Despite that, she nods. "Yes, just eager to get started."

James claps his hands together. "Me too. I am optimistic your team will be able to help our little situation."

"Little situation? You had a maid hang herself because she saw a poltergeist," Liza says in a loud incredulous tone.

James shoots his hand out, reaching for Liza's forearm. She jerks her arm back and glares at him.

After looking down the hallway of the first floor and seeing no other guests in earshot, James's demeanor calms. "We don't really know what happened to Dilly."

"Well, if you found her hanging from the chandelier with a rope around her neck, I think it's pretty safe to say she hung herself. Or somebody helped her suicide," Liza says.

"Miles, if you will, take Luis, April, and Liza up to the fourteenth." Dusty turns to Travis. "Travis, if you, Jason, and Chet can start bringing the equipment in, that would be a huge help."

The three men lumber back out the front door. Miles waves to the rest of us, and I'm eager to follow him. I don't care much for conflict.

As the four of us enter the elevator, I want to ask Liza why she is agitated. Her facial features look like a bear trap stretched to its limits, waiting to snap on the first person stupid enough to transgress the silence.

The silence is bothering me. Not Liza's, but the voices. As the elevator continues to the fourteenth floor, I gradually lower my filter and still hear no mysterious sounds. But I feel a presence. It's heavy and thick, and it makes it hard to breathe. But for whatever reason, it's holding its tongue.

When the brass gilded elevator doors open, we step into the early twentieth century. The maroon and gold wallpaper in combination with the rug of the same pattern, envelop and suffocate me.

I'd taken my filters all the way down, leaving my mind fully exposed, still nothing. Still, I feel the invisible life force breathing down my neck.

Liza staggers to a gold embroidered high-back chair in the sitting area just outside the elevator. She falls into the chair and exhales as she leans forward and cradles her head in her hands.

Luis kneels next to her. "Do you need water or aspirin?"

"I need air."

"Do you feel something, Liza?" Miles asks.

Liza snaps her head backward as she glares at Miles. "What do you think, Einstein?"

"Just asking."

Liza turns to me. "What about you?"

"I feel something." I give a quick shrug. "But I don't hear anything."

Liza drops her head back into her hands. "That's some major skill there, Snow."

Yesterday, a comment like that would've ticked me off to no end. But I'm already getting a feel for Liza. I put her in the highly self-sufficient category, not because she wants to be, but because nobody else can step up to the tasks at hand. I feel she is the type of person who has come to rely on her own abilities and doesn't anticipate any help.

"There is something more concentrated and powerful than the random voices. It's like it's—I don't know—making the rest of the spirits be quiet?"

Liza raises her now bloodshot eyes. "It's not making them do anything. They're afraid of it."

"What can I do to help?" I ask.

"Nothing for now. Just keep your antennas up. I should've brought my bag in before coming up here."

The elevator doors open. Dusty and James step out. Dusty's face contorts with concern. "Liza?"

She waves a hand at him. "Just waiting for Travis to bring me my bag."

"I thought she looked green downstairs," James offers. "I have some antacid in my office if you'd like."

"It's not like that," Liza and I say in unison.

"While we wait on your bag, I think it's important James repeats what he just told me downstairs."

James hesitates. "As I mentioned to Miles last night when we confirmed our appointment, after Dilly's death, the spirits went on hiatus. Until this morning."

I can't help myself. I look over my left shoulder and then over my right, checking the length of the hallway.

James notices, and he interjects. "Not here, not on the fourteenth. There have been no disturbances on the fourteenth since Dilly killed herself. The recent events were in the basement."

"How recent?" Miles asks.

"Yesterday," he says with a sheepish grin.

"You never mentioned a basement in our discussions," Miles comments with a perturbed tone. "I found no record of a basement in my research, either."

James raises a hand. "Truthfully, I'd forgotten about it. It was originally the cold storage for the kitchen. It was added to the design after the initial plans of the building were drawn. But after the flood of nineteen thirty-seven and with the improvement in refrigeration technology, it's been abandoned."

"We arrive today, and you just happen to remember that you have a basement?" Miles narrows his eyes. "Seems sort of convenient."

"I understand. But until the disturbance, the door to the basement had become just part of the kitchen wall. We never took notice of it. We even kept a small storage shelf in front of it."

Dusty twirls his hand forward in a 'get on with it' motion. "The disturbance?"

"The kitchen staff has been hearing chiseling for the last twenty-four hours."

"Chiseling?" Dusty asks.

"Yes, chiseling," James repeats.

"From the basement."

"Yes."

I can't help myself. "How does chiseling sound different from knocking or hammering."

"It's metal on stone. It has a distinctly different sound." James says as he shifts his stance.

"Is it going on now?" Miles leans forward as agitation is replaced with interest.

"Yes. Until you open the cellar door. Then it stops. It continues as soon as the door is closed again."

"And this is only a recent occurrence? It's not happened before today?" Miles continues to press.

James shoves his hands into his expensive trousers. "If it has happened before the staff has never mentioned it."

"But no apparitions? Just the sound of chiseling?" Dusty asks.

"Again, nothing the staff has reported. Mind you, I've never heard the noise myself."

Dusty gestures toward the hallway. "All right, first things first. We know most of the recorded disturbances over the life of the building were on the fourteenth floor. Nothing changes regarding our focus. We'll set up our gear here on the fourteenth and investigate the basement when we have the opportunity. Mr. Caldwell, if you don't mind, please walk us through the fourteenth floor."

Caldwell motions with his hand. "My pleasure. You'll notice as you investigate the building in its entirety, the fourteenth floor is quite unique from the other floors. Being the highest floor, it was designed with most upscale guests in mind. It does not have the windowless interior rooms. Its enlarged suites on the west side of the building are three times the size of a normal suite. The ten executive suites boast a spectacular view of the riverfront. In its day, the view was a huge draw."

As we wait for James to unlock the first executive suite, I study the hotel wallpaper and carpet in greater detail. It's still the suffocating maroon and gold, but now I note both appear to be new. They only appear old because they are accurate to the styles of the early twentieth century.

If I owned the hotel, I'd want to liven the place up a bit. Some bright yellows and cheery lilac pastels would do wonders for shaking off the dusty tomb ambiance. I'm not sure if the historical board requires him to keep everything in its original old geezer furnishings, or if James Caldwell is a stickler for historical details.

I steal a glance at Liza. I see the muscles clenching in her jaw, but her coloring is less green than earlier. She catches my stare and rolls her eyes at me. Stifling a laugh, I revert my attention back to James as he opens the door.

"I'll leave you a master card for the entire floor. There are no guests on this floor for the weekend. Please feel free to investigate anywhere in the hotel. Remember to be discreet when not on this floor so as not to frighten our guests."

Following James into the room, I get a prickling sensation on the back of my neck.

James faces us, and I swear I note the hint of a smirk on his face. "I would suspect this room is where you will be doing much of your investigating."

"This is it?" Miles asks.

"Right there." James points in the direction of some decorative ironwork attached to the wall above one of the monstrous plate-glass windows.

For the life of me, I can't get a read on James. When we met, he shook my hand, which is always an advantage to me. My "gifts," while less than reliable, often snap to attention and signal me if I've encountered an evil person or a person with ill intent in their heart. There was no rush of visions or even the hint of a core susceptible to ill purpose.

While his appearance, smooth voice, and polite mannerisms are magnetic, the subtle odd reactions to the seriousness of the situation at hand are more than disconcerting. I have the impression he believes the circumstances are a lark. His attitude suggests he does not believe a paranormal entity is involved, only a depressed hospitality worker who took her own life. That is a possibility.

I need to not worry about what James thinks. I need to concern myself with my job at hand. I'm here to disprove or record a paranormal existence.

If I were to cast a ballot on the existence or nonexistence of a paranormal being in the Osborne Hotel, presently, I'd vote no. My mental partitions have been totally removed and still nothing. Complete and total silence blanket my mind.

Well, not exactly nothing. Ever since we stepped foot in the room, I did notice a precipitous drop in the temperature and the uneasy feeling of being observed. Of course, the rooms may be kept cooler than the hallway and let's face it, I am on edge.

The silence, while I could consider it a positive, makes me nervous. This is a first for me. In the past, if I felt even the slightest presence and lowered my guard, spiritual chatter would flood into my mind. Sometimes so many voices at once they became inaudible. There is nothing to hear of a spiritual nature.

I turn to Liza. "Anything?" I whisper.

"Just what I said earlier."

Evil. That's what Liza said earlier. I can't tell one way or the other. All I know is it's getting even colder in the room. I rub my hands briskly over my forearms to chase away the goose-bumps.

Chapter 20

"Miles, I want the infrared cameras set up in here as well as the stationary recording system. We'll set up the headquarters in the room across the hall, and I want cameras covering the entire length of the hallway on the fourteenth." Dusty points in the direction of the hallway. "Thank you, Mr. Caldwell. I think we can take it from here." He holds his hand out. "You can just leave me the card to open the rooms."

James squints. "What about the basement?"

"As I said, first things first. We must explore the known area of disturbances first. Then hopefully, we will have time left over for the basement tomorrow."

James frowns, appears like he'll argue, and changes his mind. He holds the master key card out to Dusty. "You're the expert. Let me know when you want access to the basement."

Jason, Chet, and Travis appear with several dollies loaded with equipment. I watch the team's relaxed rhythm. They put together their control station and mount cameras and recording equipment throughout the floor. Liza pitches in and begins setting up the different computer terminals in the control station. I feel useless as tits on a boar. The last time I'd been on a paranormal investigation, our equipment consisted of a borrowed VHS tape recorder. Times have certainly changed.

"How are you feeling?" Dusty asks.

His grin indicates he is inquiring about the possibility of a psychic sign rather than my health. "Dead silence, not even a peep."

He arches a brow. "Now that's intriguing."

I nod in agreement. Intriguing, odd, or disquieting, take your pick. I catch myself rubbing my forearms again.

"Hand me your cell phone."

I pull back from Dusty's hand. "As if. What's wrong with yours?"

He chuckles. "Nothing, give me your phone. I want to load an app for you."

"What kind of app?" Usually, it's my other brother Chase, I worry about loading unwanted items on my electronic devices, but the room is making me increasingly skittish about everything.

Dusty makes a "give me" gesture with his fingers. "Something that'll replace most of this other equipment. We combined a couple of paranormal apps that include radar for electrical impulses and the ability to squelch noises to scan and zero in on spirit voices."

He is pulling my leg again. "Yeah, right."

"Give me your phone, April."

I reluctantly dig my phone out from my back pocket and hand it to him. Chase could've asked me for my phone thirty times and never gotten it from me. "You screw up my phone, and I'll kick your butt."

His fingers glide over the display. "I'm not going to mess up your phone. I think you'll like this app. We call it 'Spook Kook.' It'll assist you in locating energy disturbances too."

I squeeze in closer and stand on my toes to see what he is doing on the screen. "If it does all that, I don't know why you need me."

He turns his head and grins. "Are you for real? This is just a simple tool. I mean, it helps point you in the right direction. But news flash, artificial intelligence is still in its infancy. Besides, they'll never be able to create an app that complains as much as you do."

His cut is water off a duck's back to me. Besides, it's true. I'm just naturally talented like that.

I do wish I could believe in my "gifts" the way Dusty does. Maybe if I'd spent more time with my grandmothers learning the ins and outs of my freaky skills, I could measure up to what my brother needs.

He holds my phone out to me and points at a radar screen. "See that red dot in this upper right quadrant?"

"Yeah."

"That is why the temperature has dropped." He hands my phone back to me.

I'm shocked he felt the lower temperature too, and I'm ashamed I didn't bring it to his attention. "Why didn't you mention something?"

"We're just getting started. I expect it to take some time for you to figure out your role with the team. Besides, it's just a dot right now. Doesn't exactly make for an exciting conversation, much less an eight-thousand-word story."

"Maybe we should have pressed Caldwell on it."

"To what end? Caldwell wouldn't believe there is something in here if it reached out and pinched him on the butt." Dusty turns his back to me and unfolds a camera tripod.

"Still, I don't understand." I squint my eyes in the direction of the empty bookshelves on the far wall as I speak. The red dot from the app indicates the energy disturbance is in the top corner of the shelf.

"What's to understand? Caldwell's a simple businessman. If we prove nothing paranormal exists in his hotel, it's nice and clean for him, and he can disprove the claims. If we find something and, more importantly, can document it with a photo, it simply ups the attractiveness of his hotel to a different clientele." Dusty flashes a toothy smile. "Win-win for him either way."

I focus on the area close to the bookshelf. It's possible my mind creating what isn't there, but when I step closer, I catch the slightest glimmer in the air two feet from the ceiling.

My breathing slows, and I push everything from my mind. I focus on the small waver of light in front of me. With great concentration, I marshal the energies around me and attempt to condense the whole into a small invisible orb and hold it near my sternum. With a mental push, I force the captured energies outward in an arc directed at the shelf as I open my consciousness. The doors to my mind are open, and I welcome interaction with the spirit.

There is no expected excited chatter. No spirit attempts to recount its existence, its tragedy.

Silence. There is only silence. Still, what is it I taste and smell in the cool musty air? Fear?

I exert a more assertive push as the last of the captured energy wanes and increase my focus on the spot in the air. I sharpen my attention more than I have in years. I want to be successful and help the team.

But the tiny shimmer never grows. It never reveals more.

"Show yourself," I demand.

A quick flicker of light rains down from the shimmer. Briefly, one hundred points of small radiant lights create a silhouette that disappears as quickly as it forms. But it's enough. I'd been shown what I needed to see.

The shimmer floats to the right and disappears. The temperature in the room normalizes.

Turning, I'm surprised to see Dusty struggling to conceal a laugh. "You do realize the point of the exercise is to actually get proof on film?"

"Yeah, why?"

"It's just harder to get a picture of them if you're pushing them out of the room." Dusty holds up the "Spook Kook" app to show me the red dot is no longer in the room. A fact I already know without the fancy app.

"I was trying to get it to reveal itself. I never knew there was such a thing as a shy ghost," I gripe.

Dusty begins to laugh uncontrollably. "Shy ghost? You kill

me, April."

After I'd chased the ghost from room fourteen-thirteen things quieted down. They became mind-numbingly dull.

Luis takes the next two hours to explain the working basics on all the new cameras and recording instrumentation to me. I do my best to appear enthusiastically interested. I'm sure I do less than an admirable job of it.

Another hour of boredom is burned when Dusty is kind enough to have six large pizzas delivered to us. Jason, Chet, and Travis kill one large pizza apiece.

The three of them, while munching on their pizzas, eagerly show me how to read the EMF meter data rolling in a constant stream across one of the screens. As they show me the newest tool in their arsenal, a three-dimensional energy point plotter, I expect them to stroke the machine and chant "My precious."

Nerd boys can be over the top about their toys. Mostly when a girl is feigning interest.

I watch the sunset across the river through the glass window of fourteen-thirteen. The rich salmon-colored rays bracketed by the purple clouds above and dark river below, is a wondrous sight.

As the darkness fills the room, my aggravation builds, and I lose control of my emotions. I'm so bored I want to scratch my face off and scream.

I assumed when I accepted the position with Dusty, it would be like when we were kids and went into paranormal hot spots. Those excursions were "Crash n' Dash" events.

This is a slow burn, tedious non-adventure. Despite all the technological advantages of locating and recording an apparition, I haven't seen or heard anything since the brief silhouette earlier. I'm beginning to think the idea of a shy ghost is not far removed from the truth. Or the shimmer was just my mind playing tricks on me.

All this time, I was worried about what would happen if I went on a ghost hunt with Dusty, especially now that my "gifts" have reactivated. In hindsight, my concern shouldn't have been "What if we see a ghost?" The real danger of these adventures is if there isn't anything supernatural in the building. I'm not sure if you can die of boredom or not, but I'm certainly testing the theory thoroughly tonight.

I let the door to fourteen-thirteen close and take the three steps across the hall through the open door of our command center. The other seven team members are hard at work watching screens with nothing on them and logging times with no disturbances.

Liza notices me in the doorway and stretches her arms over her head. She gets up and makes her way to me. "You want to go for a walk?"

My severe scowl only prompts a grin from Liza. She gestures behind me to the hallway. "This thing isn't showing up anytime soon. I'm thinking you and I could walk the entire floor and see if we get a feel for it."

"Why would I want to do that?" I didn't mean for it to sound that way. It's just nothing is happening in the hotel.

Liza puts her hands on her hips. "I don't know, maybe because it's your job?"

I sigh, "Oh, all right. At least I can get some exercise, I suppose."

"Geez. Sorry to trouble you." Liza slides past me into the hallway.

"Hey, wait. Buddy team, remember?" I call at her back. She stops and waits for me without turning her head. When I'm at her side, she begins walking again.

Liza is a prickly character. I feel her harsh, unvarnished communication somehow makes her more appealing to me. She is right to call out my ill mood.

As I follow her to the far end of the hallway, my aggravation dissipates. "Are you still feeling what you felt earlier?" I ask.

"No. I'm getting a whole lot of nothing."

"How's that?" I pull up when she stops and shakes her head. I try to explain my question. "I assumed if you felt the building was evil, it wouldn't change hour by hour."

"I didn't say the building was evil. I said something evil was in it." Liza continues down the hallway.

As I follow, I attempt to comprehend the significant difference Liza believes exists in the semantics. I guess she is correct. A building in and of itself can't be evil.

Fear washes over me and chills my blood as a tingle starts at the base of my neck, running to my scalp. I realize the foolishness of my earlier aggravation of being bored. Boredom is precisely what I want from these excursions. It's stupid to be hoping to run into a spirit just so I can get an adrenaline bump to curb the assignment's tedium.

If we don't get a single picture or recording and we can inform Mr. Caldwell his hotel is not haunted, I'll be ecstatic. In retrospect, the quick silhouette visual I'd gotten earlier of the apparition is enough for me. Even though the spirit wasn't hostile at the time doesn't mean it's not.

Just thinking about the encounter now gives me an uneasy feeling in the pit of my gut. I've lived long enough to believe there are things best ignored so as not to encourage them. Still, other things should be avoided entirely. It shouldn't be my undoing because I have a brother who gets his joy from poking things anyone with common sense would leave alone.

Don't get me wrong, I know Dusty's livelihood is based on getting verifiable proof. I'm also aware these research trips are expensive. But I'm not ashamed to admit that I'm afraid to take on anything other than harmless, confused ghosts. Evil spectral entities are strictly not part of my contract.

Liza unlocks the last room on the left with the card key Dusty received from Caldwell. We enter the room. I know before the door shuts behind me, the room is empty. I don't bother pulling out my phone to confirm with the app.

"Nothing?" Liza asks, her eyes scanning the room.

"Silent as a church mouse."

She frowns. "But that's just it, isn't it? It's not that there is nothing, it's silent as a church mouse hoping we don't find it."

"The feeling could be mutual," I mumble.

We repeat the routine for the next seven rooms until we've made our way back to the team. As Liza begins to unlock room fourteen eleven, we freeze in alarm. The distinct sound of bare feet on wood flooring emanates from within the room. Liza looks over her shoulder at me. "Caldwell said no guests on this floor, right?"

"Yep." I'm afflicted with the sensation of a thousand spiders scurrying across my back.

She unlocks the door. We move inside cautiously. I hold the door open in the event we need to make a hasty retreat.

Again, there are no voices. No bare feet on wooden planks can be heard either.

"I've got nothing. You?" Liza asks.

"No. I don't..." My breath catches as I focus on a sudden sensation. I scan the room and settle on an area to the right of the closed drapes. I step toward the curtains slowly.

The door slams shut with a loud bang causing me to jump into the air and swivel toward the door.

"Son of a..." Liza yelps.

I put my hand to my chest. "That scared the living daylights out of me."

"Tell me about it. I think I almost peed myself."

I begin to giggle. "I may have a little."

"TMI, girl."

I turn my attention back to the drapes focusing all my senses on them. I listen. I exhale loudly as I prepare to call it quits, and I hear a muffled sob. My body tenses as I hear the crying a second time.

Drawing in an excited, unsteady breath, I move closer to the drapes.

"What do you see?" Liza whispers.

I hold a finger up, signaling her to wait.

The distinct sound of someone crying fills my head this time much louder as if my reception to the source has improved. Still, I don't see even a shimmer or a disturbance in the energy around the window. I pull my phone from my back pocket and tap on the "Spook Kook" app Dusty loaded. My breath rushes from me. The radar shows a red dot directly in front of me.

I swallow hard, then yell, "Reveal yourself!"

Instantly a glint cuts through the air in front of my face and begins to vacillate violently. A lightly illuminated disembodied face, with an expression of shock and terror, floats inches from me surrounded in a light metallic mist.

Sucking in forcefully, I stumble backward.

The female vision's mouth drops open. I believe she is equally shocked that I can see her. Her eyes widen, then she screams, "Leave me alone!"

Liza grabs my shoulder. "What is it, April?"

Leaning forward, I say in what I hope is a calming voice, "We're here to help you."

"No, no, no." The apparition shakes vehemently left to right as she begins to fade. "He will be angry, so angry."

"Who? Who will be angry?"

"You must leave. You will make it worse," the ghost pleads.

"Make what worse?"

It's too late. The ghost's face fades, and the last tendril of mist dissipates. Without thought, I look back to the app on my cell. The red dot is gone.

"April, what is it?"

That's an excellent question. What is it? If I had a decent idea, I'd offer it to Liza. But I'm clueless, and I don't want to alarm the rest of the team needlessly before I understand the experience.

I shake my head. "I'm not positive. I just thought I felt something for a moment. But it was too quick to be sure."

Her expression leads me to believe she is not convinced. I can't help it. I need to mull this one over for a bit before I attempt to explain it to anyone. I'm not comfortable telling everyone we have to leave because an apparition, that only I saw, recommends it.

"What about you. Did you feel anything?" If she saw something similar maybe we can share and come to a rational decision on what to tell the boys.

"No, whatever you saw at the very least isn't hostile."

The heat flash of embarrassment crosses my face. "I didn't say I saw anything."

"You had a complete conversation with something, April. I'm not stupid," she says with a huff. "Let's get the rest of the room done."

Depending on who *He* is and what he does when angry, we may all be stupid for accepting this assignment.

Chapter 21

"Did you find anything for us to film?" Chet asks enthusiastically as we enter the control room.

Liza thumbs over her shoulder in my direction. "Ask Goldilocks." I guess she is going to hold a grudge about me keeping my own consul until I am confident of what my encounter meant.

Chet's eager eyes have me stuttering, "I—uh—not really."

Dusty looks up from his laptop and studies me closely. I shrug. His brows arch briefly before relaxing. He gets it. It's not our first rodeo together. "Anybody want some fried chicken? Caldwell said it's the house specialty."

"I could eat." I'm not that hungry. I'm just interested in any activity that will get the spotlight off me.

Jason and Travis offer to go downstairs and get dinner for the rest of us. Dusty calls down and places our order.

There are times when I tell myself I'm not interested in something. Sometimes it's even true. Often, I'm trying to convince myself of a so I'll let it be because I know no good can come of it.

For example, Randy Leath. Former boyfriend extraordinaire from high school, presently dating my arch-nemesis Jackie Raines. Obviously, I shouldn't care the least bit what Randy Leath is or isn't doing. I tell myself regularly I couldn't care less what he is up to. But deep down inside, the deepest interior part of my brain, there remains a Randy Leath itch I just can't scratch. I may not want to admit I need to scratch it, but that doesn't stop it from itching.

Because of the terror building in my gut, I want to not care how this investigation turns out. Part of me, shamefully, wants to fail, so I'll have an easy out of the next excursion with Dusty.

Before you pass judgment on me, I'll ask you to remember I'm already working for my uncle. Plus, my real job right now should be passing the bar exam and finding my next job as a junior lawyer. And I like enjoy being alive

Unfortunately, the itch has already started deep in my brain. No matter how much I want not to, I know I'll eventually break down and scratch at my paranormal abilities even more.

Dusty and I are more alike than I want to admit at times. We both have a penchant for the adrenaline high only a supernatural occurrence can bring. The difference being he embraces his affinity for weirdness, I try to run from mine.

I slide into the empty chair next to Miles. "What are you working on?"

Miles pushes his glasses up the ridge of his nose. A light sheen of oil has accumulated on his forehead. "Just scanning for any electrical impulses and recording them, April."

"Taking an extended break then," I joke.

He frowns and turns his attention back to the laptop.

Okay, so my joke fell flat. I wasn't going to let that deter me from getting what I need. The itch is getting stronger. "Miles, can you show me your folder on the original owner?"

"Scott Clark or Les Blair? There were two. Remember, they were partners."

"Yeah, right. Both, please."

He shakes his head. "Honestly, April. You didn't even bother to read the historical brief I emailed you, did you?"

"Yes, I did." Speed read would be more accurate. Who knew I'd need to study the brief?

Miles opens the brief and turns his laptop so I can read the screen. He stands and stretches before stepping away.

A partnership between Scott Clark and Les Blair. Scott Clark, prominent businessman, Paducah, Kentucky family well-connected. Les Blair, local financier. Both men attended Murray State University together. Blah, blah, blah. I don't know what I'm looking for, but this isn't it so far.

I continue to read about some issues they had buying two of the lots on the block to complete the hotel foundation footprint. The project was the largest in Paducah at the time and required additional financing out of Louisville, Kentucky, to complete. The project ran over budget and over time. Blah, blah, blah.

If Miles expects everybody to read his briefs, the least he can do is put a little dirt in them to keep our interest. The brief reads drier than a bank stock prospectus.

I reach the last page of Miles's brief. Reading the very last paragraph, I grin. Why does it not surprise me it's tucked away on the final page, in the final lines of the brief? Oh right, silly me, because Miles wrote it. He is a natural at burying the lede.

Miles listed every detail of the hotel's design, creation, and history before the most important fact regarding the paranormal disturbances that were taking place.

"It was rumored in some circles that Scott and Les both sought the hand of the local debutante Renée Watson. Ms. Watson and Les Blair disappeared somewhere around November ninth nineteen thirty-two and were assumed to have eloped together."

I can't help it. It's just a natural tendency, but when I read a passage like the one at the end of Miles's brief, I rarely take it to mean happily ever after. I immediately derive a scenario. Les killed Renée and disappeared, or Renée killed Les and moved to California or some plot along that line. Unfortunately, I've never met a conspiracy theory I don't find attractive.

As I read the last passage a fifth time, I notice the JPEGs attached to the folder. I click on the first one labeled Scott Clark.

The picture appears to be from the nineteen sixties of a gray-haired, balding, short man whose eyes are hollowed with dark bags under them. I get the impression of a haunted soul.

The next JPEG is Les Blair. A strikingly handsome man with sharp, brutal facial features, he is dressed in early twentieth-century attire. Something about the man begs caution. He doesn't look like a man you'd cross without paying a dreadful penalty. Again, other than being mildly exciting background information, the photos are meaningless to me.

I hesitate the cursor over the third JPEG. A coldness creeps into me and steals my breath, and the hairs on my neck stand on end. Do I really want to scratch the itch, or can I ignore it? I believe I know what the third attachment holds. But if I don't open it, it's not my problem.

I hate my insatiable curiosity.

Steeling myself, I finally click the JPEG open. The woman in the picture is stunningly beautiful. She is laughing as if she has heard the most incredibly funny joke. I picture her at a black-tie and gown event. I can't see her hands from the neck up photo. Still, I envision a crystal glass of champagne in one hand while the other hand adorned with a large sapphire dinner ring, holds a fashionably unlit long filtered cigarette.

There are no stress lines etched across her face, and no crow's feet emanate from her squinted eyes. There were many, deeply etched in her visage that floated inches from my face earlier. Renée Watson is the female ghost in fourteen eleven.

If Renée's spirit is still in Osborne Hotel, I doubt she ever left the grounds the day she was last seen. I sober as I understand what that means. She died on site, and though she was never found, her death was most likely foul play.

The meanness that exists in the world cuts at my heart some days. It's impossible to square the picture of the vivacious laughing young woman in the picture with the knowledge that soon after that picture was taken, she was no more. Well, other than what remained of her spirit, a floating head on the fourteenth floor.

I lean back in Miles's chair and continue to study her face. If she could only talk to me. If she could tell me what happened to her. Is that what I really want to know? No. I want to know what can scare a spirit into silence and make it cower behind curtains. That's the more captivating question.

"She is quite the beauty, isn't she?" Miles takes a healthy bite of the chicken leg he holds in his hand.

"Yes, she is. You say there've been no other sightings of her or Les after that November?"

Miles chews quickly and answers, partially covering his mouth with the back of his hand. "Probably moved out to California and had like ten kids. Or that would've been my plan with a looker like that."

"Was there any more information on Les and Scott's relationship? I mean, other than Renée."

"All indications are they were like brothers. They went to the same prep school and roomed together in college." Miles gives a quick shrug. "Honestly, I can't even remember where in my research I picked up they were going after the same girl. I didn't think it important, but you know how it goes with research, put it in even if you don't think it important."

"Yep, you never know."

"You better get you a plate before Chet and Travis wipe it out."

My mind wanders as I fix my plate. It might be having been on the job for ten hours straight now, but I believe it's more to do with having identified Renée. My mind is working at warp speed. I need to understand how she ended up in the hotel and who or what has frightened her. The desperation with which she implored me to leave reminds me of the agony Charlotte had in her voice when she asked me about her children. I wonder how women such as Renée and Charlotte find themselves in relationships with men that scare them. I must believe if I ever find myself in a comparable situation, I'd just cap the man in the thigh the first time he tried to slap me, pack my bags, and leave. I might call an ambulance for him once I cleared the neighborhood.

I still have no idea how I'll get Charlotte out of her mess. Even though it doesn't feel right, because she is innocent, every passing day without a good plan for her defense, Lane's plea bargain gains attractiveness.

After eating a spoonful of paste-like mashed potatoes and half of a chicken breast, I quit eating. I toss the rest of the meal into a garbage bag and walk over to Luis. "Did you get anything interesting?"

"A slight bit of fog above fourteen-o-nine about an hour ago. But it only held together for a few minutes and then dissipated. It could've just been a filter and lighting issue."

I make a mental note to check out fourteen-o-nine again. If I take Renée's ghost literally, there remains a male ghost we haven't identified. "Not a very good day, then?"

Luis smiles. "The night is still young, señorita. Many wonders may yet be revealed."

"That's what I love about you, Luis. You're the perpetual optimist."

"Good things happen to those that expect them."

Ouch! Why did that comment sting my skin? Never mind, I know why.

"April, can I get you and Liza to discreetly check the hallways on the floors below us?" Dusty asks.

"You need to have them check out the kitchen," Chet interjects.

"Yeah, that commotion down there is for real," Travis says.

Dusty runs his hands through his hair. "Guys, we can't go chasing our tails over every knocking furnace in this hotel. It's an old building. Old buildings are always full of noises."

Something isn't right. I put my hand lightly on Dusty's forearm and immediately feel the agitation brewing through his body. "What's the matter?" I whisper.

He sighs. "Probably nothing. I just have one of those, I don't know, feelings. I haven't made my mind up about the basement just yet. I'm perturbed I didn't know about it before we planned the agenda."

I shrug. "It's no big deal. It's just one more floor on a fourteen-floor hotel."

"It's not that. It's..." He shakes his head. "You and Liza check out the rest of the hallways and let me know what you find. Take Chet and Jason with you."

I want to know what is eating at my brother but know better than to press the issue. He will talk when he is ready.

Chapter 22

I do not expect to find anything on the rest of the floors. I chalk it up as a bonus since we can kill some more of the long, dull evening if we take our time walking the hallways. Sure, I have seen a ghost tonight. There is the possibility of a murder mystery at hand, but just being honest, so far, the Osborne Hotel as far as hauntings go is on the lower end of the interest spectrum. Without the equipment picking up a spectacular picture to post with the story, it will be difficult for Dusty to dress up the story enough for it to make it into one of his books.

Let's just say it's no Freeman Plantation.

By the time the four of us make the circuit of the hallway and arrive back at the command center, it will be early morning. I can almost feel my butt in the van headed back to Guntersville now.

I'll be glad to be home in my bachelorette pad safe and curled up in my bed. That's the positive aspect of getting home to Guntersville.

The negative is Wednesday Charlotte's case goes before the grand jury. I plan to sit with her during the questioning. Still, other than answer any questions she may have, I can't even object to any of Lane's questions or presentation of evidence. My best bet is to come up with some hard evidence Lane can't overlook. I can tell the man is accustomed to winning. He won't try the case if there is credible evidence that Charlotte is innocent.

How am I coming with the evidence? I'm no further along than the day I asked for the case.

I'm beginning to feel like a failure. If I can't rise to the occasion, I'll fail Charlotte.

Making matters worse. Now, I feel like I'm failing Renée, too. Why does her death fall to me? How come somebody else didn't help her?

There is no sense whining about it when there is a job to do. That's what Mama always says. I guess it's time to be the old April and meet my fear head on. "Liza, do you mind coming with me?"

She narrows her large eyes. "What's up?"

"I just want to check something out."

She pushes up from where she sits on the floor. "Okay."

"Dusty, we're going to head down the hall a bit before we check the rest of the floors." My brother gives a brief nod as I lead the way out of the command center.

I pull my phone from my pocket and turn on the "Spook Kook" app. I pause outside room fourteen, thirteen, and read the meter. Nothing shows, and I enter the room. Still nothing on the app's radar and, more importantly, nothing on my radar.

"What are we doing?" Liza's eyes are red with exhaustion. Her body language indicates she is willing to follow me, to a point. But her energy level is dropping.

"I just have a hunch about something," I say.

I take a left exiting the room, walk halfway down the hall, and enter fourteen-o-seven. Liza begins to say something, and I hold a finger to my lip. I tap my ear with my finger.

Deliberate and slow, I draw in the energies then force my senses forward into the room next to us. There is only silence in room fourteen-o-nine. I hold my exertion level and am rewarded by a low murmur like a brook gurgling in the distance.

Two voices, one low-pitched and resonant, one slightly higher pitched and agitated. I push, stretching my powers further in hopes of understanding the voices. But they remain inaudible. I turn to Liza and arch my brow.

Liza shrugs indicating she has not heard anything. In my book, given her skill set, that's a good thing. If she can't feel anything that should indicate the spirits, whatever they are, are neutral. I like my chances with neutral spirits over evil demonically possessed ones.

Exiting room fourteen-o-seven with Liza in tow, I enter fourteen-o-nine. The chill immediately makes me cross my arms. I hold my breath and wait. The voices halt, but now, in addition to the cold on my skin, I feel eyes watching me.

I tap the screen on my phone and try "Spook Kook" again. Two red dots show to my right.

"You got anything?" Liza asks as she pulls her phone out.

I wink at her. "Not a thing. I would've sworn there was something in this room."

She angles her head before grinning. "You're probably just punch happy because it's so late in the evening. You know how it is when you're in places that are supposed to be haunted. The later it gets, the more haunted it seems even if there is nothing to see." Liza plays along.

I move toward the wall to my right. I can feel the energy level increase as I approach the wall. I pull up and demand, "Show yourselves!"

The feminine face I saw earlier briefly appears with the same horrified expression. Then melts into a mist and floats away from me across the ceiling and escapes through the closed door. The masculine silhouette of a mirage-like energy field remains stationary in front of me.

Without turning away, I ask Liza. "Do you see it?" My voice sounds high-pitched and tinny to me. The fear is building in me. Part fear for what I see and part fear that this may be *Him*.

I feel her pull up close to me. "Sorry I don't."

"Who are you?" I demand of the concentrated energy field

half hoping it will just float away like its counterpart.

A low rumble emanates from the energy field, and I lose my nerve. I know it makes no sense. A few hours earlier, the floating female ghost practically screamed at me to leave the building. Any reasonable, sane person would have just gathered up their stuff and left. But no, I stayed for more.

A hovering human face speaking English is less terrifying than a human-shaped energy field trying to communicate in a language I don't understand. It's the identified versus the unknown factor.

I turn to Liza and hiss, "I can't understand it. It's trying to communicate, and I can't understand it."

"Turn on the recorder from your app."

"What?"

"I said turn on the recorder from your... oh forget about it." She swipes at her screen then holds her phone in front of me. "The app has a feature to help discern broken language."

I fumble with the controls on my screen. Finally, I see a long squelch line stretching across the screen horizontally. I hold my phone in the direction of the entity, too.

"Who are you?"

The same low rumble comes from the undulating mass of energy. I capture the rumble and hit the replay button listening to the translation intently. Liza listens to her phone first, then moves closer to me and listens to mine when I replay it.

"I hear something, but I can't make it out," Liza says.

I look back to the energy force to ask it to repeat itself. It's gone. My heart sinks as I turn and survey the suite.

"What's the matter, April?"

"It's gone."

"Okay. How about we take the recording back to the others. Maybe one of them will be able to make sense of it."

The adrenaline and fear release the hold on my muscles. I'm suddenly exhausted. "Okay. That sounds like a plan." This time I follow Liza as she leads us back to the command center.

"Hey, I think April has something for you," Liza alerts Luis and Dusty as we enter the command center.

Dusty leans forward in his chair. "With the paranormal app?"

"Yes. But it just sounds like a squelch," I say.

"And?" Dusty asks.

"She saw something, but the princess refuses to tell me what," Liza says as she crosses her arms.

I give her a look I hope conveys I'm not happy with her accusing me of withholding information. I'm not. I'm just cautious about reporting things others can't see. I like to be sure of what I've seen before I get everyone's dander raised.

I look back to Dusty. "I might've seen a masculine silhouette."

"Shadow?"

"No more of an energy field. Sort of like looking at a mirage that's shaped like a man."

Dusty studies me for a moment. I can tell he is running different hypotheses through his head. He turns to Luis. "That fog you captured on video outside fourteen-o-nine after the girls entered it. Did it ever form?"

Luis shakes his head. "No. It didn't even hang around the doorway like it had earlier. It came through the doorway and then disappeared down the hall."

"That was when she left the room..." Me and my stupid mouth! I freeze, hoping Dusty missed my slip. But it's Liza who hops on it first.

"You said it was masculine," Liza insists.

"There were two spirits at the same time?" Dusty asks.

I shift on my feet. They feel sore and battered. "Well, they were sort of having a discussion."

"Two spirits were having a discussion?" Dusty's brow rises.

"That's what it sounded like."

Luis holds out his hand. "Let's hear your tape, April."

I give my phone to Luis. It's bad enough I'm the only one who can hear or see these apparitions. It's starting to tick me off. Everyone is getting tense with me because I'm not telling them when I see ghosts. But if they can't see them, they can't get photos or videos of them anyway. So, what is the point?

I know what is required for us to be able to capture on film or audio. Relaying every detail I experience is futile.

Plus, the woman's warning chills me to the bone. Until I can make better sense of it I feel it best not to alarm everyone.

Luis hits the play button and frowns. He slides his finger on the screen and replays the short audio once again.

"Run the laptop program," Dusty suggests.

Luis downloads the audio directly onto his laptop. He fidgets with a bar on the right of the screen and then plays the recording. This time the recording resembles something closer to English.

Dusty twirls his finger as the recording ends, and Luis plays it again.

"I thought you said there was a male and a female spirit in the room, April."

I shrug at Dusty. "Yeah, there was. But the female left."

"What do you hear?" Dusty asks Luis.

"Theona?"

"Context. April, how did you direct the spirit."

The feeling of being cross-examined is agitating me. I attempt to keep the sarcasm out of my tone when I reply, "I asked it to show itself, that's all."

"That doesn't make any sense. It's apparently trying to communicate something to you and asking it to show itself would simply be an action."

I don't want to play this game anymore. Maybe I wasn't taking it as seriously as I should. Still, it was Dusty's idea to begin with. Now it seems like he wants to direct anger toward me I don't feel I have earned. "I don't know, Dusty. It's not like a witness on the stand. It's a freaking ghost."

Dusty holds up his hands. "Calm down, April."

Oh no, he didn't. "I am calm. You're the one jumping down my throat because I can't get a ghost to answer me the way you want it to."

"I'm not jumping down your throat."

Liza steps forward with a finger raised. "Wait, that's not it."

"He is too jumping down my throat."

"No. I mean, that's not what you said. You asked it to show itself. Then you asked it who it was."

"Theona? I thought you said it was a male spirit?"

I give my brother an extra-long dose of my patented 'Look of death.' "It was a mirage. It's a guess. It's not exactly anatomically correct."

"I'm just going on what you said. What made you think it was a male spirit?"

I toss my hands in the air. "I don't know, Dusty. What makes me think of any of this stuff? I felt a male presence. Maybe it was just some big female ghost with a lot of testosterone left over."

Luis covers a laugh.

"Not funny, Luis," I say.

He takes his headset off and turns to me. "I'm on your side, April." He looks up at Dusty. "The voice rates a ninety-nine percent probability male. We're obviously misinterpreting what it's saying."

Dusty plops down in his chair. "Great, simply great. The first report of a full apparition in three months and we've got zip. We've got EMF blips all over the spectrometer when we first walk-in. Eighteen hours later, all we have is a garbled ten-second tape of a sexually confused ghost."

"We have the mist floating out of fourteen-o-seven," Luis adds hesitantly.

Wrinkling his face in apparent disgust, Dusty says, "You know that looks like an amateur set off a firecracker in the hallway."

Luis drops his head and begins to flick at the pen on his notepad.

"I need fresh material for the next book, people. Fans of this organization are expecting a book to be available on the internet within the next eight weeks. I've got some decent material for the back pages, but I need that big lead story. Real pictures, real audio, and really scary." Dusty pushes his laptop away from him. "Right now, I've got a little bit of smoke on top of an old hotel ceiling and a ghost calling itself Theona on a crappy recording. Whoa, I'm shaking in my boots, folks."

My brother's outburst shocks me. He rarely loses his temper, and to do it with sarcasm and complaints, well, those are my usual ways of dealing with frustration, not his.

It forces me to reflect and realize that once again, I've been so caught up in my own issues I assumed nobody else has problems. Least of all, a multimillionaire like my older brother. Who would think he has got any difficulties to worry about?

I sober as I realize he is more than a little concerned about the sales of the next edition. Like he said, he needs a strong lead story, and he doesn't have one right now. I can understand that it must be a lot of pressure. I guess there might be more work involved in being a business owner than just cashing those big royalty checks.

I understand why Dusty is tense with me. Even without newfangled ghost finding apps and expensive equipment, I know there exists plenty of paranormal in this hotel to create a solid, spooky tale, if not a lead story. But I can't explain why the ghosts are hiding. The whole situation is just off, and the longer it continues being abnormal, the creepier it gets to me. Usually, spirits wouldn't allow a person like me, who can pierce the veil, a moment's peace.

There is also Liza's experience to consider. Like me, she was nauseated when she entered the hotel. We've been in the hotel for hours now, and she hasn't had the first bit of nausea since. For that matter, she claims she has not felt a twinge of anything spiritual in the building. Odd does not even begin to describe that.

"We could try the basement, Dusty," I whisper.

Luis looks up. "The guys said it was humming with activity, boss."

"No." Dusty grabs at the back of his neck.

"Why not?"

"I don't know, April. Why do you know that your ghost is a male? You just know. That's not good enough for me. I'm just not prepared to walk blindly into something we didn't prepare for."

"It's a stupid basement, Dusty," I argue.

He glares at me. "Not prepared. If anyone should know the dangers of going in unprepared, I would think it would be you."

I turn to Dusty's wingman. "Hey Miles, did you find anything about the basement since Caldwell told us about it?"

Miles, who's been across the room attempting to make himself invisible, looks up from his laptop. "Yes. It is conceivable that Caldwell forgot about it."

Dusty breaks his glare from me and directs a look of interest toward Miles. "How so?"

Pushing his glasses up the bridge of his nose. Miles clears his throat. "Well, I didn't catch the basement because it wasn't on the original architectural drawings. It seems Caldwell was correct that the cellar was dug out and added as an afterthought shortly after the building was completed."

"Why?" I ask.

"Good question, April. Despite all the elaborate designs and planning for the building, they left off one important detail." Miles pauses for effect. "Storage for the kitchen area. They tried to make do with a pantry upstairs and eventually decided there was no way to work around it. I'd suspect it was a pretty costly mistake given it would not be easy to excavate with the building already completed."

"Why do we know this just now?" Dusty remains in a less than amicable mood.

Miles clears his throat again. "Well before Caldwell mentioned the basement, I thought we were dealing with a complete set of blueprints. Since this morning, I accessed another building permit on file. As it turns out, there was a second one just a year after the hotel was completed. One was pulled last week, too."

"What?" Dusty squints his eyes.

"I did notice on the way in, there is a slight tilt to the structure. When they initially dug out the cellar, they damaged some of the footings at the front of the building. Consequently, the building began to tilt toward the street. In the mid-thirties, new pylons had to be driven at the front of the building to shore up the foundation. This took place only weeks before the great flood."

"But you said recently," Dusty presses.

"Yes, another permit was pulled last week to repair the foundation a second time. I suppose the original fix has finally failed."

We watch Miles in anticipation of additional information. That was it. No further speculation or analysis on the knowledge he acquired.

"So, Caldwell lied about just remembering the basement in the last day." Dusty was like a dog with a bone. The bone was James Caldwell.

Miles shrugs. "I don't know, Dusty. I can understand where to a layman, an abandoned basement would hold no interest. I mean, the reported sightings and suicide happened on this floor. Why bring up a basement with nothing in it?"

Dusty relaxes his shoulders. "All right, valuable information, Miles. Make a note we need to touch base with Caldwell first thing in the morning and see what else we can find out about the basement."

"Does that mean we're going to investigate it?" I ask.

"I think we should leave it be." Liza has been so quiet I'd forgotten she was standing next to me.

"Why?" Luis asks.

She shakes her head. "I agree with Dusty. We don't have any information on the area. Caldwell needs to provide some additional history before we go down there to research."

I fail to conceal a snorted laugh. "You just heard Dusty say we need an incredible lead story for his next book. This floor is obviously not going to turn up a picture or audio, I think the least we can do is try the basement."

"I didn't say we shouldn't check out the basement. I'm simply saying we need better information. Just being cautious, April. Better safe than sorry." Liza turns her back on me and walks over to Chet and Travis.

Man, I hate the way Liza can dismiss me from a conversation. That sort of thing gets under my skin. It's all I can do not to run after her and jerk her bald.

I also don't understand why suddenly everybody is so cautious about the basement. The research Miles did on the rest of the building, as far as I'm concerned, is just vanilla details that can be pulled from any old microfiche or database at the public library. For that matter, the most crucial part of the information he omitted from his report.

The facts are after eighteen hours on site, all we have as far as the rest of the team is concerned is a little bit of smoke and a garbled squelch. If they could take a picture from my memory, they'd have a photo of a screaming floating head and a giant mirage of a man that would make great photos for the dust cover. But they can't, and we don't.

"Miles, when you can, find Caldwell. Ask him about the cellar. I want to know what they've used it for and what the recent construction was about." Dusty turns his attention to me. "April, I want you to go with Miles for that conversation. I can't put my finger on it, but I still think there is something off with Caldwell. I must admit, this small omission has me a little concerned about his trustworthiness."

Chapter 23

Dusty looks up from his laptop. "All right, it's four a.m. We'll spend two more hours up here, let Miles speak with Caldwell at breakfast, huddle up and decide if we want to tackle the basement."

"Sounds good," Miles agrees.

"Luis, what do you think about trying out the electronic Ouija board?"

Luis snaps to attention as he smiles broadly. "I'd love to, Boss."

"Are you sure about that, Dusty?" Miles rubs his hand over his mouth. "I mean before we get an accurate identification of the negative disturbance Liza felt at the start of our investigation."

"Liza hasn't felt anything since yesterday morning." Dusty's hardens his expression as if daring Miles to continue with the questioning. "There is no point in having all these expensive toys if they don't assist in locating some material to publish."

"I suppose," Miles mutters.

"How long will it take you to get set up, Luis?" Dusty asks.

"Five, ten minutes at the most."

A bead of sweat trickles down my spine. To say I'm less than fond of Ouija boards is like saying I'm less than fond of having my molars pulled without anesthesia. Nana once told me when you use a Ouija board for communication, you open a portal through the veil. I have enough holes in the veil to contend with, I don't understand the need to create new ones. I've never touched one of the ominous-looking boards.

I despise the way my mind can slip through the veil. I would never give permission to some paranormal, especially one I don't know, to come through whenever it wished.

In the worst way, I suddenly want to be back home in Guntersville. My anxiety is pitching to an uncontrollable level as I watch with unexplained dread as Luis prepares his equipment. This field trip has progressed from boring to disconcerting awkwardness to what now feels like recklessness in a fevered pitch to salvage something useful from the investigation.

I know Dusty is tired and irritable. We all are. Still, I can't understand his reticence to check out some bumping noises in the basement, but he wants to open a gaping hole in the veil? A paranormal portal in the epicenter of where the supernatural occurrences have all been historically reported. What sort of logic is that?

Luis calls out to Travis, Jason, and Chet to help him put the more extensive equipment pieces together. They pull out what resembles a four-foot-by-four-foot whiteboard. It's laser-etched with the alphabet, numbers, and 'Yes' and 'No' in an exact replica of a standard-sized Ouija board if it were electronic and made for a giant. They mount the board to a base they place against the far wall. Luis connects the USB cords between the sinister-looking device and his laptop. He sits and adjusts the cursor on his computer.

"I'm setting the cursor to the most sensitive. We can adjust if it's too unstable." Luis's excitement to try out the equipment is evident.

Luis isn't the only one. Chet, Travis, and Jason are standing back with broad grins on their faces as if they're about to watch a rocket launch. Miles remains concerned. I'm debating if I should just run out of the hotel, and Liza has backed into a corner, her skin implausibly whiter.

"Sure," Dusty says.

I go to Liza on the other side of the suite. I reach out and take one of her fidgeting hands in mine. She flinches and resists. Then she exhales and grips my hand. At least we can be scared in solidarity since we have a free ticket to what I fear is an impending train wreck.

It wasn't my intention. Usually, I don't receive reads from people I've become familiar with. Still, her emotions are high and flowing out from her freely into the energy around her. I feel the raw anger and fear emanating from her.

If I was scared a moment ago, now I'm terrified.

"Don't be stupid, Dusty," Liza blurts out.

"Excuse me?" Dusty says.

"You know better than this. Just because we need a piece doesn't mean we can quit taking precautions."

"Liza, you're the one who said you haven't felt anything. Has that changed?" Dusty leans back in his chair and crosses his arms.

Liza opens her mouth—then closes it.

"Well?"

"No. I haven't felt anything since we've been upstairs."

Dusty gestures with his hands, palms up. "There you go. The coast is clear."

"Dusty, I know you feel it too. Something is here, and it's not revealing itself," Liza says.

"I don't know what you're talking about." Dusty turns his back to Liza. "Start your experiment, Luis."

Involuntarily I take a step back and bump into the wall.

Luis turns on the whiteboard, and the laptop's cursor appears in the middle of the screen. Seeing the cursor on the screen and the whiteboard fill in with the parchment's color makes my pulse quicken.

"Just let it sit there for the first few minutes," Dusty whispers to Luis.

Luis gives a curt nod with his chin.

I'm torn between my fear and my loyalty to my brother. My fear insists I close off my mind and find a way out of the building with Liza and Miles if they want to come with me. I've never seen Dusty like this before. It's as if he has turned into some mad scientist, disregarding his own safety protocols in the quest for his experiment to be successful.

That's the conflict. I want Dusty to be successful. My desire to help my brother is almost as strong as my fear. I could assist by pushing out with my mind to lure the two apparitions to the Ouija board.

No chance. The last thing I need to do is throw my gallon of gasoline into this dumpster fire.

The temperature in the room drops precipitously. I know Dusty feels it too. Heck. The whole team feels the drop in temperature. Every one of the men has their bare arms hugged tight to their chests.

Dusty locks eyes with me. I hesitate, then give him the smallest nod. I'm only confirming what he knows as a fact anyway. It's not like I can stop him in his current determined state.

He turns his attention to the creepy board and speaks to it as if the ghosts derive from it. "Welcome, Spirit. We mean you no harm, we only wish to communicate with you." Dusty speaks the words calmly.

I realize I'm holding my breath, and I force myself to breathe. My heart rate is increasing exponentially.

"Spirit, please speak with us. Or, if you prefer to move the cursor on this tool."

The cursor on the whiteboard shudders briefly. It's so infinitesimal I wonder if the monitor simply had a momentary glitch from a power surge.

"Please, have no fear. Speak to us," Dusty continues.

Goose pimples pop up on my arms as the temperature drops further. Instinctively, I let go of Liza's hand and fold my arms over my chest to protect against the dramatic change. The hairs on the back of my neck stand at attention, not because of the frigid temperature. I can feel eyes on me that I can't see.

I glance at Liza in my peripheral. She shakes so violently the tips of her jet-black hair are quivering against her porcelain skin.

The cursor moves, and my knees give out, forcing me to lean against the wall. Acid dumps by the gallon into my stomach as the room spins on its axis.

I must get control of myself before fear overwhelms my senses. Widening my stance, I take measured breaths.

The first cursor movement is a jump across the screen. The cursor slides back to the center slowly, where it remains motionless.

Dusty loses his patience, runs his hands through his red hair before settling his gaze back to Luis. Luis gestures with his hand for Dusty to be patient. I realize Luis is tracking something with the "Spook Kook" on one of his screens. I could pull my phone out and use the app.

Why? I know something is in here.

The cursor begins a long-measured track to the top of the whiteboard. I'm horrified that the boys have added an annoying scratching noise to the program to emulate the sound of the gliding piece across an actual board. The creepy sound has the same effect on me as fingernails dragging across a blackboard.

The cursor finally rests on the letter 'H.' 'H' is for hotel, hate, happy, hello, or h-e double hockey sticks. I run the possibilities through my mind. About half the options are good, and half are terrible. Why don't I like those odds?

A shorter slow track and the cursor rests on the letter 'E.' All right, I'm game. The spirit has spelled 'HE.' I breathe a cautious sigh of relief. We've summoned Renée and she is attempting to warn us again about the male spirit since I didn't heed her earlier warning and leave.

The spooky sound signaling cursor movement begins again. The black arrow stops on 'L.' My heart sinks as fear grips every muscle in my body. This stupid game is making me crazy with its highs and lows.

One thing's certain if that cursor comes back around for another 'L' nobody better get in my way. I'll be running out of the hotel like Beelzebub himself is chasing me. As bad as Ouija boards scare me, I can't think of a worse scenario than having one spell out hell.

The cursor jumps to life again. I hold my breath in anticipation.

The cursor stops on 'P.' HELP? Fear squeezes in on me as I struggle to think of an alternate word. The only thing I could come up with is "helper," I have a sickening feeling that isn't where Renée is going with her spelled message from the grave.

"Lord, please no," Liza mumbles.

The cursor speeds to the center circles once before going up to the letters. It begins to glide over letters quickly, resting for the briefest of time before dropping to the center and circling once and returning to the letter rows. My eyes can't follow the movement after the first few letters.

The black dot continues its frantic blurred pace, and with each passing letter unseen, my fear builds. When it stops, resting in the center of the board, I'm not relieved. I'm frozen with terror. It's the only reason I haven't run out of the room.

I have no idea what Renée has spelled.

"Luis?" Dusty asks.

Luis runs his finger across his laptop screen. The software they created must have been able to record each letter signaled.

Luis's voice cracks with excitement. "Help he is risen from his tomb and rides the steel coach."

"What the devil does that mean?" Jason whispers.

"Shh..." Liza hisses.

We wait in silence. The cursor remains lifeless in the middle of the yellowed board.

Dusty calls out, "Spirit, who is risen?"

The cursor does not move.

"Spirit, who is risen?"

I hear the pulse of blood in my eardrums. The cursor does not move.

"Spirit, identify yourself."

The cursor lurches forward. The pace is deliberate, the scratching noise chilling. I want to tell Luis to turn off the audio effects, but I am mesmerized by the cursor's spelling. As the cursor selects the letter 'D' and stops in the center, I understand it has identified itself merely as 'BAD.'

The room spins on its axis again, this time faster with no end. I'm off balance and begin to slide down the wall as the world starts to close in a foggy ring.

"I told you not to mess with this, Dusty!" Liza says through gritted teeth.

"It could be initials, Liza. Bill Albert Davis for all we know," Dusty growls back. I don't think he even believes what he just said.

"Yeah, go ahead and tell yourself that."

The cursor jerks to life. Its movement is so quick it looks like the blur of a laser light show.

Recovering, I mean to move to the board and unplug it. Someone needs to stop this reckless madness.

Liza grabs my arm. I turn to explain to her, assuming she plans to keep me from my new mission then realize she is catching her balance. Her knees buckle, and I dive to put my arm behind her to keep her head from striking the floor.

"Chet, give me a hand," I call out to the man closest to us. He comes to my aid and extends Liza's legs. I hold her head in my lap as we continue to watch the rest of the team.

"Dusty, we need to call this," Miles warns.

Luis runs his finger across the laptop screen. "He is here, I can't help you, run while you still can."

"Renée," I whisper. The words create a fissure in my mind, and I'm filled with impending doom as thousands of pinpricks electrify my skin.

The lights dim, creating shadows in the room. A breeze begins to push loose papers from the desks, and the rancid smell of rotten eggs wafts through the room. I cover my mouth to quell the urge to vomit.

Cognizant that we will need an expeller soon, I look down at Liza. Her mouth is open, and she is barely breathing. Liza is out of commission and will not be able to assist the team.

"What is it?" Chet asks me under his breath. I can only shake my head. I've no idea, but I know it's strong and harbors ill intent.

"Luis!" Dusty hollers.

"I don't know!" he answers as he frantically types on the keyboard.

"Uh, you guys, something is covering up the entire room on the 'Spook Kook!'" Jason alerts us.

"Can't be," Miles says. "Nothing's that big."

Lighting tripods at the front of the suite fall to the floor in alternating directions. It looks like a skier slapping slalom sticks on the way down a snow-covered mountain. The bulbs explode as they strike the floor. A thick nauseating black gas floods quickly into the room. It splits as if a river against a rock, half flowing to me and a half to Luis.

"Dusty, are you seeing this?" I scream.

"See what?" Chet asks, his head swiveling wildly.

"Yes, I see it. Jason, get that recorder back on. Travis the cameras!" Dusty yells.

"For what?" Travis asks as he reaches for the camera's remote activator. He is fully swathed in the black fog.

As he flips the switch on, a spark of electricity emanates from the dark cloud traveling up his right arm. Travis pulls back, immediately dropping the controls as he cradles his arm. "Man, that smarts!"

I want to run to him and see if I can help, but I'm just a spectator now. I'm tending to Liza, and even if I wasn't, I'm in a near-catatonic state of terror.

The black fog fully encases Liza and me now. Flashes of lightning illuminate the murky entity causing my hair to stand on end. I curve my body over Liza in a protective movement and pull her farther into my lap. I try to wake her as I realize she may be our last hope to end this assault.

"Luis, Chet, help Jason get those cameras back on," Dusty commands.

As Luis stands, his laptop flies across the room, striking the whiteboard on the wall. It explodes unnaturally into a hundred pieces. Despite the destruction of the communication device, the whiteboard Ouija remains illuminated with the cursor making small circles in the center of the board. The scratching noises are impossibly louder now.

"What the devil?" Miles remarks.

"Don't say that," I plead.

I didn't need Liza's higher skill level of paranormal discernment to understand what's entered the suite is all kinds of unwelcome news. As a matter of self-preservation, I pull my thoughts in tight and throw up my partitions to their maximum power. The last thing I need is some spirit with a bad attitude to hijack my mind.

I continue to try and wake Liza. As I pat her face, I look in the direction of my brother. His jaw is set, a portrait of determination.

"Show yourself, Spirit," Dusty commands.

The entire team, save for Liza, looks at Dusty as if he has lost his mind. I'm beginning to think black fog isn't so bad compared to an evil full apparition.

A deep raucous laugh echoes throughout the suite. I'm quite sure Tiffany will be giving me that hair color treatment soon. I swear I feel my hair turn gray from fright.

The cursor reappears on the whiteboard. Which I know can't be happening because Luis's laptop is in a hundred tiny pieces on the floor.

We watch intently as all motion and noise in the suite, except the movement of the cursor and the earsplitting loud, incessant scratching has stopped. The entity wants our full attention to its message.

Slowly it spells "F O O L S D I E."

Yep. I've had enough fun for one weekend. I'll be seeing y'all. I'm ready to go home now. I can't even remember how much

Dusty is paying me for this excursion, but I know it's not close to being enough.

As my fear reaches a crescendo, the black fog begins to recede from the room. As it flows off me, one tendril stretches back toward me, forming a hand that caresses the bottom of my chin before retreating. We have a spirit who enjoys pulling the wings off its victims before ending their life.

As the last of the fog rolls out of the room, Liza regains consciousness. She gasps for oxygen as if she didn't breathe during the event.

"What happened?" She looks around the room, her eyes wide.

I think about it for a second, because I'm not sure myself. "I think we just met the spirit who made you queasy on the way in."

She pushes up on her arms. "What did he look like?"

"Hmm—Big dark and inky."

She nods as she finishes sitting up. "I didn't miss it then, that's what I dreamed."

"Well, no offense, but you sure did pick a fine time to pass out."

She tries to stand and braces against the wall. "I didn't pass out. It's as if something was, I don't know, holding me under."

"What did we get?" Dusty asks.

"A whole bunch of nothing," Jason says. "The camera wasn't rolling until the laptop already hit the wall. Other than that, I have a cursor flying around the whiteboard, which isn't exactly compelling."

"What about the fog?"

Jason shrugs at Dusty's question. "What fog?"

"For Pete's sake, can't we catch a break? Tell me you've got something, Miles."

"I got something Dusty, but it's not what I heard."

Dusty twirls his finger at Miles.

"I distinctly heard a male laugh," Miles says.

"The rest of you?"

We all nod in stunned silence at Dusty.

"Okay. That's good. We all heard the same thing."

"Would be, except this is what we recorded." Miles replays the audio. The silence is broken by static in six short successions. That's it, no laugh, just static in the cadence of the male laughter we all heard boom through the room.

Collapsing onto his chair, Dusty says, "That doesn't make a bit of sense."

Dusty is correct. None of this makes sense. An apparition capable of throwing a keyboard across the room, while remaining concealed, is an extremely powerful entity. Yet, why stay anonymous. Antagonistic, powerful individuals tend to flaunt their presence.

"April, what can you tell me?"

I consider my brother's question carefully. "Hostile..."

"No need to state the obvious," Dusty interrupts.

When did Dusty become such a snark-hurler? The Dusty I know is nurturing and complimentary. I don't know Dusty the businessman, and I don't like him much. His attitude is covered in a thick layer of passive-aggressive sarcasm because he is stressed.

"Male."

"The energy field from room fourteen-o-seven?" he asks.

"Silhouette," I correct him. "Definitely not. This one is totally different."

Dusty is intense as he studies my face. He pulls at his beard. "And?"

"And what?"

"What else did you feel?"

"Nothing. Strong as it was, I was afraid to push out too much to it."

Dusty closes his eyes and appears to be struggling to maintain his composure. I watch his chest expand and then release. "All right then. This rogue spirit got the best of us. We'll need to put our heads together and develop a plan. At least we now know the disturbance on the fourteenth floor is still our target.

We'll just need to retrace our steps to draw it out again and figure out what we'll do to get some decent audio and video."

"We could switch to electrical impulse video," Travis offers.

"I wouldn't be comfortable putting all our eggs in one basket," Luis says. "We haven't tested it fully, and this is too important."

"Luis is right. We'll want to run standard black and white, the electrical impulse equipment, and even though it is a long shot, the passive infrared equipment."

"Excuse me. That spirit is some seriously bad mojo there, Dusty," Liza interjects.

"Yeah, Liza? Somehow I thought we were past thinking all of our research subjects would be Casper the Friendly Ghost," Dusty says pointedly.

"I think I could use some coffee." Miles inserts to break the tension between Dusty and Liza.

"I'll go see if the kitchen is open." I pull on Liza's hand. "Liza can help me carry it up." Her eyes squint, and I gesture with my head toward the door.

"If we don't come back, don't come looking for us," Liza says as we exit the suite.

Chapter 24

Liza rants as we walk to the elevator. "Mark my word, I'll cut your brother the next time he embarrasses me in front of the team."

"Well, I may help you. I don't know what's gotten into Dusty."

"I know darn well what's wrong with him. That she-demon ex-wife of his, Bethany's come back for more blood."

That is a name I wasn't expecting to hear anytime soon. Bethany Roberts was Dusty's wife, for a hot minute a month after he graduated from college with his undergraduate degree.

She was under the impression he would take over the family marina business from Mama. She liked the idea of being a business owner's wife. The summer after his graduation, when Dusty began graduate school, Bethany realized her dreams may not happen. After numerous fights that required family members to intervene, Dusty finally did them both a favor and filed for a divorce before anyone got hurt. That should've been the end of it. But after Dusty's first book hit the bestsellers list, Bethany sued for a portion of the proceeds. She convinced a Birmingham judge she had been instrumental in the layout and research of the first book. I know for a fact Bethany never read, much less outlined Dusty's first book. Nonetheless, she ended up with twenty-five percent of all the net earnings from the first book and ten percent from all the subsequent books.

"Dusty is too smart to get mixed up with her again."

"Sure, he is. I'm sure if your brother had his way, he'd never talk to her again. But that's not going to happen if he is earning money. She refiled against the judgment, and the twenty-five percent has been prorated against all his earnings. Retroactive."

"All?"

"All. As in including the books that were originally at ten percent. That means Dusty has three books he must make up a fifteen percent royalty on and cut her a check for."

"That can't be right. How do you know that?"

"You'd be surprised what your brother talks about after a beer or two."

I'm not saying I know everything about Dusty. But I have my doubts Dusty would talk loosely about personal money matters to his teammates after a few beers. I spent the weekend with him at the Renaissance fair earlier in the month, and he didn't mention Bethany taking him back to court. And we had way more than a few beers together.

I almost let the leash off my curiosity and reach out to see what else I can glean from Liza. She may have guessed my intentions as she steps further away from me as we walk.

"Maybe a good cup of coffee will help everybody's nerves. Hopefully, the kitchen is already in gear," she says as she slaps the elevator down button on the wall.

Her face contorts into a grimace. "Oh, for the love of..."

"What is it?"

"Our nasty little friend left something on the elevator buttons." Liza rubs her hand on the back of her jeans.

"That's the first time I've heard of a spirit needing to use an elevator."

"I seriously doubt he used the elevator." Liza scoffs. "The evil ones like to toy with you. He must have figured one of us would come along and touch the elevator button eventually. And he was right."

I consider how the formless black fog developed a hand complete with fingers to stroke under my chin before it exited the suite. An involuntary shudder racks my body.

"On a scale of one to ten, with ten being the worst, where would you rate this one with what you've witnessed before?"

Liza steps into the elevator as it opens. "Little early to say. But if things keep going in the direction they're going; it may end up at the top."

I stay quiet until the tenth floor. Which I consider exceptionally disciplined given all the questions bouncing around in my head.

"Have you been knocked out like that before?"

"I wasn't knocked out."

"You could have fooled me," I grumble.

I'm not reaching out to her. But we're terribly close in the elevator, and her emotions are extraordinarily charged. The energy is bouncing off her. I can feel—I wouldn't call it fear—but her extreme concern. I'm sure if she had my "gifts" rather than the skill of discernment, she'd be reading the same of me.

It's not just that we've encountered a violent and evil spirit. My more significant concern is nothing is going to plan. None of this compares to any of the cases I worked with Dusty, nor any of the multitude of studies listed in his books.

Most unsettling is the continued lack of voices in my mind. Even black and icky cloud spirit didn't vocalize his anger. I can't help it; I like things to be familiar.

Continuity is my friend.

The elevator opens to the hotel's first-floor hallway. The front desk is presently unmanned, and the lights are dimmed. We take a right to the formal dining room, which the boys told us leads to the kitchen.

"Pay dirt. The staff already put out the coffee urns." Liza points to the far wall.

I may be curious, but I really believe I'm just feeling rebellious toward Dusty. "Let's check the kitchen."

"Why? I'm sure they have some Styrofoam cups by the coffee urns."

"Don't you want to check out the cellar door in the kitchen?"

Liza purses her lips. "No. Not really."

"Who was it just a few hours ago, making me feel guilty about not giving my job one-hundred percent?"

"Yes, well, that's before the eight-hundred-pound gorilla held me unconscious on the floor against my will. That's a bit of a perspective changer."

I'll have to concede her that point. I can't speak from experience, but I suppose that would be beyond terrifying.

"I'll check it out myself. You stay here and get the coffee."

"Right. And if something happens to you, I'm supposed to explain this to Dusty how?"

"Just tell him you didn't notice I left your side. But if you don't mind, do send the guys after me if something goes wrong."

Liza shakes her head in disgust. "Your decision process is conflicted at best."

"I know." I wrinkle my nose. "I have serious issues."

"That's an understatement. I'm coming with."

Thank you for small favors. "If you want."

For some reason, I slink to the kitchen on my toes and peer through the porthole window as if I'm a cat burglar preparing to steal a pound of bacon. As I suspect, because of the coffee urns, the kitchen help is preparing breakfast. Stealth is out.

Steeling my nerves, I push through the swinging door. I hope the smile on my face is casual as I stroll with purpose through the kitchen as if I own the hotel. I feel the worker's watching me with perplexed interest, and I ignore them.

Whatever remained of my hair straightening from the prior morning goes up in the first few seconds as the heavy steam collects on my face. My attempt at looking nonchalant is flagging, and I don't dare turn to see if Liza is faring any better.

Determined to see what I came for; I walk along the perimeter of the noisy kitchen. I figure the cellar door must be on one of the peripheral walls.

"Ms. Snow and Ms. Gowen, what a pleasure to see you this morning."

James Caldwell's voice comes from behind me. I slip and catch myself on the wet floor when I pivot to face him.

"Has your group decided to begin investigating the cellar noise?" His grin tells me everything I need to know about his level of belief in the paranormal.

"Uh... no. What gave you that idea?" How does he look so put together this early in the morning? He should be sweating in the heat of this kitchen, yet there isn't the first bead of perspiration on his forehead. If he were a female, I'd be envious.

He grins. "I suppose because the kitchen is not on the fourteenth floor?"

"True that, Sherlock," Liza interjects. "We just came down to get a shot of caffeine for the crew, but since you brought it up and it sounds like such a lark, where's the stupid cellar door anyway?"

James's cringes at Liza's coarseness, much like she flinched in disgust when she pressed the elevator button earlier. "Yes, of course. My apologies. I should've thought to have coffee sent up to your team earlier. I will have my staff gather something together for you immediately. There is no need to bother yourselves."

"Well, that's rather genteel of you, Jamie." Liza slaps her hands together and rubs them briskly. "Now, where's this cellar door?"

"It's James," he says, then shakes his head in an offended manner. "Follow me, ladies."

James leads us through a small doorway at the back of the kitchen. An unpainted pine door rough in finish stands in the middle of an old off-white plaster wall. James lays his hand on the wood.

"It is unfortunate you'll not be able to hear the chiseling noise I mentioned yesterday with the clamor of the kitchen."

I hear it with complete clarity. Rhythmic, clack, clack,

clack. It does indeed sound like chiseling or someone striking two stones together, attempting to start a campfire. My mind scrambles for an explanation. Nothing probable comes to mind.

"And I'd let you go down into the cellar, but I'm afraid the noise ceases the moment the door opens. Truthfully, I've come to believe somebody is playing a trick on us." He points at the framework of the door. "Somehow, they have a sensor in the door that stops the recording whenever the door is opened, perhaps."

"Does the noise begin up again when you close the door behind you?" I ask James.

His lips part as he considers the question. "I'm not fully sure. I can't recollect if I actually shut the door behind me once I went into the cellar."

"I wouldn't blame you there. You never know when you'll need to beat a quick path back up the stairs," Liza says.

The tension working in her jaws means I don't have to ask her. I know she feels something or hears precisely what I'm hearing.

"Let's just check that theory out." James opens the door before I can protest. Liza and I both suck in our breath. Some men never learned the count to three rule.

It stops. The clacking noise stops. But whatever is creating the sound has only opted to cease the activity and take up watching us on the stairwell. I can feel its hungry interest.

James steps through the doorway and signals for us to follow him. "Come on. We replaced the old light bulbs. Let's check it out together."

"That's okay, James. Maybe some other time," Liza says.

"Seriously? We're right here. Don't tell me you ladies are afraid to solve this little mystery."

I don't do well with folks inferring I'm chicken. I step through the doorway. "Are you coming, Liza?"

"Like you left me a choice," she grouses as she stomps across the threshold.

Before we close the door, we turn and examine the frame for any wires. Not finding any, we pull the door to. The cellar immediately plunges into darkness save for the sixty-watt incandescent light bulb at the base of the stairs hanging from the ceiling. The noise does not restart.

"Well, there goes your recorder theory, Jamie," Liza quips.

"It's James. It might be on some sort of a timer, too." He starts down the stairs. "I should have put an end to this stupidity two days ago."

"Where are you going?" I sound frantic.

"I'm going to find that stupid recorder."

Liza pulls on my arm. "You do know it's not a recorder."

"Yes," I say before I follow James into the darkness.

Chapter 25

As I reach the bottom step, the vastness of the cellar, an entire city block, stuns me. The packed dirt and rocks form the flooring of the creepy subterranean level of the old hotel.

The cavernous hole is lit by a dozen strategically placed bare light bulbs. Each hang on a thin foot of power cord attached to the floor beams six feet above the earthen floor.

It boggles my mind that the cellar was dug out after the building was completed.

A moist, dank odor hangs in the air, and the temperature has dropped enough to make me wish I had a hoodie with me. Something to remember on the next excursion. Assuming we get out of this one alive.

"April. This is a horrible idea," Liza warns.

Probably. But something tweaks my curiosity. I nod my agreement to Liza. "James, seriously, let's get some lanterns or portable lighting, and we'll come back and give it a thorough search after breakfast."

He marches toward the front of the building. "This will only take a few minutes. There are only so many places to hide an MP3 player down here."

"And turn it on and off?" I struggle to keep the incredulous tone from my voice.

"Motion sensor, of course."

Right. I'll let James go on his wild goose chase no matter how silly he sounds. It'll give me a couple of minutes to have a look at the basement.

"April."

I turn to Liza. "It's not going to hurt anything for him to check it out."

"No." She shakes her finger toward the stairs. "Look!"

A single light bulb at the base of the stairs swings gently on its cord. I wonder why Liza is so concerned she bumped one of the lights.

The bulb's cord whips upward, and the glass shatters against the floorboard with a violent pop and a bright flash. Peaches. That's not good.

I swivel and find James at the concrete footers at the front of the building. "James!"

"What?"

"We need to go." I notice the three lights illuminating his path sway side to side on their cords. "Right now, James."

"Hold your horses," he says.

The light bulb at the front of the hotel whips up and explodes against the floor. James stands up straight and bumps his head on a lower beam.

The lights behind him blow in quick succession. This sets into motion choreographed destruction flowing to the back of the building. Each bulb explodes with a violent pop as if someone is running through the cellar with a baseball bat, shattering each dim globe as they pass.

We're plunged into utter darkness. I panic, anxiety squeezes the air out of me. I pull my phone from my back pocket, swiping wildly until I successfully turn on the flashlight. The pale blue light illuminates Liza's face.

"Now, can we leave?" she asks with a heavy dose of sarcasm.

"What was that?" James rubs his head.

"I'd say it's either the spirit you keep denying exists or your light bulbs had a suicide pact."

Liza adds her phone's light to mine. "April, let's go. If he stays, that's on him."

I laugh as a thought crosses my mind. The spirit took immense joy in traveling to the fourteenth floor and trashing our control station. But now we're in its safe space, and it doesn't like it one bit. No, it's still not communicating, yet I sense its aggravation.

The sudden cold on my right side confirms the spirit has sidled up next to me to intimidate me. It's not taking kindly to my visit into its lair, crowding me in the hopes we'll leave.

No, screw that. Mr. Paranormal Bully thinks he can come upstairs, tear up our laptops, throw Liza to the ground squeezing the breath out of her, and expect no consequences? I believe I'll take my sweet time investigating the basement properly.

"If I were to hide an MP3 device down here, I'd put it over by this wall." James stumbles toward the support columns into the darkness. He is in denial.

"Are you brain-dead?" Liza yells at James.

Fudge. I follow James to allow him some light. I don't want him to bean his head on a board again. If he knocks himself out, I'm not sure I could carry him up the stairs. "Are those the additional support columns you added to adjust the lean in the building, James?" I raise my phone a little higher to get better light distribution as I approach.

He pulls up and stares at the columns. He resumes progress toward them, his steps are heavy and with purpose. "What in the world is going on here?"

I follow him to the side of the columns. "What's wrong?" I feel our unfriendly ghost tracking directly behind me. It feels as if I were to stop too quickly, it would merge into my body.

"These concrete columns, they're doing exactly the same thing the original units did." He points at the base where large chunks of concrete have flaked off, leaving the ironwork bare. "This doesn't make any sense. It's not too damp down here for concrete to cure properly. This is unacceptable work."

"You have some things in here that need to be cured, but I don't think it's concrete." Liza is trailing a few feet behind us.

I move closer to inspect the columns. They are chipped severely at the bottom three feet. "This is the most recent work?"

"Yes, but it looks like they're going to have to tear this out and pour the columns again. I see no way to fix this." James appears distraught. "I thought the lean in the building had returned. I didn't want to believe it, though."

The sound of metal rolling and clanking into something substantial makes me jump to the left. I shine my phone light to the right. From behind one of the chipped columns, a thirty-six-inch-long steel bar rolls into view. Oddly, it moves over three large rocks. Physically impossible in the ordinary world. It comes to a stop. Then it rotates twice, nudging forward four more inches.

Okay. Now I'm imagining things.

"That, that's not right," James complains.

"April, I've had enough."

Liza's statement dumbfounds me. Had enough? You think? It's one thing to be crowded by an angry spirit, but this covert intimidation is unnerving. Whatever fascination I have for the cellar dissolves, and I turn to leave. "Time to go."

"We need to leave now. It's getting agitated." Liza leads the way toward the stairs.

"See, this would be the best place to hide an electronic device."

Stopping, I pivot and confirm James doesn't follow group instructions well. I can see his silhouette in front of me. "James, you're in denial. There are no speakers down here. Now get over here before we leave you." I march back in his direction so I can share my light.

I make my way to him, past the columns until I'm directly under the front desk and the hotel entry stairs. The disturbance is even more significant at the front of the building. I feel rage, not mine, roiling the energy of the area.

I'm trying to remain calm. I know panic will only make it more challenging to get all of us out of the basement. "James, enough is enough. We'll come back down with the team and lights."

Spinning in a three-sixty, I shine my light around us. An odd shape on the floor catches my eye. I toe at the dust and dirt with my sneakers and lift the object for a closer view.

It's a brooch. The antique jewelry is crusted with years of dust and grime. I'd not be able to identify it if not for the rusted pin on its back. I slip it into my pocket. "Come on, James. You can see there is no recorder down here."

"There are a few more spots it might be."

"April. Leave him."

The steel bar levitates off the floor; it hovers at waist height. I gape at it, and it flies end over end toward me. I duck to the left just in time as the bar strikes the wall behind me.

I backup in the direction of the stairs as the disgusting smell of rotten eggs permeates the cellar. "Do you smell that, Liza?"

"Yes, April. We've got to get out of here!"

Having a thirty-pound solid steel bar miss my head by inches has a galvanizing effect on my fear, turning it to purposeful anger. I push out with my "gifts" and catch the spirit unaware. It bucks hard as I tap into its emotions.

Intense anger and indignation pulse through my mind like flames licking up from a bonfire. Old, but not ancient. We are in its home, its sanctuary, and it will defend its territory at all costs.

A wave of vertigo scrambles my balance, and I stumble backward as the spirit throws me from its mind. It counterattacks with a psychic intrusion I barely hold at bay.

I continue to backpedal toward the stairs, not yet ready to abandon James. "Get your butt over here, James! I'm not kidding!" I scream.

His shape, barely visible, turns. My yelling seems to have finally earned his attention.

A blast of cold slams into my side. I stumble and cut my palm on the point of a rock as I save myself from falling to the ground. My self-control fades as the spirit's anger presses into the energy around me. I can't see an apparition, but I know I'm in its ghostly invisible embrace.

It wants me to cower, to pull away in fear as it pushes to enter my mind. I do the opposite and thrust hard toward its essence with all the force I can muster.

The entity is surprised as I reverse the game. For the briefest of moments, I read and feel his thoughts directly. He clamps his mind hard and squeezes me out like a wet watermelon seed.

Liza grasps my hand as she tugs me toward the stairs. "April, we have to go!"

My toe catches on another stone when I turn to follow her. She continues to pull me, and I nearly fall. I manage to get my legs under me, and my heart threatens to pound out of my chest as we run to the stairs.

We reach the first step. I can't do it. Nobody would blame us for leaving James behind, but he isn't thinking clearly. I pull Liza to a stop. "Wait for, James."

"April no. Please."

I want to get out of here as much as Liza does. My hand hurts, I'm hyperventilating, and I have the mother of all migraines slamming me at the base of my skull. But James, in his confused state of denial, is a pathetic figure. I can't leave him down here alone.

"But how can a bar just fly through the air?" James asks. He leans down and lifts the steel bar. His screams of pain fill the basement and eerily echo back from the walls far behind us in the dark. "What?" Liza hollers as she flashes her phone's light toward James.

James holds his right hand in his left. Tears leak from the corners of his eyes. "It's so cold it burned my hand."

Liza's phone light goes out. Then my phone goes dead, and we are plummeted into pitch-dark. She squeezes my arm tighter.

It's silent again. Except for small groans of pain coming from where I know James is dealing with his hand injury and erratic short breaths from Liza behind me. Her palm, damp and clammy, slides down to my wrist, and she renews her grip.

"Is it gone?" James asks.

I don't want to answer James's question. Still, I know he'll continue to ask if I don't say anything.

"Stay quiet, James. It's still in here," Liza hisses.

The sound of slow, unsure footfalls begin. They start in front of me but sound as if they are going to the left. "James?" I tense my body when I hear a loud thud.

"Monkey's uncle," James yells.

"What are you doing?" I ask.

"I want to get out of here," he says.

"Can you see?" Liza asks.

"No, but I can feel my way out of here."

I know Liza quit pulling me toward the stairs in hopes our eyes would adjust to the darkness first. But when there is not enough light to see your hand in front of your face, we could be down here for a month and be as blind as we are now. "Aren't the stairs just twelve feet over to our right?" I ask Liza.

"Yes, but I don't trust our creepy ghost friend not to put a pitchfork or sharp blade in our path," Liza says.

"We'll give it a few more seconds. But then I'm with James. I'll feel my way out," I tell her.

James trips, and I hear him tumble to the dirt and rock floor. I cringe when I hear his grunt on impact. That'll leave a mark.

"Stop moving before you hurt yourself," Liza demands.

The creak of rusty hinges, echo through the underbelly of the hotel. The irritating noise makes me cringe. Liza squeezes my wrist tighter.

A series of eight metal on metal taps rings through the inky black atmosphere. I think it's coming from the back of the hotel. Opposite where we were searching.

James has stopped moving. Liza must be holding her breath since I can't hear her.

The unmistakable sound of a cast burner's gas catching flame whooshes through the cellar. An angry red glow illumin-ates the back of the basement.

"What the..." James fixates on the cast burner I now see at the back of the building. I did not notice it earlier.

Liza points. "Look, the stairs." She pulls me toward them, my eyes still watching the red and orange flames in disbelief.

To the left of the flame is a supporting column. Next to the column, I see the profile of a shadowy tall, thin man. His emergence catches me off guard, and I feel my stomach flip.

The shadow vanishes.

"Come on, James," Liza urges as we reach the stairs.

We take the first stair together, and as we step on the second, the fourth plank explodes upward like a cannonball has ripped through the middle of it. The fifth, sixth, seventh, and eighth planks explode into the air in sequence.

The last of the wood splinters come to rest around us. My jaw hangs open.

"Not good, not good," Liza chants.

Seeing our mode of escape now gone, I do the only thing I can. I strike against the spirit. This time he is ready for me. I think the show of force may have been designed to encourage me to lash out and lean too far forward with my attack. He uses my momentum against me, pulling my mind into him.

I stumble forward in his direction as he clamps around my mind and takes control. I'm off balance, and he chooses what to show me.

The taste of copper on my tongue nauseates me as I search about the broken dirt floor. Flames dance against the concrete block wall. The smell of sulfur and mold clings heavily in my nostrils. Splashes of darkness discolor parts of the back wall, the same hue as the small oval puddle I'm standing in.

I'm cold. Wet and frozen. My mind seeks the source of the flames and locates the iron trash incinerator. The grate is open, and the burners on full as flames lick outward from its boundary.

I need to turn it down before it starts a fire.

I shake my head, attempting to clear real-life from force-fed illusion.

Stumbling toward the incinerator, I notice my shoes are discolored red by the mud. "I just got these last week."

Did I? I can't remember now. Where am I?

Stopping in front of the incinerator, I'm desperate to remember why I came here. I'm no longer cold, I'm hot, burning up even. That's it. On fire, I need to turn the furnace off. I look to both sides of the incinerator before finding the gas valve at the back of the enormous iron box.

I turn the knob counterclockwise until the valve has worked almost flush with the pipe. It does not decrease the volume of flame flaring out from the incinerator.

The valve head is mounted directly on a black pipe that leads back to the concrete brick wall. The last four feet on a mesh hose. I turn the coupling on the mesh hose until the hose detaches and falls to the ground.

The odor of rotten eggs engulfs me. The detached hose whips wildly in air from the pressure of the escaping gas. I panic. Surely the flame will ignite the gas leak. Why is there still a flame?

Backing away from the hose toward the front of the incinerator, I wonder if there is a second gas line. I watch the detached hose snake across the floor. The flames inexplicably intensify from the front of the incinerator. I struggle to reconcile what I'm seeing and fail.

I can only shift my attention from the incinerator to the whipping gas line and back. In a delayed reaction, my gut clamps an alarm goes off in my head that screams: 'get out of the building.'

Turning to make my escape, a skeletal hand extends out from the incinerator. Its bony fingers stretch up as fierce flames swirl around the forearm stripped of flesh. Three fingers close back toward the rest, and the pointer finger curls forward then back, making a 'come hither' gesture.

Something strikes me across the face. It's so violent I cradle my nose in my hands.

The weight on my chest makes it impossible to breathe. This

must be what Liza felt. No wonder she is gun shy. Who knew a ghost could hold you down?

I know that voice. The voice chanting in my ear.

The disorientation is too high for me to understand what is happening to me.

But I feel him, and he is irate. I'm spent, but for him, the battle is just beginning.

Chapter 26

Black smoke billows toward me from the lake house as the wind shifts. Acrid smoke envelops me before I can react, stinging my eyes and burning my lungs. Gasping, I suck in another noxious mixture of toxic plastic and wood fumes, forcing me to my knees as I choke.

Sweet air. I suck in greedily as I focus through my blurry vision at my parents' lake house. My home.

Above the roar of the flames licking twenty feet into the air and plate-glass windows exploding, I hear the extended whine of an animal mortally wounded. When I suck in another breath, the animal's cry stops, and I realize I'm the source of the sorrowful noise.

My family's faces flash in my mind, and I am filled with purpose. I must make sure they're out of the home. The concrete driveway cuts my hands and bare knees as I crawl toward the back deck.

One of the picture windows that look out onto the serene lake explodes outward into a thousand tiny diamonds that shower me like a hailstorm. The companion window does the same as I lift my vision again.

The orange flames roll out the gaping holes in the side of the home. A thick column of inky black smoke dances up into the pristine powder blue sky, smudging its perfect beauty.

They're gone. My family cannot have escaped a fire of this ferocity. The only reason I am alive is that my room is above the boat house.

No. They're not home. I know it's not true as I see all five of our vehicles in the driveway. Still, I convince myself they rode somewhere with another family member.

Mama walks through the kitchen. The flames blurring my view of her. She stops, waits, then takes Daddy's hand, and they step through the badly cracked sliding glass door.

They're smiling as they step out onto the deck that has just begun to burn. My brothers, laughing at one another, follow close behind. The ghostly progression comes down the deck stairs as a group like I have seen them do a thousand times before in my life, and as they come within feet of me turn toward the dock.

I know I have lost them forever. The tears flow freely, and as the sobs come, I am too tired to fight them. Instead, I fall to my side and curl into a ball, wishing I were going with them.

The volume of the noise from the crackling of the fire, as well as my own sobs, decreases. I hear a low hum floating above my head.

The hum has a cadence. As its volume increases and the sounds of the fire squelch from existence, the hum becomes a chant of unintelligible words.

From sorrow, I turn my attention from the chant and long to go back to the flames. Where my family remains. Where I belong.

The chanting pulls me back. Away from the flames and tragedy.

I feel a warm and moist breath on my ear. Liza's voice repeats, "Heavenly Father, I beseech you to cast out this evil spirit. Heavenly Son, I implore you to protect this child of God. Holy Spirit, I request you cleanse this area."

Repeatedly she chants. Each stanza she repeats becomes clearer as the mental fog dissipates.

My temples throb from the lack of oxygen. I struggle to rise and am held down by weight across my chest.

Opening my eyes, I ascertain Liza is draped over me as she chants for intervention. I study her profile, her eyes closed tight, and her full lips moving quickly at their task. A light sheen of oil on her face gleams in the blue-tinted light.

I'm looking for the light source and see my phone is next to my hip in the dirt and has come back on. I reach for it as again; I try to roll to my side; Liza stops her chant. She lifts her weight off me, and the pressure point releases across my chest, allowing an immediate influx of oxygen into my lungs. It is undeniably complete ecstasy to get a full breath again.

"April?"

I reach for my phone, still disoriented, but knowing I need it in my hand.

"Is it you, April?"

That's an odd thing for Liza to say. I mean to answer her with something smart like 'Who were you expecting,' but I feel like someone poured a container of baby powder in my mouth. I swallow, trying to clear the dust so I can speak.

"Yes," I croak.

She sits back on her haunches and heaves a sigh of relief.

I rise to my knees, and the light flashes across James. He sits at the base of the stairs with his knees tucked under his chin. The slow rocking motion he makes is disconcerting, as is the concerned expression on Liza's face as she stares at me.

My survivor instinct kicks into gear, and I remember why I had such an affinity for my phone. I call Dusty's number. As I wait for Dusty to answer, I feel an evil entity watching us with interest from the far back corner of the basement.

"Where are you?" Dusty demands.

"Come to the basement now." My phone flickers, and we're in the dark. I feel Liza press against my back.

The spirit does not advance from its far corner. He keeps his distance now.

I'm doing the same. Despite our formed connection, I'm only reaching out enough to locate Les Blair. It feels good to know our spirit by name.

At this point, we've developed a respect for one another. In some relationships, respect is just another name for fear.

Our small team of three is quiet as we wait for our rescue. I believe Liza can sense the spirit has had enough for now, too. Neither of us cares to provoke his wrath until we are at full support. If Les Blair's ghost will stay in his corner and leave us alone, it's enough to make me happy for now.

The cellar door clicks open, and my shoulders relax. The fight with Les has consumed my mental and physical energy, but now I'm safe. My big brother is on the way.

"April," Dusty calls out. "Liza?"

"We're down here, Dusty. Can you get us some light?" Liza hops to her feet.

Dusty comes down the stairs. A lantern light bounces at waist height with each hasty step.

"Watch it!" Liza hollers.

Dusty stops with his right foot hovering over the hole in the staircase. "What the..." He sets his foot down on the last stair.

I have a moment of déjà vu thinking about the Freeman Plantation all those years ago.

He ducks his head from the stairwell and shines his light in our direction. His eyes are wide and wild, his mouth parted. "What happened to these stairs? He looks to James and me, and why are you two in the dirt?"

"How about you get us out of here, and I'll be the first to fill you in?" I smart off.

"How about I fire you for not being able to follow simple instructions. Safety is key."

I stand and wipe my hands on my jeans. "Don't do me any favors by firing me." There is an awkward pause as I knock gravel loose from my jeans.

Liza walks toward the light, shielding her eyes with her hand. "There are bigger things at work here, Dusty."

"I know," he says.

Liza's ominous tone already piqued my interest. Dusty's answer surprised me. I stop knocking the dirt from my jeans and look in his direction. His stare is inscrutable.

"I felt you were in trouble shortly after you left the control station for coffee. Miles and I've been looking for you ever since, and nobody knew where you were." He exhales. "Don't do that to me again, you gave me the scare of my life."

"That would make two of us," I say.

"It wasn't enjoyable for the three of us in this dungeon if it makes you feel better," Liza adds.

James drops a plank of wood on one of the stairs with a thud. He shifts it side to side, making sure it will stay.

"Where did you find those?" I ask.

James's features have a hard edge he has not shown previously. "Once all the religious mumbo jumbo she started calmed down" —he gestures toward Liza— "the first thing I did was look for some way to make the stairs passable. I found some old scaffolding in the back. No offense ladies, I enjoy your company, but I'm ready to get out of here."

I recognize his expression. Anger as your mind processes the new reality.

Individuals with paranormal "gifts" must cross the bridge every time they witness a new phenomenon to add to their library of "weird" catalog. Most people don't have any psychic abilities. They are blessed with never having to reconcile events and reset their perceptions of what is real in the world.

James's expression tells me all I need to know. After three decades of believing in the fundamental rules of science, his belief system has been completely obliterated in an hour.

Everything James knew to be sure, and a fact has been pureed like a stick of celery in a blender. No matter how he tries to rationalize what he just experienced, his stick of celery will never be the same.

The level of survivor instincts he portrays is commendable. His jaw is set, and his demeanor calm, full of immediate purpose. James is holding it together, which is more than most people can manage. For the first time since we met, I think of him, not as a pretty face but a man of at least fair measure.

He slings the third board onto the destroyed stairwell. Again, he slides it back and forth until he is satisfied with its fit. James tromps back into the darkness to retrieve another board.

Dusty stretches out a long leg while balancing on the rail. He manages to clear the hole left by the two still missing stairs. He is on me before I realize what he plans to do. He picks me up in a bear hug.

"Put me down, you big lug." When he sits me down, I punch at his chest. "I told you I shouldn't do this."

"That's crazy. You're a natural at this. I was just worried I lost you."

"You were just worried you'd have to explain it to Mama. You knew she'd kill you."

Dusty laughs. "Mama wouldn't kill me. I'm her favorite."

"You're probably right. Which makes me hate you even more."

"That's not true. I'm too loveable for you to hate." He turns to Liza. "Are you all right, spitfire?"

"Barely. It was a lot closer than I care to admit."

Dusty tugs at his beard. "Really? Worse than what happened on the fourteenth?"

Liza shrugs. "He just held me down on the fourteenth. He was attempting to keep me from using any of my training. But he didn't take over my mind."

Liza really is shook up. That's the second time her syntax is off. "You say that like he did possess someone?"

"He did."

"Who?" I ask, looking to where James is searching for another board.

Liza squints her eyes. "Really? *You.* Unless there is some other reason you were screaming, 'The fire is hungry and needs to be fed.'"

I let a nervous bark of laughter escape. "Yeah, right."

James throws another board onto the staircase. "Had me

convinced the hotel was on fire."

James's comment brings the memory, false memory, forward into my mind. The lake house fire images elicit strong emotions still. I act nonchalant and roll my eyes. "You're crazy."

Dusty is having none of it. "April, this is not the time to keep to yourself about what you know."

"I don't *know* anything you don't." I'm not obligated to tell him about dreams I have while passed out. Again, until Dusty figures out a way to record my thoughts, dragging everyone through my torturous visions is pointless. Plus, I think if I must recount them aloud I will break down.

What good would that do for the team.

"April."

"What. I don't know what you're talking about." I stare at him defiantly. I'll admit it's awkward, with all three of them staring at me, but I'm not about to cave to peer pressure. I refuse to recount the vision of my family burning to death in our home. If I have my rathers, I'll never tell a soul about the terrible image and hope it fades away into the recesses of my mind.

Improbable, but a girl can hope.

James shakes his head, mumbling something unintelligible while returning to the lumber pile.

Dusty loses interest in his cross examination of me.

"Was this spirit much more talkative than the ones upstairs?" Dusty asks Liza.

"I never heard a voice during the attack," Liza says.

That reminds me. "Hey, how did I end up on the floor anyway?"

"You don't remember." Liza's voice rises in pitch. "We were on the first step, then you swiveled as if somebody hit you in the jaw. Hard. Before I could move, you face-planted into the dirt."

James throws the last of the replacement boards onto the staircase. "You were screaming the house was on fire. When you began to sob about it exploding—well, that's just not cool. You had me convinced you saw some vision about the kitchen upstairs going up in flames, and we were trapped down here to meet our doom."

"You did cry that someone was trapped." Liza shrugs. "With your abilities, it was unnerving."

Her comments bother me. The dream-hijacking of my brain was not the standard images I receive from spirits. In those images, it's like I'm passively watching a movie.

The visions Les forced on me were participative, as if I were sleepwalking. Which leads me to the idea he had control of my mind. An involuntary shudder wracks my body, and I can't shake the thought of having been so violated.

The rest of the team starts down the stairs as James sets the final replacement board. James squeezes past them and stands halfway up the stairwell.

"April, it's imperative I know if you heard a voice?" I know Dusty still believes I'm holding out. One of the negatives of being close with someone your entire life.

Yeah. I heard an evil laugh. But nothing that could be recorded. "No. I'm sorry, Dusty. Still nothing."

The frustration is evident on his face. "Still no recording or photo. Just a few more hours, and this will be a total washout of time and resources."

"Wait, I did see a shadow figure right before the stairs blew up."

"You didn't say anything," Liza protests.

I turn my left hand palm up. "Well, things got kind of weird really quick after that. We didn't exactly have time to discuss it."

"Where?" Liza asks.

"By the incinerator."

"Where?" Her eyes narrow.

"The incinerator." I point toward the back-left corner of the cellar where the large cast box with the menacing metal grate face and wild array of hoses is stationed.

James squats down on the middle stair so we can see his face in the cellar "There was an old incinerator down here before the flood of thirty-seven. But you couldn't have known about that."

I take a few steps toward the back of the cellar, squinting my eyes against the darkness. The inky formation that is Les Blair shifts nervously along the back wall, but I'm not concerned about him for now.

I turn to Dusty. "Give me that." I take the LED lantern from him.

Shining the light to the back of the cellar, I see the pile of scaffolding lumber James used for makeshift stairs. There are a few rotting wooden shelves that look to not have been used in decades along the walls. There is nothing else. "I don't understand. There was an incinerator back there." I turn to Liza. "That's why we could see after our phones went out."

Liza shakes her head. "April, we've been in pitch-dark since the stairs blew up."

"But the light. From the fire."

"No light, April. Just darkness," Liza says grimly.

"Can't see my hand in front of my face darkness," James adds.

Miles clears his throat. "Dusty, it sounds like we've got way more opportunity down here than the fourteenth."

"I agree," Dusty says. "Luis, will you organize the movement of the equipment so we can set up command center down here for the rest of the day."

"You got it, Boss," Luis says.

"You're not mad at me?" I ask Dusty.

"I didn't say that. But, I knew in my gut there might be something down here that's at the limit of our capabilities. I was right. But since we're here." He rubs his huge hands together roughly. "What do y'all say to a strategy discussion over a celebration breakfast. We need to celebrate."

"Celebrate what?" I ask.

Dusty raises his arms into the air. "That everyone is safe and sound, of course."

Chapter 27

While it's true the Osborne Hotel will never be on my top five list of places to spend a relaxing weekend, I must admit James's team really has it going on with the breakfast. Between the made-to-order, lighter than air omelets, and the pancakes sweeter than wedding cake, I discover I worked up a considerable appetite while fighting off the evil spirit in the cellar.

I'll never recommend the Osborne to anybody for accommodations, still I'd certainly not be ashamed to recommend them for breakfast.

I'm halfway through a stack of pancakes only an adolescent boy should attempt to eat. James is sitting next to me. Which is a killjoy since it's hard to keep up the appearance of being a proper lady while power eating a huge breakfast.

"Are you really okay?" James asks.

"Uh huh." I conceal my mouth with my hand.

"I don't see how you do it."

I look down at the pancakes and feel an unwelcomed blush on my cheeks. "I'm just hungry."

James favors me with a good-humored grin. "No. How you deal with that nightmare downstairs and then snap back as if nothing happened."

I'm relieved he is referring to my other oddity, not my eating habits. "It wasn't like he gave us much choice."

"I suppose I'm still having difficulty processing it all."

"Give it time. The possibility it's real is brand new to you."

"That's just it. Everything in my head is denying it." He puts his hands around his head. "It's not possible. Yet I can't deny what I saw down there. The floating metal rod, the light bulbs —and let's not forget exploding stairs. There is nothing to explain that away."

"Yeah, when stuff starts flying around, and you can't see anyone doing it, it tends to make you a believer in ghosts fast."

James folds his hands in front of him on the table. "It's just a lot to take in. Not to mention what do I do with the knowledge? Do I market the hotel as a haunted experience?"

I choke and begin to question James's intelligence. "Not with the hostile entity downstairs. It's got to go."

James leans in closer to me. "So how do we convince it to go?"

"We don't. Once Dusty has all the photos and audio we can collect, we'll hook you up with a good priest to exorcize the spirit." I pause. "If that's what you choose to do."

"I thought that's what your team does."

Giving up on the pancakes, I set my fork down. "Yes, sort of, sometimes. Whatever you have downstairs has more mojo than most. It's way beyond our capabilities of expulsion. We're more of an identifying and documentation crew."

James sighs. "Nothing has been simple about this reclamation project. It only holds I'd have a stronger and angrier than normal ghost in my hotel. But I must work through it and bring this project to fruition."

"After all—tomorrow is another day." The words pop out of my mouth.

James raises his eyebrows and chuckles. "I suppose I do sound a bit overly dramatic."

"You channel Vivien Leigh quite well," I tease.

James sobers. "You know there are a lot of stories about what happened to Les Blair and Renée Watson. I only mention it because you said you saw the incinerator."

That gets my attention. It's as if I'm a tuning fork and James just smacked me hard on the edge of the table. "What about the incinerator?"

He looks down at his hands. I can tell he is considering whether he should share with me. "Whenever something unexplained happens, especially in a place as public as a hotel the public manufactures theories. One of the more popular theories for the decades was Renée Watson was killed and her body dismembered and burned in the incinerator."

"By Les Blair?"

James frowns. "Not necessarily. It never seemed an important part of the story as to who killed her as much as what happened to her."

"That's stupid. I'd prefer to know who killed Renée rather than the macabre details of the killer's disposal of her body."

"But that's the norm with rumors and theories, isn't it? They're often just stupid."

"What happened to the incinerator?"

James shakes his head. "It went underwater in the thirty-seven flood. If I venture a guess the flood corroded the burners rendering it useless and it would have coincided with the startup of citywide trash pickup. It was most likely pulled out and sold for scrap metal."

"I suppose nobody checked for bone fragments when it was taken out."

"How old do you think I am? No, I would assume nobody did. But that was half a century before I was born."

"Well, thank you for sharing. Dusty always says the more historical information we can get the better the chance we have of solving a mystery. Sometimes it's the most mundane facts that solve these."

"I feel bad now. I always thought all this talk about spirits was just people with too much imagination getting carried away."

"Well, don't beat yourself up about it. It's hard to believe in something you've never seen before."

James gives a wry laugh. "Yes, and I would think near impossible to forget once you do see one."

I almost let his comment slip by me. It's one of the moments where I'm done with the conversation, and I have expectations to what the other person is about to say. But James said something I didn't expect.

He too thought the conversation complete. His interest floats to the end of the table before his stare falls on the cellar door. I don't reach out to check with my "gifts." I don't need to.

"What did you see?" He flinches and I wait until he turns his attention back to me.

An insincere smile graces his face. "Excuse me."

"Don't play games with me. Tell me what you saw."

A tortured expression cracks the thin veneer of his smile. "I..." He closes his mouth and frowns before starting again. "I did see a red glow at the back of the cellar."

"Then why did you make light of the discussion when I was explaining it to Dusty."

"I never saw the incinerator," he protests. "I only saw the red glow. It's almost as if I saw it through a dark sheet or a piece of black plastic."

"The veil."

His upper lip draws upward, exposing his teeth. "Do I want to know what that is?"

"It's what separates the living from the paranormal. You shouldn't have been able to see it. Assuming you don't have psychic abilities."

"Surely not." He tugs at his hair. "I saw it standing over you and Liza."

Now I'm shocked. "Explain yourself."

"I'm so ashamed." He lets out a long sigh and seems to deflate. "I—I just knew I was about to die, that we were all about to die, and I froze."

"Saw what standing over us, James?"

He stands. "Like I said, it was as if I were looking through a dark sheet. I can't be sure what I saw. It could have been the darkness getting to me. It was dark down there once the voltage spike blew the light bulbs."

I grab hold of his wrist so he can't walk away, especially since he has chosen to rationalize away the event again. I didn't intend to violate him, but the visions come anyway. I drop his wrist. We stare at one another.

"Was that him?"

James nods slowly. "Les Blair. I'm certain of it."

I knew from my interaction with what remains of Les's tainted soul, but confirmation from another source when dealing with the paranormal is always welcome. The pieces of the puzzle are falling into place in my mind. If I were to bet, neither Renée nor Les left Osborne Hotel alive.

It should make me happy to put the story together. But it isn't. If Renée were disposed of in the incinerator it makes sense she remained at the hotel. There were sightings of mist and smoke forming humanlike shapes on the fourteenth floor as far back as the early forties. Everyone has always commented they felt it was a female presence. A peaceful entity.

Where has Les been? According to James, the disturbances in the cellar began this week. Why now? Why break silence after eighty years?

Another troubling fact in the loose ends topic, who is the male presence on the fourteenth floor. The male silhouette meeting with Renée's ghost in fourteen-o-nine.

I'm confident Les is the spirit who paid us the rude visit in our command center, but most definitely not the male spirit in fourteen-o-nine. The more things come together, the more information I still need to understand the situation in the hotel. But we're a few hours out from completing our investigation.

We also haven't determined what happened to Dilly. Was she a case of an unhappy woman taking her life, or was there paranormal interventions in her suicide?

What a hot mess. With a time crunch to boot.

After hours of boredom yesterday, we have a spectacular breakthrough today. But we're running out of time, and I have more questions than answers.

"If you really want us to solve this, James, you can't withhold information from us."

His eyes harden. "I don't see how you can accuse me of lying. I still don't know what I saw. If I were sure, I would've told you sooner."

It's best I let it go. James knows he is in the wrong. But pressing the issue and trying to get an apology out of him would only make him belligerent and isn't helpful.

I nod in agreement. To my surprise, he doesn't move away from me. Instead, he reclaims his seat next to me.

"Speaking of honesty, I have a question to ask you."

I'm nervous how suddenly the tables have turned in the questioning game. My stomach rolls as I search my mind for when I was not honest with James. I do some frantic mental housekeeping. I am suddenly aware of my half-truth in the cellar regarding the vision of the burning lake house Les showed me. But how could James know that?

"I just." He measures his words. "April, are you seeing anyone?"

When I'm not prepared for interludes by the other sex, it tends to short-circuit my brain. While I did notice James is attractive in his own metro sort of way, I wasn't attracted to him. It could be he is only a couple of inches taller than me, or that he has a thin build. More likely, his stick up his butt attitude just clashes with my personality.

Still, given I find a wide range of men sexually attractive it's interesting I feel neutral about him. Yes, he is a guy, but that is about it on my interest meter.

The silence is awkward and then becomes embarrassing. Then I convince myself I read too much into the question, as I am known to do, and I misread the question entirely. His question isn't an overture at all. I seriously need to get over myself if I thought he was asking me out. "No, James. I haven't seen any spirits since we left the cellar."

A smirk graces his face. "I was referring to your dating

status."

Bless it. I knew that was too convenient.

"I want to know if you're available or if you're in a committed relationship."

Now that's an interesting question? My mind drifts to my phone call with Shane. After all that's presently the closest thing I have to an actual love interest. The apparent issue being I'm interested, and Shane is yet to be determined. Being honest with myself, I can't say Shane and I are an item. If wishes were gold and all that. The sad truth is, April May Snow is totally available.

"No, at the moment I'm not seeing anyone."

James smiles, exposing his white teeth. It's the first time he has smiled so broad and it's an attractive smile, it suits him. It almost makes him handsome. "Do you think you'd be up to me showing you the town once we are done with this haunting investigation? Next Saturday perhaps?"

Next weekend? What's going on next weekend? Think, April, think. Oh, the fishing tournament. Shane is coming into town. Does that qualify as a deal killer? If so, how do I explain that one? 'Hey, don't take this personal, I'd really like to go out with you, but this really hot guy is fishing with my older brother next weekend, and I want to desperately flaunt my nearly nude bikini-clad body in front of him in hopes I get his attention.' Right, I'm sure no guy would take that manner of rejection personal.

"Actually, I'm entered in a fishing contest with my brother next Saturday."

His well-practiced smirk reappears. "You fish?"

"Of course, I fish." Three or four times a year, whether I want to or not, at my brother's insistence. Besides, it is the truth. I'd be fishing, James doesn't have to know that what I'll be fishing for is named Shane.

"All right, how about Sunday?"

I can tell he thinks I'll turn him down with another excuse. I appreciate the persistence and consider the new offer.

Rule of thumb, if a man doesn't put a little fire in my belly, going out with him will be a waste of time. I also know sitting alone in my apartment and posting to Pinterest is a boring drag. "I think that'll work."

"That's great. I can't wait to show you my town." He pushes his chair back. "And I promise you if it goes well, I'll reciprocate, and you can show me your town."

Oh, goody. That should take all of ten minutes. "You better."

"All right. Good deal." He gestures over his shoulder as he stands. "Well, I guess I better get busy; this hotel isn't going to run itself."

"No, I suppose not." I give him a smile sweeter than Mama's iced tea.

Don't. I know what you're thinking. Why accept a date from a man who can't get my motor hot? You feel I'm just leading him on and I'm the worst sort of tease. Well, one person's tease is another person's insecurity issues.

This recent dry spell has me concerned that I'm setting my goals a little high. It's not lost on me dating, courtship and marriage is a lot like playing musical chairs. If you spend too much time listening to the music circling the chairs and don't get busy putting your butt down on a seat, you might be standing the rest of your life. Alone. Somewhere along the line unconsciously I think I've made the decision being married to a man I don't have the hots for is monumentally better than being an old maid.

I mean if I'm married and other women look at my husband and say, 'I don't get it', they still must assume I married the man I wanted and accept our marriage. If I become an old maid, that'll be a 'Kick me' sign permanently taped to my back.

My logic might be a tad wacky, but I do have a reputation to uphold.

Chapter 28

"You two were awfully chatty." Liza slides into the chair James vacated. "What was that all about?"

"This?" I waggle a finger between the two of us. "I don't do girl talk."

Liza attempts to conceal a smile. "I wasn't that interested anyway."

"Liar."

She snorts as she shakes her head. "Was he confessing his belief in the paranormal now?"

"Oh yeah. James even has big plans of turning the hotel into a haunted attraction."

"You can't do that with a maniac spirit running through this facility."

"I think I convinced him of that finally." I face her directly. "What are we dealing with?"

Liza wrinkles her nose. "It's some seriously major bad mojo."

"I told him it was more than what we could deal with."

"Thank you for the vote of confidence."

"Well it is, isn't it?"

"I don't think so. I mean, I've expelled some bad spirits in the past. But this one's strong enough I don't want to run the risk of being in the middle of asking it politely to leave and realize it can squash me like a bug." She shrugs. "Besides, they're not paying me for that. I'm here to protect the crew and relay any information I find."

"The trip's almost over and I feel like we have more questions than when we got here."

"Yeah, that's the nature of it sometimes." Liza stretches her arms over her head. "Eight hours of boredom followed by eight minutes of extreme adrenaline rush and a bunch of unanswered questions."

"I know Dusty wants to go back in the cellar right after breakfast. Part of me hopes the spirit will show itself again so he can get what he needs for his book, then part of me hopes I never see that shadow again." Liza nods her head as she listens.

Oh, why not share? Presently Liza is the only person I can share this news with. "James asked me out."

She arches an eyebrow. "Really now?"

"Don't act so surprised."

"You took it wrong. I was just beginning to get the impression James might play on the other team. He seems sort of— prissy."

Chapter 29

The LED work lights the guys set up change the feel of the cellar dramatically. No longer does it feel like a tomb.

With the entire area lit, I walk to the back-left corner where the incinerator in my vision was located. As I near, I see the steel plates and bolts where the huge unit was once fastened to the old hotel's concrete footers. I look up and find the hole the smokestack once rose through all fourteen floors. The opening had long since been sealed with a steel plate. I hear footsteps crunching the rock behind me as I examine the stained metal above me.

"April?"

I touch one of the anchor bolts sheared from the wall with my finger. "Yes?"

"Dusty said you sensed a lot of activity over here."

I don't answer Travis as I continue to search for the stain I'd seen on the wall in my vision.

"I set up a battery of two different electric energy videos and one passive infrared in a crossfire pattern here," he says.

Travis Early and I played together when we both wore disposable diapers for undergarments. Our mamas were good friends from high school when they were on the same dance team. There is something to be said about having seen a guy's weenie when you were both learning to walk that just naturally pushes him into the brother-light category. If it weren't for our history, he might be suitable date material, especially since I've floated to the bottom of the barrel with James.

Travis's blue eyes aren't exceptionally bright. His nose has been broken in several fights, and his blond hair reminds you of a haystack since it points in all different directions at once. What he lacks above the neck he makes up for below. His shoulders are broad, and his arms are thick and corded with muscles, his waist tapers down, connecting to a well-formed buttocks.

His physique and athletic prowess in high school gave him the reputation of a womanizer. In truth, it isn't his looks that earned him the player moniker. It is his predisposition to date multiple girls at the same time, often behind one another's back, and often best-of-friends. He likes girls a lot and doesn't understand the most basic of dating etiquette.

To me, he is just Travis.

"Is that electrical energy camera Luis and Miles rave about doing any good?"

Travis shrugs. "You know them, they oversell everything. But it's better than nothing. It's like connect the dots. You might have to use your imagination, but if you stare at the pattern long enough, you can make something out of the reading. At least it allows you to get a better feel for what you're looking at." He flashes a brilliant smile. "But if you're expecting some sort of technicolor picture or anything, you'll be sorely disappointed."

"Sometimes, I wish you could plug into my brain for your pictures. Then it would look like a full technicolor."

He waves his hands in the air in jest. "Ooh... straight from the brain of a veil walker. Dusty's fans would eat that up. We'd all be millionaires no matter how small the cut we're getting."

Did I mention Travis tends to be a dick sometimes? It doesn't bother me a bit. It's just part of his personality, and if one day he quit being that way, I'd worry he contracted a terminal illness.

"Don't you have some equipment to hook up."

He clutches at his heart. "Our Majesty has dismissed me. Ow. Oh yeah, where were you and Joan of Arc when Casper slapped you into the dust?"

"Where were Liza and I when the hostile spirit attacked us?"

Travis jams his thumbs in his jean pockets. "That's what I asked."

I point back to the stairs. "Right at the base there."

He nods his head. "I'm on it."

I turn my attention to the front of the cellar, where the rod had flown at us earlier. Miles, Luis, Dusty, and Liza are all busy on their laptops close to the area. Chet and Jason are putting more lights around the support pylons.

A chill runs up my spine. The spirit is watching us. I did not feel him until now, and I had thought he fled to a different part of the hotel since we know he can travel with free rein.

He is giving me space. He isn't scared, but wary.

Fear squeezes my heart. I look frantically to the left and then right as I move between the pylons. "Jason, Chet, did either of you move the solid steel bar laying between here and the stairwell?"

They look at each other and then to me with a blank stare.

"I didn't see a bar, April," Chet says.

"Me, either."

I stomp quickly to Dusty and Liza. "Tell me you picked up the steel bar."

Liza's eyes widen. "It wasn't here when we came down after breakfast."

"I didn't see a bar of any sort when we found you two earlier. Maybe James moved it? Either way, I'm sure it'll show up eventually."

"That's what I'm worried about," I grumble as I relive how close it came to bashing in my brains earlier.

Chet and Jason finish the lighting and cross in front of me on their way to help Travis. The three of them were a group since elementary school. Jason Early is Travis' cousin. Chet

Lambert's family owns land next to Jason's parents. All three boys are within six months of the same age and played on every football, basketball, and baseball team together coming through school. Jason is the same height as Travis, a little thinner and a lot quieter. Chet is equally tall but twice as broad as Jason and has no waist. Jason tends to laugh at everything, his laugh so contagious if you aren't careful, you'll be crying after talking to him for a few minutes.

The "clink" reverberates through the cellar. All eyes come to me.

I pivot toward the pylons. I stop breathing as my gut clenches. If that is what I think I heard, the spirit isn't only evil; it has a twisted, diabolical nature.

My lungs began to ache, and I exhale. My breath forms tiny ice crystals that float to the dirt floor below.

"April, hold up, we don't have video equipment over there," Dusty calls out.

I push forward into the frigid air. I've about had enough of this cocky spirit. I've been dealing with men too big for their britches my entire life. I'm about to yank a knot in this one's tail, whether he has a corporeal body or not.

Mama always says it's a virtue to keep your cool. 'Don't let people get under your skin.' No matter how hard she tried, she was never able to teach me the skill entirely. A lot has to do with the fact I do like the adrenaline rush I get when I've had enough and decide to come out of the corner swinging. The spirit has just earned a complimentary ticket to see my crazy side.

I stomp past the oldest set of pylons. I know it's aggravated about us being in its place, now I'm going to see how it likes me being in its head.

"Travis, you and Jason get some cameras over there," Dusty yells.

Yeah, get some cameras over here. You're about to see a spirit wet its pants when I get a hold of it. This old codger is not gonna know what hit him.

I hear the crunching of stone behind me as I draw level with the newest support columns. My adrenaline is at a pitched level, my face so flushed the frigid air feels good against my skin, and I'm fully ready for battle.

I examine the front of the column as I pass it. I give a start and stumble backward, almost falling onto the rock-strewn floor. The steel bar floats at waist height above the floor just in front of the column.

"Dusty?" My voice sounds as if my vocal cords are too tight.

From my left peripheral, I see Travis and Jason clearing the old columns. I hold up my hand, signaling them to stop.

"What is it, April?" Travis asks.

I know what it is. What I don't know is how to explain it to Travis. What I don't know is what it will do when Travis and Jason come around the column and try to film it. I'm also afraid it will try to whack me in the head again like it intended to do earlier this morning.

With all the questions, I decide it best to be patient and let the spirit make the first move.

"Come on, April. If you have something, I want to film it," Travis complains as he starts forward.

I raise my hand at him again. "Travis, stay put."

When I look back at the floating steel bar, I notice the forward tip of it is swaying back and forth in a six-inch arc. I believe the movement is meant to intimidate. I can vouch for its effectiveness as it was scaring the bejesus out of me. I feel the last of my adrenaline rush drain from me and be replaced with fear, and a powerful desire to run outside fills me.

I take a step back, and the arc doubles. When I take a second step, the bar slaps the column, and concrete chips spray forward.

"What is it?" Travis whispers.

"It's that steel bar I was looking for."

I identify confusion in Travis's eyes. But he'll be more confused if he comes around the column and sees what I'm watching.

The bar pulls back and slams into the column again. This time a large chunk of concrete falls out from between the ironwork and chips rain onto the dirt floor.

The concrete chips resemble something. Without thinking, I shove my right hand into my pocket and touch the brooch I picked up earlier. I pull it out of my pocket and rub it with my thumb.

The small distraction helps calm what is left of my nerves. The rod swings an additional foot upward and points directly at my face. It's as if a six-foot-tall man has picked the bar up and decided to point me out in a crowd.

I shove the brooch back in my pocket and try to take another step backward. The bar swings back and comes forward so forcefully another large chunk of concrete rolls out from the ironwork. There is no more of the light tap, tap, James and his people heard. This ghost is taking Albert Pujols type batter swings at the columns now. At this rate, he will have the column he is working on destroyed in another fifteen minutes.

There is a click up and to my left. A voice floats down from above.

"What's going on down there?"

James's shoes click a hot trail down the stairs.

"I'm thinking Mr. Blair is taking out his frustrations on your concrete supports again with that steel bar."

"And she won't let us film it," Travis adds.

"April, if there is a shot to be had..." Dusty begins.

"Fine! If you want Travis to get beat up by a floating piece of metal, send him on over."

Travis doesn't wait for Dusty's command. He is fearless if nothing else.

He sees the floating bar as he comes around the column, his knees come out from under him, and he stumbles backward. "That's just messed up!"

Jason follows close behind with the second camera. He makes no comment as he spots the levitating metal. The color drains from his face.

Whether the spirit is distracted or overconfident, it lets its guard down. As the bar takes another swing at the support columns, I push hard against his energy with my "gifts."

I slide easily into his mind. It has an oily and repulsive feeling—red with purple flashes—a thought pattern incoherent peppered liberally with hate.

Focus, April, focus. Get past the emotion. Is there a thought pattern?

From the corner of my eye, I catch Travis lifting the camera to his shoulder. Good, I think, as the light indicates he is filming. The floating bar will be an excellent bit of footage for Dusty.

The flow of the thought pattern changes direction. The color quickly turns to black and gray. A piece of concrete the size of a grapefruit floats into the air. The bar swings and explodes the concrete into thousands of tiny shrapnel flakes hurtling through the air. I lift a hand to my face and feel five pieces bite into my palm and wrist. As I lower my hand, I see a second softball explode into shrapnel.

He let it slip. I don't understand what it means. It does not make sense. "Destroy the supports, collect the insurance." It's etched on his mind just like his name, Les Blair, the one and only.

Chapter 30

"Are you getting this, Travis?"

"Yes, ma'am."

"Me too," Jason says.

"How much damage has this maniac done?" James scowls as he approaches the old columns.

Another concrete softball floats into the air. The bar does not swing.

I read Les's thoughts. "Duck, James!" I yell.

The large chunk of concrete impossibly zooms forward toward James with unbelievable speed. James steps to his left, but the concrete bounces off his right shoulder. He clutches his shoulder and slides behind a column in search of cover. "What the heck."

I'm noticing a trend. Les becomes more violent whenever James is present.

With James out of view, Les returns his attention to me. With great force, he pushes me from his mind.

The lights around the column flicker spasmodically. Les's shadow appears. He stands six feet tall, lean, and appears agile.

Exceptionally malicious energy swirls around him. An offensive odor wafts between us leaving a bitter taste on my tongue. His shadow flickers in indirect concert with the lights blinking, and he fills in with colors. I fear I may have accidentally slipped through the veil. I turn to Travis. "Please tell me you see that."

"Oh, I'm getting it all right." He is entirely too gleeful.

"I'm not getting any audio, guys!" Dusty hollers.

"I got this," Luis says as he moves toward me.

I'm wise to Les's tricks now. Like earlier with the stairs, he allows himself to be open once again in hopes I'd come rushing in. If I do, he will use my momentum to pull me through. Even with the planning, Les almost overpowers me. I almost slip across the veil and into a world where he would hold all the advantage.

"Liza, come here." I'm beginning to believe Liza is our only hope.

Truly obsessed. The spirit talks over and over about killing her and collecting the insurance. That makes no sense to me. Miles's meticulous report never mentions a claim filed against the property's insurance. But the spirit is like a broken record discussing murders and insurance claims.

The bar slaps against a pillar three times again in quick succession.

"April, I don't know what to do," Liza says as she slides in next to me.

"Something's not jiving true. Just try the Lord's Prayer for starters."

Les becomes more agitated. Different from the increased anger when he saw James. He hates James and wants to kill James. Liza, he fears.

"Thy kingdom come; thy will be done..."

The silhouette blinks bright with three short bursts. It takes the full apparition form of a thirty-something man, albeit transparent.

"Travis?" I ask.

"I'm getting it. Keep drawing it out." He laughs with joy as he moves closer to Les.

"The feed is perfect. Keep it up, April!" Dusty cheers.

A scream of rage echoes through the cellar. The vision

swings the steel bar against a column again, knocking free a chunk of concrete.

"Luis, did you get that?"

"I got something. What, I have no clue," Luis mumbles.

Liza continues chanting the Lord's Prayer. Her eyes close tight as she focuses on her task at hand despite the rest of us yelling and the disconcerting sound of exploding concrete.

I see Jason swinging wide to change angles from the view Travis is filming. Both men are well past their initial shock and are now moving closer to the floating steel bar.

Between Liza's confrontation and the film team's aggressive nature, I'm expecting Mr. Blair to retreat into the corners and bide his time or float to a quieter floor.

Contrary to my prediction, the translucent man glimmers with an exceptional brilliance forcing me to shield my eyes. I lower my hand and see Les Blair standing before me as clearly as any human being I've ever met. His eyes a dull-gray-blue resemble opaque marbles from a child's game.

He glares at me with his ghoulish eyes void of pupils. The hairs on my neck stand on end as the left corner of his lip curls into a smile. He drops the steel pipe, and it bounces off one of his shoes.

Oh no. The ghost is solid. That can't be.

Les turns toward Liza and squats until his face is inches from her face. She continues to pray fervently on her knees. Les raises both hands and claps them in front of her face.

Liza flies backward several feet as if struck by an explosion, landing on the cellar floor. She rolls over and curls into a ball as she clutches the back of her head.

Luis jumps from his chair and runs toward her. I know he will help her, and I focus my attention on Les.

Les wiggles his eyebrows at me. I know now we've poked a ghost we should have left alone, and I must fight back the fear growing inside me.

The worst thought clarifies in my mind. I'm the only person, besides Liza who may be unconscious, who realizes just how much danger we are in now.

I'm not a real fan of aha moments. Those brief seconds of reflection where something hidden from my mind is revealed. They always tend to make me feel like I was a little daft for not figuring it out sooner. This is one of those moments.

All seven of the men in the room are in pitched excitement. My experience has always been men live for the hunt. The problem is sometimes they're so intent on the pursuit of their prey they don't realize when the tables have turned, and they've been lured into a deadly snare.

The grin on the once handsome face of Les Blair continues to grow as the lids above his cataract ravaged eyes opened wider. His ruby lips pull back, exposing teeth filed to points.

That only confirms my aha moment. We hold a tiger by the tail with one hand, and our grip is slipping. I now understand Les has been playing us to lure us all in close. His excited energy forces are building and climbing to a crescendo. I know there is nothing I can do to improve our situation.

I glance over my shoulder at our only hope. Liza is shaking off the effects of the impact and struggling to her feet with Luis's help. Her uncharacteristically jerky movements signal me she'll not be able to bring her abilities to the fight in time to help us.

"Chet, the audio boom over there." Dusty's voice echoes in my head as I consolidate my powers in my core.

"Stay at a ninety-degree-angle from me, Jason. You're getting in my shot," Travis complains.

The noise fades and I marshal the available energy around me, focusing on the general area of my sternum. My breathing settles, the shaking of my knees and hands subsides, and the need to blink ends as I stare into the blue-gray marbled eyes of Les.

Desperate times demand desperate actions. I'll have to deal with Liza's anger later.

I consolidate my energy for as long as I can hold it and then throw it outward. Liza is my target, and I slip easily into her

consciousness since she is already disoriented and comprom-
ised.

Her memories are cluttered with relationships from years
past, visions from childhood, and snippets of ceremonies
strange to me. It's as if her mind were a drawer that has been
turned upside down.

That's it, upside down. I dive deep down, searching for the
most recent events at the bottom and begin to sort quickly as I
feel precious moments slipping away from us. Finding a recent
memory, I realize I am close to the information I need to save
us.

Pushing through the last of her jumbled thoughts I locate
what I'm searching for in her mind. I'm sure it's the correct
thought. I can feel her recent touch on it.

The language is strange, and I can't read it. Grabbing the
mental note, I pull it to me.

Something strikes me in the solar plexus. My vision reverts
to the current reality as I double over and watch a baseball-
sized chunk of concrete bounce off my chest. I struggle to pull
in my next breath as I clutch my hands to my chest.

A short burst of high-pitched static fills the air. My skin
crawls as the sound mimics fingernails across a chalkboard.

The remnants of the handsome man continue to rock with
laughter. The anger created by his cruel injustice coils inside
me and heats like a nuclear core.

Les's laugh cuts short as he tilts his head slightly. His smile
relaxes as he smirks then leans over and casually lifts another
chunk of concrete into the air.

It's no mystery he intends to throw another piece of concrete, but I don't predict the speed of his throwing motion. He
catches me off guard. I have no time to avoid his throw. My
hands come up to protect myself and, in my mind, I scream,
"no!".

The concrete explodes into talcum powder a few inches
from my hands. The cement dust floats upward and to the
sides before settling like fog to the cellar floor.

Les's upper lip curls exposing his pointy front teeth. More high-pitched static spews from his mouth as he screams at me.

His anger builds, and I realize belatedly Les has been playing with us. I clamp my mind around the only thing I believe may give us a fighting chance. With purpose, I chant in a calm manner that belies my fear.

"Domine Deus purificat cast de loco isto in terram gloria tua primos patronos corporum fluens abluere luciferi."

I falter when Les chortles. He clutches at his heart or where it should've been, mocking like I've caused him tremendous pain.

I assume the chant is having no effect on him. I don't even know what I'm saying. I took Spanish, not Latin in high school.

All I know is Liza recently accessed the memory, and it feels right for some reason. My selection is a guess, based on a hunch. Not exactly confidence inspiring.

But it's too late to worry about it now. What little I know about chants is that often your belief in them is more important than the actual words. Well, my faith is as low as ever, but my need is high. At this point, I believe I should fake it until I make it.

"Domine Deus purificat cast de loco isto in terram gloria tua primos patronos corporum fluens abluere luciferi." I chant a second time, and I adjust my tone in hopes of it sounding more convincing. My conviction grows as Les quits laughing. His amusement melts from his face and is replaced by a stoic expression.

I complete the chant a third time, and I am aware of its meaning now. 'Lord God purify this place cast out the patrons of Lucifer, cleanse this land for your glory.' A bit ominous sounding, but I think it's about right.

The fourth time I say the Latin version, I practically spit the words at Les as I force my energy in his direction too as I step forward. The snarl returns to his face as he reaches for the steel bar.

My heart skips, and I falter in the recitation of the chant. Les slings his arm outward toward me, the steel bar arcing a few feet from my face. Involuntarily I take a step back, and he grins. He lifts the steel bar level to my face and makes small undulating circles with its tip as he taunts me again.

The words are frozen on my tongue. The muscles of my jaw clench shut, preventing any sound even if my tongue were free.

As the tip of the steel bar comes closer to my face, I lift my hands and attempt to force it back with my mind. He continues closer to my face forcing me to step back again. Again, Les's horrendous screech of pleasure fills the air as he backs me through the cellar.

I hear the chant in my ears. At first, I think it's words trapped in my mind. Or I was able to vocalize over my fear. Liza steps past me, and I realize she is chanting the very article I borrowed from her mind.

She clutches her left arm over her ribs as she moves slowly forward. Each step, she cringes with pain, and drops of perspiration flow freely from her temples as she spits the chant at Les.

The spirit holds his ground until Liza presses against the steel bar he clutches. Reluctantly Les steps back, his eyes growing wide, fear collecting in his energy force. Uncertainty nips at his understanding.

Moving forward with Liza, I join in the chant. I copy her cadence as if I were spitting the words out. I have no idea what I'm doing. But the aggressiveness of the speech and the forward motion presses the bully spirit backward, making my own energy grow as my confidence and faith are fed.

"Hey, wait a minute. Don't push it through the wall," Travis warns.

As if I'm going to stop so Travis can get a better shot. If I have the ability, and now with Liza's help I feel I do, I'll push Les Blair all the way back to Hades.

Chapter 31

Les Blair levitates until his back is against the far wall of the cellar. Then he stops. I'd anticipated, more likely hoped, he'd take the opportunity to disappear since he was out of room to maneuver.

Throwing the steel bar to the floor, he stops and his lip curls into a snarl. He pushes his hand toward me in an abrupt move, and something strikes the right side of my face with such force I stumble to my left and take a knee.

Man, that stings. Even dead jerks know how to hit a girl.

"You've done it now, Mister!" Liza screams.

Her face contorts into a mask of such complete hatred, I lean away from her. I don't know if Les fears Liza. I do know Liza is way scarier looking than Les ever could manage. I scramble to my feet, so I don't accidentally get hit by friendly fire.

Liza rips her long-sleeved cotton tee-shirt over her head. In a menacing gesture, she thrusts her wrist outwards toward Les, as her body tenses. The veins rise in her arms and neck as she strains. It's as if Liza's lifting an incredible weight.

A streak on her left forearm emits a blinding white light. I shield my eyes with my hands, yet my curiosity draws me closer. The serpentine chain tattooed on her forearm changes colors from the intricate black ink design to a brilliant copper. The two-dimensional artwork rises from her arm, the copper turning to bronze and finally a lustrous gold. The ornate chain slides free from her forearm, the length running down to the floor coiling neatly at her feet. When the last link positions in the center of the coil, the tinkling sound of the chain unraveling ceases, and the cellar is silent.

Nobody moves. Les watches Liza warily, and I get the odd feeling I now know what it feels like to wait for two gunslingers to draw.

In a single fluid motion, Liza picks up the odd gold chain and whips the length in Les's direction. The links grab fast around the ghost's wrist, writhing and twisting like a thin constrictor securing its dinner.

He lets out a screech that forces me to cover my ears as he backpedals. His right heel moves through the wall as the rest of his body begins to fragmentize, becoming transparent. He is attempting to leave in a rush.

Les pulls against the chain, managing to free a leg out of the cellar as he drags Liza forward. I quickly wrap my arms around her waist to anchor her in place.

I cringe against his terrible howl of despair. Its unnatural volume and pitch turns my blood ice-cold with fear.

As his howl stops and he begins to rail violently against his binds, I realize Liza is chanting. Her tone is venomous and full of rage. I struggle to clear the ringing from my ears to join her in the chant.

We're losing the tug of war with Les. The boys are either too far away to help or standing in shock, those who can't see the ghost. All still visible of the spirit is his elbows down to his hands. But Liza refuses to let him go, and we are within feet of the concrete wall.

"We lost him!" Dusty hollers.

"I still have him," Liza growls.

Les's wrists, bound by Liza's chain, are inches from the wall now, and I realize Liza is in a mood. She doesn't plan on giving up. I also become concerned about what happens if Liza's remarkable magical chain is pulled through to the other side of the wall. What if Les is retreating to the other side of the veil, not the wall? What if he has help on the other side of the veil to pull us through?

"Liza, let him go," I say.

"I almost have him."

"No, Liza. Get your chain back."

With a quick snap of her wrist, the chain falls away from Les's wrists as they disappear into the wall. "I hate losing!"

I ignore her momentarily as I push toward the wall with my "gifts." I search as long as I can manage to hold my energy stable.

He is gone.

The cellar is silent except for the hum of our electronic equipment, as Liza and I attempt to catch our breath. The air feels heavy, and my temples are pounding.

"That was freaking awesome!" Jason raves.

"I can't wait to edit this," Travis adds.

Dusty laughs. "And I had given up hope this trip was gonna payout. Luis, do you think you can do anything with that audio?"

"If I can find the right filter, I'm sure we have something worthy of a trailer advertisement."

Liza drops to her knees. I squat next to her and put a stabilizing arm around her. The gold chain in her hand disintegrates into glitter and tracks back up her arm like pitch-black mercury. I watch in amazement as the black chain tattooed on her left forearm reforms.

I'm thankful Les is gone, and I'm equally grateful for Liza's tremendous talent. I feel ashamed I ever questioned her ability.

I'm also angry and aggravated. I don't know if it's residual from the battle we fought, but I'm about to start slapping the boys. The least they can do is acknowledge that Liza and I have taken some hits during the fight.

I feel a hand on my shoulder and pivot, ready to fight. My shoulders relax as I see it's Luis.

"How are you two?" he asks.

It's impossible to be angry with Luis. This is especially so when he stares at me with his big dark, doleful eyes of concern. The adrenaline flows away from me. I touch my chest and flinch from the tremendous shooting pain. My sternum feels like it is severely bruised, compliments of Les Blair. What a jerk.

"Hey, Dusty. I think we need to get the girls to the hospital," Luis says.

"Seriously?" His heavy footsteps crunch stone loudly as he trots to us. He squats in front of me, and his face so full of concern brings tears to my eyes. "April?" His eyes go from me to Liza. "Oh no, her coloring isn't right at all."

"I'll go get the van," Travis says.

"The equipment," Chet complains.

James hands Travis a set of car keys. "Take my Mercedes instead. It's the black one out front."

Chapter 32

I was raised with a bunch of gearheads. While I have a healthy appreciation for vehicles, especially antiques, I've never understood some people's obsession with foreign luxury sedans. As I lay curled up on the leather back seat of James's Mercedes sedan, I begin to be persuaded there are some excellent amenities about the cars.

The pain in my solar plexus is increasing. It hurts to draw in more than half a breath at a time, which gives me a sense of panting. The more I fixate on it, the quicker my breath, the less air I get in my oxygen-deprived lungs. It's a vicious circle, my climbing anxiety only adding to the issue. I can't wait to be examined by a doctor.

Travis repeatedly asks Liza how she feels. Liza is not in a talkative mood.

Travis was not her first choice to chauffeur us. That's sad considering his body language toward her. But understandable given what I accidentally gleaned from her when forced to rummage her mind for the chant while she was unconscious.

I wonder if Dusty has any idea how she feels about him? Probably not. Considering it's Dusty, she'd be best advised to write him a manifesto explaining her feeling and include illustrations.

She'll need to figure that one out on her own. I think it best she doesn't know I'm aware of her feelings.

We pull into the emergency room driveway, and I realize I'm as hungry as I am bruised. I check my phone and see it's one in the afternoon. That raises my heart rate and blood pressure. I need to get home to Guntersville if I plan to get any sleep tonight, so I'm rested for work in the morning.

Two hours is a long time to wait when you're hungry.

I sit in the semiprivate room with Liza. She has four cracked ribs and a concussion. The doctor requires her to stay the night for observation.

They inform me I have a bruised sternum; I didn't need a medical degree to self-diagnose that. The physician's assistant tells me a handful of ibuprofen and a heating pad is about all I can do to help the injury heal. Basically, they're giving me a pat on the butt and telling me to walk it off.

I'm antsy to get on the road to Guntersville. But Travis promised he'd be right back with a chicken fillet sandwich for me. Given they're my favorite and I'm starving and broke, I think I can keep Liza company for a little while longer. Sometimes keeping Liza company means sitting still if she isn't in a talkative mood.

She pulls the covers up over her arms. "You're staring again."

My cheeks flush with heat. "Sorry. I just keep trying to figure it out."

"I'm just a freak," she mumbles.

I'm horrified. "Don't you say that. You do realize you saved our bacon today. Without your skill, there is no telling what would've happened. I don't think anybody else on the team realizes how deep over our heads we were."

"Well, don't be going all emotional on me."

My face clenches into a knot. "What's wrong with you? Why do you have to be so hard?"

She stares at me for a few seconds as if measuring me before turning away.

"I get it. I don't expect you to be my best friend or anything. But you don't have to be so dismissive."

She turns back, her eyes narrow. "I'm just a bit aggravated."

"Cracked ribs and a concussion? I'd say it's understandable."

"It's not that. It's just what you did was wrong."

I struggle to look nonchalant and not let my jaw drop. I didn't think she knew. "What did I do?"

She arches her eyebrows. "The chant?"

"It's not like I wanted to," I plead.

"Yeah, well, not cool."

I can't conceal a derisive snort. "Seriously? It would've been better to let the spirit pummel all of us to death with concrete chips."

She sits up straighter in the bed. "No. It's just… What else did you see?"

Nope. I'm not going to do it. People who say it's always best, to tell the truth, don't have much interaction with people. There are times when a little side stepping the question is far superior to the truth. My trouble is even little fibs make my face light up with guilt. If ever there were a time to float one, now is an appropriate time.

"I didn't see anything else, Liza. The chant was right at the forefront of your thought."

She studies my face intently. I struggle not to crack a smile. Her left eye squints, then she lets it go. "I just felt violated."

"I understand fully. If I thought there was any other option, I wouldn't have done it."

"Now that I believe." She exhales loudly. "Is Travis ever gonna get here with those chicken sandwiches?"

"Tell me about it, I feel like my stomach is eating my spine."

Chapter 33

Travis drives me home in a rental from the hospital. We arrive in Guntersville so late it seems pointless to attempt to review the Charlotte King case. I decide I'd be better served to get a good night's rest and get to the office early in the morning.

I'm incredibly proud of myself as I unlock the law office at six a.m. and lock the door behind me. Something about taking my responsibilities seriously tells me I'm genuinely joining the world of adulthood. As proud of myself as I am, I can't shake the fact I don't have a clue how I plan to help Charlotte King avoid being convicted of murder.

Despite the impending doom of my only client's case, it does feel good to be back in the office. I much prefer dealing with real problems and real people rather than the paranormal. Dusty and the remainder of the team stayed behind to help Father Finnegan from the Louisville diocese bless the hotel. Making sure Les Blair doesn't ever show himself back into the Osborne Hotel is a priority. Dusty wants to tape the blessing for the potential future documentary *The Making of the Thirteen* and pick up Liza from the hospital on the way home to Alabama.

The ability to square in my mind what happened over the weekend still eludes me. I have unresolved questions about the case. Why Les Blair's ghost suddenly decided after eighty years to animate and what the two entities on the fourteenth floor were about. Not to mention we still haven't cleared up if the maid, Dottie, committed suicide or if she had some "Spiritual" coaxing to help her along her way.

I also have some questions for my hospitalized partner once she feels up to them. The tattoo popping from her body and creating three-dimensional objects, way too cool not to get the backstory.

There are some impressive new skills in my repertoire too. I don't know how, but me being able to focus energy like a battering ram that turned a chunk of concrete into dust—so awesome! I can't quit grinning about that one. Even if it's a little creepy and unnerving.

I flip through the King folder again and layout the photos. I rearrange the pictures. Staring at them, I hope to see some minor bit of information I somehow overlooked the first hundred times I studied the photos.

The office phone rings, and I jump. Irritated at my reaction, I pick it up.

"Oh, thank goodness you're already there, April," Howard says.

I think to mention, he can reach me twenty-four-seven on my cell phone rather than remain a slave of the eighties. Then again, it might be convenient for him to always call me on the office phone. "What's up?"

"I'm down in Mobile this morning and have car trouble."

"Why are you in Mobile?"

"I have an old friend down here who invited me for the weekend. A little road trip down to the beach just sounded like a great idea."

"Are you going to take your car into the shop?"

"Yes, that's exactly what I plan to do."

Odd. I'm still trying to understand what this has to do with me. "Okay. Is there something you need?"

"Right, yes. I'm sorry, I'm just a little flabbergasted now. I'm scheduled for a meeting with Brad Mathis this morning. He is a small-time crook Lane assigned to us on Friday. I'm scheduled at the jail to have a sit down with him at nine, but obviously, I'm not going to be able to make it."

I check my phone and note it's already seven-thirty. Mobile is a six-hour drive from Guntersville. "You wouldn't make it on time, even if your car were fixed."

He laughs. "I suppose not. Listen, I need you to do the initial interview with Brad. Lane believes he should accept a plea bargain, but you know Lane, he wants to plead out everything."

That rings awfully true. I'm starting to wonder if I should have accepted Lane's plea deal for Charlotte. If I can't get creative soon, I'll rue the day I turned it down.

"Okay. So, what, just take notes and then put them on your desk for when you get here?"

"No, we'll just let this one be yours. Assuming it doesn't go to trial."

My chest tightens. "I've got the King case."

"Well darlin', if you want to make a living, you'll have to learn how to chew gum and walk simultaneously. Unless you're trying to get a multimillionaire off for murdering his trophy wife, you don't normally get to work one case at a time."

Howard is correct, I know he is. But that doesn't decrease the anxiety level I presently feel. "You're right."

"Great! I'll see you on Wednesday then."

"Wednesday? It's gonna take that long to get your car fixed?"

"Oh no, I just need to get a new battery. But since I'm already down here, I figure I'll spend a couple more days. It sure is good to have someone I can count on helping me."

No! He played the compliment leading into a shame card. That's just messed up. "All right, well, I've got things under control here. Enjoy your stay at the beach."

"Oh. I will."

I'm hyperventilating as I hang up the phone. How can Howard do this to me? I only have two days until Charlotte King's case goes to the grand jury, and now I'm saddled with my uncle's workload too. Getting Brad Mathis to take a plea bargain just became my top priority because I sure don't have time to plan his defense too.

Chapter 34

I'm familiar with men like Brad Mathis. As the guard leads him into the interview room, his exaggerated swagger and disinterested expression insinuates that the world owes him a high debt of gratitude. Brad sits, rests his handcuffed wrists on the table, then slouches low in his chair.

My client is a tall, thin man, his harsh chiseled face is framed by an abundance of long mud-colored hair. Brad's large blue, hazel eyes demand attention, and they make my skin crawl. They're what I commonly refer to as 'Crazy Eyes,' the eyes of an unstable predator.

"I told them I didn't need no lawyer. I'm probably smarter than you are anyway."

This is going to be a joy. "Great! Because my schedule's full as a tick on a hound dog right now. I'm glad you can take care of yourself," I say with an overly cheery voice as I make a show of shoving my planner in my brief as I stand.

"Wait. You're just gonna leave?"

"I thought you had this handled Mr. Smart Guy."

His crazy eyes glint before he glares down at his hands. "Well, it might be helpful if I could ask you a few pointers first."

I pull my chair across the floor, making a loud grating noise on the concrete, then sit. "Shoot."

He stares. His expression is inscrutable.

"You were going to ask?"

He leans forward across the table. "I suppose I could use a little bit of lawyering."

I draw a deep breath as I pull his folder from my brief. "Hmm..." I flip the multitude of pages casually. "Armed robbery, video documentation, and three eyewitnesses." I look him dead in the eye. "I'd say you're screwed, Mr. Mathis."

His lips tighten as his eyes narrow, then he chuckles. "You're a real ball buster, lady. I like that. I don't need a pushover for a lawyer." He sobers, then clicks his tongue. "So, what's the play?"

"Well, it's your lucky day. I'm not sure if the DA and your parents are close friends, but he has offered you five years in medium security and five years of probation for a guilty plea. I'd suggest you hop on that quick."

Brad's jaw comes unhinged. "Are you serious?"

"Serious as a heart attack. Again, I'd accept before the DA changes his mind."

"But I didn't do it."

I can't repress a laugh. "Nobody ever does."

He slams his chained wrist against the table, and I nearly pee myself. The aggressive energy emanating from him is the sort that would make me cross the street to get away from him even in broad daylight.

"No, I mean, I didn't steal any money."

I exhale loudly as I try to appear uninterested. In a way, I am. I don't have time for Brad's stupidity. Charlotte King is an innocent client. I need to get busy with her case. To free the time to develop her defense, I must get this yahoo to understand Lane has offered him a lenient sentence.

"Just so you understand, if this goes to the jury and you're found guilty of armed robbery, you will be looking at twenty-five years."

"But you're not listening. I didn't steal any money."

I push my chair back and stomp to the electronic equipment at the front of the room. With a dramatic wave of my hand, I insert the memory stick and pull up the video Lane included in the brief.

A black-and-white, high-quality video appears. The video was shot from over the right-hand shoulder of the clerk and affords a perfect view of Brad's face. He waves a gun in a menacing manner.

The cashier appears to attempt to explain something to the robber. His gun arm extends, the barrel of the pistol taps the clerk's head. She quickly opens the register, pulls the cash from the tray, and shoves it in the direction of the bag the robber holds in his other hand.

I stop the film. "Care to explain how you didn't steal anything?"

"You don't believe me."

The nerve of this guy. "No, I don't. More importantly, no jury will believe you after watching this film."

"Take it back farther."

"Why?"

"You have to go back farther in the tape." He narrows his eyes. "You have to trust me."

Trust? Brad Mathis will never be someone I trust.

He must have noticed my body language. "I didn't do it. If you take the time to watch the whole video, you'd see what I'm talking about."

"For Pete's sake." Liars, thieves, and stupid people. I have a challenging time suffering any of them, and Brad Mathis qualifies for all classifications.

Stewing with anger, I search for the uncut file. When I find it, I run the footage in reverse until I see Brad enter the establishment. He appears agitated as he makes a show of looking at the merchandise. He selects a small porcelain figurine and approaches the cash register. The clerk rings up the purchase, and Brad hands her some cash. Everything looks like a normal customer interaction to this point.

As the clerk's attention goes to the drawer, Brad pulls a pistol from his pants. The rest of the video was the shorter version

Lane had queued up for me on the flash drive.

"See, I told you."

"What I see is a video documentation of you committing a crime."

"Man, it figures they'd send me a stupid lawyer."

My steam valve blows. "Listen, mister, the state is required to offer you legal defense if you can't afford it. But there is nothing that says I have to be the one who works with your sorry butt."

Brad presses his lips tight as he shakes his head. "They can't accuse me of stealing money when I lost money on the deal."

My head is beginning to hurt, and I feel my stomach rumble. I came in early this morning to work on the Charlotte King case, and I now realize I didn't eat breakfast. Mr. Mathis is treading on thin ice, and he can't know how close I am to showing him my crazy. "Explain."

Brad rolls his wrists on the table, exposing his palms. "I handed her a twenty-dollar bill."

"And?"

"There were only twelve dollars in the drawer. Technically I paid the clerk eight dollars."

I freeze as the information sinks in. Despite my best effort, I giggle. "Let me get this straight. You handed the clerk a twenty-dollar bill, so she'd open the drawer, but all she had in the drawer was twelve dollars?"

"Yeah. So, I didn't steal anything. If anything, the clerk took eight dollars from me."

"What about the twenty?" He gives me a dumb look. "The twenty you gave her."

"She set it to the side until she finished making change. When she started blabbing to me, I got tense that it was taking too long and forgot about it."

"She was probably trying to tell you she didn't have any cash."

Brad rolls his eyes. "Duh, do you think." He shakes his hands, rattling the chain. "Regardless, I didn't rob anyone."

I shake my head in disbelief. "You honestly can't believe that."

"It's a true story. Ask the clerk."

One of these days, people's idiotic explanations will quit shocking me. It's amazing what folks will convince themselves of when they've gotten themselves into a pinch.

"Okay, Brad. Let's play a little game for a minute. You pretend you're one of the jurors and let me explain how my client should be found innocent." I don't wait for him to accept my offer.

"Ladies and gentlemen of the jury, my client is innocent of the armed robbery charge and should be freed immediately. Mr. Mathis is innocent of the robbery by way of having paid the establishment eight dollars. In truth, he did not steal anything, he made a cash donation to the local establishment. And yes, Mr. Mathis did hold a revolver to the clerk's head. Still, he was simply expressing his second amendment rights. He never intended to hurt anyone with the firearm, so he can't be found culpable for the 'Armed' aspect of the charge. As you can understand, my client is not guilty of either the armed or the robbery aspect of the charges wrongfully leveled against him. Therefore, you must see justice done by acquitting my client of all charges."

I arch my eyebrows. "How convincing is that, Brad?"

The sides of his lips twitch into a smile. "That's what I'm talking about."

I can't help myself. "Are you delusional, Brad?"

"I don't think so."

"You sure could fool me. You really believe a jury is going to buy the second amendment explanation for you poking a loaded gun in the cashier's face?"

Contempt flashes across his face as he slides down in his chair. "See, this is why I didn't want no chick lawyer. You don't even realize that wasn't a real gun."

I clutch the pen in my hand tighter. As I glare at Brad, my eyes focus on his aortic artery throbbing in his neck. Lucky me, my civilized brain lobes can convince my primal desires that Mr. Mathis is not worth fifteen years in prison. Even if skewering him with my pen would be satisfying on so many levels.

"Again, Mr. Mathis, you're more than welcome to seek a change in counsel," I say with my jaw clenched.

He grins lazily. "Nah, that's okay. You're sorta easy on the eye."

Mama said there would be days God would test me. It must be a double bonus week for April. However, the thought that this sack of refuse in front of me is a test sent from a higher being does help me calm. I dig deep for the training I received from Mama and the church when I was growing up and fight to tamp down my crazy.

"Mr. Mathis, I understand you do not believe you stole any cash. I'll have to investigate your claim that the gun was not real." I point my pen at him. "But in the rule of law, perceptions count. The cashier had no way of knowing the pistol was fake. If she had shoved your twenty in the bag with the rest of the cash, you'd have stolen money. I hope you see where this is leading."

"Yeah," he answers. "It leads me straight to a jail cell for something I didn't do."

Oh, Lord, give me strength. I want to stab him in the neck so bad. "Just to get this straight. You want me to put together a defense that claims since you lost money, and you used a toy gun; it's basically no harm, no foul?"

Brad sits up straight and points at me. "Finally, you got it through that pretty little head of yours."

I turn that over in my mind, and my anger turns to complete joy. Yes, it would be a loss on my win-loss tally sheet, but it suddenly seems like a small price to pay to get Brad off the streets of Guntersville. He didn't hurt anyone this time. But it's easy to understand he'll escalate his stupid criminal acts and get himself, or worse, an innocent Guntersville resident killed.

I gather my folders. "All right, Mr. Mathis. We'll proceed with the defense you've requested. I'll discuss your denial of the plea deal with district attorney Jameson today."

"There you go. I had faith you'd be able to get on board."

I turn to leave as I've nothing else to say to the jerk that's now my client.

"Oh, baby!"

I turn back in alarm. Brad's eyes are leveled at the top of my legs. "Excuse me?"

Brad turns his hands over as he favors me, his lazy grin again. "Sorry, ma'am, but you've got an onion butt. When I saw it, well, it just made me want to cry."

The eye of death I give Brad, I'm sure, is not understood. It's all I can do to turn and leave instead of backing out the door. Some days it amazes me how close some men dance to the fire. I doubt they ever know how close they've come to being killed by a furious female.

Chapter 35

I'm short on time, but I'm also famished. I swing into Jerry's sub shop on the way back to the office, and against my better judgment, buy a double Reuben. All of Jerry's sandwiches are heavy on the meat and cheese and light on the vegetables. They're designed to fill large gaping holes in your stomach, not to be artistic culinary affairs.

The weight of the sandwich in the paper bag I carry to the front door of the office makes me smile as my stomach continues to rumble in anticipation. I can't wait to unwrap the heavy wax paper and watch the aromatic steam trail up toward my nostrils.

Ms. Castle is waiting in the small alcove of the office's front door. She examines her diamond tennis watch pointedly. "I was wondering what sort of office hours this establishment keeps now."

"Hello, Ms. Castle. I had an interview with a client if you must know." I make a shooing gesture with my hand to get enough room between her and the door to unlock the office.

"I will definitely have to let Howard know I am not happy."

That makes two of us.

I cringe as I turn the key and the lock clicks. I wait for Ms. Castle to reply in anger to my smart comment. When she doesn't, I realize I didn't vocalize my thoughts for a change. I'm getting much better at this dealing with people thing.

"I have an absolute emergency."

That gets my attention. I study Ms. Castle's demeanor. "What's troubling you?"

"Word has come to me; my grandniece Tiffany has been helping Charlotte build a case to get her off for murdering her husband."

"Tiffany Bates?" I'm not really asking for confirmation. I'm shocked Ms. Castle is upset Tiffany is helping Charlotte.

"Yes! I simply cannot have my family harboring a criminal. Even if it is one of our own."

"Ms. Castle, Charlotte hasn't even had her day in court yet. She may be innocent of any wrongdoing in Alan's death."

Her nose wrinkles severely. "Oh, she did it. That little harlot was always the wild child. I told her mother to get control of her. I knew she would turn out to be trash."

Mama promised me God would never give me more than I can handle. Between Brad and Ms. Castle, and the delicious Reuben sandwich now cooling in my bag, I really hope God hasn't overestimated my ability to cope. For the second time today, I feel the violent urge to pummel someone, and I'm not sure I won't beat Ms. Castle black and blue with a Reuben sandwich.

"Well, considering I have to defend Ms. King, I think it best we don't discuss it any further. Conflict of interest and all."

Ms. Castle draws back in horror. "You're defending her?"

"Yes." I round my desk and stand in front of my chair as I set my Reuben on the table. "Now, what can I do for you, Ms. Castle."

"Isn't it obvious?" She trembles with rage.

"Uh, no."

"Tiffany is scheduled to receive five percent of my estate when I pass. Obviously, I need to write her out of the will."

Let's see five percent of nothing, that's a tough one, oh yeah nothing. "Obviously."

"Just a bit of helpful advice dear, you would be a much better attorney if you bothered to pay a little more attention to your client's documents."

I'm positive a Reuben sandwich is more dangerous the colder it gets. I think the action of the corned beef and sauerkraut congealing would allow the sandwich to solidify. Like a brick on rye. "Yes, ma'am."

Chapter 36

I clear Ms. Castle from the office, nuke my Reuben in the microwave and settle in reviewing the King case for what must be the hundredth time. I'm hoping for an epiphany that is slow to come.

Slamming the folder shut, I make up my mind. Desperate times demand desperate measures. We're a day and a half away from the grand jury, I still have no angle to play, and I'm a fool if I don't use my "gifts" if there is an opportunity for them to help build a case.

I hate to admit it, but the craziness that was the Osborne Hotel weekend has forced me to confront my fears of my talents. If I can use them always for good, clearing the hotel or freeing an innocent woman, that's something I should be proud of, not fearful. Right?

I must get over to the King's home today. I jot down their address in my notebook.

The office door opens. "Hello?"

A little tingle shoots through me. Bless it, that man has a sexy voice.

Lane smiles as he closes the door behind him. "I heard you had a chance to talk with our model citizen Brad Mathis this morning."

I snort. That's ladylike. "If Brad is a model citizen, this town is doomed."

"Just another country boy brought up a little rough." When I wrinkle my face in disgust, Lane laughs. "He is indeed walking, talking, excrement."

"I was wondering about you there for a second."

"Making matters worse, Brad is one of the wildcard guys. When he is calm and working, he is incredibly smart and industrious. When he is out of work or broken up with his girlfriend, he becomes dumb as a rock and as dangerous as a lit stick of dynamite. Too bad, he stays unemployed most of the time."

That does an adequate job of summing up the anomaly I witnessed during our interview. Lane's correct evaluation of Brad makes it easier to share Brad's decision. "He has requested I deny the plea bargain you offered."

Lane jams his hands into his trousers. "Why in the world would he do that?"

I laugh as I fill Lane in on Brad's logic. "He contends there was no robbery since he walked away with less cash than what he had when he came in the store. Also, since it was a toy gun, he contends there was no armed robbery."

The humorous smile plastered on my face fades as I watch Lane consider the argument. He frowns, and I become concerned. "What?"

Lane's face creases aging him at least a decade. "That slippery snake. He may actually have a point."

He must be joking again. When he doesn't clarify, I ask, "You're not serious?"

"Strictly speaking from the law standpoint, of course not. But this is a felony, April. A judge won't decide this. This will go to the jury."

"Right."

The left side of his face tics up. "I'm not sure we can sit twelve jurors, and there not be one of them that'll think Brad has a point."

"You can't really believe that."

Lane locks his eyes with mine with no humor in his expression. "I want you to consider everyone you know in town and tell me not one of them would believe Brad's explanation."

Lane is right. Brad's theory would be hogwash with most residents, but with twelve jurors... "What now?"

"Give me a day. I want to talk to Judge Rossi before moving forward on this. In the meantime, I don't want you to talk to Brad."

"Gee, I'm crushed."

"I'm sure you are. I hope to let you know something tomorrow afternoon."

The wheels of justice move slow because they're not round, they're square and dysfunctional. Such is the profession I have chosen.

I struggle to shake off the injustice of Brad's case after Lane leaves. To say it bothers me that such a lowlife might get off with a slap on the wrist on a thinly disguised lie of intent is an understatement.

My focus goes back to Charlotte's case, and after a few moments, I berate myself for getting off track. I meant to get to her home to investigate for residual energy.

I read the name of the reporting officer and do a mental head slap. How had I forgotten Jacob Hurley, one of my best friends from high school, was the reporting officer.

It slipped my mind because it seems so improbable. Jacob as a police officer? Will wonders never cease?

Jacob was a big boy who played both ways on the lines of Guntersville High School's football team when we were in school. He asked me to be his girlfriend several times as a freshman, finally retiring to "friend" status when he got it through his head I wasn't interested. We weren't just friends; we were tight buddies sharing each other's breakups and dreams, allowing us each a good look into how the other sex thinks.

Rumors persisted about our relationship until I left for Tuscaloosa. Our friendship, which was natural to us, was a weird concept to everyone else in town.

Odd, now that I think about it. I've not seen Jacob since I left for college. I would have thought we would have bumped into each other around town when I visited my parents on the holidays.

I dial the police station and identify myself as the defense attorney for Charlotte King and request to speak to Officer Hurley. He is off duty, but Kimberly Meeks, an older cousin of Randy Leath, is running dispatch, and she is more than happy to give me Jacob's cell phone number.

A little twinge hits my gut hard. I'm nervous. When I left for Tuscaloosa, I sent Jacob a birthday card during my freshman year and never bothered to call him. Worse, the times he called me at school the first year at Alabama were always the worst timing, and I had to cut him short.

There were no calls after my freshman year. I heard he joined the Marines and shipped off to Afghanistan, but either way, I lost track of him. It's not going to be an easy call from a personal standpoint, but I guess it's time to put my big girl pants on and be a professional for my client's sake.

But I really am a sucky friend.

I dial his number and imagine touring the scene with Jacob will kill two birds with one stone. He'll be able to describe everything he saw the day he arrived on the scene, and at the same time, I'll be able to get a feel for his thoughts about the case.

"Hello?"

His voice sounds fuller, more assured than I remembered. "Hey, Jacob. This is April Snow."

"Hey, April. Some of the guys told me you were back in town."

What guys? I get knocked off my game by his statement. "Yeah, it's only been a week or so. Listen, I'm the defense attorney for Charlotte King." The pause has a chill about it. "I understand you were the first officer on the scene."

"That's right. Why?"

Defensive. Interesting. "I haven't been to the King's home yet. I was wondering if you'd mind meeting me there and walking me through what you saw."

"I guess that would be all right. When?"

"I can meet you there in thirty minutes. If that'll work for you."

"Tonight?" he sounds panicked.

"The grand jury is Wednesday. If possible, I need it to be tonight. I can go without you if you can't make it."

There is another pause. Awkward—not a chill pause this time. "It's just, I've already had a couple of beers tonight."

"Are you drunk?" I'd think it would take more than a few beers to get a man his size drunk.

He laughs. "Not hardly, I just didn't want you to be offended."

"I think I can get over my sensibilities for the sake of my client."

"Good deal, counselor. I'll see you in a few."

Chapter 37

The King's house is set in a small meadow with a tree line to the right and back of the house. The gravel road leading to the clapboard home was pocked and in need of leveling.

I am stepping out of my car when Jacob pulls up in an older pickup. He moves toward me, and I notice he dropped the extra thirty pounds he used to carry during high school. He remains broad-shouldered and handsome in a rugged mountain man style. Jacob is, easily, one of the most attractive men in Guntersville, next to my brother Chase. Oddly, I recognize Jacob's natural good looks but have never felt a spark between us.

His grin threatens to swallow his face as he holds his arms out. "April Snow." He embraces me, and I pat him on his broad back. He smells terrific. "I wasn't sure you would ever come back to this tiny town."

"Well, I still have family here." I squirm free. "So I suppose I'll always have a reason to come back."

His gaze bores through me. "Good. I'm glad to hear that."

I clear my throat to break the awkward silence. "What can you tell me about the King case?"

He sighs as he shoves his fingers into his tight jeans. "I'm afraid I won't have much more than what's written down in my report. With the body found where it was, Charlotte's interview and the murder weapon in the garage, it's a very cut and dry crime scene."

"Murder weapon?"

"The nail gun."

I think I might get more if I play a little dumb. "Nail gun?"

Jacob frowns. "You did read my report, didn't you, counselor?"

"Yes, but I didn't see any photos of a nail gun."

Jacob narrows his gaze. He is suspicious. Somewhere over the years, his intelligence has increased exponentially, or I misread him in our youth. "No need to photograph it since we turned it in with evidence."

"Oh, so there isn't a photo showing the location of the nail gun when you found it."

He hesitates before answering. "It wasn't possible."

"Because?"

"The suspect buried it under some other tools."

Interesting. Charlotte went through the trouble of concealing the murder weapon, indicating she knew it would be a problem if it were found. But why not dispose of the nail gun?

I incline my head toward the house. "Care to show me around?"

"Sure." He unlocks the door and remarks. "Of course nothing of any merit is inside the house. We found Alan just under the house and the murder weapon in his workshop out back."

The familiarity catches my ear. "Did you know the victim?"

His shoulders tense, and a light blush colors his stubbled cheeks. "We've been known to share a pizza on game night at Torino's or a couple of beers at Jester's before."

"Y'all ever talk about his wife?"

"No. I don't remember Charlotte ever coming up."

His lie shakes through me. It's a funny thing about lies. Some people genuinely are pathological liars. Liars of that ilk have nearly convinced themselves their lies are so justified it's a greater good than telling the truth. A lie told by such a person is like throwing a grain of sand into a still surfaced pond. Does it have a reverberation? Certainly. But it is imperceptible.

Folks who don't typically lie are the polar opposite. The lie Jacob tells is like dropping a boulder into a puddle of water. He is hiding something. But his lie disturbs him as much as the truth he is concealing.

I wander from the foyer to the kitchen of the small house, leaving Jacob up at the front door. I push out with my mind clutching at any energy residuals of sounds, smells, or visuals. Nothing out of the ordinary comes to me as I feel equal measures of happiness and disappointments.

Continuing my investigation, I walk down the hallway. Sounds of both anger and love play through my system. In both rooms, the children stayed in a high measure of laughter and bright colors flashing through my mind. This brings a smile to my face.

Finally, I enter the master bedroom. There is such a conflict of sounds and color I must calm myself and sort through the rush of emotions. A great sadness rolls over me. What I feel confirms what I already believed true.

"It's best we hurry up to check the outside. It's going to be dark soon," Jacob remarks as I walk out of the master bedroom.

"Was there any sign of a struggle?" I ask Jacob as he leads me out.

"No. But there wouldn't be a struggle if she did it while he slept." Jacob leans over and removes the metal plate from the crawl space entry. "Besides, it's the only way she could have used the nail gun with the guard still on."

So, he did consider the guard still being on the nail gun. As much as I don't want to admit it, Charlotte may have ambushed her husband in his sleep and driven a twenty-penny nail into his forehead. The thought makes me shudder.

"He was lying right here face down." Jacob points a few feet back through the crawl space entry."

I notice the plastic lining covering the dirt floor is covered in coagulated blood teeming with maggots. "Is that blood?"

Jacob sucks his lips in. "Yeah. Sorry. The cleanup crew was

supposed to take care of that."

"Why so much blood here?"

"She must have pulled the nail out once she moved him here."

It isn't funny, but for some reason, I chuckle. "Well, why would she have done that?"

"How would I know?" Jacob's face turns beet red. "Chick is just crazy, I guess."

No. That isn't it, and Jacob knows it. He can't explain it because it makes no sense.

Something is eating at Jacob. He knows something isn't quite right with his cut and dry case, but he has become too stubborn to move off it. I squat and peer past the bloodied muck into the dark crawlspace.

"What's back there?" I ask.

Jacob pulls a flashlight magically from behind his back and squats next to me. I can smell the musk of his liberal aftershave floating on the air as he squeezes in closer to gain access to the door.

"Not really sure." He flashes the beam into the darkness. The three-foot-tall crawl space becomes shallower until at the back of the house no more than a foot and a half clearance between the ground and the floor beams remains. "It doesn't look like much to me. It's too small of an area to store much of anything."

As Jacob clicks off the flashlight, something catches my eye. "Hey, wait. Shine the light over there."

His direction is off. I pull his wrist to the right. "What's that there?"

"Looks like a plumbing wrench," he says absently. I stare at Jacob until he turns toward me. "What?"

"Well, don't you think that's important?"

"No. Contractors are always leaving tools behind. Shoot, a lot of the tools are guaranteed for life. Do you think those tool stores would still be in business if guys kept up with all their tools?"

Men are always complaining about not understanding women? I know for sure that if I lost a thirty-dollar tool, I'd backtrack until I figured out where I left it.

My expectation had been if there were any place at the house, I'd receive a vision it would be here where Alan's body was found. I centered my energy, then pushed out with all my might.

It's like scanning a whole lot of nothingness. No visions, no sound, no feelings. Only the subtlest scent of sweat. The smell of the sweat is slightly off, but I can't put my finger on what it's telling me.

Jacob cheerfully replaces the metal closure plate of the crawlspace. "We better check the shop before it's dark. They cut the power to the house off the other day."

Man, what is with that sweat? It isn't like work sweat or gym sweat, it has a high tang to it that I can taste.

"Like I said, we didn't find the weapon right off. We figured it had to be here somewhere. It's not likely a man is going to let somebody drive a nail into their head with a hammer."

"It's not like it would be impossible."

"Yeah, it would be pretty impossible," he counters.

Maybe with Jacob, considering he is showing what a hard head he has. "One good whack with a twenty-eight-ounce hammer ought to do the trick."

"If they didn't wake up when you held the nail to their forehead."

Fair. Jacob makes a good point.

I follow Jacob into the workshop at the back of the gravel drive. The rip saw, and the planer are either new or extremely well-kept. To the right is a cherry cabinet, three-fourths complete. I'd love to have a home where I could have a piece of furniture as stunning as the cabinet Alan was working on.

Jacob pulls a yellow milk crate from under a well-ordered workbench. "I found it in here under a stapler and some drop cloths."

Alan's energy signature is most active in his shop. There are exponentially stronger energy signatures here than anywhere in the house, including where he slept. I feel pride, determination, and expectations. There is no anger, and the color is deeply ingrained mahogany. I'd say Glenda was right on about her assessment. Knowing only what I feel now, I, too, believe Alan was an exceptional carpenter.

"April?"

Jacob comes into focus as if through fog. I shake my head. "Sorry, I was just trying to imagine him working here."

"Alan had some sick skill as a carpenter." His eyes narrow. "You sure you're okay? You look sort of green around the lips."

"Yes, I think I might just be hungry."

"Awesome, I was about to ask if you'd like to get a burger and beer with me. You know, catch up on old times."

I feel a rush of panic come over me, which makes no sense given I'm talking to Jacob. "Aw, I don't know Jacob. I need to go over my case notes again, and I'll have to open the law office early tomorrow."

He shoves his hands in his back pockets. "Darn April. I wasn't asking you out for a date. I have to be in at six in the morning too, I just figured we both have to eat."

Chapter 38

Going with Jacob to Rex's continues to bother me. Either it's a bad idea because I'm leading Jacob on or Jacob is equally uninterested in me, and it's another case of April get over yourself. Waiting to order my stomach rumbles loud enough to draw his attention.

"Dang Snow, you're not about to have an alien pop out of your chest or anything are you."

Jacob's feigned disgust bruises my pride, and I favor him the eye of death. He also answered my question. It's a case of April get over yourself.

Rex's has a light crowd, but it's Monday evening and still early. Jacob selects a booth big enough for six people at the back of the restaurant.

"Anything new here in the last few years?" I ask.

"You can get Dijon mustard on your chili fries now."

"Why would I want that?"

He laughs briefly. Jacob has always had a great laugh. "I didn't say you'd want it. I just said it was new."

I pull out a menu and study it. Jacob sits with his arms crossed, staring at me. "Are you not gonna look at the menu?"

"No, I already know what I want," he says with a wicked grin.

Oh, boy. Double entendre. Danger, danger. I pay enough attention to the twelve disgusting toppings available for chili fries long enough to commit them to memory. I know darn well I don't want any.

"Oh my gosh."

I look up from the laminated menu to see a familiar face. "Barbara."

Barbara leans down and gives me a shoulder hug burying my face in her mass of flaming red hair. "My goodness, you're all grown up. I heard you were back in town." Her eyes dart to Jacob. She wags her finger back and forth. "You two aren't..."

"No," I say a little too eagerly.

Barbara Elliott and my brother Chase dated from middle school until they graduated from high school. It was long assumed in our family she would be a part of the Snow family eventually. Barbara is fun, sweet, and if PhDs were handed out for social adeptness, she would undoubtedly have an honorary one. I never knew why she and Chase broke up. They certainly made a handsome couple, but I suppose it takes more than mutual good looks to make a relationship work.

"Chase told me you finished law school." Her jade eyes sparkle. "I don't know I've ever seen him so proud of something."

"What have you been up to?" I ask.

"Oh, just teaching dance a couple days a week and then working tables at nights."

What do I say? I know Barbara's dreams well. For the seven years, she was a fixture in my household. She talked about when she would go to New York and be a dancer. She had the looks, the legs, the moves, and here she is aging out of her dancing prime. "That sounds like fun."

"Some days. It's not exactly dancing on Broadway or Vegas."

I have nothing for that comment. I sit in the booth with a silly thin smile pasted on my face as I nod my head at one of the women I used to look up to. The fear grips me. If I don't find employment within my profession soon, I too will have to explain to folks why I'm working part-time at my uncle's law firm and chasing ghosts with one of my brothers. That does not appeal to me.

"So, what will it be?" She holds a pen to her order pad.

The knot in my stomach about my career has knocked my hunger down a few notches. I order a grilled cheese sandwich and a cup of tomato soup.

Jacob waits until Barbara leaves for the kitchen. He leans across the table. "I'm afraid she still has a thing for your brother."

"If he had half a brain, he'd get back together with her. Knowing my brother Chase, he is probably still in love with her too."

"Maybe. Sometimes the hardest thing to do is come full circle and pick up something you never should've left."

Something is different about Jacob. If I add up all his deep thoughts during our prior conversations as high school students, they wouldn't equal the statement he just made. "I suppose, but I wouldn't know since I haven't had the need yet to circle back around for anything."

He grins and fidgets with his napkin. "If you don't mind me asking, what makes you so certain Charlotte is innocent?"

"I never said I thought she was innocent. I'm just defending her. Everybody deserves counsel."

"Cut the crap, Snow. I can tell, you believe her. Otherwise, you wouldn't be going through the trouble you are."

My face flushes with anger. "Are you implying if I thought Charlotte was guilty, I wouldn't be working to defend her."

"Not as hard."

I rock back as if he slapped me. "That's a heck of an insult."

"I didn't mean it like that. I'm just saying when you believe in something, you tend to work extra hard at it."

I avert my eyes from him. I don't care to talk anymore.

"You didn't answer my question."

Nope. I sure didn't. And I become incredibly interested in the old jukebox on the far wall that hasn't played since I was a child.

Jacob is a "Just the facts ma'am" sort of guy. His world has always been based on solid facts and definitive answers of yes and no. He is ill-suited for the gray areas that are my life. The last thing I need is for him to scoff at my gut feeling that Charlotte is innocent.

Maybe if he knew about my "gifts." I kept them a secret from him while we were best friends, I won't reveal them to him now.

Barbara saves me with our meal. "Now honey, watch the soup; it's hot. I also had Juan smash the grilled cheese for you. I know you like it that way. Oh, and whatever you do, don't get your hands too close to Jacob's plate while he is eating. You don't want to come up missing any fingers."

"Ha, ha," Jacob mocks as he squirts mustard onto his hamburger.

My anxiety dissipates as I taste my soup, and a comfortable, familiar warmth cocoons my frazzled mind. Jacob is excellent company when he remains quiet. His energy has a steady, solid thrum to it that calms my soul.

He wipes his hands on a napkin he tosses onto his plate then drapes a thickly muscled arm over the back of the booth. "How are you liking being home so far?"

"Hard to beat the rent. It's just temporary anyway."

"That's two."

"Two what?"

He lifts two fingers from his hand on the back of the booth. "Two times, I've asked a direct question, and you've avoided answering. That's not a very friendly way to have a conversation. One more and I'll have to leave."

"Well, don't let me stop you."

"You know, trying to be your friend is like hugging a porcupine."

As much as I hate to admit it, he is right. Whatever I believed Jacob once hoped was between us, he no longer feels. Jacob is trying to be a good friend by welcoming me home, and I'm being difficult.

He sighs. "Why are you going to be at the grand jury Wednesday?"

"To help my client."

"You know you don't get to say anything."

What? Does Jacob think they don't even teach the basics at the University of Alabama Law School? "I can speak to my client."

"True. If it goes to trial, do you feel you have a good defense strategy mapped out?"

"I think I have a pretty good plan." In my mind I'm being optimistic, not stretching the truth.

"I hope so." His eyes bore into me with unfathomable intensity. "There is a lot to lose if this goes to a jury, April. Mind you, it wouldn't hurt my feelings any if you can prove her innocence. I keep thinking of those four kids growing up without a mama or daddy. It breaks my heart. I can't understand what gets into some people."

I realize my mouth has fallen open. With a clack of my teeth, I snap it shut.

He looks away. "I don't mean to tell you how to do your job. You saw the body, and you have to know there isn't another way to explain what took place."

Saw the body. The words stick in my head, and I zone out of the present. The words seem uniquely important now.

"April, you did see Alan's body."

"I saw the pictures." My voice is a high-pitched whine.

Jacob pauses before replying. "It's your case, counselor. But as a friend, I have to say seeing the condition of the deceased firsthand is like seeing their home firsthand. It may be nothing, but then again, it may take you one step further toward understanding what transpired leading up to Alan's death."

"I just didn't think about it."

"There is no shame in that. You're still learning the ropes."

"I'm surprised Howard didn't mention it to me."

Jacob uncorks another laugh. "I'm not surprised. He and district attorney Jameson are hoping you'll take the plea bargain. I guess Charlotte is lucky you're not easily convinced."

My face tightens in anger again. Jacob's comment rings true.

Howard's possible manipulation is a bitter pill to swallow.

"Listen, Old Doc Crowder is still the medical examiner. I can run you out to his farm tomorrow morning so you can see Alan."

"I can take myself."

He twists his face. "You're sure? It's really out in the boonies." He watches my facial expression and adds. "Let me do this for you. I need to catch up with him anyway."

Chapter 39

Jacob picks me up the next morning at the law office. I can't help but notice his police uniform looks commanding on him like a superhero's cape. Somehow it makes him look even larger and more formidable. I'm still having some difficulty getting my mind wrapped around him in a position of responsibility and authority.

He reaches to open the passenger's door of the police cruiser for me, and I beat him to the handle. He laughs while trotting around the front of the police car. There is something about that man's laugh that makes me warm all over. Too bad I don't find anything else attractive about him. Mostly.

He buckles his seat belt. "You see that handle right there." He points to the handle above my door.

"Yeah."

He starts the cruiser. "If you hear me report on the radio, I'm responding to a call, you grab hold of that handle for dear life."

I don't like the sound of that at all. "You're kidding."

He tilts his chin up and laughs again. "I had you for a second. No, Tuesday mornings are usually incredibly boring. If you're buckled up, we should be okay."

I tug at my seat belt before I realize it. I trust the Jacob I grew up with, but don't know this version of my high school friend.

If I tried to find Doc Crowder's farm on my own, I would

have been late to court Wednesday. Jacob turns down several old county highways before turning onto the three separate packed gravel roads. The cruiser is leaving a massive rooster tail of dust behind us as he speeds along at a pace that has me wanting to grab for the "oh crap" handle Jacob pointed out earlier.

"I know it may seem like a waste of time to travel all the way out here to look at a hole in a man's head. But I do believe once you see it, you'll realize it had to be the nail gun." Jacob has the unnerving habit of looking at me while talking when I'd prefer he focus on the curves in the gravel road.

Jacob slides the cruiser to a stop in front of a chain-link gate. He hops out of the squad car, opens the gate, and slides back into the driver's seat. "He doesn't have goats anymore."

I suppose that was to explain why we didn't close the gate.

We take two quick turns, and a large farmhouse in the middle of a sunny pasture materializes from the woods. The green metal roof is a charming accent to the white two-story home. There are six rocking chairs on the wraparound porch which look very inviting.

The Rottweiler, who greets us with growls and foaming mouth, is less welcoming. Jacob steps out of the cruiser, and the dog quits growling. It tracks toward Jacob, joyfully wagging its butt.

"Hey Bubbles, how are you doing, girl?" Jacob pulls something from his pocket and feeds it to Bubbles as he scratches her on the back of the neck. "You can get out."

Easy for the beast whisperer to say. I'd feel more at ease if I had a pocket full of whatever Jacob has for Bubbles. I get out of the cruiser and walk to him. Bubbles growls at me.

"Bubbles, that's not nice." Jacob pushes at her shoulders. "Go on if you can't play nice."

"Is she like this with everybody?"

Jacob watches the Rottweiler trot off toward the barn. "Couldn't tell you, it's the first time I've been out here with anyone else. Let's get on inside, Doc is waiting for us."

We step onto the large porch. Jacob surprises me by opening the front door rather than ringing the bell. He motions for me to follow him in.

The scent of stale tobacco, cheap whiskey, and old man hangs in the air.

I follow Jacob down a wide hallway past a kitchen and then an office. The hall ends in front of an elevator.

Jacob presses the down button, and the elevator opens. He steps in, and I follow.

"Doc is in the lab downstairs," he says.

The elevator opens, and my sense of smell is assaulted by a myriad of chemicals. I didn't think to close my mind before entering the autopsy room, and voices barely audible fill my mind. I reach out and steady myself against the interior of the elevator.

Jacob looks back at me. "I know. It stinks. But you do get used to it."

I push out with my energy and form a barrier around my mind. The voices draw down to a murmur and I follow Jacob out of the elevator.

Harsh lights spill into the hallway from the right. We turn through the doorway, and I see a little man hunched over a gurney.

"You and your girlfriend are just in time, Jacob."

I'm shocked Doc knew we entered his work area until I spot the round reflective mirror in the corner of his lab. He motions with his gloved right hand speckled with blood, for us to move closer.

I recognize the body on the gurney from photos in the file to be Alan King. Albeit a very pale and purple Alan King.

"I hope y'all didn't eat a big breakfast." Doc's mouth is so insignificant compared to his substantial bulbous nose; his smile barely registers. He makes two quick incisions in Alan's hairline. He then pulls the dead man's scalp over his face.

"Hand me the saw, Jacob."

Jacob hands Doc the power tool. The diminutive man sets to

work with the care of a jeweler cutting a forty-carat diamond. If Doc Crowder intended to shock me with this activity, he is out of luck. I once seriously considered studying to be a surgeon and sat in on the dissection of a human body one day. That and my recent weekend with Dusty, had my shock meter busted.

"Lane's been after me to cut cost on the lab by twenty-five percent. I told him he might as well go ahead and change my title to medical guesser instead of examiner if he doesn't allow me to do full autopsies." Doc taps the skull with a mallet and pulls. A sucking sound fills the room as the boney cap pops free. "It's been bothering me ever since we discussed it."

Jacob crowds the smaller man. "What's that?"

Doc pulls Alan's brain from his skull and sets it on the stainless-steel tray. He picks up a scalpel and cuts the frontal lobe. "When we reconstructed the scene, we decided that the perpetrator must have pulled out the nail." Doc grabs a ruler and takes a measurement of the incision he made. Then he measures the skull thickness. "I've got just under one and a half inches."

Jacob's expression changes to one of confusion. "How's that? The only nail ribbons we found were two and three-quarter inches."

Doc holds up a gloved bloody finger. "Check this out." He pulls Alan's face back into place and points to the entry wound. "What's missing here?"

Jacob examines Alan intently, then shrugs.

Doc lifts his left hand and smacks his right fist into his palm. "There should be an impact mark of some sort left from the nail gun's impact. We just have a hole."

Jacob put his hands on his hips. "So, what do I have here?"

Doc opens his little mouth wide and releases a ghoulish cackle. "That's for you and Lane to figure out. Cause of death remains the same as far as I'm concerned."

"No, Doc. I'm serious."

Doc begins to stitch Alan's scalp together. "I can tell you

what you don't have, and that's a murder weapon. A nail is still what killed him, but it did not come from that nail gun. You make sure to back me up on this extra autopsy charge if Lane asks."

The tangy metallic scent overrides the multitude of chemicals and other body fluid scents in the room. I move closer to Alan. The scent increases, and before I realize it, I'm leaning over Alan, sniffing him from chest to neck. Fear. I smell a massive dump of fear in chemical forms layered in a thin sheen across his body. Something scared him, and Alan had been aware of his impending demise.

I push out with my energy toward him in search of his soul. But Alan has already moved on. His body is just a shell.

That's disappointing. But I continue to float my energy across Alan's body. I've already been rewarded with the scent of his fear. Possibly there is some other residual emotional energy he left behind for me—something useful to clue me into who killed him.

I'm cast into pitch darkness, and I recoil as I lose my sight. A solitary scream echoes loudly through my mind, and I cover my ears with no improvement.

"April?"

I come back to the present, and Jacob comes into focus as my eyesight returns. "Oh, sorry."

Doc lets another ghoulish cackle escape that makes the hair on the back of my neck stand up. "Maybe I should give you some of that iodine rub to use for aftershave there, Jacob. It almost made her pass out with desire."

"That's all right, I'll pass, Doc."

The little old man gives a quick shrug. "The girl likes what she likes."

"I appreciate you taking the time to show us, Doc. We need to push off and get back to work."

"My pleasure, Jacob." Doc lifts the body that outweighs him by sixty pounds from the autopsy table onto a stainless-steel gurney as if lifting a small bag of dog food. "You tell your Nana this old man sure could use a taste of cherry pie if she ever gets the mind to visit me."

I barely contain a laugh as Jacob turns red. "I'll let her know you said hi."

Chapter 40

I see Chase on the back porch grilling as I pull into my parents' driveway. Grilling is only second to fishing on his list of favorite activities.

The heavenly scent of barbecue wafts in the late evening air as I open the door to my Prius. My mouth begins to water. Didn't I just eat?

No. I can't visit him and bum a plate. Not with a full night's work ahead of me. There is no time to socialize no matter how delicious the grill smells.

I'll sneak down the path toward the boathouse. He is too intent on the grill to notice me.

Taking care to be silent, I ease my car door shut. It groans as I close it.

"Hey, April, have you eaten yet?" Chase is watching me across the drive.

"I had a late lunch." I ignore my complaining stomach. "I can run to get me something a little later if I get hungry."

"Don't be silly. It's just Dusty and me. Besides, you know the grocery store makes you buy an eight-pack to get the chicken breast with the ribs still in them."

That changes the complexion of the situation. I'd hate for my brother's to be inconvenienced by a bunch of leftover chicken. How can I refuse to help?

Yes, I have a tremendous amount of newfound information, of the psychic sort, to process about Charlotte's case. I also know my mind will wander back to the heavenly smell of barbecue. "What's the occasion?"

"Mom and Dad are having a date night." He grins over his shoulder. "Some traditions are too good to let die. There is beer in the cooler if you want one."

I grab a beer from the cooler and pull up one of the lawn chairs. I watch my handsome brother as he works the grill like it's a grand piano. The glass door slides open, and Dusty comes out with an eight-cup glass bowl.

"Hey, hey. Look what the cat drug up onto the porch."

"She was skulking in the shadows."

My face heats up. "I wasn't skulking. Plus, I don't even know what that means, Chase."

He laughs. "No, but if I have to guess, it's what you were doing."

Dusty set the bowl on the wooden table we use for outdoor meals. "Probably afraid she'll have to cook dessert. That is your specialty, isn't it?"

"What's that stuff she cooked all the time?"

"Rice Krispies Treats," I grumble.

Chase shakes his grilling fork at me. "That was it. I probably haven't had those in seven years."

"It's not like they are tough to make," Dusty says.

"Well, she didn't leave me the recipe. How am I supposed to know what goes in them?" Chase asks.

"Only on every box of Rice Krispies ever made, Chase."

"I'm not much of a cereal man."

Dusty shakes his head and walks back into the kitchen. I try to cover my laugh by taking another sip of my beer.

A bittersweet sadness flows over me as I realize the date night cooking sessions didn't end with my departure. My brothers simply carried on their tradition minus the dessert. Chase has always taken care of the grill, tonight barbecue chicken breast bone-in. Dusty takes care of the sides. Tonight, potato salad, baked beans, and fried okra.

I remember asking them when I was younger what I could do to participate. They suggested dessert. Mama showed me how to make Rice Krispies Treats, I was eleven at the time. That is the apex of my culinary accomplishments. I haven't progressed much further.

I now realize how important this tradition is to keep their relationship strong and healthy. Sure, my brothers love each other fiercely. But there is no denying they are as opposite as two men can be in most respects.

There is some magic family glue that comes from cooking a meal together and sharing your labors of love. It confirms both, you are equals and valued family. For the first time in years, I have the itch to make some Rice Krispies Treats.

"Dusty, how did the blessing of the hotel go?"

He stops his fork in the air. "Good, it was sort of odd."

"How?"

He pulls apart his chicken breast with a fork. "Real quiet, given all the disturbances we experienced. Too quiet. But it's done."

"Liza?"

He rolls his eyes. "Liza's too tough to be down for long. The nurses were more than happy to get her out of their hair the next day. I dropped her off at her house earlier this morning."

I'm glad to hear she feels better. Liza, and I will never see eye to eye or be BFFs, but I do respect her mad skills of manifestation and psychic prowess.

Plus, I would be dead if not for her protection from the ghost of Les Blair.

"I'm glad to hear that," I say.

"It's one of the prerequisites of a successful trip. Everybody comes home in one piece, and we get some good material. This trip was a raving success."

"That's wonderful, Dusty." My secret desire is our trip to Paducah has given Dusty enough material to finish his book. If he decides to take a yearlong sabbatical now, I'm good with it.

I'm in no hurry to go on another ghost hunt excursion.

"Almost forgot." He wipes the barbecue sauce from his fingers and pulls an envelope from his back-jean pocket. "Your pay for last weekend."

Awesome. I'm going to open this and want to go every weekend. "Thank you." I take the envelope from him and the check inside even feels heavy. My imagination is getting the best of me.

"My pleasure. I think we'll have another trip in a month. I'll give you the schedule so you and Uncle Howard can work out the dates."

I'm positive this is how I get sucked back into my small town. I make a little money, enjoy a few dinners with pleasant company, and get a work routine that is livable for me. Next thing I know, I'm fifty years old and wondering what happened to my dreams. That reminds me. "Hey, Chase. Guess who I ran into today?"

Chase licks barbecue sauce from his fingers while wrinkling his face in thought. "Jackie Rains."

"No! Why would you even say that?" I can't believe he would even mention my former best friend turned nemesis.

"You said guess."

Man, he can be stupid at times. "Barbara."

"Oh, how is she?" His expression loses some of its joy.

"She is fine. As pretty and nice as ever. She works at Rex's as a waitress."

Chase becomes more interested in his okra. "I told her she needs to quit that job."

"Whatever happened to you two anyway?" My jaw drops as soon as I hear myself. I want to grab the knife off the picnic table and stab my hand a couple of times.

Dusty squints his eyes at me while shaking his head, acknowledging my lousy play.

Chase turns, pulls another beer from the cooler, and twists the cap. "Don't know, maybe she can tell you."

I'm the worst about asking the question everyone else

knows to leave alone. The awkward silence goes on for what seems an eternity, and I feel awful I've ruined the festive mood for my brothers.

I fear in the future they'll pretend not to notice me when I come home and not extend an invitation to their sibling dinners. I couldn't blame them if they did. The thought makes me sad. I'll have to make some extra special Rice Krispies Treats next time. If there is a next time.

During my time away, I've forgotten my family more than anything is built on a code of acceptance. Each of us is a little odd in our own way. Our oddities are accepted, and many times celebrated.

I'm known for blurting things before thinking about what I'm saying. It's not precisely an endearing quality.

Thankfully, after a few minutes of silence, my faux pas is forgiven. My brother's share details about their days—Chase about the latest happenings at the marina and Dusty about a discussion he had with his publisher.

"Has Uncle Howard got you doing any ambulance chasing yet?" Chase asks.

"No, but he may be skirt-chasing the best I can tell. That's why he is still down in Mobile."

Chase nearly knocks over his beer. "Uncle Howard is shacked up with somebody down in Mobile?"

"Yeah, he left me to take care of the entire office while I'm getting ready for the grand jury Wednesday."

"You're not jealous much, are you?" Dusty smirks.

"Well, it's just pretty irresponsible, considering this is my first case."

"No. It's only irresponsible if he doesn't wear protection." Both my brothers roll with laughter.

"Eww. Thanks for the bad visuals, Chase."

"You started it."

I try not to crack a smile while I watch their laughter die down. It's incredible how much can change in seven years and how much can stay the same. They're bigger, more experienced, and a lot hairier than they were when we were kids, but mostly my brothers are the same two goofballs.

"Tell me what information you found that you're gonna use to get Charlotte off with." Chase eyes me over the lip of his beer.

Good question. "You know I can't talk about a case. It's a homicide."

Chase blows a raspberry. "Who are we gonna tell?"

"Like everybody. You two have a bigger social network and talk more than anyone I know."

"I resemble that remark. But we wouldn't put your career at risk." Dusty jerks his bearded chin into the air. "Go ahead, play like we're the judge."

"Yeah, Judge Snow. I mean Snows," Chase kicks in.

Of course, I know better. But it isn't fair since my brothers ganged up on me. I don't think it's ever in doubt I would share the gory details with them. "We learned today that the nail gun was not the murder weapon."

Chase's face contorts. "Ouch, I always assumed he'd been shot in the head with a gun. Not nailed."

"We need to keep some stuff out of the paper just in case they find out Charlotte isn't the murderer."

Dusty makes a clicking noise with his tongue. "So how does that clear Charlotte?"

"I'm not sure it does. It highlights that not everything is so cut and dry."

My brothers' stares change. Their eyes are open, but I can tell they're far back in the recesses of their minds, turning the facts over.

"Why was the prosecutor so sure Charlotte killed Alan?" Dusty asks.

"The police had been out to their house several times for domestic disputes."

Chase snorts. "Heck, I know a bunch of people the Po-Po visit every Friday night to break up arguments after the boys come home from the bar and have drunk the grocery money for the week. It always puts a bad spin on the weekend, but it doesn't prove anybody killed anyone."

"There was also a fifty-thousand-dollar accidental life insurance policy."

"It would cost you half that to get a decent hitman for the job." Chase and I both turn and stare at Dusty. He shrugs. "I mean, that's what I've heard."

I think I'll table Dusty's response for a conversation later. Especially considering he has someone he wishes would disappear.

"I guess I agree with Dusty. Not about the hitman thing. But I think fifty-thousand-dollars will buy a nice boat, but I'd have to balance that against the possibility of getting caught and spending the rest of my life in jail." Chase turns both hands palm up and makes an up-and-down motion with them. "Fast bass boat, life in prison? Yeah, that's not enough money to make me move on it."

"That's what I keep telling everybody. A mother of four would never kill her husband over fifty-thousand dollars."

"So other than her, who's the most likely suspect?" Dusty leans in closer.

I feel the anxiety building in the pit of my stomach. Being objective, it's easy to see why the police feel Charlotte is the perpetrator. "I don't know."

"There has to be somebody. April, a jury is not gonna just let the most likely person walk unless you give them another plausible suspect. Did Charlotte not suggest anybody?"

"No." My voice sounds like a three-year-old whining. "Everybody I talked to said he had been wild in his younger days but had settled down into his career as a carpenter."

"It must've been some kind of random killing. Probably an occult sacrifice. Except instead of a knife to the heart, it's a nail to the forehead."

Chase looks serious. That makes his comment even more disturbing. "Why would you even say that?"

"That's what happens on TV. Anytime the Po-Po tries to make somebody fit the crime, and it feels like a square peg in a round hole, it always ends up being something random like an occult killing. It takes them an hour to tell you what they could've told you in fifteen minutes, but all the same, if Charlotte feels like a square peg to you, you probably have a random killing. You already said you don't have a murder weapon. I'd be checking his wrist and ankles for strap marks. I bet he has them where he was held down while they drove the nail into his head. Poor fella. That must have been rough."

Note to self. Don't share case information with your brothers, not because you're worried about them telling other people but because you can't handle the stupid theories.

Dusty shakes his head. "I don't think there are any occults in Guntersville, Chase."

His jaw drops open momentarily. "Seriously? Our own nana is a witch."

"That's different, Chase."

"Oh, right because she is Dorothy, the good witch."

"Dorothy wasn't a witch. Besides, what Dusty is trying to say is just because there are witches, it doesn't mean there is an occult sacrifice going on."

Chase raises his eyebrows. "Potato, tomato, they're first cousins to one another."

Neither Dusty nor I have a comment for that.

Chapter 41

I stay up until one in the morning, going over my notes. Maybe I didn't press Charlotte hard enough for alternate suspects. Perhaps I need to dig deeper into Alan's business acquaintances as well. Somebody had it out for him. Enough so they'd want to drive a nail into his forehead.

But that leads me back to Charlotte. If the nail gun is not the weapon, and somebody had it out for Alan, why hide his body under the house? Why not roll him into a ditch? Or dump him into the lake? Maybe they were trying to scare Charlotte and the kids.

Nah. If that were their goal, they'd have hung him up at the front door or something, not hidden him under the house where it took a few days to find him.

Then there is the nail. What was with the odd length compared to the nails at the house? Did the killer bring their own nail and then remove it? Did Charlotte?

I let out a scream of frustration. It makes me feel a little calmer even though my vocal cords now feel like a flame has scorched them. Why, oh why, can I not figure this out? There must be a simple explanation if Charlotte didn't do it.

Flipping open my calendar, I jot down that in the morning, I'll need to speak with Charlotte again. I circle Friday when Shane comes to town for the tournament and underline my

Sunday trip to Paducah.

After sitting motionless for a moment, I send Howard a text reminding him I'll be off Monday and ask him when he plans to return. If he plans on coming home.

I turn off the lights and slip under the covers. The tap, tap noise against the bottom of the boathouse keeps me awake. An unreasonable fear of camel crickets jumping on me from out of the darkness pervades my thoughts.

The next morning, I bring a sausage and egg biscuit and a coffee into the jail for Charlotte. Typically, they don't allow food items, but I'm feeling lucky. As it turns out, Jade Woodson is now a security guard at the jail. Her brother Javaris and Chase played baseball together in high school. We catch up for a few minutes, and she takes me to see Charlotte without questioning the food.

Charlotte has puffed up like a balloon over the last few days. The bags under her eyes look more like black pillows, and her coloring is a pasty gray. If she looks like this after only a few days, I can only imagine what an extended sentence would do to her.

"Are my babies all right? I haven't heard from Rachel in two days now."

I'm such a loser. It never occurred to me to check in on Charlotte's children. Wait, is that even in my job description? No, but it falls under the heading of being a decent human being. "No, but I'll see what I can find out for you."

She stares down at her hands and goes mute. She is physically present, but her mind appears far away. Or wherever her babies are.

"Charlotte, we have to talk." She doesn't look up from her hands. "Charlotte, I need your help. You must tell me who might have wanted Alan dead. I don't care how unlikely it is, we have to identify somebody besides you."

"Doesn't matter now." Her whisper is barely audible.

"What do you mean, it doesn't matter? Of course, it matters."

She looks up from her hands, and tears roll down her cheeks. "They already have their minds made up. I don't necessarily blame them. I understand what they think about our past issues. The truth is, I can't think of anybody who would want to hurt him. That includes me."

I'm not getting through to her. A sick feeling overcomes me as I realize I can handle many things, except for someone giving up hope. "Charlotte, stay with me here. I need you to give me the names of some people to talk to."

"The police done talked to all of them. They have alibis. I don't because I lived with a man I loved, and I have four kids who take up all my time. I never had a reason to go carousing at all hours of the night, where everybody remembers seeing me. No, I was just at home, and the only person who can back me up on that is dead."

"Charlotte, believe me, I get it. But we need new names. Anybody, anything that can shed new light on this."

Her lifeless eyes level with mine. She shakes her head slowly back and forth.

"Charlotte, think of your babies. For your babies' sake."

"I am thinking of my babies. Rachel and her husband have a nice house. He makes good money. What am I supposed to do to raise my babies now?" A clear stream of snot runs from her right nostril.

Charlotte's comment is a gut-shot to my attitude. Even if we win the case and keep her out of jail, she now believes her babies are better off without her. The situation is more than I can bear. I reach out and put my hands over hers. She doesn't move, but her tears increase exponentially. I must get out of here before I break down and begin to cry too. "Okay, Charlotte. I'll see you tomorrow in court, okay."

I wait, hoping for a response that never comes. I pat her hands and leave the room.

As I walk out to my car, the fatigue from being up all night hits me full force, and I feel I need a nap. I admonish myself for worrying about phantom camel crickets jumping on my face. Still, the thought of the spooky insect makes my skin crawl, and I give an involuntary shudder of disgust.

Chapter 42

Lane waits in his car in front of Snow and Associates. He waves as I pull into a parking space. I open my door to get out of my car, and it comes to me in a panicked rush. Bless it, I forgot about Brad Mathis, my oversexed, little punk convenience store robber.

"You run this place like your Howard. I always told him he should've been a banker."

"I was meeting with Charlotte King, clearing up some last-minute details."

"Right."

My back is to Lane as I unlock the front door, but I can sense his frustration. I glance over my shoulder. "What?"

"I didn't say a thing."

"You thought about it."

He follows me in. "Last I checked, that's inadmissible."

I toss my keys on my desk and move toward the coffee machine. "It would be a lot easier if Howard just gave you a spare key. Then you could start the coffee for us. Do you want one?"

"I'd love that, but this isn't a social call. I talked to Judge Rossi, and she agrees we need to offer Brad Mathis five years' probation."

I nearly drop the coffee urn. "For armed robbery? He brandished a gun in the clerk's face, and he is only getting five years' probation?"

"Fake gun," Lane corrects me.

"She didn't know it was fake!" I can feel my crazy pulling at its chains. Lord help us if it breaks free this early in the morning.

"But it was, and he ended up inadvertently paying for what he took. I know it sucks, but the judge agrees with me. It's a fifty-fifty chance we'd have a juror who would vote to acquit and hang the jury. If he accepts five years' probation, it's just a matter of time before he makes another boneheaded decision. Then we'll add the five years to whatever his new crime is."

"If he doesn't hurt somebody next time."

Lane presses his lips together tightly. "There is always that. There is also the chance he walks free if it goes to trial. At least this way we're able to track him."

All I can think presently is thank goodness I'm not a parole officer. I can't imagine having that misogynistic little jerk reporting to me regularly for five years. It doesn't seem right there is actual footage of Brad committing his crime, but he will only get probation when nobody has any evidence on Charlotte. Yet, she is liable to be convicted of murdering her husband.

"Do you think you can convince him to take the deal?"

"He'd be stupid not to." I think about that as soon as I say it. That's sort of the crux of the issue. Brad has shown he is not particularly bright. "I'll do my best to convince him."

Lane's expression brightens with a smile. "Excellent. I have more than I can say grace over without that wildcard."

Lane appears to be debating whether to leave or not. "You're still committed to seeing the King case through the trial?"

"I don't know. Do you have a better deal to offer than the last one?"

I see I've caught him off guard, and he chuckles. "After you and your client have forced me to prepare for the grand jury, the last offer isn't even on the table anymore."

"That's your last chance of keeping her in jail. Judge Rossi will be releasing her tomorrow."

"Is that so?" His grin reveals his perfect white teeth. "Well, if you'd be so kind, please point me in the direction of the real killer. We hate for empty jail cells to go to waste. We try to maximize the taxpayer money."

"It's a poor use of taxpayer money to hold an innocent woman too."

Lane sobers, then nods his head. "That would be true. I do wish you and Ms. King the best of luck tomorrow."

Chapter 43

What wonderful news. I just returned from the jail, and now I must return to convince Brad to accept the plea deal. I don't know how I'm supposed to cover the office and take care of our clients. Not that the phones are ringing, or anybody is at the law office, but if there were.

Since I'm not having fun, I think I'll ruin Howard's day too. I mentally load the double-barrel shotgun with double aught buckshot and rack it in my mind. I'm gonna blast him with both barrels.

Howard's phone only rings twice before he answers. "Oh April, that's the most fun I've had in twenty years. I am so thankful I had you there to watch my business while I was visiting my friend in Mobile. I know it's only temporary, but having your help at the office has allowed me to do things I have wanted to do for an awfully long time."

Well, how the heck can I argue with that? Here I'm locked and loaded for bear, and Winnie the Pooh shows up offering me a jar of honey. "My pleasure, Howard. I just want to check and make sure you're okay."

"I am better than okay. I am absolutely splendid!"

I can almost smell the pheromones through the phone. "Good, well I was curious when you would be back. You know I have the grand jury tomorrow."

"Absolutely. I'm on the road right now, and I should be home late this evening, probably around midnight."

"All right then. You be careful coming home."

"Sure thing, April. Hey and April?"

"Yes, sir?"

"I really mean it. You covering the office for me these last three days is the nicest thing anybody's done for me in twenty years."

"No trouble at all, Howard. I'll see you tomorrow morning." As I disconnect, I can't help but think how bad I want to hit somebody. Suddenly it seems like a perfect time to go have a discussion with Brad Mathis.

Chapter 44

"Girl, I need to get you an all-day pass."

Despite the growing hostility I feel due to my circumstances, I laugh at Jade's jest. Part because it's humorous, and part because Jade outweighs me by a good hundred pounds and could easily crush me like a bug.

"When business is good, business is good," I say.

"Business is always good in this city. Too many crazy people."

There is a lot more truth to that statement than most citizens of Guntersville will ever admit to an outsider. But extended family to extended family, we know almost everybody in Guntersville has a healthy helping of crazy in their blood. Some of us are just able to hide it better than others.

Jade opens the interrogation room for me and informs me it will be just a minute for Brad. I clear out old emails while I wait.

The door opens, and Brad appears with Jade behind him. He wears a sweat-covered sleeveless shirt. He rubs his left hand over his right bicep. "I hope my guns won't be too distracting for you. I was working out with the rest of the boys in the yard."

"I'll try to contain myself."

"Boy, shut your mouth." Jade sits him down and chains his cuffs to the table. "Mind your manners like your mama taught

FOOLISH ASPIRATIONS; APRIL MAY SNOW PSYCHIC MYSTERY NOVEL #1

you some."

"Yes, ma'am," he favors Jade, an amused smile.

Jade rolls her eyes as she leaves the room. The door clicks shut.

He gives me his now-familiar lazy smile. "You just couldn't stay away, could you, Blondie?"

"Right, that's it." I open my planner. "I came to inform you that you won the lottery."

"Excellent. My baby's mama will be thrilled she has some child-support coming her way."

Man, this guy is such a winner. "Unfortunately for her, not that kind of lottery. The prosecutor has altered the plea bargain. Actually, they sweetened it considerably for you, given the circumstances."

"Considering I didn't do anything?"

Geez. Please, Lord, keep me from slapping him. I don't want to be disbarred over this slime bucket. "Yes. Considering you were so inept, you didn't actually earn anything off the deal."

"Inept. Are you calling me stupid?"

Somehow, I manage to keep a snarky smirk from flashing across my face. "No, I'm calling you inept. And in this case, lucky. The prosecutor has a couple other pending cases of higher priority and has decided to offer you five years of probation."

Brad slides lower in his chair. "I don't know, five years sounds like an awfully long time."

"Dude, five years of reporting into a parole officer, is nothing compared to twenty years in a maximum-security prison. Don't look a gift horse in the mouth. Take the deal."

His facial features pinch with confusion when I say gift horse. He stays silent for a moment. He studies his hands before he speaks.

"Do you really think it's the best deal we can get?"

Now I'm suddenly his confidant and resource. I seriously need to throttle him. "It's far better than we could've hoped for. Plus, if this goes to the jury, it's always like rolling the dice. You never know what's going to come up."

That he appears to understand. "Okay. Tell them we'll take the deal."

I'm momentarily shocked. This has gone much easier than I anticipated. I gather my backpack as I stand to leave.

"Hey, April. I mean Ms. Snow. Thank you. I wouldn't have known what to do without your help."

"Just doing my job Mr. Mathis." Releasing the world's stupidest criminals back onto the street of Guntersville. "Please try to stay on the right side of the law. Remember, if you do anything to break your parole, it becomes a five-year prison sentence immediately."

"Yes, ma'am. But you don't have to worry about me. I'm good."

Yeah, I wasn't exactly worried about Brad. It's the rest of Guntersville I'm concerned for.

Chapter 45

I sit in my car for fifteen minutes, debating if I'm going to cry or not. I can't believe how screwy the justice system is to release Brad but be bent on sending Charlotte away from her kids until they are adults. I also can't believe they put the woman's life in the hands of a rookie attorney. One who doesn't have a clue what she is doing much less a coherent defense probable of freeing her client.

Seeing the defeat in Charlotte's eyes this morning has undone me. Hearing her justify how her children will be better with her sister-in-law just because of money breaks my heart.

I've played my best cards already. Even my "gifts" failed to reveal anything to help. The game is ending, and it's time to play the last card I hold. A real deuce, but a two of clubs is better than no card left to play.

I drive back out to the King's home. This time, without Jacob's energy field, I hope I might be able to pick up on the family's residual energy a little easier.

The window I unlocked during my prior visit to the girl's bedroom allows me access. The house is hot and stale from baking in the high afternoon sun with no air conditioning. I make my way to the master bedroom as that was the only strong residual energy forces left of Alan other than his workshop.

Standing in the center of the room, I marshal all the energy around me and push out forcefully. I locate Alan's frequency again. Brilliant flashes of color change behind my eyelids. Yellows, oranges, royal blues, and soothing browns. His voice bubbles up from the floor. He has a forceful, steady voice. I can understand how men like Jacob would take to his voice. Even the moments of anger that remain in the room have a sarcastic tone of disbelief to them. Hardly a hint of contempt or cruelty exists.

There is one overriding emotion in the electrical impulses that remain. It's what convinces me Charlotte did not, could not have killed Alan.

What overpowers all else is a desperate electric current of passionate love for his wife. I'm sure he failed to display it correctly at times, given the domestic dispute calls. But it's there nonetheless, and I'm sure Charlotte has always been aware of his true feelings.

I understand how Charlotte, armed with the knowledge of her husband's passionate love for her, might overlook his shortcoming. She might consider them sharp edges meant to be filed and smoothed by her love over time like the river over a stone.

She would never kill a man who loved her that completely. Charlotte might swing an occasional skillet to knock a rough edge off his hard head but would never consider offing him.

It is essential knowledge. But I'd never be able to explain it to a judge without revealing my "gifts" and being committed to a psychiatric ward. I need concrete proof that the ordinary world can understand.

I scratch my arms mindlessly as the night vision of camel crickets hopping on my face afflicts me once again. Believe me, when I say, nobody can ever doubt my dedication to getting Charlotte cleared from the charges. I cringe as I try to steel myself for what must be done; the real reason I made the trip to the King home.

I venture out the back door. Crawling under the house is the last thing I want to do. But the only clue left unexamined that I can imagine is in there.

Removing the metal plate from the crawlspace, I nearly gag. The maggots have multiplied from the day before, and I fight the impulse to turn and leave. I direct my phone's light to the back of the house, but it's not as bright as Jacob's flashlight was the other day.

The crawlspace is tall enough for me to hunch over, throw my left leg in before I pull my right one in, finishing in a squatting position. I duck walk ten feet toward the back of the house before I'm forced to go the rest the way on my hands and knees. I move forward a few feet then flash my light forward. The metallic reflection of the pipe wrench makes me grin.

It's been an abstract dream. One that lingers with me longer than the familiar ones because my mind is trying to comprehend what I'm looking at. More importantly, its meaning, if anything.

The pipe wrench has played over and over in my dreams. In the vision, the wrench falls a short distance and then bounces. The entire sequence is always in slow motion. I have memorized it. The wrench turns head down, bounces once off the ground, rotates in the air, falls flat with its handle toward me on the plastic lining of the crawlspace.

The significance of it all? I haven't a clue. But I hold hope I'll be able to ascertain the importance of the vision as soon as I touch the metal tool. Metal always holds residual energy better than other materials.

My joy of seeing the wrench is short-lived as the bottom of the house floor pushes me closer and closer to the ground until I'm army crawling. With fifteen feet left to go to the wrench, I bump the top of my head against one of the floor beams. It's not what I want to do, but I resolve I'll need to lay on my back and wiggle the remainder of the way to the wrench.

As I work my way to the wrench on my back, anxiety eats away at my resolve. I'm painfully aware of how small of an area my body is now confined in and how limited my response would be if I were to meet something unexpected.

Granny Snow always says you get what you think about the most. I'm struggling to force any thoughts of ghosts or demons from my head. There is still no sign of Alan, so I pray he doesn't decide to reveal himself to me until I am out from under his home.

I twist my head around to locate the wrench. I continue sliding on the plastic liner until the wrench is at my shoulder. In triumph, I cross my body with my left hand and pull the wrench to me.

It is Alan's. I'd know it even if it weren't marked AK with a permanent marker. I can also feel it's Alan's least favorite. He despises this tool. Is that why he left it under the house?

No. Guys don't abandon tools on purpose.

I push with my feet until I clear the next beam to see if I can determine what he might have been repairing. A PVC plumbing elbow is concealed just on the other side of the thick wood stud. I can feel the back of my T-shirt absorb the moisture from the slow leak. The best I can tell I'm directly under the kitchen.

Okay. I've established Alan attempted to fix a clogged sewer line. And this tells me? Nothing. Yet, for some reason, it seems significant and incredibly important to the case.

I'm running out of time. If there was ever a moment where I need my talent to manifest into something useful, it's now. I close my eyes, slow my breathing, and draw all available energy to me. Slowly and deliberately, I push out with my mind in hopes of gleaning some information.

All I sense is darkness. Then I smell that funny metallic sweat I detected on the earlier visit. The spiked fear sweat I smelled on Alan's corpse. I concentrate as hard as I can on that one characteristic scent in search of an answer to what scared Alan.

I open my eyes in frustration. By the blue light of my phone, I barely identify the little booger before it drops onto my face. I scream as I sit up to make my escape.

Chapter 46

I wake with a start and almost sit up and brain myself a second time on the floor beam. Slowly I remember where I am and fight to calm my spidey-senses, or in this case camel cricket.

I rub vigorously the area on my cheek, the nasty little dude used as a landing pad earlier. I hate those strange little bugs. They always show up at the most inopportune time.

If they'd act like spiders and snakes and leave me alone if I don't bother them, it would be one thing. But camel crickets have the unnerving habit of jumping at me. I don't care for things with antenna and hairy legs jumping at me.

My hand finds the welt on my forehead. At least it's pushing out. Good for brain swelling, not so good for public appearances in court in the morning. I grab my phone to check how long I've been out. It's only been a few minutes.

Besides a new conversation icebreaker imprinted across my forehead, I have absolutely zilch for my effort today.

I rotate my head to see if I can locate my four-legged nemesis. I must have sufficiently scared him by trying to kill myself. He is nowhere to be found.

There is an odd block of wood attached to one of the floor joists the best I can tell it's there to act as a support spacer between the beam and the drainage elbow. The southern engineering is not what draws my attention. Whoever attached the two by four block used the wrong length of nails. The nails protrude through the lumber by a couple of inches. Three of the nails are brass colored. The fourth on the bottom and closest to me is the color of iron ore.

I reach up and gently touch the tip of the ore-colored nail with my fingertip. Intense fear rips through my body, and I begin to sweat profusely. The high tang sweat scent, not mine, permeates my sense of smell again—Alan's sweat.

Now I know, Alan was a fearless man. But at that moment, he knew he was in imminent danger. His body responded by dumping a motherlode of chemical cocktails into his bloodstream.

My nose twitches, and it becomes difficult to breathe. I try not to think about it. I know if I think about it too much, I'll become a sobbing wreck.

Alan wasn't a plumber, and he didn't like to do plumbing. Even so, he had been under the house trying to fix something for his family. Something broke his attention. My money is on the kamikaze camel cricket, and he inadvertently pierced his head with two inches of a nail. Mortally wounded and afraid, he struggled to get out from under the house. Before he could, he lost consciousness and died.

I know this to be fact. I read it off the nail. For the rest of the world to understand, I'll need more conventional proof. I wiggle my way back toward the exit until I can crawl. Once free of the darkness, I dial Jacob's phone number I'd saved.

"Hello?"

"Jacob, it's April. Where are you right now?"

"Well, if you have to know, mom."

"Funny."

"I'm on duty. I just left the marina. Why?"

"Can you come over to the King's place?"

He hesitates. "I suppose."

"It's important. I found something that'll exonerate Charlotte."

"Now, April."

The aggravation in his tone doesn't anger me. I understand it because I was there too just before the camel cricket made me knock myself out. "Let me ask you a question, Jacob."

"Sure."

"When you found Alan, you only looked into the crawlspace because the plate was missing."

He is silent for so long I think he might not answer.

"You couldn't have known that April."

"It bothered you that it was open. This whole time that's been eating at you."

"Well, yeah. The premise is Alan was under the house because Charlotte was hiding him. It didn't make much sense that she left the cover off. Then I got to thinking about it, and a lot of women have trouble putting those covers back on. So, I just assumed she couldn't get it fixed right."

I might not be able to figure out how to put the cover back on correctly. But Charlotte had enough country in her I'm sure she could've if she needed to. I let his sexist opinion slide. "What if it were open because Alan was under the house repairing something. What if he injured himself severely while he was under the house?"

"Do you have proof?" His tone is excited.

"I believe so. We'll want Doc Crowder to confirm for us."

"Let me call this into dispatch. I'll call Doc as well to let him know we're coming over."

"Hey, bring one of those thingy cutters too."

"The what?"

Dang, I can't remember what they're called. "We'll need it to cut a nail."

Jacob's deep laugh reverberates from the phone, tickling me right below my navel. "I think I have one of those thingy cutters in my trunk. I'll see you in ten minutes, April."

Chapter 47

Jacob does not share the same reservations as me about getting under the house. I'm barely able to explain to him where to find the drain elbow before he starts into the crawlspace. I watch in awe as he works his way to the wrench.

He pauses with his light trained, where I know the block of wood is attached to the beam, then pulls a tool from his shirt and works on the board.

"I've got it," he grunts.

"Got what?"

"The nail," he says as he rolls over and begins to crawl out. "You need to come with me to Doc Crowder's."

"I do?"

He holds a plastic bag toward me that contains half a nail. "Your find. Plus, I think it might be the missing part of the puzzle."

He turns and starts around the house. I have no choice but to follow him.

My adrenaline is pumping as we get to his squad car. I'm getting used to riding shotgun in a police car. I have to say it beats riding in the back. A firsthand experience I had compliment of the Pensacola police department a few months back. I won't be sharing that story with Jacob.

I admire Jacob's attitude. From my "gifts" I already know the nail he has in the plastic bag is the nail that killed Alan. Jacob won't know that conclusively until Doc Crowder confirms the blood is Alan's. To him, it is still a maybe. A maybe that could prove his initial crime scene determination incorrect. Yet, that doesn't slow his quest for the truth.

His energy and emotions grow as we speed down the curvy dirt road toward the laboratory. Bright beams of joy shine off him. Without trying, I read his excitement over the prospects of clearing Charlotte of her husband's murder.

Doc Crowder is sitting in a tall white rocking chair on his front porch. Bubbles rises from a nap at his side. The dog walks out to greet Jacob, her butt wagging, as Jacob approaches the house. I lag behind Jacob in case Bubbles hasn't eaten dinner yet.

"Don't keep me in suspense. Let me see it," Doc says as he pushes up from the rocker.

Stepping onto the porch, Jacob holds the baggy up. Doc takes it from him and turns it over slowly as he inspects it.

"We'll double-check it inside, but the blood coat looks to be exactly an inch and a half." Doc's small mouth turns upward. "You may figure this mystery out yet, young man."

"April did." Jacob motions over his shoulder. "She went out to the King house by herself and found it."

"That is some fine detective work, young lady." Doc winces as he focuses on my forehead. "Did someone whack you with a baseball bat?"

My hand goes instinctively to my forehead. It's incredibly sore, and the pressure stings. "I had a spatial disagreement with a camel cricket."

Doc shudders. "Creepy little boogers. Always jumping unnaturally. They practically dare you to kill them."

"I know, right."

He appears to shift into more profound thought as he takes

another look at the nail in the baggy. "DNA can take up to eight weeks, Jacob."

Inadvertently I gasp, "Oh Doc, we don't have eight weeks. I need to know something in the morning."

He bites his lower lip. "You know, we may not need a DNA test right off. If I can determine the blood type on the nail and match it to Alan, that might be sufficient from a probability standpoint considering where it was located."

"You can do that? I mean tonight?"

"You bet I can. I'll do you one better too, Alan was AB negative. The chances on someone with that blood type other than Alan being under the house would be one heck of a coincidence."

Doc gestures for us to follow him into the house. Jacob and I follow him to the elevator when Doc points in the opposite direction. "You two get some ice out of the freezer and put it on her forehead before that horn grows."

I checked my bump in the mirror on Jacob's car visor when we left the Kings'. I didn't think it looked that bad.

Jacob leads me into a kitchen and pulls out a drawer that holds dishtowels. He dumps two handfuls of ice into the towel and folds the ends over to form a compress. "I'm sorry—I should have thought of this earlier. I guess the discovery of a possible out for Charlotte has me a little excited," he says as he puts the compress in my hand.

I press the ice to my forehead and wince. The pressure hurts, and I pull it away before trying again much gentler.

"You're going to want to keep that on it."

"Has the bump gotten bigger or something."

He grins, and I know at first he doesn't want to tell me. "Let's just say I keep thinking I need to step back because I don't know how much more it's going to grow."

That's embarrassing. "I don't think I like you."

"Story of my life with pretty women." He laughs as he leads the way out of the kitchen.

His laugh tickles something inside me again. Did Jacob just

say I was pretty? I trail after him with the compress to my forehead.

We ride down the elevator in silence. I'm trying to confirm if I heard Jacob right or if I imagined his comment. Maybe he meant other women?

Doc looks up from a microscope as we enter the lab. His eyes go to my head, and he smiles.

"I was right. The blood coating the nail tip is the exact depth of the puncture of Alan's skull," Doc says.

"So that's it, right?" Jacob asks.

"Should be. It will be a heck of a coincidence if it's not. But —" Doc points to a machine on the counter. "The blood analysis will be done soon. That will take it from a highly likely it's Alan to a definitive yes."

I get antsy waiting on the machine to finish its analysis. After the last trip to Doc's, I know to put up a sturdy barricade in my mind in case a Chatty Cathy spirit notices I can hear them.

It's comforting to know I can shut the door on the voices whenever I want to concentrate on blocking them out. What would be more useful, especially when working with Dusty, is if I could select with which ones I block. If I could block out all the voices except for the ones I conjure, that would be helpful.

I make a tiny hole, a doorway, in the barricade around my mind and push out for Alan. He wasn't here the other night. His body was just a shell, so my expectations are low. Still, I focus on him.

The bright colors and passion-filled visions I experienced in my mind's eye at his workshop the other night are gone. Despite me standing next to Alan's body, gone too is the tangy scent of sweat that had been present under the King home.

Either the barricade I formed is too formidable for him to pierce even with the doorway I created, or he has indeed moved on. As I open my eyes back to the harsh LED lighting in the laboratory, I almost miss it. It's so quiet it sounds like damp summer wind through a pine bough.

"Thank you."

I'm paralyzed. My heart aches as my eyes water. "You're welcome." I push out toward the voice as hard as I dare. I wait. I relax and wait some more. Nothing.

Now I know Alan is gone.

"Winner, winner, chicken dinner!"

Doc's exclamation pulls me back to the living.

"AB negative as if there were any doubt."

"Thank goodness. So, Alan wasn't murdered." It isn't a question from Jacob.

"Just an unfortunate accident," Doc agrees.

"Unless we can bring manslaughter charges against the camel cricket," I grumble.

Jacob turns to me, his eyes soften. "Why so sad? You just got your girl a get out of jail card."

I don't know why, and I can't explain it, but I break into an all-out waterworks session, and I can't stop the flood of tears. Both men's eyes widen as they lean away from me. Then Jacob raises his hands and steps toward me.

"Hey, now. Those better be tears of joy. You did something special here, April. You stopped us from making a terrible mistake."

Jacob speaks the truth, but the tears are coming anyway, and I don't know why. Probably because nothing I do can piece the King family back together again. Or it could be I realize how close I came to failing Charlotte and causing her to miss her children's childhood while she was in jail. Then again it could be I'm filthy, my shirt's wet, and I have a tumor growing out of my forehead that would make a unicorn envious.

Whatever it is, I move from full waterworks to jerky sobs. Jacob opens his arms and invites me in for a hug. Against my better judgment, I accept. His muscular arms drape around me. With a few more sniffles and deep breaths, I'm able to get control of my emotions.

I push away from him. "I'm sorry."

"Don't be. You've been under a lot of stress." Jacob turns to

Doc. "Doc, can you email those results over to D.A. Jameson?"

"It'll be done before you leave."

"Thank you. I need to drive April back to her car and follow her home."

I move to hand Doc the ice compress. He holds his hand up to me.

"Don't even think about it. Just bring it back to me the next time you visit."

"Next time?" I ask.

Doc chuckles. "Honey, if you keep working as a defense attorney, you and I will get to be best of friends. Who knows, Bubbles might even take a liking to you."

"Hope springs eternal, I guess."

Chapter 48

I turn off my car in my parents' driveway then text Lane and Howard a cryptic message about having found the information to exonerate Charlotte. I grin. That ought to chap Lane's butt. He deserves it for nearly wrecking the lives of an already hurting family.

The grand jury is scheduled for ten a.m., and Lane texts back he wants to meet Howard and me at our office at seven. I can't help poking Lane when I reply, *Don't forget the doughnuts.*

The night air smells of fresh pine as the breeze caresses my cheek. Reveling in my victory, I tilt my head back and look at the stars shining bright against the velvet black sky. The wind chases a gray cloud across the sky, momentarily smudging the silver moon.

I pull in a deep breath. How long has it been since I was able to just enjoy a night without stress? Oh, how I miss this feeling.

Sure, I still have work to do in the morning, but I know the outcome now. It is a certainty that Charlotte will be free.

I visualize the scene when I inform Charlotte in the morning of what I've learned about Alan's death and that her freedom is imminent. Not to deceive myself, it won't be all joyous.

It's a blessing she will be able to raise her children. The thought of the four children losing both parents in this tragedy has hounded me from the second I asked for the case. Still, the grave reality that Alan won't be in their life, a man who loved them dearly, is incredibly sad. I was able to facilitate a part of the family remaining intact, but nobody can make them whole again. There will be difficult days in the future for the family.

Oddly, what is absent from my mind is any congratulatory self-praise. I'd just gotten lucky. It's a truth I can't get out of my head. I know Daddy always says he'd rather be lucky than good, that's all fine and dandy until your luck runs out. In this case, I wouldn't have been the one paying for the lack of luck. The thought is enough to make me feel like I, or more correctly Charlotte, just dodged a cannonball.

Do better, April.

This law profession is a lot different from what I imagined it to be. Of course, I'm practicing as a jack-of-all-trades attorney in a small market, but I have a hunch a large market will be similar. I always desired the obscenely large paychecks, the excitement of the litigation in front of the jury, power lunches, power skirt suits, and hundreds of pairs of shoes. What I'd not expected is to have to connect with my clients.

I mean, I'm actually rooting for a total slime ball like Brad Mathis and hoping he doesn't do something stupid that lands his butt back in jail for five years. I hope he pulls his act together.

Why do I care? Because under his sexist "I'm a big deal," façade is a genuinely smart guy. If he could overcome his glaring issues, Brad could do something great in this world. Even if it's just to raise a family with a wife who loves him like Alan was doing.

Do I believe Brad will? No. I'm not stupid, and I understand history is the best indicator of the future. But it could happen. I hope it happens.

I didn't ask for that. It may seem odd, but I never considered I might interject my own hope and desire into what should be just a transaction of legal services for a fee. My expectation was I would do my job get paid well and be done with it.

They didn't mention emotional entanglement in law school.

I consider turning off my laptop to get some much-needed rest when a ding from it alerts me to a new message. Opening the email, I'm confused about what I'm looking at until I read it a second time.

The law firm in Louisville had responded to my request for an interview. They request I meet them at their office at one o'clock on Monday.

My date with James is Sunday. Still, if I leave early enough Monday morning, I should be able to make a one o'clock meeting even considering the one-hour time change. I accept the meeting in Outlook and set myself a reminder for Sunday evening.

Lane and Howard are deep into the biscuits and coffee breakfast when I arrive. I'm disappointed Lane didn't bring doughnuts. Not that I'd be able to eat anything as the butterflies take flight in my stomach the moment I see them together.

"Well, if it isn't Mrs. Matlock." Lane's eyes shine with what looks to be appreciation. Suddenly, I feel like a schoolgirl who just got two gold stars.

"Grab a biscuit and have a seat, April."

"Your uncle and I were catching up on the rounds of golf he played during his trip to Mobile."

"Is golf what they call it nowadays?" I joke as I select a biscuit and pull up a seat.

"He wishes," Lane starts. "I won't keep you long, April. Doc Crowder called me last night and forwarded his finding to me. I also had a lovely conversation with Judge Rossi this morning. It's my decision, but I like to bounce these things off the judge when we get so close to a grand jury, so the judges understand why we backed off at the last moment. Given the new evidence you brought to light, Judge Rossi agrees we can't bring charges at this time for what has the appearance of an accident. We are set to release Charlotte this morning at nine."

He leans closer and locks eyes with me. "Charlotte is unaware of her pending release, April. It would be a nice touch since you were the one who secured her freedom, for you to give her the good news."

I don't know what to say. With the latest information I was confident I'd be able to get Charlotte released; I just never anticipated it to go this smoothly. "Yes. I'd like that. I'd like that very much."

"Good." Lane stands, gathering the remainder of his biscuit and coffee. "Unlike some people who can take half a week off, I am slammed. If you don't mind, I will take my leave."

At the threshold of Howard's office, Lane turns back. "Good defense attorneys are hard to find, Howard. If I were you, I would figure out a way to pay for her free agent's contract." Lane shrugs. "Of course not that I would ever tell you how to run your business."

"No, you would never do that," Howard says.

Chapter 49

Jade is as excited as I am about the turn of events when I explain them to her on the phone. She already has Charlotte in one of the interrogation rooms for me and left her uncuffed, as I requested.

Charlotte appears fifty percent larger than she did the first time I met her. She has some significant stress-related water retention going on. Her hair even looks thinner to me. She sits directly in front of me, but her stare goes through me. Her general demeanor is blank and soulless. "Are you ready to go home, Charlotte?"

She draws a deep, faltering breath. "At least you have spunk. I'll give you that."

"No. I'm serious, are you ready to go home?"

"God willing and a miracle," she whispers.

"Okay, let me try a different angle. Charlotte, the prosecutor has dropped the charges against you. Last night Jacob Hurley and I were able to confirm some information we found on your property. The medical examiner concluded Alan's death was an unfortunate accident."

She shakes her head slowly. "I don't understand."

A smile stretches across my face, and my skin tingles as I lean in. "Charlotte, you're going home to your babies."

"I am?"

"Yes, you are." I reach across the table and take her hands into mine.

"When?"

"Right now?" I laugh.

Her eyes widen as she stands. "Are you serious?"

"Serious as a heart attack. Is there anything back in your cell you need to get before we leave? A book or a letter?"

She surprises me with an embrace. "No, there is nothing here for me."

I reiterate, they never mentioned emotional entanglements in law school. I relax and lean into Charlotte's hug and then reciprocate with a tighter embrace. It feels surprisingly good.

The next two days are as close to perfect as I've experienced in my life. Charlotte got her kids back from her sister-in-law. We also learned Alan's life insurance had a double indemnity clause for accidental death. A hundred thousand dollars will not replace his income. Still, the money will at least allow Charlotte to get her feet under her.

Having Howard back at the office is nice too. I know it was only a couple of days, but I did miss his consistent coaching and insight.

In many ways I wish I'd interned with him instead of the big city law firms I chose each summer. I figure it has more to do with his need to be proficient in all subsets of law. Then again, he might just be an exceptional mentor.

Dusty broke down the audio, stills, and video from our Paducah trip. Wednesday night, we sat down together for a couple of hours while he showed me what we captured on our investigation. I really don't care for the ghost hunting excursions. But it's difficult not to get excited when Dusty explains, with his usual high passion, how he plans to use the information in his next book.

Oh, yeah. I almost forgot. It's Friday afternoon, and Shane

is supposed to be arriving within the hour. Not that I've been looking forward to it or anything. I mean, really—I have way too much on my mind thinking about my lovely date planned in Paducah with James on Sunday. Did I mention James owns a hotel? And then the interview with my future dream job Monday afternoon in Louisville.

As you can see, I'm way too busy to be concerned about Shane White coming into town.

To say things are going excellent would be a significant understatement. That's also why I have this incredible uneasy feeling the good times will come to a screeching halt sometime soon. I'm not a pessimist. Really, I'm not. I'm what I like to call a life equilibrist.

Over time, things tend to even out. For whatever good there is, there'll be some pain on the backside. When you have a tough go, you fight through because you know that there will be some good times just over the hill. Everything averages out. Presently my good cup overfloweth, and that is a cause for concern.

From the window of the boathouse, I see Shane drive up in his black ground hugging sports car. My skin, including the tips of my toes and fingers, tingle wildly. When he steps out of the car and makes his way to the front door with his nonchalant swagger, I feel my lungs constrict. The man moves with the grace of a panther. I'm not sure if the fact that he has the heart of a kitten makes him more or less sexy. I can't get past his physique long enough to contemplate the sexiness of a personality trait.

My plan is to give him and Chase half an hour to catch up and get the fish talk out of the way. Five minutes after he arrives, I stroll as casually as possible over to the house.

I open the sliding glass door to the kitchen. Chase and Shane are sitting at the kitchen counter, dipping chips into salsa, and drinking beer. I do my best "oh my gosh" voice and smile as I enter the kitchen. "Well, hey there, Shane. I didn't see you drive up." I may have overdone it just a bit.

His eyes glide up-and-down me leisurely. "Hey, April. You are a sight for sore eyes."

Is that a compliment? Or just a Shane salutation. What is it about him that makes me overthink everything? I sway to the counter, pick up a chip, and run it through the salsa. It breaks in half, and I abandon the half-buried chip in the salsa as if nothing happened and pop the plain half into my mouth. Both men stare at the bowl of salsa as if they're expecting the abandoned chip to levitate to the surface.

"Are you talking about where all the magic holes are?" I ask.

Shane rolls his lips inwards as he squelches a laugh.

My face flushes hot. "It's important to have a game plan and know where all those fish are in advance."

Chase clears his throat. "Yeah, I'd gotten some opportunity to check out a number of the alcoves over the last few weeks. We're all mapped out and ready for the morning. The only thing we're trying to figure out is the weather."

Shane drags a chip through the salsa, expertly circling the one I buried. "The Weather Bureau can't make up its mind if it's going to be overcast or sunny. Until we know for sure, it's hard to decide which color lures will work the best."

"And that's why you take all of them," I chirp.

Chase exhales loudly. "Well, yeah. But there is sort of a time limit on this. If you can figure out the right lures to start with, you leave yourself time to get to each of the destinations you want to try."

I remember why I stopped doing tournament fishing with Chase. It's not because I'm a total girly girl. If it's in the spring or fall and if I don't have anything else to do, I'll occasionally go fishing with Chase, just to have some alone time with my brother.

Chase is a wealth of information on how guys think, or instead sometimes don't think. If I need to determine if a boyfriend is acting weird or just "like a guy," Chase is my number one go-to.

One thing about Chase, he is from the hundred percent all-male club. If I'm confused how a boy will react to a situation, I ask Chase how he would feel about it and presto, I have an instant window into alpha manhood.

It's like having my own boyfriend relationship simulator. I can crash Chase a couple of times until I get my wording right and not burn a relationship with a boyfriend.

When I was sixteen, Chase entered the Guntersville fishing tournament, and his partner came up with a terrible stomach virus. Daddy and Dusty already had plans that weekend out of town, and as a last resort, Chase asked me to fill in as his fishing partner. It was the last week of July. I remember two things from the day. Sweating so profusely in the July heat, I developed a severe case of swamp butt and the fear of being bucked out of the bass boat every time we changed locations. Chase would open the boat's throttle wide, and we would skip along the water like a flat stone barely touching the surface. How anybody calls that fun, I'm not sure.

Hindsight being twenty-twenty, if I had paid attention to my gut and never gone fishing with Chase again I wouldn't be having the sudden surge of paranormal events in my life. It was after our boat accident in March that all my "gifts" came back to life.

Being fair, it wasn't the accident. It was the weird glowing amulet that a ghost named Dionis gave me that brought the surge in powers, an amulet presently frozen in a bowl in my freezer so I can't touch it.

"So, what have you been up to, Shane?"

"Just working. You?"

I purse my lips as if I'm deep in thought. "Same."

"Chase tells me you got a mom off a murder charge the other day by doing some slick investigating. Congratulations."

"Thank you." I'm shocked. I wasn't even sure Chase knew, and I certainly didn't think he would care enough to mention it.

Needing something to do with my hands, I grab a beer from the fridge. Not because I want one, I just don't want to leave the room yet. Unfortunately, there doesn't seem to be anything left for me to say.

The boys go back to their strategizing. Their passion is enviable.

I wish I could have their level of enthusiasm about something in my life right now. The high from Charlotte's case is already waning, and I'm looking around at what is April's life.

I'm a hot mess. No real job, no real boyfriend, no real place to call my own, and most of all, after a couple of weeks in retreat to my parents' home, I'm truthfully no closer to solving those issues.

When I drove home from Atlanta, I believed this would be a three-week process at the most. Why doesn't anything ever go to plan for me?

The kitchen door opens. Dusty carries eight plastic grocery bags hung from his arms.

"Can you make room on that grill for some ears of corn, Chase?"

"We can always make room for more. More is good," Chase says.

All three men laugh heartily. I feel like a tourist in a foreign land, and my male language skills are broken at best.

"Good, it was too pretty to pass up for a quarter an ear even though I'm gonna bake some potatoes too."

"Mama is going to have a fit. Double starch, gotta love it!" Chase grins as he helps unload Dusty's arms.

"Got it covered." Dusty lifts two bunches of asparagus into the air. "It's a thinking man's game."

"Stinky urine tonight." Chase laughs.

"We'll have to pee in a beer bottle tomorrow. Peeing in the water would scare all the fish away," Shane adds.

"I guess that solves the bottle versus aluminum can issue for you two tomorrow," Dusty says.

I've spent most of my life in the company of men. In some ways, that's where I believe my healthy appreciation for them is derived. Sometimes too strong of an appreciation.

Despite thousands of hours with all the different men, I remain at the appreciation stage. I would hope, at some point, to move to a state of understanding. Maybe fifty years from now, but for the time being, I don't have any more of an understanding of masculinity than any other woman I know.

I watch silently as my two brothers and Shane prep the vegetables and steaks. They cook them to perfection and create yet another festive feast for my family. When my parents arrive home from work, the six of us sit down and enjoy each other's company on the back porch.

My melancholy will not give way to everyone else's joy. Regardless of the culinary delights that dance on my tongue, I cannot get a bitter taste out of my mouth. The bitter taste that Shane has moved us to friend status, and there is nothing I can do to change that.

Granny always said that if you had a lousy yesterday, put all your focus on today. That's precisely what I do during my drive up to Paducah Sunday. I'd come to grips with the state of Shane and my relationship. Or non-relationship if you prefer.

Saturday, after a few moments of irrational shunned lover anger, I accepted what I already knew for weeks. Shane is a thoughtful friend, and I'm better to have him in my life than not. Plus, it's near impossible to move a relationship from a friend to a lover when you live four hours apart. Not saying I'm expecting Shane's feelings to change. Just that being long distance dashes even the long shot romanticist notion it might happen.

The lunch date with James should be a pleasant diversion. True, James doesn't possess the physique or quiet sexiness of Shane, but he is a guy, and he seems kind enough. Plus, he has some level of success, which has to be a good thing. Right?

Okay, James is a consolation prize of sorts, and my expectations are depressingly low. But I'm turning over a new leaf and trying to go into things with no preconceived notion. There is always the possibility James is surprisingly sexy and has a super-cut body underneath his starched white shirt and tie.

Chapter 50

As I get out of my car, I hear the distorted whispers. I close my eyes as I build the barricade around my mind. I know better. Some areas are a hotbed regardless of how much blessing is done. Besides, nobody really knows what lies below us from hundreds of years earlier. There is no telling how many unmarked graves of frontiersmen and indigenous people lie at the edge of these old county roads that were initially cut by deer.

James is at the front desk. He appears taller, and his hair is different, an admirable try for the sexy mussed look. His expression changes to joy when he sees me. Flattery, which stokes a warm feeling in my chest. It's good to be wanted.

"I wanted to commission an oil painting of the riverside for the lobby. You've changed my mind. I'm going to display a life-size picture of you instead."

I shake my head. "Did you have to think all week to come up with that line?"

He comes from behind the counter. "You inspired it just now."

When he holds out his hands, I feel obliged to put mine in his. I sense the energy of his genuine excitement, and I'm flattered again.

"I'm so glad you agreed to this today. You won't regret it."

My eyebrows arch. James has exploded the "over the top meter."

"Good," I say.

"Yes, good." He stares into my eyes as if he is searching for something. Grinning, he releases my hands, allowing them to return to my side. "Give me just a minute, and we'll head out to the river."

I think about the river while he is gone. James did not give me any details about the date. In fairness, I hadn't asked anything about his plans for us today. The word river reminds me of what Shane was doing with my brother the day before. Shane, the hot sexy man who sees me only as a friend. Despite trying to take Granny's advice, I'm doomed to be stuck in the past, and my melancholy returns.

The click of James walking down the hall draws my attention down, and I see he wears cowboy boots with a substantial heel. That explains the increase in height.

Snap out of it, April. The man has gone through some trouble to prepare a fun day for you. Stop picking at him. Open your mind. There is the possibility that James might be "him."

I know it can happen. I don't have to look any further than my own parents.

Pictures from her youth show Mama to be a cross between a World War II pinup and a top-notch bridal model. She was a ten before the scale was ever conceived.

Daddy was—well, Daddy was my daddy. He is average height, average looks, glasses, and a little on the geeky side in a cute way. If I had been a matchmaker forty years ago, I never would have put those two together.

There is no doubt somehow, Daddy stokes Mama's fire. You can still feel the passion in the air like electricity crackling across the room when they're together.

Mama didn't pass that gene down to me. Geeky guys just don't crank my motor.

"Okay, we'll take the Benz down to the river walk, and Demarius is going to have the pontoon ready for us."

James motions toward the front door, and as I turned to exit, he places his warm small hand on my lower back. I can't help it, I cringe. Tell me I'm not awful.

Chapter 51

The river is eight short blocks from the hotel. With the bright summer sky, it would've been a pleasant walk from the hotel if it weren't hotter than a goat's butt in a pepper patch.

The Paducah Riverwalk District reminds me of a ninety-year-old movie star who's had a few too many bad facelifts in a failed attempt to regain her youth. The brick buildings with few exceptions are without character and of an early twentieth-century utilitarian style.

James pulls the car up to the small dock area, which allows boaters to land their craft and eat at the local establishments before continuing upriver. A young man approaches us as we exit the car. James exchanges keys with him and beckons for me to follow.

Let's see, it's ninety degrees out and ninety percent humidity, and I'm dressed in jeans. A man I barely know is beckoning me to join him alone on a boat, and I have no idea where he plans to take us. What's wrong with this picture?

I follow James down to the dock. Okay, this settles it. I'm either crazy or stupid. Most likely both.

"I hope you don't think this too presumptuous of me. It's just my two favorite things in the world are beautiful women and riding a boat on the river."

Presumptuous? Who says that? "No, I'm sure it'll be fun. I

just wish I'd known to wear shorts."

I see disappointment register on his face before he successfully recovers. "Oh, I assure you, once we get on the water, you'll be glad you wore jeans. Besides, Demarius pulled the awning up for us. It's always markedly cooler under the awning."

It is a spectacular pontoon boat. At least thirty feet long with a second sundeck above a third of the length. The other two-thirds of the lower deck is covered with a striped awning. James offers his hand and helps me board.

I prefer lakes to rivers. The rivers around Paducah are still commerce lifeblood for the communities. The commercial vessels are far more numerous on the Paducah rivers than what I've experienced on Guntersville Lake. On the flip side, we're able to go exploring longer distances without having to worry about a lock system to slow us down.

James and Shane differ from each other like lakes and rivers. Undoubtedly Shane is hotter. It's futile to argue the point. But James isn't exactly ugly.

One of the pluses I must credit James with, he is an excellent conversationalist. He brings up topics and is adept at adding thoughtful comments balanced against his careful consideration of my opinion. With Shane, I often only got the attentive listening and no comment back from him. The irony is not lost on me that James if he hadn't already made his romantic intentions entirely clear, is by far the better friend material.

James drops anchor a few miles north of town after an hour ride. He pulls items out of a cabinet built into the boat. Looking at the condensation on the plastic containers, I realize it's a working refrigerator. Who has a working refrigerator on a pontoon? How cool is that?

He lifts two different colored plastic containers toward me. "Chicken or tuna salad?"

"Chicken, definitely."

He grins knowingly. "The tuna was packed in water, not oil."

"I'll take your word on it."

He sets a loaf of bread on the table. "You sure? You're missing out."

"I've had an unpleasant experience with tuna before. If it's all the same to you, I'll just leave more for you."

"Suit yourself." He pushes the chicken salad toward me with a fork on top.

"Water or wine?"

"Water for now." I scoop out some chicken salad. It's my favorite kind, loaded with grapes, pecans, and apples.

"I have to admit I'm pleasantly surprised you accepted."

"Really? Why surprised?"

James shrugs as he opens another container revealing a colorful pasta salad. "Let's just say I'm not so blind I don't know I'm playing out of my league. But then again, I've been doing that my entire life."

Interesting. This is where April keeps her mouth shut, so things don't turn intimate. Of course, I have the right to remain silent but not the willpower. "How do you mean?"

"This hotel, the Osborne, it will never be able to break even."

"Why in the world would you say that? Dusty told me the blessing went well, your business should be able to operate without any fear of further disruptions."

James laughs, then holds his hand up in apology. "Oh April, you're so sweet. Seriously though, you've been around Paducah enough. Its best days are behind it. There is no need for a five-star hotel here. And if there were, you surely wouldn't put it downtown." He waves his hand in the air. "You would put it next to one of the exit ramps from the interstate. The interstates are today's riverway. The downtown area is just on life support. Give it a few more years it will be a ghost town except for law offices and banks."

"James, if you believe that, why put such an effort into bringing back the hotel?"

"Love, pride. You see, I grew up dirt poor. My mother had me out of wedlock, and my natural father killed himself when I was only three. But I always had a talent for making money."

He looks down at the boat floor. "I don't have any college degrees like you do. By the time I was twenty-three, I had three different service companies. By the time I was twenty-five, I had cashed out with a couple million in my back pocket and became a successful day trader. In short, I just have a nose for money. It's just in my blood."

I must admit I'm from the school of thought where the more you talk about having something, the less of it you possess. But either James is one of the best liars I've ever come across, or he is one-hundred percent sincere. I want to reach out and confirm one way or another, but I believe if I start reading people regularly, it'll be a slippery slope I don't come back from.

I keep my hands on my sandwich.

"I can tell you that you can earn more money than you can spend." He shakes his head. "That's not quite right. You can earn more money than you can spend if you keep the same lifestyle."

"As I was approaching thirty, I realized all I was doing was creating wealth. That's what I did in the morning, the afternoon and late at night. Money without a purpose, it becomes as pointless as watching TV.

"When I came back to town to bury my mother two years ago, I took a drive through town. There she was, the Osborne, the decrepit old lady that once was a showplace of the South being used as a homeless shelter. I knew what I had to do. I had to restore her to her former glory."

On one level, I admire James's passion. I never see myself driving through Guntersville and suddenly saying, "Hey, I remember that building. I want to make it look like it did when it was first built." Yeah, no. That's not gonna happen. That goes double if it means I'd have to shell out a couple of grand every month to keep the project afloat.

"I guess I understand wanting to have something more concrete to show for your effort than owning a bunch of stocks and bonds. But that doesn't answer the question of why Paducah? Why the Osborne? There are plenty of old structures in Louisville and Nashville and even Indianapolis. Areas where people are paying a premium for these type of hotels."

"I know. Like I said, I have a nose for money, and the skill set to start a successful business from scratch. But this was never supposed to be a moneymaker. It was just something I needed to do."

"Sorry, I just don't get it."

"It was my legacy, April. It was my birthright. Circumstances, before I was born, stole it from me."

I'm stunned. Something turns in my gut as it sounds like Miles missed an important factoid during his extensive research of the Osborne. The shock must wear off before I can ask the question. "What do you mean by legacy, James?"

"I mean, the hotel should've been mine. I am the last living member of the Clark line."

I slowly shake my head. "That's not possible. Miles and Dusty researched the family tree. There haven't been any living relatives of Scott Clark since the sixties."

James laughs. It has a bitter edge to it. "Scott Clark had an older brother, Eugene. Eugene and his wife died in a boating mishap in the forties. Their only son Leonard shot himself with a pistol in sixty-three, but not before he sired an illegitimate daughter, Jennifer Caldwell, my mother.

"Scott also had a younger sister named Mildred. Mildred became pregnant at the age of fourteen and had a daughter, Tansy. Tansy is the grandmother of Dilly. Dilly was one of the first people I hired when I reopened the hotel. I do believe the adage you can't trust anybody quite like you can trust your family."

"You knew. You knew, and you put her in danger," I accuse him.

James's face twists violently. "I would've never put Dilly in danger. We both heard the legends, the rumors. That's all we believed them to be. In a lot of ways, we thought they were intended to keep us from bringing the hotel back."

My anxiety is peaking. I'm trying desperately to get hold of

my emotions before they put me into a full-fledged panic attack. "James, you need to tell me everything. Miles didn't find
any legends about the property. Just a few reports of some cold
spots and odd noises, no legends attached to it."

James rubs a finger across his chin. "It's not exactly the sort
of thing you let out if your goal is to have paying guests."

"What legends?" I insist.

"Okay fine. I can't stress enough; this is all old hand-me-
downs from family member to family member," he sighs dramatically. "Clark Scott and Les Blair were equal partners in
the Osborne. That's public record, and you must know that
already. You may have also found information about Renée
Watson. Renée was a young socialite in the twenties, and the
Watsons were a family of considerable wealth. Originally the
three of them were simply good friends, and then it became an
unworkable love triangle."

"Clark and Renée were engaged, but then she ran off with
Les," I interject.

"So, the public story goes." James grins. "The story in the
family is a little more complicated than that. Shortly after
Clark won Renée's favor, Les lost his wealth in the stock market
crash. Rumor has it that the hotel's original foundation issues
were not caused by the ground shifting due to being built on
sediment and not rock. The original pylons were driven deep
enough to support the building. Instead someone had worked
to compromise the pylons."

"Les?"

"Again, rumor, that was never confirmed. But the thought
being Les needed cash more than a hotel. He knew Scott would
never agree to sell the hotel, but if it collapsed." James shrugs.
"An insurance check is as good as a check at closing."

If James's intent is to clear matters up for me, the added details only confuse me. "What does this have to do with Renée's
disappearance?"

"This comes from my great-uncle Scott just before he died,
by way of Dilly's great-grandmother Mildred. Renée caught Les

compromising one of the pylons. It's unclear if he meant to or not, but a struggle ensued, and Renée ended up splitting her head open from a fall.

"Les panicked. Rather than report the accident to the police, he disposed of her body. He cut her up with an ax and burned her body in the incinerator.

"By happenstance, Scott noticed smoke from the incinerator stack and went to investigate in the basement. There he found Les trying to clean blood off the ax.

"Scott was able to put the scene together quickly. One of Renée's shoes and a brooch Scott had given her at Christmas were still on the ground."

The horror Scott must have experienced when he realized what his partner had done is beyond comprehension. At the same time, a chill runs up my spine as I understand there is no way I found Renée's brooch in the basement by chance after eight decades.

"Scott lost his mind, understandably. The two men fought. Scott wrestled the ax away from Les and whacked him upside the head with the intent of knocking him unconscious. But he couldn't kill him. He told Mildred that instead…"

James stops and frowns. He runs his hands through his hair and looks out over the water.

"What?" I ask.

James sighs. "He told her he bricked Les up between two of the pylons in an area just big enough for him to stand."

The shock messes with my equilibrium giving me a momentary bout of vertigo. The horror washes over me as the story just went from evil to diabolical. "That's worse than death."

James arches his eyebrows. "Absolute purgatory. How long can you hold out, three, six, eight days without water? And if by chance Les was hoping for water on the third day, he got all he could stand. Because the third day of his entombment was the great flood of thirty-seven, and the water rose to the second floor of the hotel."

"He drowned?"

"Maybe it was merciful? Either way, it had to be horrible."

He was a murderer, but the manner of his death, if true, had been horrific. "What happened to Scott?"

"He made the fourteenth floor of the hotel his personal home. He continued to complain of hearing voices, one more than all others. The state took the hotel for back taxes in the forties. They allowed him to stay on as a tenant. Finally, in the early fifties, he had dwindled away to a hundred pounds and was stark raving mad. Ultimately, he quit eating and died of starvation. But he always warned Mildred that Les Blair had placed a curse on our entire family."

"That is a horrible story. It's so sad."

James brightens immediately. "But it is just that, a story. Besides, the hotel has been blessed, and there are no more spirits to contend with benevolent or malicious."

I want to mention to James that curses have nothing to do with ghosts. Just because a spirit has been banished does not automatically lift a curse placed against a place or person. There is a specific ritual for removing every type of classification of curses.

Nana has made this point painstakingly clear to me as her experience in the dark arts has run afoul of curses from time to time. But James seems at peace, and I can't bring myself to rain on his parade.

There is something about James I'm beginning to warm to. His ability to overcome obstacles and continue with an optimistic faith in the face of insurmountable odds appeals to me. It's a strength I would do well to emulate.

"Oh man, it's almost four o'clock. We have dinner reservations for six-thirty," James says as he pulls on the anchor chain.

"We're not eating at the hotel?"

"Not when a good friend of mine is a four-star chef and has his own place downtown." His jaw drops. "I didn't ask you to bring a dress."

"Nope. You didn't tell me anything. And I'm an idiot for not asking."

"I can fix this." He texts someone with his phone. "What are you, a size four?"

I roll my eyes. "Eight."

He frowns. "An eight would swallow you whole. But who am I to judge if you like your clothes baggy?"

"What did you just do?"

"Order you a dress?"

"Don't you ever do that again." That was thoughtful. Weird probably, awkward heck yes, but it's a first by anyone I've dated.

"I'm sorry. I won't ever do it again without your permission first."

"I guess I can let it slide this time."

Chapter 52

We ride the elevator to the fourteenth floor when we arrive back to the Osborne. As I enter room fourteen-o-seven, I find a strapless black cocktail dress that hits just above the knees that I'm concerned might show way too much cleavage. But I'm distracted by the uber-cute silver pumps lying next to the dress on my bed.

I take a quick shower to wash the sweat off and apply minimal makeup. As I pick up my hairdryer, I hear the shower door in fourteen-o-nine shut. James takes longer to get ready than the average female. He better hurry it up, or we'll miss our reservations.

As I dry my hair, I keep hearing a voice shouting in my head. I pause to reinforce the partitions in my mind, but it has no effect.

A bloodcurdling scream tears through the bathroom wall. I turn the hairdryer off and listen intently to identify the sound.

James is still in the shower; I can hear it running. But I do not hear the scream again and am about to turn the hairdryer back on.

Another scream echoes in the bathroom, and I realize it's not in my head. It's coming from fourteen-o-nine. It sounds like James.

I drop the hairdryer and run out of my room directly to the

door of fourteen-o-nine. It's locked. I hammer my fist against it to no avail. "James! James, let me in!"

He doesn't answer, and the only thing I can think to do is call the front desk. As I wait for them to pick up the phone, muddy water pours out from under the door into the hallway. It catches a crease near the wall and forms a small stream turning the crimson carpet maroon as it soaks into the plush fabric.

The front office picks up. "I need a key!"

"Hello?"

"Send a key for fourteen-o-nine now! Something is happening to James, and the door is locked!"

The stream from under the door intensifies. I hear fire engines start to wail; the front desk must have called the emergency rescue.

The elevator door pops open, and Demarius runs out. He slides between me and the door and unlocks it in one smooth movement.

The water, ankle-deep in the room, gushes out as we open the door. There is no sign of James.

"The bathroom. I heard James scream in the bathroom."

Demarius opens the bathroom door, and a wave of putrid brown river water strikes us taking our legs out from under us. The stench of the stale water makes me gag as I stand. I push past Demarius into the bathroom in search of James.

James is floating unconscious inside the shower stall. His nude body barely visible in the brackish water.

I jerk on the shower stall handle, but it doesn't open. I try again in vain.

"Move over," Demarius says. When I do, he kicks at the plate-glass with his boot, but nothing happens.

The laughter draws my attention. I wish I had been expecting Les as I pee myself a little and am grateful I'm already soaking wet.

He is a good-looking man my age, a year or two older. He holds a brandy snifter in one hand and a soggy cigar in the other. His suit, circa nineteen-twenties, drips water profusely.

His eyes are a marbled blue-gray with no iris.

"How fitting." He smiles, exposing yellowed filed teeth.

"You did this!" I scream.

Les Blair laughs and takes a drag on his soggy cigar.

Demarius crashes into the glass door and bounces off, falling to the floor. He sits in the water, rubbing his injured shoulder.

"He is gone! That's the last of them I scream at Les."

Squinting his revolting eyes, he clacks his pointed teeth together in a menacing gesture. He shrugs his shoulders and swirls the brackish water in his brandy sniffer as he samples its bouquet.

"Leave now!" I scream. In my peripheral, Demarius is watching me warily as he crab crawls away from me.

Les tilts his head and stares at me.

I lock eyes with his lifeless gaze and scream again, "Now!"

The outline of Les immediately lights as small particles break away from his solid form. The disintegration gains speed, and in a matter of seconds, he no longer stands in front of me. As the last of Les disappears, the shower stall opens in a flood, and James washes out, taking my legs out from under me a second time.

Scrambling to my hands and knees, I pull James to me. I check for a pulse.

"What just happened? Who were you screaming at?" Demarius yells.

James doesn't have a pulse. I hesitate since I know what it will take out of me, then I lay over the dead man and squeeze tight against his chest. The warmth flows from my body immediately.

The energy it consumes from me is unfathomable, and I consider stopping. But I'm so close. At least I feel close to success.

"He is gone, ma'am." Demarius pulls at my bare shoulder.

I force more of my dwindling energy at James, and our bodies feel super heated. He convulses. I look to see if his eyes have opened, and he vomits water into my face.

Chapter 53

The police question me until midnight in a futile search for answers. I have all the answers to their questions, but I don't tell them anything. They don't want to hear the truth anyway. They want to hear something they are comfortable with; they would never be at ease with the truth if I shared it with them.

When they release me at midnight, they request I return to the local station at nine in the morning. I call the law firm in Louisville to explain my situation and attempt to reschedule the interview. They inform me rescheduling is not an option and remove me from their list of candidates.

I can't bring myself to stay the night at the Osborne, free room or not. Nana always says the world moves in circular patterns. Somehow, I end up at the motel where the paranormal team spent the night before we investigated the Osborne. It feels like poetic closure.

Numbness covers my body. My mind is skipping gears, and I'm exhausted from using my paranormal "gifts."

When I think not having a job and not having a boyfriend is the worst, I get an excellent opportunity pulled out from under me, and a prospective boyfriend drowns in a shower stall. The police are acting all sketchy like I tried to kill James.

I can't tell them I saved him. That I brought James back from the dead, and he is in critical but stable condition at Lourdes Hospital because I can bring people back if they haven't been dead too long.

I'm losing my mind. I need to talk to someone before I have a complete breakdown. Someone needs to distract me from the awful events of tonight.

It's a bad idea, stupid even, but I dial the number anyway.

"Hey, April."

I smile, and the tears run down my face. "Hey, Shane. I didn't wake you, did I?"

"I hope not, I'm on third shift tonight."

"Anything interesting happening tonight?"

"Nah, it's dead here tonight. What about you?"

"About the same."

I can sense the concern in his silence.

"Are you okay?" Shane asks.

"Yeah, I am now." Drawing a deep breath, I'm able to get a hold of my nerves. "Well, I just wanted to check in with you. I guess I should get some sleep now."

"Okay, that's cool. I appreciate the call. You sure you're all right?"

"Right as rain."

"Good deal. If you change your mind and need to talk, I'll be here all night."

We hang up and I can't help but compare where I was this spring to my present situation. Real-life is giving me a severe case of low self-esteem. All those years of studying and grinding through the system now feel like nothing more than foolish aspirations.

Mama is right. I'm just a foolish girl.

No. That's not true. I've just been dealt a lot of atrocious cards in a row, and with a little affirmation, I'll find my way one day soon. The world might be able to knock April May Snow to the ground, but I will get up again bloody lip and all.

I dial her number without any thought. "Hi, Mama. Are you up?"

"Baby, I'm always here for you. What's the trouble?"

The End

*Don't miss the next April May Snow
release date. Join the reader's club now.*

www.mscottswanson.com

April's story continues with
Foolish Beliefs

Have you read the prequels? *The Gifts Awaken* stories are the prequel series to the *Foolish* novel series of April May Snow.

Click to get your copies today!

The Gifts Awaken Prequel Series

Throw the Bouquet
Throw the Cap
Throw the Dice
Throw the Elbow
Throw the Fastball
Throw the Gauntlet
Throw the Hissy

M. Scott lives outside of Nashville, Tennessee, with his wife and two guard chihuahuas. When he's not writing, he's cooking or taking long walks to smooth out plotlines for the next April May Snow adventure.

Dear Reader,

Thank you for reading April's story. You make her adventures possible. Without you, there would be no point in creating her story.

I'd like to encourage you to post a review on Amazon. A favorable critique from you is a powerful way to support authors you enjoy. It allows our books to be found by additional readers, and frankly, motivates us to continue to produce books. This is especially true for your independents.

Once again, thank you for the support. You are the magic that breathes life into these characters.

M. Scott Swanson

*The best way to stay in touch
is to join the reader's club!*
www.mscottswanson.com

Other ways to stay in touch are:

Like on Amazon

Like on Facebook

Like on Goodreads

You can also reach me at mscottswanson@gmail.com.

I hope your life is filled with

magic and LOVE!

Printed in Great Britain
by Amazon

80408799R10190